GEORGE & LIZZIE

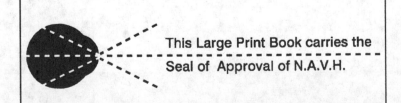

GEORGE & LIZZIE

NANCY PEARL

WHEELER PUBLISHING
A part of Gale, a Cengage Company

GALE
A Cengage Company

Farmington Hills, Mich • San Francisco • New York • Waterville, Maine
Meriden, Conn • Mason, Ohio • Chicago

Wheeler Publishing, a part of Gale, a Cengage Company.

Wheeler Publishing Large Print Hardcover.
The text of this Large Print edition is unabridged.
Other aspects of the book may vary from the original edition.
Set in 16 pt. Plantin.

LIBRARY OF CONGRESS CIP DATA ON FILE.
CATALOGUING IN PUBLICATION FOR THIS BOOK
IS AVAILABLE FROM THE LIBRARY OF CONGRESS.

ISBN-13: 978-1-4328-4254-3 (hardcover)
ISBN-10: 1-4328-4254-4 (hardcover)

Published in 2017 by arrangement with Touchstone, an imprint of Simon & Schuster, Inc.

Printed in Mexico
1 2 3 4 5 6 7 21 20 19 18 17

To my husband Joe,
who makes my life possible and
without whom this novel wouldn't exist.
Fifty-one years and counting!

If you are involved in a fantasy
relationship with someone
in which the sex is so good
it's like a fantasy
and things happen
between you that are
incredibly private and
unmentionable that
you could never do with
anyone else ever again
so much so that you moan with
pleasure in bed and can't
believe it's really happening
and don't even
bother fantasizing about
anyone else or any
situation other than the
one you're in, then you
are in very very serious trouble
and good luck
to you. It won't last and
when it ends, you'll

walk the floor and wear out your shoes.

If, on the other hand,
you are involved with someone
with whom you have regular, decent sex
that feels good and normal,
but that you
would never think about for a moment
when masturbating — which is
by no means to put
it down — then the chances of
this relationship lasting
a very long time, of the two of you
growing old together,
are very good. But often this
is simply not enough.
Or it *is* enough when what is wanted,
unfortunately
or not, is more than enough.
— Terence Winch,
"The Bells Are Ringing for Me and Chagall"

HOW THEY MET

The night Lizzie and George met — it was at the Bowlarama way out on Washtenaw — she was flying high on some awfully good weed because her heart was broken. For the past several weeks she'd been subsisting on mugs of Stoli and popcorn. It was Leon Daly who'd told her that drinking vodka that'd been kept in the freezer was what got you through the bad times. Lizzie had known (with the small part of her brain that still seemed to work during the difficult months since Jack McConaghey disappeared from her life) that Leon meant bad times due to football injuries (he was then the right defensive tackle on their high school team), but Lizzie figured, what the hell, anything to mellow the sadness was worth a try. So vodka, taken directly from the freezer and poured seemingly nonstop down Lizzie's throat by Lizzie herself, had infected her arms and legs and brain with welcome numbness. She could see how it might even improve her football game. The popcorn was her own idea.

But Marla, tired of the emotional and physical sloppiness of her roommate and best friend's drunkenness, and engaged, as she was, to the campus supplier of superior dope (as well as being a major pothead himself), suggested Lizzie switch. Good plan! After only a few days it was clear to Lizzie that, for what she wanted, weed was the drug of choice.

Lizzie had never been in the Bowlarama, or any bowling alley, for that matter. During the years when she might have gone as a kid, her parents had insisted that Sheila, her babysitter, take her to ballets, museums, libraries, operas, theaters, and planetariums. Marla had dragged her to the bowling alley because she loved Lizzie and she was exhausted by sharing an apartment with someone whose broken heart still showed no signs of mending, though months had passed.

Marla thought that bowling, an activity far removed from their normal lives, might bring Lizzie to her senses. And was she ever right. Lizzie was immediately entranced. The noise! The swoosh of the balls hurtling down the alley! (Although she didn't yet know it was called an alley.) The satisfying thunks when the ball reached its targets! The excited yips and heys of the bowlers! Those cunning shoes with the numbers on the back! The smell of the place — a combination of stale beer and sweat and a hint of talcum powder. Weird! Those tiny pencils? Fabulous! And those balls — some black, some zigzagged with color!

On the other hand, George was high as a kite on happiness and pride because he was not only out on a date with the current woman of his dreams, but he was also about to bowl the best game of his life since 1982, when he was twelve years old.

In October of his first year in dental school, George developed a serious crush on Julia Draznin. Julia was beautiful and had an intelligence that was said to be stratospheric. It was rumored (although never confirmed) that she had gone straight into dental school after her junior year at Bryn Mawr. She was the subject of both the waking and sleeping dreams of her fellow students, some of whom had already dated her. You could see Julia and her current boyfriend at the movies, Rollerblading on spring evenings in Ann Arbor, or sitting around in coffee shops, talking animatedly. The word on tooth street was that she'd go

11

out with you for a few times and then let you down gently while explaining that she didn't intend to get serious about anyone until after she'd established her practice, several years in the future. This left many of her suitors emotionally bereft.

George intended to change all this. Before he finally asked Julia out, he considered several options for what they should actually do on the date. Whatever they did had to be unique and sophisticated, or ironically quotidian, that was the main thing. George immediately rejected fishing in the Huron River (much better for a second or third date, he felt), a concert (not original enough), and that old standby, dinner and a movie (ditto). So what was left? Bowling was left. George would give you odds that not one of their fellow dentists-to-be had taken her bowling. It would be great, right? Even though he himself had not been bowling in, let's see, almost a decade. But the good times he'd had in bowling alleys were among the many pleasant memories from George's childhood.

George saw himself as a suave bowler, definitely not a dork, someone Julia would surely recognize as worthy of her attention. He was trying to decide whether he should admit to Julia that bowling was something he was good at, or used to be pretty good at. Would that charm her? Or would she think it was ridiculous to be pleased that you're good at throwing a ball down a lane? Would she go home and tell her roommate that George was handsome, smart, and frequently able to convert the 7-10 split?

That's the setup, George sometime later explained to Lizzie, with just the two corner pins left, one on either side of the alley. It's possible to convert the spare by hitting the inside of one of the pins, causing it to rebound off the wall and slide briskly back across the alley to take down the other pin, but it's not easy. Lizzie tried, it must be said not very hard, to show some enthusiasm for this tidbit of information.

However, George knew that very likely there were some women, perhaps especially smart and attractive ones like Julia, who would be bored silly with a man whose major talent appeared to be that he could aim a ball down a wooden lane and knock down the requisite number of pins. When George discussed this with Lizzie, long after they were married, she told him that she could only confirm that, yes, she was bored beyond bored with him whenever he brought up bowling, but not during the rest of the time they were together. So that was sort of okay.

And now Lizzie was at the Bowlarama, stoned on dope from James, and George was there stoned on happiness, etc. etc. etc. Marla instructed Lizzie on the intricacies of scoring, although she immediately assured Lizzie that she wasn't expecting her to actually keep score. That would be Marla's job. While Marla talked on, Lizzie was mumbling "score," "spare," and "strike" over and over because she liked the sound of the words in her mouth.

Marla showed her where to stand and demonstrated how to send the ball spinning down the alley. Lizzie thought "alley" was a funny word in this context, and added it to her mantra, so it now read "alley, score, spare, strike." Then she decided that it sounded better as "sass": score, alley, spare, strike. She didn't seem able both to remember those four words in that order and at the same time listen to Marla's explanations. This is likely the reason that she hadn't really gotten the sense of what "send the ball spinning down the alley" actually meant. In any case, it appeared that she interpreted "send" somewhat differently from how Marla intended she should.

Meanwhile, George, bowling with Julia in the very next lane, was on a roll. This was the one word in the how-we-met story that George truly loved. "Roll," with its double meanings, was the kind of pun that he was prone to make, always accompanied by a certain expression on his face that meant: Isn't that clever, do you get it? Lizzie always appreciated George's puns, but that expression drove her crazy. Anyway, George and Julia had just finished the eighth frame, and George's score was an amazing 152, which meant that he could break 200 if he was both careful and tremendously lucky.

So Lizzie went up to the foul line, which Marla had carefully pointed out to her, for her first try at bowling. They'd agreed that it was best if Lizzie didn't attempt the much more complicated option of starting farther back and taking three strides to the foul line. Neither she nor Marla was confident that Lizzie could coordinate walking, carrying the ball, counting the steps, stopping at the right spot, and then throwing the ball, especially because she was still occasionally mumbling "score, alley, spare, strike." She stood there with the ball held out in front of her, thumb in its correct hole, two middle fingers in theirs. All the pot she'd already smoked that night had made her hyperalert to every move she was making. Her palms were sweaty. She didn't notice that George was lining up to bowl, and in any case was unaware of the protocol that if someone in the lane next to you is getting ready to bowl, you should wait until the ball has left his hands to begin your turn.

"But, George, why didn't you wait until I was done?" Lizzie once asked, years after the fiasco, their courtship and marriage.

"Didn't even see you standing there," George admitted.

There they both were, Lizzie and George, in their separate worlds, surely a clue to what their future relationship would be. George steps toward the line, brings his arm forward and smoothly lets go of his ball, and at the same moment Lizzie tries to throw her ball spinning down the alley, but something immediately goes wrong. (Or right, depending on what's important to you.) Lizzie's ball hits the floor with an awesome crash and somehow leaps over the ball-return mechanism that separates the lanes and crashes right into George's ball, which until that moment had been rolling straight and true toward what certainly looked like an imminent strike, and now both balls make their separate but causally related ways to the gutter.

Pandemonium ensued within the confines of lanes 38 and 39. Lizzie, laughing uncontrollably in response to the shock of watching and hearing the collision, sat down on the floor. If anyone had been close enough to her, what they would have heard was a sequence of whimper, gasp, snort, gasp, snort, whimper, gasp. She felt a strong desire to pee, but was unable to make herself stand up. Also, the particular pattern of the floor seemed to be worth studying in depth, which served to take her mind off the prospect of wetting her pants but did nothing to stop the gasp, whimper, snort sequence.

George was devastated and, quite frankly, more than a little annoyed with Julia, who was also laughing and didn't appear to be on the verge of consoling him. Marla, seeing that Lizzie didn't seem inclined to get up, or for that matter to be able to stop the routine of snorting, whimpering, and gasping, rushed over to apologize to George.

"I'm so sorry," Marla said. "I'm Marla, and she's Lizzie. I don't know how this happened, but we're really sorry."

"I know how it happened," George said coldly. "She shouldn't even be here. She obviously can't bowl. She totally ruined my game." His voice rose. "My game, maybe my two-hundred game. Everything was going so well."

"George, get a grip," Julia ordered. "It's just a game; don't make it into a big deal." She turned to Marla. "I'm Julia, by the way, and this ridiculous man is George."

Marla nodded at Julia but addressed George. "Look, give me your phone number and we'll call and set up a time to get together for a drink. We owe you one for ruining things. Or Lizzie does."

"My game," George moaned again, but Julia hushed him.

"Here," she said as she tore off a piece of the scoring sheet, "write down your name and phone number and give it to them." George obeyed her, but it was clear the evening was spoiled. He never went out with Julia again.

THE GREAT GAME

Although it was Lizzie who carried it out, Lizzie who, for many months afterward, lived with the slights and the snubs and the nasty comments from her female classmates and the knowing looks, leers, and wolfish grins from every boy at school, even the freshmen; although it was Lizzie who got an unsigned note passed to her in chemistry class that was addressed "Dear Slut" and went on to threaten her with bodily harm if she ever again so much as looked at the writer's boyfriend (who was Leonardo deSica, currently the football team's strong safety); although it was Lizzie who didn't go to her own senior prom because nobody asked her; although it was Lizzie who suffered all the consequences, it was actually Andrea who came up with the idea that became the Great Game.

It was the first week of their senior year. Lizzie and Andrea were both on the yearbook staff, which met during the last period of classes and inevitably ran late. They were slowly walking home along the fence line that enclosed the football field. They could hear shouts, whistles, and occasionally the thwack of a ball being kicked or the crashing sound of bodies colliding. The sounds reminded Lizzie of Maverick Brevard, the team's starting wide receiver and her excellent boyfriend during their junior year. She couldn't decide if she wished they'd get back together. If they did, it would make the next few months more interesting. Maybe.

"Football team's practicing," Lizzie murmured, mostly to herself.

"You think?"

"Do irony much?" Lizzie asked her best friend. "I was wondering if it'll be a good team this year."

"Do I really care?"

"Don't criticize what you don't know. It's so un-American of you not to like football. And you've never even been to a game. You didn't come with me at all last year, when they were playing great."

"I wasn't criticizing. I was just expressing my feelings." Andrea paused. "Sorry. I'm just feeling awful today. I miss Jon so much. I know it's a good idea for us to date other people now that he's at Duke. I mean, he's like eight hundred miles away, so obviously there's not much chance of us getting together regularly. But I really wish he'd stayed here, or at least gone someplace closer. Why'd he have to choose Duke, anyway?"

Another pause. "Do you think he'll sleep with a lot of girls there? That's what bothers me the most, honestly, especially because this year is going to be so useless. What are we going to do with ourselves except take the SATs again and fill out college applications? It's basically no fair that he's off at Duke having a great time and we're stuck here. Plus, there's no one in school I'd want to date anyway."

"Yeah, you're right. There isn't anyone. I was just wondering if I should get back together with Maverick," Lizzie admitted.

"At least you have a choice," Andrea said bitterly, "at least Maverick's still around. I keep imagining Jon making passionate, sweaty love with all those smart southern belles."

"Well," Lizzie said, trying to be comforting, "first of all, I've heard that those southern girls don't actually sweat because their bodies have adjusted to the heat."

"You made that up," Andrea complained.

Lizzie pretended Andrea hadn't said anything. "Secondly, I don't know what the national average is for freshman sex in college, but I don't imagine that Jon'll go much above that. He's much too conservative."

"Yeah, but the way I'm feeling is that even one or two is too many. Really, Lizzie, we need to do something drastic that'll stop my imagination from working overtime."

They walked on, not talking. The football sounds grew louder when they turned the corner. Now they could see the team practicing. Lizzie could pick out Maverick, his blond hair reflected in the setting sun. She was just beginning to imagine a detailed scenario in which she and Maverick started dating again and ended up at the same college next year, when Andrea turned to her and gripped her arm, hard.

"Ow," Lizzie said. "That hurts. Let go."

Andrea ignored her. "Lizzie, listen, I have a totally crazy idea. Wouldn't it be something," she went on, "if we both slept our way through the football team this fall? Then I wouldn't care what Jon did, because I'd be doing it too."

"Whoa," Lizzie said, not quite believing that Andrea was serious. Still, her mind began to race through the possibilities that the idea presented. "I'd have thought that only a true football fan would come up with a plan like that. But I kind of like it. It would be a great game that only the two of us knew the rules to. If we seduced every player on the team, then we'd be winners of the Great Game and Champions of the West, just like the fight song they sing all the time at Michigan football games."

Andrea tried to look modest but failed. "Whether I'm a fan or not, if we do this it'll be like being the first men on the moon: they never had to achieve anything else in their life because they always had that giant leap for mankind to fall back on. And we'll have all those boys to show that once we really did something adventurous with our lives. It's like a sign that we really lived."

"We'd be legends in our own time," Lizzie said, willing to play along.

"Not legends," Andrea said, slightly

alarmed. "We'd only be legends if people knew, right? And we can't tell anyone about it."

"Don't be ridiculous. We don't have to tell anyone, but do you honestly think the guys we have sex with will keep quiet about it? They'll broadcast it far and wide."

"My parents would kill me if they found out."

"Your parents would ground you until you were thirty," Lizzie said. "Then they'd kill you. But you know what my parents would do?" Without waiting for Andrea to respond, she said, "They'd want to watch. Maybe they'd bring along a grad student or two to take notes."

"Oh, ick, Lizzie, don't even think that. That's disgusting. Nobody's parents would do that. Not even yours."

Lizzie shook her head in disagreement. "They definitely would. Then they'd write articles about Girl X, a high school senior acting out sexually. More stuff to add to their overflowing CVs. So of course I don't want them to know about it. I don't want it to show up next year in some adolescent psychology journal. This is ours, ours and the team's."

Lizzie thought about what she'd just said to Andrea. Was it true? She wondered what it would mean to her parents to discover that their daughter — their little developmental psychology project, as she often thought of herself when she felt especially unloved by them — had had meaningless sex with multiple members of the football team. Lizzie knew that Mendel and Lydia believed that they were uniquely qualified to raise a psychologically healthy child just because they happened to have devoted their lives, professionally and personally, to psychology. And Lizzie had done nothing to dissuade them from that belief. She had been, in their eyes, a more or less perfect daughter. She had been well behaved, seemingly untroubled, a good student (that had been easy for her), and surely headed for a successful life; a daughter who validated all their theories about children and child-rearing. When she was young, she had just wanted to please them. As she got older, especially once she reached adolescence, she saw how her collaboration with them on that view of her (and of themselves as parents) kept them off her back. But she'd also begun to understand the price that she'd paid for that collaboration: they had no idea who she really was. Some of her teachers probably knew her better than her parents did. Heck, Andrea's mother almost certainly did — that was why she didn't want Andrea to spend so much time with her. She wanted Mendel and Lydia to see her, Elizabeth Frieda Bultmann, as she really was (or at least as she saw herself, from the inside). She wanted them to be curious about her, to want to know what went on below her polished surface. She wanted them to know her sadness, and her fears that she wasn't attractive, that she'd never be happy, that she felt lost and frightened most of the time, that she was, deep down, in her bones, a terrible person, a liar and a cheat. Maybe if they did find out about the Great Game, it would wake them up enough to finally see her.

"All right, I'm in," she said abruptly.

"You are?" Andrea's voice came back into focus. "That's terrific."

As they got farther from the high school, the sounds of the football practice receded. After a few minutes Lizzie asked, "Would it be just the starters, or all the seniors on the team? Which, d'you think?"

"I think it makes more sense to do the starters, don't you?"

"Yeah, maybe so. Easier to keep track of, anyhow."

"I think we should do them in alphabetical order."

"Last name or first name?"

"Actually, I was thinking more in order of their positions."

"Missionary, et cetera?"

"Be serious, Lizzie, this will be the defining act of our lives. If we did it alphabetically, who would we start with?"

"The center — and nobody pays much attention to the center, so he'll be easy to convince, although they'll all be easy to convince. After all, we're offering them sex with no commitment and no guilt. It's all on us."

"Too true," Andrea agreed. "You're right; it shouldn't be too hard at all."

Lizzie might have made another jokey comment ("Oh, they'll all be hard enough, I bet" or "I certainly hope they will"), but she was still thinking about the center, whose name she didn't then know. (It was Thad Cornish, and he was pathetically grateful to Lizzie for the rest of his life.)

" 'The center cannot hold.' That's from a poem by Yeats."

"Don't show off. This isn't the time for poetry. We need to get this settled really soon. We only have a couple months until the season ends, and twenty-two guys to go, eleven each."

"Twenty-three if we include the kicker,

which you'd know if you'd ever been to a game. I guess we can flip a coin to see whose team he's on, yours or mine."

"Yeah, good idea. Twenty-three it is." Andrea laughed. "Eleven, possibly twelve boys, eleven, possibly twelve weeks. It definitely sounds like something exciting to look forward to."

"Yeah," Lizzie agreed, "and think of how much fun we'll have."

They arrived at Lizzie's house. "I'll call you if I have any more brilliant ideas," Andrea said.

"It'll be hard to top the Great Game, for sure," Lizzie said as she started up the stairs to her front door.

The next day Lizzie took her tray to the farthest corner of the lunchroom so that there was no possibility of being overheard. She waved Andrea over and waited impatiently for her to sit down before she began. "So I thought about it a lot last night and this is how I think it should go: let's divide the team up so that one of us takes the defense and the other the offense. You should take the offense, because of Maverick." She stopped for a moment. "Or maybe it should be the other way around, and I should take the offense? Never mind, we can figure that out later. Anyway, if we each take half the team, we can help each other out if we have to deal with clingers, although I suspect they'll all be clingers, don't you?"

While Lizzie stopped to take a breath, Andrea started to respond but didn't get a chance, as Lizzie began talking faster and faster. "I was thinking that we'd take, like, a week with each guy. Two days flirting, two days fooling around, and then a sex-filled Friday night with whoever's turn it is. We could call it like the Three-*F* tactical approach. If my math is correct, that should take us into December, and gives us some wiggle room in case something comes up." She grinned. "And I'm about ninety-nine-point-nine-percent sure that something will come up, every week."

She took some books out of her backpack. "Look at what I got from the library last night: everything they had in on football, both coaching and strategy. I put all the others on hold, so hopefully we'll get them before we start."

Andrea looked puzzled. "Why'd you check out those books?"

"Because I figured we needed to know more about football. Well, *you* need to. I already know enough to get by. We're going to have to talk to those guys too, in addition to everything else we're doing with them.

We don't want to seem dumb, like we're just after them for sex, even if we are."

"But, Lizzie, listen, we don't need those books." Andrea's face had unease written all over it. "That was just a joke, my idea, the Great Game and all that. It was just to sort of preemptively punish Jon. But he called last night, and I'm not so worried. Besides, my mother said that I could go down to Durham sometime this fall to see him. And he'll be back here for Thanksgiving and Christmas."

"A joke? Really?" Lizzie was incredulous. "Yesterday you sounded awfully serious for it to be a joke. And why shouldn't we go ahead and do it, even if you're feeling better about Jon? Maybe tomorrow you'll start feeling insecure again."

"You can do what you want, Lizzie, but I'm not going to do it."

"But you thought of it."

"It was a joke," Andrea repeated. "I changed my mind. I'm not going to do it. And you shouldn't either."

"But, Andrea," Lizzie sputtered. "It's such a good idea. Why won't you do it?"

"I just can't," Andrea said doggedly. "I don't think it is."

"Well, you did think it was. You came up with the whole plan."

"Yeah, well, I was joking."

"Don't rewrite what happened yesterday. You weren't joking. You weren't. You loved the idea."

"No. Maybe. But now I don't love it. It's an awful idea. It's nuts. It's wrong."

"Like a sin, you mean?" Lizzie knew that Andrea's family belonged to a Conservative synagogue. (She herself had never set foot inside it. When Andrea had her bat mitzvah, Lydia had forbidden Lizzie to attend the services. "Religion," she'd admonished thirteen-year-old Lizzie, "is not the opiate of the masses, as Marx thought, but rather an excuse to kill others in its name. You need to learn that. History tells us that more people have been killed in the name of religion than any other justification for murder." There and then Lizzie crossed history off her list of interesting subjects to pursue.)

"Not a sin, not exactly a sin. Just wrong."

"Did your mother find out about it already? Did you tell her?"

"God, no, of course not. You know she suspects that Jon and I slept together last year, but she really isn't sure. I don't tell her anything. You know that."

Lizzie did know, but still couldn't figure out why Andrea had changed her mind. It was Andrea's overactive conscience, she decided. Andrea's conscience was evidently in overdrive.

Andrea interrupted her thoughts. "I . . . I don't know, I started thinking about me and Jon, and how I'd feel if he had sex with someone he didn't care about, how I'd hate that. And this would just be fucking; it wouldn't mean anything at all. That's not me."

"But wouldn't you hate it more if Jon had sex with someone he was in love with? I think that's the whole point. What we're doing isn't supposed to be meaningful. It'll be a diversion. A way to get us through the months until we graduate." And a way to get back at my parents, she added silently.

"Yeah, in a way it would be worse if he fell in love with another girl. It would be horrible, but at least it would mean that he wasn't having sex just to have sex. Trust me, Lizzie. You're crazy if you go ahead with it. Why's it so important to you, anyway? You could get Maverick back anytime you wanted to, you know that. Maybe I can find someone I could stand to go out with so we can double date like last year. Wouldn't that be more fun than having sex with a bunch of football players? I just don't understand why this stupid Big Game or whatever you called it is so important to you."

"Because when my parents find out about it, and I think everyone's going to find out about it, they'll finally have to realize that I'm not who they think I am. Parents are supposed to love their children even though the kids aren't perfect, but they don't love me like that. You know Mendel and Lydia: they think they can get rid of any behavior they don't approve of by treating me like I'm some rat they can retrain to do better. I honestly think they never loved me at all."

Andrea reached out to touch Lizzie's hand in sympathy, but Lizzie twisted away from her. "Lizzie, listen to yourself. You're going to do something totally asinine just to show your parents you can do something asinine? That's ridiculous."

"If you think it's so ridiculous, then, okay, don't do it. I couldn't care less. But I'm going to."

Andrea had almost the last word as they walked out of the lunchroom. "You know, Lizzie, I think my mother was right when she said you needed therapy."

"Wait, your mother said I needed therapy? When did she have that great insight? When you told her about the Great Game?"

"I didn't tell her, I already told you that."

"When, then?"

"I don't know, back in the sixth grade, maybe. She was talking to my dad."

"How come you never told me?"

"Because I knew how angry you'd be."

"But now you're telling me?"

"Yes, because you're making a huge mistake and you won't admit it, even to yourself, so I don't care how angry you are. I'm your best friend and I feel like I'm trying to save you from yourself."

That was the end of Lizzie and Andrea's friendship. After the yearbook staff meeting that afternoon, Lizzie walked home alone, making a list in her mind of all that she needed to do before the next day and the first F of the Great Game. She had to choose what to wear and decide what she was going to say to Thad Cornish. Finding out the location of Thad's locker was third on the list. Homework was easily neglected in favor of the more important stuff.

From the middle of September to the middle of April Lizzie was consumed by sex. It wasn't great sex. It wasn't even good sex. It was pretty awful. It was nothing like sex with Maverick had been. When she and Maverick slept together, it was exciting and a lot of fun. They learned the basics from one another, and then a little bit more. It felt as though they were fellow explorers, gingerly (and often not so gingerly) filling in all those blank spaces on the map of the body. It didn't have to do with passion or need, but rather good fellowship and camaraderie. Friendship. It was totally satisfying and Lizzie never regretted a moment she spent with Maverick.

But after the first four or five guys, the sex involved in the Great Game wasn't even fun. Still, she charged on, grimly and doggedly. At first the flirting was diverting, but once she got to the eighth or ninth player on the list even that palled and became more and more like a boringly repetitive homework assignment, something she had to do to get a good grade. In the midst of intercourse she often found herself reciting poems in her head. She wished she could talk to Andrea about what was happening. She'd come home after the deed was done, take a shower, brush her teeth, get the Great Game notebook from one of the drawers in her desk, cross off a name, and then crawl into bed, falling instantly and thoroughly into sleep. She came to count on those dreamless Friday nights that somehow seemed so much more restful than the other nights of the week.

THE CENTER

Thad "Cornball" Cornish was the team's center for his sophomore, junior, and senior years. As a born-again Christian, he was the player who led the team in their pre- and postgame prayers. He was very selective about the sins he'd commit, and it turned out, luckily for the Great Game, that fornication, or maybe just fornication with Lizzie, wasn't on his proscribed list.

LIZZIE MEETS MARLA

Lizzie was lying on her bed, reading *I Capture the Castle,* waiting for her roommate to arrive. It was a little nervous-making. She'd never shared a room with anyone before, although she and Andrea, in their younger and friendlier days, had often spent the night at each other's house. Earlier that morning, the first day the dorms opened to incoming freshmen, Mendel had driven her to Martha Cook, where she'd be living for the next year. Together they'd carried up the heaviest of the cartons, filled with whatever she couldn't bear to leave at home. When Lizzie opened the door of her third-floor room, what she noticed first were the many boxes piled in one corner. They were from someone named Marla Cantor, from Ohio. Marla Cantor, whoever she turned out to be, was going to be her room-mate.

She almost started to tell Mendel about how anxious she was but saw that, after putting down the last box from the car on the floor, he was heading toward the door. He stopped before he reached it and hesitated; for a moment or two Lizzie thought that her father might, weirdly, want to shake her hand before he left. But instead he reached out and gave her one of the typical Bultmann hugs, a sort of sideways embrace that denied any concession to actually touching one another except in those places that absolutely couldn't be avoided.

When he was gone, Lizzie closed her eyes and turned around a few times and pointed. When she opened her eyes she saw she'd selected the room's left side, with its uniform and institutionally bland bed, desk, chair, and dresser. No matter what sort of person her roommate was, Lizzie couldn't imagine Marla might possibly think one set of furniture was more desirable than the other. She began unpacking her books; she had a brief discussion with herself about the best method to arrange them on the bookshelves and decided just higgledy-piggledy in whatever order they came out of the boxes was fine. There were some of her favorite novels, books that she thought she'd better read if she wanted to be an English major, as well as books by the eclectic group of poets she loved most: A. E. Housman, Randall Jarrell, W. H. Auden, Edna St. Vincent Millay, Philip Larkin, and Dorothy Parker. Once she'd finished unpacking, she made several trips back and forth from the dorm to Mendel and Lydia's (as she'd always thought of the house where she'd lived her whole life) to get clothes, sheets, and towels. By the time she finished the last trip, unpacked everything, and made the bed, it was early afternoon.

She'd just gotten to one of her favorite parts in Dodie Smith's novel, the incident with the bear, when she heard voices at the door.

"Hi," she said, getting up. "You must be Marla. I'm Lizzie."

"Wow, you sure got here early. It felt like we left at the crack of dawn."

"Well, I live here. I mean, in Ann Arbor. Easy walking distance. Practically on the campus." She knew she sounded ridiculous but didn't know what to do about it.

"Oh, that's terrific; you can show me around."

There was a slight cough from the woman who'd come in the door right behind Marla.

"Oh, sorry, Mom. Lizzie, this is my mother, Abby Cantor."

Mrs. Cantor smiled at Lizzie, who gamely smiled back. "It's nice to meet you, Lizzie. How would you girls like to have a late lunch or a very early dinner with me before I leave?"

Marla spoke before Lizzie had a chance to say anything.

"Can we wait till next time you come up? I want to get my stuff put away and then I want Lizzie to give me the grand tour. And you have a long drive home by yourself. You should probably get going before it starts getting dark."

Mrs. Cantor nodded, admitting that her daughter's observation was correct, but clearly not happy about the conclusion. "Well, if you're sure you'll be okay, I suppose I should really get started."

"I'll be fine, Mom." Marla grinned at Lizzie. "Lizzie will take care of me, won't you, Lizzie?"

Although she wasn't quite sure what was going on, Lizzie assured Mrs. Cantor that, yes, she would take care of her daughter, although it seemed to her on not much evidence that Marla could take good care of herself.

Watching Marla's mother envelop her

daughter in a huge hug gave Lizzie a small, jealous pang. "Listen," Mrs. Cantor said as she gently pulled away from Marla, "college is a new beginning. It's a chance to start over. You'll meet tons of new people and take interesting classes. You'll discover yourself or reinvent yourself. It can be a way to outrun your past." She stopped, her voice cracking a little.

For a panicked moment, Lizzie wondered whether news of the Great Game had somehow reached the shores of Lake Erie and she was now hearing the lecture certainly due her for playing the leading role in it. But, no, Mrs. Cantor wasn't looking at her; it was Marla she was addressing these words to.

"Are you girls absolutely sure you don't want to go to dinner?"

"Mom," Marla said patiently, "I'll be fine. You go. We can talk this weekend."

"Just —" But Mrs. Cantor didn't finish. She started walking toward the elevator, the heels of her shoes clicking on the wooden floor of the hall.

"God, I thought she'd never leave," Marla sighed. "Well, I'm not entirely a liar, so how about if I put away some of this stuff first and then you can show me the campus? I came on a tour with my dad and stepmom last year, but since I never thought I'd end up here, I didn't pay much attention."

That was fine with Lizzie. For the next hour or so she continued paging through Dodie Smith's novel, turning back to earlier sections whenever she came too near the end. And in between chapters she studied Marla.

She was taller than Lizzie, which was not saying much, since Lizzie herself was only a smidge above five feet. Her wavy shoulder-length hair was the color of wet sand, and her face and arms were dotted with freckles of the same color. She moved with a competent ease from box to box, sorting and arranging their contents on her side of the room, humming a song Lizzie didn't recognize. She quickly made her bed, but, unlike Lizzie, Marla didn't bother with hospital corners. Mendel was a stickler for them (neatness in general was second only to cleanliness in his pantheon of greatest goods), and it was the first habit Lizzie intended to break herself of, although it was now so ingrained that it might be a little more difficult than she'd originally thought. Lacking hospital corners, the blanket and sheets immediately came away from the bottom of the mattress when Marla threw herself down on it with a grand whoosh.

"Unpacking is exhausting. Worse than packing, I think. Well, come on, time's a-wasting. Show me around the campus a little before we have to be back for dinner."

They walked through the Law Quad to State Street and then turned right. Lizzie pointed out the Union, where John Kennedy gave his "Ask not what your country can do for you — ask what you can do for your country" speech when he was running for president and, farther up State, Shaman Drum, her favorite bookstore.

"Looks great," Marla commented. "If they have a good section of art books, this'll definitely be where my allowance goes."

"Oh, they do," Lizzie assured her, although she had no idea if this was true. "And this is called the Diag," Lizzie told Marla as they reentered the campus. "There's where most of our classes will be, I think, in those buildings," pointing to Mason and Haven Halls. "And over there" — she gestured — "is the UGLI."

"Ugly?"

"U-G-L-I." Lizzie spelled out the abbreviation for the Undergraduate Library. "Although lots of people think it actually is. Ugly, I mean."

"Mmm," Marla responded absently, not particularly interested in the aesthetics of libraries. By then they were back at Martha Cook, just in time for an uneventful dinner during which Lizzie kept glancing around and thankfully failing to find anyone who looked even vaguely familiar, and then there was a seemingly endless orientation meeting.

Afterward, as they made their way through a crowd of girls up to their room, Marla nudged Lizzie.

"Well, that was all pretty sobering, I thought. Way too many rules; now I know why my mother wanted me to live here. So tell me, why are you here and not one of the other dorms?"

"Uh, I don't know. It just seemed like a good thing. No men."

Marla shook her head in mock wonder, put her arm around Lizzie, and gave her a hug. "No men. Clearly, there's a story behind that sentence. I can't wait to hear it."

Later that night, when Lizzie was wriggling around, trying to make herself comfortable and wondering if she'd ever get used to the thin mattress, Marla spoke into the darkness.

"Do you think we'll be friends?"

Lizzie got a sick feeling in her stomach, although maybe it was a result of the pizza at dinner. "I'm not so good with friends," she muttered.

"Really? That's interesting. My stepmom, Taylor, says that the typical pattern with roommates is that first they adore each other, then they can't stand one another, and then they come back to being friends. But maybe we can skip the middle part of not liking each other. I sort of have a feeling we can."

Oh God, Lizzie thought. Was Marla one of those woo-woo people who believed she could predict the future? She would absolutely change rooms tomorrow if that was the case.

But Marla seemed to read her mind and went on to say, "No, no, it's not like there's an angel sitting on my shoulder telling me what's going to happen. I just get these feelings about things. Big things. Not like passing tests or getting a date, but the deep, important future."

Although Lizzie wasn't sure that she saw the distinction that Marla was making, she was interested in what Marla would say next. "And I kind of need a friend right now, to talk to. To tell something to. A sort of secret. I mean a real secret. About me. That nobody except my parents and the other people involved in it know about."

But Lizzie wasn't ready for that quite yet. She wasn't sure she wanted to tell her own secret. "So what about our future?"

"Okay, here goes. When we're really really old, like in sixty years or so, I see us sitting on a porch, in rocking chairs, and one of my great-granddaughters will say, 'Mama Marla' — because that's what I've decided I want to be called — 'how did you and Auntie Lizzie meet?' And we'll tell them that we met the very first day of college, because we were assigned to the same room, and that first night we lay in our beds and told each other great secrets about our lives. And she'll say, 'What are those secrets?' And I'll say, 'Oh, baby, they're secrets; they're not for telling, not now or ever.' "

"Why are you all of a sudden talking in a southern accent?" Lizzie asked suspiciously. "You're from Cleveland."

Marla said, just a tad defensively, "I'm from Brecksville, actually, which is south of Cleveland. But that seems to me how that little story needed to be told."

Lizzie, enchanted despite herself with the picture of Mama Marla and Auntie Lizzie, took a deep breath and sat up in bed.

"Okay, you go first with the secrets," she said.

Marla nodded, which of course Lizzie

couldn't see, and began. "Well, my mother was so weird this afternoon because she's worried about me."

"Is that the secret? Because of course I got that."

"Hey, don't interrupt, it's hard enough as it is."

"Okay, sorry."

"I had this boyfriend, James. Well, I still have him. I mean, he's here, going to school here. And I got pregnant last fall." She hurried on. "James and I talked about it, what we should do, should we get married, because we are going to get married sometime, of course, and then we talked to our parents. And then . . ."

Marla paused so long that Lizzie thought she might have stopped talking for good.

Finally she continued. "And then," she repeated, "nobody thought we should get married, we were way too young, and that I should have an abortion and put it all behind me. But I realized that I wanted to have it, the baby, that I wanted to keep it, that I wanted to get married. I didn't want to have an abortion. And then everyone started arguing with everybody else, and with me, except James, who felt the same way I did, and finally we came to this terrible compromise, which was that I would

45

have the baby and then some lucky couple would get to adopt it.

"So that's what happened. I spent my senior year being pregnant and having the baby in June, and then it was gone, poof, off to live with another family. So technically I didn't graduate from high school but they let me in here anyway, and I don't even know if it was a boy or a girl, and everyone is just tiptoeing around me, even James, and though I guess that it was the sensible thing to do — I mean, how could we raise a baby and go to college, even if we did get married; I mean, I know people do it, but it didn't seem that people like us did it — it's turned out to be really hard, and I spent most of the summer crying and not wanting to see anybody, sometimes even James, who I love more than anything in the world. I mean, honestly, nobody wants me to see James anymore, especially his parents, who did like me once, so that's why my mother is freaked out about me. She doesn't know what I'm going to do next.

"And you're the only one here who knows, besides James." Marla took a deep breath and let it out slowly.

Lizzie couldn't think of anything to say. Everything she tested out in her mind — "Oh, wow," or "That's terrible," or "I think

46

you're really brave," for example — sounded lame, insensitive, or just plain dumb. She got out of bed and went over and sat down next to Marla and took her hand. Of all the secrets that passed through Lizzie's life, Marla's was the one she never revealed, never retelling it as a good story or a terrible heartache, not divulging it to friends or George. Or even Jack, to whom she'd told everything else.

"Now you," Marla said, when Lizzie was back in her own bed.

"Okay. My secret is that I had sex with my entire high school football team last winter and spring. Well," Lizzie corrected herself, "not the entire team; just the starters."

There was silence for a few moments, then Marla said, "Oh, Lizzie, I'm so sorry."

Of all the responses Marla could have made, that was the most unexpected. Lizzie felt tears well up behind her eyes.

"It was supposed to be fun. We called it the Great Game."

"Do people know?"

"Well, the whole school knew by the time it was over. Everybody stopped talking to me, and I kind of stopped functioning at all my last semester. And in a horribly weak moment I told my parents, which was probably a mistake. They're totally different than your parents."

Marla started laughing, which shocked Lizzie. "Oh my God, Lizzie, you screwed two dozen different guys and you didn't get pregnant? Are you kidding me?"

"Twenty-three, actually," Lizzie admitted, uncomfortably.

"You know, kiddo, it would have been so much less crazy, not to mention less destructive, if you'd picked the basketball team to fuck."

MAVERICK AND THE GREAT GAME

Maverick Brevard was Lizzie's first real boyfriend.

The Brevards were a family that lived and breathed football. Wyatt, the father, grew up in Baton Rouge in an exceptionally large Cajun family. He'd always planned on playing for LSU (Geaux Tigers!) but was wooed away by a damned good recruiter for the University of Michigan (Go Blue!) who basically promised him the moon, including a free ride financially and no redshirt year: he would start at wide receiver as a true freshman. And the guy absolutely delivered on his promises. In return, Wyatt played his heart out for Michigan and Coach Bump Elliott. During his years there the team had one winning season, his freshman year, when they lost only a single game and were the Big 10 champions. The next three seasons — which he never liked talking (or even thinking) about — would have destroyed a lesser man's love of the game in general and University of Michigan football in particular, but Wyatt remained a Wolverine fan forever. His greatest disappointment, at least prior to his realization that his two oldest sons showed some talent but probably not enough to play pro ball, was that he was never mentioned as a possible Heisman Trophy candidate. He'd chosen to play the wrong position.

"Should have been a quarterback," he'd say to his three boys, Maverick, Ranger, and Colton. Still, he was plenty good enough at wide receiver to be drafted by the New Orleans Saints, much to the delight of the hometown fans, who still remembered the good hands and fleetness of foot he'd possessed in high school. He spent his steady and successful career there, making the Pro Bowl once, but was cursed again with being on a team that was mediocre at best. He was happy that he'd chosen to retire in 1979, because the next season many of the Saints' frustrated and angry fans started calling the team the "Aints" and coming to the games wearing brown paper bags on their heads so that nobody could recognize them for the fools they were, throwing away good money to watch a consistently losing team. Right after Wyatt retired and was casting about for how to fill his life post-football, Bo Schembechler, then the head coach of the Wolverines, asked him to come back to Ann Arbor to coach the receivers.

Maverick's mother, Pammie, grew up in suburban Detroit. She was tiny, blond, and cute, and reveled in being all three. She'd been captain of the U of M cheerleading squad (which is how she and Wyatt met), president of the Tri-Delts, and still wore her hair in a ponytail. Under the right conditions and after a glass or two of wine, she was reliably bouncy. Dispensing with the dot, she put a heart over the lowercase *i* in her name. She loved her sons to distraction. Her cheerleading background came in handy at their football games. And she'd never missed one.

Maverick, like his father before him, was a wide receiver; his brother Ranger, ten months younger but also a junior (the vagaries of birthdays: Ranger was a young junior, Maverick an old one), backed up the quarterback but was projected to be a starter his senior year. Their younger

50

brother, Colton, quarterbacked his Pee-Wee football team. Maverick was a good football player but not an excellent one. Ranger was excellent but not great. The family's football hopes and dreams resided in Colt, who at thirteen was starting to get noticed by college football scouts. In fact, Colt went on to win the Heisman twice, joining Archie Griffin as the only two players to achieve that distinction. He had a superb NFL career with the Kansas City Chiefs and would eventually be inducted into the Football Hall of Fame.

Before she started dating Maverick, Lizzie had never given much thought to football. Oh, she went to the occasional high school game, because that's what everyone (except Andrea) did on Friday nights. At the beginning, though, when Maverick and Lizzie couldn't bear to be out of sight of one another, she spent her afternoons watching the team practice. Evenings, she helped Maverick memorize the playbook. He diagrammed various pass routes and defensive alignments, went through the rosters, and described to Lizzie the strengths and weaknesses of each player on the opposing team. He told her stories about the great coaches: Vince Lombardi, Bill Walsh, Don Shula, Tom Landry (Lizzie would hear that name again — and again — from George); and the great tragedies: Ernie Davis, the first African American to win the Heisman Trophy, dead of leukemia at twenty-four before he could ever play a down as a pro; Darryl Stingley and Mike Utley, whose football careers were cut short by spinal cord injuries.

Maverick lent Lizzie all of his favorite football books to read, which included not only George Plimpton's *Paper Lion* and Don DeLillo's *End Zone* but also *Mr. Quarterback* and *Mr. Halfback,* two children's books by William Campbell Gault that Wyatt had read as a boy growing up in Louisiana and passed on to his sons. Under Maverick's tutelage she rooted wholeheartedly for the holy triumvirate: the Pioneers (High School), the Wolverines (U of M), and the Lions, Detroit's pro football team, which had never won a Super Bowl.

Even before she was a teenager, Lizzie discovered novels like *Double Date* and *Going Steady* and *Fifteen* at the library and read and reread them regularly. Set mostly in the 1950s and early 1960s, they described a world that she couldn't quite relate to but that was totally fascinating. She learned from them that it was always a mixed blessing to have a steady boyfriend in high school. Yes, you sometimes got to wear his football varsity jacket (Lizzie did) or his ID bracelet (Lizzie didn't, but that was because by the time she'd read those books, in the middle of the 1980s, no one wore ID bracelets any longer). The main characters in those novels, who were all named Jane or Sally or Penny, loved the fact that they knew who was taking them to the sock hops and spring flings and who they'd share lemon Cokes with at the drugstore, but in between the lines on the page there was always the lurking problem of sex, specifically, how far to go. Jealousy ran rampant in those books. Girls you thought were your friends became enemies whose goal in life was to get your boyfriend away from you. And breakups always broke your heart.

But none of this was true for Lizzie and Maverick. Instead, it was all good fun. Because they'd known each other since kindergarten, everything was familiar. They started dating because they found themselves always laughing at the same jokes in class, because Maverick could help Lizzie in trig and Lizzie could help him in English comp, and both of them really liked listening to duets, although neither could carry a tune, a fact that they both lamented. "I've Had the Time of My Life" and "Somewhere

Out There" were two of their favorites. They had sex because it seemed silly not to. They broke up when Maverick went to spend the summer with his dad's family in Baton Rouge and wanted the freedom to date other girls; he didn't want to feel he was sneaking around behind Lizzie's back. That was Maverick, blond and sweet and fearless, an Eagle Scout always insisting on the truth.

Lizzie had (still has, in fact) a less-than-comfortable relationship with honesty. By the time Maverick told her this, she'd been feeling a little burdened with twosomeness. She'd started to think wistfully of weekends without a date; she wanted to spend some time by herself. She'd grown tired of football and football statistics, at least for a while, but she never would have told him that. She drove Maverick to the airport; she enthusiastically kissed him good-bye and went home, completely fine. The year that she was seventeen and Maverick Brevard's girlfriend was the lightest of heart Lizzie would ever feel, but back then she thought it was just the way her life was supposed to arrange itself.

Once she'd decided to go on with the Great Game, even without Andrea, Lizzie thought she should move Maverick up to the second week, right after Thad Cornish, since the Game involved also having sex with his brother Ranger, which would be a little awkward. She wanted to explain the situation to Maverick and see what he thought. When they met on the Wednesday night of his week and she told him her plans for the next twenty weeks or so, Maverick immediately responded that he thought playing the Great Game verged on lunacy. Plus it didn't sound like the Lizzie he'd dated all last year. Because Lizzie couldn't explain why it wasn't an insane thing to do, there was little left to say. There was no flirting involved. Thursday night they picked up the argument right where they'd left off. Lizzie finally told him what a stick-in-the-mud he was being. She'd slept with him, hadn't she? And he enjoyed it. A lot. Hadn't he?

"That was different," Maverick said. "I'm pretty sure Ranger's a virgin. It's not fair to him that the first girl he's going to have sex with is someone who doesn't love him. You were the first girl I slept with, but we were dating, we loved each other. Don't you see how different that is?" There was no fooling around that night.

Friday night after the game, when they were due to have sex, they drove out to the park and walked along the river. "Can't you just go along with it?" Lizzie pleaded. "Just because we were happy together?"

"Oh, crap," Maverick said, "you are certifiably nuts. I know I'm going to regret this," but he gave in, as she knew he would.

GEORGE'S CHILDHOOD

By any objective standard, George had a pretty wonderful childhood. In fact, there were only three downsides to it that he'd ever been able to identify: his conflicted feelings about his father, his conflicted feelings about his older brother, Todd, and the frustration of riding the Hebrew school bus.

He lived in Tulsa, Oklahoma. Elaine, his mother, occasionally tutored students in French, but was mostly a stay-at-home mom. His father, Allan, was the Jewish orthodontist. What this meant was that whenever the sons and daughters of members of the Jewish community needed orthodontia — which was almost always — it was Allan to whom they turned. He understood the importance of teeth in bat and bar mitzvah photos, and it was not unknown for him to remove a set of braces for the big day and then reattach them when the festivities were over. For no extra charge, of course. Because he deserved his excellent reputation as an orthodontist, a large number of Tulsa's non-Jewish community also brought their offspring to him when they were in need of braces. It was not uncommon for George to see someone from middle school, his bowling league, or his Sunday school class whenever he went to his father's office.

It was because of his father's profession that George hated pain. Even though Allan was the soul of generosity, kindness, and care — he'd purchased three large arcade games so everyone, parents included, would have something to do while the kids waited to be called into the treatment rooms — he still inflicted a great deal of pain on his patients. George never forgot those awful monthly appointments when his braces needed to be tightened. He understood even as a kid that while the shoemaker's children may go barefoot, the orthodontist's sons must have perfect teeth. Hence those dreaded visits to his father's office.

George likened his father's smile — fake, false, and totally fearsome — to the grin left behind by the Cheshire cat. And who smiles like that when they're about to hurt you? Sadists, that's who. He knew, even at thirteen, that Allan was smiling in order to try to reassure each patient that it would all be okay, it might hurt a little, just for a second or two, but that straight teeth were a necessity for a certain type of young person in Tulsa, Oklahoma, in the 1980s, and this small step, done every four to six weeks, was a necessary part of the treatment. George knew this, and knew for certain that his father loved him, but he couldn't get over the fact that the torturer/orthodontist was his own father, coming toward him in order to dispense some not inconsiderable pain on his own son. For his own good.

George didn't read the ne plus ultra example of dental malfeasance, William Goldman's *Marathon Man,* until he was in dental school. When he did his hands shook so much that he had trouble holding the book; he found it so distressing that he never finished it, although he never seriously considered changing his career plans.

But for the three weeks and six days between visits, George deeply loved and admired his father. He was proud that Allan worked in a free dental clinic twice a month, and that he braced up (as George thought the verb should be) poor adults and kids in his office for free. There were scrapbooks in the waiting room filled with pictures of before (buckteeth) and after (the ultimate dental ideal), as well as letters of appreciation from patients, praising Allan for his concern, skill, and pleasing manner. Dopey Annette Silverberg, who went to dancing class with George, once told him during a waltz that his father was "jovial." Jovial! How could you be considered jovial when you were inflicting pain on someone?

The biggest lesson he learned from his childhood was this: that he wanted to grow up to be exactly like Allan, except that he knew that he would never, under any circumstances, become an orthodontist. In his junior year of college George had had a passing thought that maybe he'd become a gerontologist, but the thought of Allan and Elaine being old enough to possibly need his services made him sick to his stomach.

It had perhaps been a mistake to later share these thoughts with Lizzie, who was given to an abiding interest about George's childhood, so different from her own. Although she was also devoted to Allan (she couldn't imagine a better father-in-law, or father, if it came to that), she wanted George to think deeply about his relationship to his dad. She pointed out that his older brother, Todd, having presumably suffered similarly at his father's hands, was a surfer bum, with no connection to teeth at all.

"But of course," Lizzie told George, "you never ever see a surfer with bad teeth. Maybe we should move to Sydney, too, and you could become the dentist who specializes in kids who want to be surfers."

George was not particularly introspective and only occasionally wondered why, given what he'd felt about his father and pain, he had decided to go into anything relating to teeth at all and had not studied engineering or agronomy or really anything else. What he thought about a lot, though, during the long years of his greatest successes, was whether those months and months of getting his braces tightened had been the source of his slowly developing belief that perhaps pain could be rendered mute and weaponless.

"But, George, don't you think it's a bit weird that you, someone who denies the existence of pain, became a dentist? I bet you inflict as much pain or more on your patients than your dad did. I bet Freud would say that what you were really doing, what you needed to do to grow up, was to deny pain and Allan's power over you."

"First of all," George answered patiently, "I don't deny the existence of pain. What I think I'm denying is that pain, or at least suffering, is ever really necessary. And I'm

60

certainly not causing the pain. People come to me when they're in pain. Great pain, sometimes. My job is to make the pain go away by fixing what's wrong. Which I do. And thirdly, I'm not denying my dad's influence on me. He's — he was — a terrific father. You know that. If I could be even half as good a father to my own kids, I'd be thrilled. I just didn't want to be responsible for that fucking monthly tightening-of-braces routine for any other kid in the world."

"Well, why'd you go to your dad for braces? I know I read somewhere that doctors shouldn't treat their own families."

"He was the best in Tulsa," George said simply, and not without pride. "Everyone knew that. All my friends went to him, whether they were Jewish or not. For those who were, it was like a rite of passage. Hebrew school. Learning your haftorah portion. Braces from Dr. Goldrosen."

Lizzie was far from convinced that George's career had been a purely free choice and not some working out of an ancient father–son curse, but that particular day she let the matter drop, though she continued to ponder it all.

The second downside was Todd. He was only twenty-one months older than George, but because Todd skipped the sixth grade, they were three grades apart. In some ways this was a relief to George, because each year there was then the chance that Todd's teachers would have transferred to a different school, moved out of state, or retired, and the people hired in their place would be unaware of Todd's unnerving combination of superior intelligence and scorn for the human race and its ridiculous conventions. But more often than not, what happened on the first day of classes in September was that the teacher, taking attendance, would say, "George Goldrosen." Pause. Sigh. "Any relation to Todd Goldrosen?" And when George acknowledged that, yes, indeed, he was Todd's younger brother, the teacher would look at him for a long time, assessing what he saw, before finally going on to the next name. George guessed that the teacher was hoping that he was as smart as his older brother but that he lacked Todd's interest in defying authority. Actually, both of these were true.

There wasn't a physical resemblance between the brothers. Todd inherited a mixture of all of Allan's and Elaine's most attractive physical qualities and out of that olio of genes he became himself. He had dark eyes, skin that tanned easily and evenly, thick black hair, and eyelashes to die for (this was according to their Stillwater grandmother; their Montreal grandmother wasn't interested in such trivialities). His eyes were dark brown, he had no need of glasses, and he possessed a killer smile both before and after orthodontia. In short, he looked like Adonis. George knew this last fact about Todd because one of Todd's many girlfriends had told him so, and he knew which girlfriend it was because George happened to regularly read Todd's journal, which included intimate details about his girlfriends and who said what and what was done, and Todd had no trouble with including all the graphic details. George would often feel that he needed to wash his hands after putting the journal back in the top drawer of Todd's desk, but he never felt so dirty that he stopped sneaking into Todd's room whenever Todd was out on a date, and reading it.

George, on the other hand, resembled nobody else in the family. He was much fairer skinned, with red hair that curled up into short, tight ringlets on his head and that, sadly, began receding when George was in his early twenties, just when he and Lizzie became a couple. The sun was his enemy; during those impossibly hot Oklahoma summers of his childhood he couldn't stay outside nearly as long as Todd did. He'd have to huddle under a towel when he came out of the pool at the Jewish Center.

There was also no getting around the fact that, in sharp contrast with his parents and brother, George was, as a kid and early teen, although by no means fat, definitely pudgy. "Chunky" was perhaps a kinder, more masculine-sounding description. The worst part of being more than a tad overweight was having to shop for his clothes in the Husky Department at Dillard's, praying hard from start to finish that nobody would see him there. He hated those shopping trips.

When he began to become really interested in girls, George feared that his was the sort of face that only his closest relatives could love, the kind of person that's always described as having a great personality. George didn't undervalue the benefits of a good personality, but he also aspired to handsomeness. Cuteness at the very very least. He almost got his wish. By the time he started college he'd lost some of the pudginess of his youth and his face had become thinner and more defined. He started working out a lot, so if physique was what you were interested in, there George's muscles were. Lizzie thought the best part of George's face, besides the general fact of liking that it was George's face, was his eyes. They were a variable sort of hazel and, depending on the color of the shirt or sweater he wore, they'd become grayish or bluish or greenish. Lizzie adored George's eyes and thought he looked most handsome in deep-blue shirts. There was still no way anyone would describe George as Adonis-like, but on the attractiveness spectrum that stretched from handsome to downright ugly, he'd ended up somewhere between cute and handsome.

Both sets of his grandparents were face pinchers, sometimes painfully so. Invariably, whenever they saw him they'd first hug him and then step back and take a piece of his cheek between their thumb and forefinger, "Oy, what a *punim,*" they'd murmur. "A *sheyn eyngl.*" They marveled that they couldn't think of anyone in the long and proud history of both sides of the family that he resembled, living or long dead. He was sui generis. One of a kind in the Goldrosen and Lowen clans. His Stillwater grandparents would look accusingly at Elaine. Had there been a randy car salesman in his mother's recent past? His Montreal grandparents would look reproachfully at Allan, their expressions clearly indicating that they blamed him entirely. If she didn't keep her marriage vows, you *ganef*, it's all your own fault for being such a rotten husband. Of course nobody said any of this out loud; George just imagined that's what they were thinking.

But the main reason that all his grandparents doted on George was that he had a marshmallow heart. He cried when he watched sad movies and he cried when he read sad books (*Beautiful Joe* almost did him in). Even commercials on television could bring tears to his eyes. Todd couldn't stand it. "That is so goddamn sappy," he'd say scornfully, watching George weep at an ad for dog food. "Yeesh. Can't you see how they're just manipulating you?" No, George couldn't.

One result of being softhearted was that George constantly felt sorry for people. He would empty his pockets of change for a man sitting on the ground in front of Swenson's holding a sign saying "War Veteran. No Home. No Job. Anything Will Help." If the vet looked hungry (and they all looked hungry) he'd go in and buy the guy a hamburger and fries. If he got to choose kids for his class spelling bee team, the first three people he chose were the least popular, the outsider, and the worst speller in class.

George's attitude infuriated Todd. "Don't you see how presumptuous it is to assign unhappiness to someone? What right do you have to do that? Maybe they don't mind how they're living, even if it is different from what other people think is a good life. Maybe they feel sorry for you and your little bourgeois life, taking a shower every day, getting good grades, going to dances, living in a big house, and some woman is paid a pittance to vacuum up the dirt you bring in and wash your clothes and iron your oxford cloth shirts. Yes," he'd continue in a fake judicious tone, "I believe they must definitely pity you, because *I* certainly do."

It wasn't only people that he cared about to excess. He regularly brought home stray animals and begged his mother to let him keep them. Elaine relented only once, for a three-legged kitten George named Twinkie, who he'd found shivering in a storm drain. When George was ten he stole a small stuffed animal from his cousin Shelley's house in Montreal because he thought the rabbit was neglected and in need of a great deal of love, a task George was eager to take on. As far as George knew, no one even realized that the rabbit was gone, which only went to show that he'd been right. He named it Rabbit Elias, after the Goldrosen's rabbi, and in an early example of George's already well-developed sense of humor, he realized that Rabbit Elias was actually a pretty good pun, so he changed its name to Rabbit Pun Elias, known familiarly as Pun. The first Christmas Lizzie visited the Goldrosens, George introduced her to Twinkie and Pun, who by that time were both suffering from age-related conditions. Twinkie was basically incontinent and Pun had lost most of his stuffing.

One afternoon when George was twelve he was walking home from Hebrew school and encountered a sick squirrel resting under a tree.

"But how did you know he was sick?" Lizzie asked years later, which was one of the litany of questions his parents had asked when he arrived home and explained why his wrist was bleeding.

"He had this look, like he wanted me to help him. So I did. Or tried to."

After he bit George, the squirrel leaped out of his grasp and ran away, clearly not very sick, or even sick at all. The result for George was a painful series of rabies shots.

Lizzie kissed the tiny squirrel scar on his wrist. "You would think," she commented, "that would teach you that no good deed goes unpunished. But it didn't, did it?"

No, George admitted. It didn't teach him anything, except perhaps that it was harder to read a squirrel's state of health or state of mind than he had once thought.

"But he let me pick him up," he told his parents. "If he wasn't sick, why would he do that?"

No one at the time had an answer for him, but years later Lizzie came up with one. "Maybe he'd just had a miraculous escape from a man driving way too fast, and wanted revenge on humanity. He probably immediately saw that you were the perfect mark."

George doubted that theory but couldn't totally dispute it. He *was* the perfect mark.

For all of Todd's relentless criticisms of him, George didn't hate his brother. He idolized him, until the day that Todd, at seventeen, either intentionally or not (nobody except Todd knew for sure), mishandled an experiment in chemistry class and blew out all the windows in the lab. He walked outside with the rest of his class when the school was evacuated but then never walked back inside. Late that night, or early the next morning, he bailed from his bourgeois life in Tulsa and left home, first for Boulder, then Portland (where he worked on an organic farm and changed his name to Kale), and then Sydney, where he started surfing. When George saw how all this had devastated his parents — his mother cried constantly for what seemed like the whole next year and couldn't be comforted, and his father started behaving weirdly, smoking a pipe and loudly guffawing at odd and inappropriate times — he realized that while he still loved Todd, he didn't, any longer, want to be him, Adonis or not.

The third blemish on his otherwise blue-skies childhood was the situation with the Hebrew school bus. This bus picked up all the twelve-year-old Jewish boys after school two days a week and took them to the temple to study with Rabbi Elias and Cantor Ferber in preparation for their bar mitzvahs. Two hours later the lucky boys who lived on the other side of Thirty-First Street got driven home. The talk on the bus, both to and from Hebrew school, was almost exclusively about sex and girls. Generations of Jewish boys in Tulsa learned about sex on the Hebrew school bus. The problem was that George rode the bus only one way, since he could walk home when Hebrew school was over. This meant that he learned only half as much as Michael Minter, say, or all the other boys who got to ride the bus both ways. George worried about this a lot and wondered how he could possibly measure up to them when they started sleeping with girls and all the other boys knew things of which George was unaware.

Lizzie thought this was a perfectly wonderful story and wondered whether there was some kinky sexual practice that occurred among Jewish men bar mitzvah'd in Tulsa at a rate much higher than the national average and that could be ascribed to the erroneous information the boys had exchanged. "In any case," she told George when they were lying in bed one night, "you don't seem to have missed anything important." George was greatly relieved that Lizzie felt that way.

THE WIDE RECEIVER

Maverick was one of the wide receivers. The other was Loren "Speedy" Gonzalez, probably the worst player on the team, although a lot of the reason for that was genetics, not lack of enthusiasm or desire. Speedy was slim verging on skinny and, under orders from the coaches, he ate constantly and spent a lot of time trying to muscle up in the weight room, to no good effect. Ranger avoided throwing to him as much as possible, but of course the opposing teams would double- and triple-team Maverick. It was discouraging for everyone. When Speedy wasn't on the football field, in class, or the weight room, he played bass in a rock band. What Lizzie remembered best about Speedy was that even away from his bass he was always tapping his foot to some rhythm only he could hear. During sex too. It was more than a bit distracting.

JACK McCONAGHEY

Lizzie overslept the first day of classes spring quarter of her freshman year and, after running across the campus and dashing up four flights of stairs, she was out of breath and already late to her twentieth-century poetry class. It was taught by the best-known poet on the English faculty, Addison "The Terror" Terrell. Keeping his nickname in mind helped Lizzie, and no doubt others, remember that Terrell, who had won or been nominated for the Pulitzer and National Book Award several times in his distant and not-so-distant past, pronounced his name with the accent on the first syllable, Terrell like terror, not like Tuh-RELL. His fellow poets and departmental colleagues knew Terrell as a formidable and ferocious critic who brooked no careless language, who hated loosey-goosey pronouns, who knew exactly what he liked and what was good (very little and nothing by a woman or anyone under, say, the age of forty). No surprise that the same group of poets made up each category. He didn't hesitate to let you (especially if you were a student) know what he thought, whether you'd asked or not. He was equally venomous in deconstructing a pantoum or a petition to the dean. He delighted (or seemed to, anyway) in using your own words to impale you, then somehow twisting them so that he left a gaping wound in your writing hand, or your head, or your heart. No real writer — although Terrell never actually acknowledged that there was another one besides himself — wanted him to review his (never her: Terrell refused to acknowledge the existence of what he invariably called "poetesses") new book of poetry, even if a bad review generated the same amount of publicity that you'd get with a good one, or even more, sometimes, if you happened to write a letter back to the editor complaining about the perfidious Terrell's review.

Lizzie read and wrote a lot of poetry. At sixteen she'd won a contest sponsored by

Seventeen, and her poem was published in the magazine. She approached poetry in a careless, loving sort of way. She planned to major in English knowing it would, at the very least, seriously annoy Mendel and Lydia. Hence, the need to spend time with the Terror every Tuesday, Thursday, and Saturday from eight to nine (that's a.m.), April 1 to June 24.

"Hah! No foolin' about that startin' date," George would have added, had she known him then.

She entered the room just as Terrell finished calling roll and then made her way to the first open seat, which happened to be in the middle of the first row and thus involved climbing over four unhappy pairs of knees. "Sorry, sorry, sorry, sorry" she muttered as she sat down.

"Your name?"

"Uh, Bultmann, Lizzie."

"Ah," he said grimly. Did he know her parents? Surely he didn't. It was a huge faculty and she couldn't imagine what they would have to say to one another if they had ever met at a cocktail party. To which her parents never went, anyway.

"Well, now that the late Miss Bultmann has arrived, hand her a syllabus, Mr. Mc-Conaghey, so we can then begin. This is a class, as I'm sure you're aware, devoted to the major poets of the twentieth century, the century that is drawing to a close. Ours was a century that produced much remarkable writing, both prose and poetry. But, one could argue, and I do" he smirked "the achievements of the poets far outweigh those of the writers of prose. What else can you can conclude from one hundred years that began with John Betjeman, included Ted Hughes, Theodore Roethke, Richard Hugo, and Philip Larkin, and will conclude with John Ashbery and W. S. Merwin?"

This was clearly a rhetorical question, but the boy sitting next to Lizzie — the one who'd given her the syllabus — raised his hand. "Yes, McConaghey, what is it?" Terrell asked without any enthusiasm, as though he knew what was coming next and was already finished with it.

"You know, the reading that I've done about Eliot and Pound, in preparation for this class . . ."

(In preparation for this class? Lizzie thought incredulously. Who is this guy?)

"Yes?" Dismissively.

"Well, I wonder why we consider them major poets when they were not, in fact, particularly nice men. How can someone who's — well, 'evil' is too strong a term —

but at least someone who behaves immorally in significant ways, as well as being slimy in their interpersonal relationships —"

Terrell heaved a dramatic sigh. "Didn't we go through this last quarter, McConaghey? Didn't we discuss this for more hours than I, personally, care to remember? When we talked about all those Romantic poets? I'm sure we did. Perhaps you weren't paying quite enough attention. 'Mad, bad, and dangerous to know' — doesn't that convey a certain je ne sais quoi when it comes to the treatment of the women in one's life? And didn't I argue convincingly enough for you that Byron was a great poet, though you wouldn't want to leave him and your girlfriend together unchaperoned? Or your boyfriend, for that matter. Do you have such a person in your life, sir?"

Uneasy laughter rolled through the class. Without waiting for an answer, he went on. "And, Mr. McConaghey, don't I recall from some of our ex parte conversations that at least two of your favorites — Housman, wasn't it, and Larkin? — were not such upstanding individuals? Hadn't they a few quirks, shall we call them, here and there? Anti-Semitism and so forth. Nastiness. Yet, in the case of Larkin, who amongst us could not be moved by 'Dockery and Son' or

76

'Church Going'? Not you. Nor I. But don't let me get started on Housman, of whom I'm not nearly as fond as you've indicated you are. Duh DUH duh DUH duh DUH duh DUH. 'From Clee to heaven,' forsooth. Spare me those green hills and dales of Shropshire." He mimicked the voice of a young woman. 'Oh, soldier, show me your sword.' I don't call that poetry but rather nausea-inducing."

Lizzie immediately felt offended on behalf of the long-dead Housman, and she suspected that Mr. McConaghey, sitting beside her, did as well. There was more laughter from the class. It seemed that The Terror knew how to command his audience.

At this point in what could only be termed a rant, Terrell made an amazing face. It somehow combined a leer and a sneer. Lizzie felt sure she had seen both a leer and a sneer before, but never the two together. Assuming someone who was not Addison Terrell could ever duplicate it, it deserved its own name. Perhaps 'sleer'?

"As for Pound, well, any man who can write that perfect poem 'In a Station of the Metro' has no need to fear for his immortal soul. Or any defense by me, particularly in front of a class of undergraduates who can barely distinguish between blank verse, free verse, and bad verse. Now, any more questions before I dismiss class so that you can all begin work on the first assignment?"

Some poor fool seated right behind Lizzie said, "Uh, Professor Terrell?"

"Yes," Terrell said with exaggerated patience.

"How do you spell 'Housman'?"

"Good Lord, who cares? There's no possible reason you would ever need to write his name down."

Lizzie, heart sinking as she listened to Terrell's monologue, had been scanning the syllabus. She raised her hand.

"Ah, it seems that the late Miss — make that Ms., of course, in deference to the feminists that I am sure are amongst us — Bultmann has a question. Or a comment?"

"Question," Lizzie said. "I don't see Edna St. Vincent Millay on the syllabus. Are we going to read her this semester?"

Terrell stared at her with interest. "Are you demented?" he asked, sounding genuinely curious. Then, without waiting for her answer, went on, "You're referring, I trust, to Edna St. Vincent O'Lay? That 'Oh God, the pain' girl? I can't imagine that you would really think I'd include anyone, any poetess, who wrote about burning her candle at both ends." Wiggling his eyebrows, he went on. "What in the world is that supposed to mean? That she was careless with matches? That she was a pyromaniac? But that's not the worst of it — the line that makes me blench is 'He turned to me at midnight with a cry.' What was that cry? I wonder. 'Yeeoww!'? 'Whoopee!'? 'Man the barricades!'? 'Up and at 'em!'? Good Lord, the possibilities are seemingly endless.

"You, Jack," he said, turning to Lizzie's fellow Housman admirer. "You're a great success with the girls, I suspect. Correct?"

"Not bad, I'd say, but by no means perfect."

"Yet surely you can enlighten us: What is that particular cry at midnight?"

It took long enough for Jack to answer that Lizzie thought he might be ignoring the question. Then, with a wicked, knowing grin, he said, "I believe, sir, that it was probably something like 'Oh, my God, I think I left the iron on.' "

Lizzie giggled, slightly ahead of the whole class breaking into laughter. Terrell chose not to respond to this directly. Instead he turned to Lizzie, who had been hoping that he'd forgotten her. But no.

"You, the O'Lay fan." He scanned the class list. "Bultmann, wasn't it?" She nodded.

"Let me hazard a guess in the form of a few declarative sentences. You write poetry. Little rhyming verses about the pain of young love, the agony of adolescence, each packed with trite observations on the beauty of the world and your own personal hell."

Lizzie heard a sharp intake of breath from the boy — Jack — sitting next to her. He moved restlessly in his chair and she could feel him getting ready to speak.

"Wait a —" he began.

"Well, listen, Ms. Bultmann," Terrell continued, his voice getting louder and louder. He slammed the grade book on the table in front of him and screamed, "I want no little-girl poets, no O'Lay wannabes, in my class. Do you hear me? Stop writing whatever sloppy verses come out of that head of yours or drop this class. Now."

He flicked his hand, dismissing them all. "I have no high hopes for any of you. Go, thou, and, if you dare, read some poetry. Not your own poems, Ms. Bultmann. Never your own," he concluded. "In fact, I'd suggest you burn them."

Lizzie sat, red-faced and stunned, as the rest of students drifted out of the classroom, a few coming by her desk to pat her back in solidarity, or just smile at her in what looked like sympathy. She knew what Marla would do in a similar situation: she'd march herself to the dean of Arts and Sciences and make a formal complaint about Terrell. She wasn't sure she had the fortitude to take that step. Jack waited for Lizzie to get up before he stood and spoke to her. "So. Millay. And another Housman fan. I think I just might be in love."

Lizzie looked at him. All her life she would remember that the perfect response came to her unbidden, as though it were a gift from the gods, a line from a poem they'd been assigned in AP English last year. "Really? 'Who ever loved, that loved not at first sight?' That's your position, is it?"

He laughed and took her arm. "Yes, Christopher Marlowe and I are more alike than you might think. Let's get coffee and be poetry lovers together. You can bind my wounds, and I'll bind yours. Do you have another class right now?"

At that moment Lizzie would have gladly given up the rest of the quarter's classes to spend time with Jack. "I have anthro at eleven but nothing until then."

"Great. Let's go."

As they walked, Jack said, "I'm really sorry you went through that with Terrell. He's always been pretty nasty, but that was much farther than I've ever heard him go with a student."

"What does he have against Millay, or me, for that matter?"

"It isn't you, or Millay. It's just that he's a miserable human being. My guess is that he resents being regarded by the critics as second-rate, plus he has to teach a bunch of undergraduates whose idea of poetry is probably nursery rhymes. He's stuck with this life he hates."

"That all may be true," Lizzie said, "but it doesn't give him a special dispensation to be nasty."

"No, of course not. But there's a line by Housman that I've always felt applied to Terrell: 'The mortal sickness of a mind / Too unhappy to be kind.' That helps me deal with him."

They walked to Gilmore's, one of the many coffee shops close to the quad that sprang up, shut down, and shortly reopened under a different name with amazing regularity. It was, as usual, packed with other students.

"Um," Lizzie said when they finally found an empty table. "Do you think you could empty that ashtray? I'll get sick if I look at it."

"Ah, there's a contradiction, a poetic sensibility and yet lacking a love of smoking

82

to complete the very picture of a dissolute soul."

"Hardly dissolute. My parents are serial smokers and when I was little I used to go around hiding all the ashtrays and hoping that would make them stop. I thought it was disgusting. And, as you can see, I still do."

"I take it they never did."

"Nope. Probably even as we speak one or both of them are lighting up. And they don't have a speck of poetry between them. They like it that way."

Jack grabbed the full ashtray and went up to the counter. When he came back with their coffees and a lemon poppy seed muffin for them to share, she said, "I know I'm probably irrational about this, but did you wash your hands after emptying the ashtray?"

"Wow. You're just a little intense, aren't you?"

"Well, yes, I guess so. About this, anyway."

"I'm awfully glad I don't smoke," Jack said, sitting down. "We almost certainly wouldn't be here together."

He held out his hands for her inspection. His nails were short and very clean. His black hair fell into his eyes and she wanted more than anything to brush it off his forehead. She could smell the shampoo he

83

must have used that morning; it contrasted sharply with Mendel's, which was tangy and unpleasant, something to keep dandruff at bay. Oh, why was she sitting here with this gorgeous, smart (and poetry-loving!) guy and thinking about her father's shampoo?

"Me too," Lizzie assured him. "Otherwise I'd probably get up and leave."

"You've never smoked? Not even to see what it's like?"

"Well, not cigarettes, anyway. 'I neither smoke nor drink, but I have my memories,' " she said, mock tendentiously.

Jack laughed. "Did you make that up? Is it true?"

"No," Lizzie told him. "I read it somewhere. And the drinking part is definitely not true. I do love beer."

"Really? Beer? You don't look like a beer girl to me."

"What does a beer girl look like?"

Jack thought about it for a while.

"Well, where I come from, the beer-drinking girls are fast and loose, with loud laughs and big voices and big hair."

She laughed and then sighed and thought of all those Friday nights, all those boys, during the football season and afterward. "I guess I'd have to say that being fast and loose doesn't come in one style. Hey," she said, changing the subject. "Did you really suffer through a different class with Terrell?"

"I did. Honestly, he's not so bad. He's a bully, of course, and just a little full of himself. But he has this sly sense of humor."

"Ha ha," Lizzie said dryly. "Save me from whatever sly sense of humor he might have. And don't for a moment think I didn't get the oh-so-not-humorous implications of 'you bind my wounds,' et cetera."

Jack grinned. "I'm so glad you told me. If you hadn't gotten it, I would've been really disappointed in you."

They stared at each other for a few moments.

"I still think he's an insensitive, pretentious asshole whom I already dislike intensely. Maybe nobody reads Millay these days except me, but isn't that what he should be doing? Introducing us to poets who might not be so popular now?"

"Okay, okay, don't despise me for this, but I've never actually read her."

"As long as you start to remedy that condition, I'll forgive you."

"Thank you, Lizzie," Jack said formally. "I appreciate your generosity. Do you think I'll like her?"

"Honestly, I'm not going to pretend that Millay's not romantic or doesn't write almost always about being in love and having your heart broken, and her poems always rhyme, like Housman, which I'm quite sure Terrell despises, but she's so good at making you understand how love and loss feel. I mean, they're not light verses, like Dorothy Parker, who I also read obsessively, and she's not ironic and detached at all. She writes these wonderful lyrical poems that I find so moving and true. They just work for me," Lizzie finished, somewhat apologetically.

Jack had been listening intently, leaning toward her. "So where should I begin? What's your favorite poem?"

"Mostly it's individual lines that capture my imagination. 'Neither with you nor with myself, I spend / Loud days that have no meaning and no end.' I suppose that a man could have written that, but he probably wouldn't. I mean, I bet that a lot of the poets Terrell admires might have had that feeling about someone, but they'd never admit it in a poem. Don't start with 'Renascence,' which is the poem she first became famous for when she was a teenager. Maybe read the sonnets." She thought a moment. "Yeah, start with those. I can lend you my copy if you want."

"Sounds great," Jack said. "Bring it to

86

class on Thursday."

For some reason Lizzie felt unaccountably shy and quickly changed the subject. "So, what's your favorite Housman poem?"

"No," Jack said decidedly. "Housman's too depressing for spring, or at least this spring. Let's wait until it snows to talk about him."

Can you fall in love this quickly? Lizzie wondered. And that was the beginning.

WHAT WE NEED TO KNOW
ABOUT GEORGE

George rarely got annoyed at anyone, never at his patients (even if they obviously weren't flossing enough) or his parents. Even when Lizzie pushed him beyond endurance (and he could endure a lot), he'd usually only sigh heavily, clamp his lips together, and somehow radiate an air of frustration tinged with regret. Probably very few people besides Lizzie, or maybe Elaine as well, would notice anything different about him in those situations.

George even looked like the perfect purveyor of happiness. He radiated health. He looked steady and safe, dependable and kind. You just knew that he could competently handle any situation that might arise. He had an infectious smile (and, of course, perfect teeth), and he smiled a lot. To those who had been his patients from the beginning, when he and Lizzie were newly married and he was straight out of dental school, those patients who had been through cleanings and routine fillings and impacted wisdom teeth and gum disease and root canals and crowns, who had suffered more than once through the dreaded tap test to determine which tooth, exactly, it was that hurt so badly, he was held in high esteem, even loved.

He had one seemingly impossible desire, which was to do a standing backflip. He had fantasies of entertaining his patients, while they were waiting patiently in the dental chair as their gums numbed, with a flashy (and to all appearances effortless) little backward twirl into space and back to earth again. He didn't aspire to the Olympics. He didn't necessarily want to be known as the dentist-who-excelled-at-backflips. He just wanted to be free of gravity for a few short seconds, launching himself into the space behind him and then returning to his normal existence.

On Saturdays and Sundays, watching football, he would gnash his teeth in envy as lithe and superbly muscled tight ends or wide receivers would do an insouciant backflip after scoring a touchdown. This happened so frequently that George began worrying about the state of his molars and took to wearing his plastic night guard while he was watching the games.

George had always dealt affirmatively with his desires. For several years, beginning in college, he had subscribed to an early online motivational website called LiveYourDream-.com. On the day he signed up, he had to submit a list of what he wanted to accomplish that year: getting an A in organic chemistry and losing fifteen pounds were what he remembered he'd included. He'd then receive daily messages urging him on toward the fulfillment of those goals. ("Pay attention to your desires." "Don't be discouraged by setbacks." "Affirm. Affirm." "Forge on." "Breathe deeply and go forward.") He had never included his dream of doing a backflip, feeling that it was too frivolous. But later, when he was in dental school, he decided to come clean and e-mailed the company. "I would like to revise my automated online goals for the coming year. My new goal is to conquer the standing backflip. Thank you. George Goldrosen."

Lizzie felt that the advice the company proffered was puerile and altogether useless, but couldn't convince George to see it that way.

THE GUARDS

Brendan "Toker" Tolkin, the right guard, was the biggest stoner in high school. He smoked dope before, during, and after games. Maybe all that pot left him too zonked for any semblance of enthusiastic sex. Or maybe it was Lizzie. He was also way too spaced-out to have any sort of sensible conversation with. All in all, a week lost in Lizzie's life, one she'd never get back again.

Billy Jim Estes was just about what you'd expect from a left guard named Billy Jim. Billy Jim was always sweaty, always smelling faintly but noticeably of BO. Each time he successfully blocked someone, he'd rub his hands together in a gesture that indicated that he'd been there, done that, and succeeded beyond everyone's expectations. He took to the idea and practice of the Great Game with great enthusiasm. Though Lizzie had to breathe through her mouth when she was with him, it made for a nice change after her experience with Toker.

THE LAST DOWN

By the time it was finally Leo deSica's week in the Great Game, Lizzie was counting the minutes until the whole project was done and she could get on with what was left of her life. She was sick of sex in the backseats of cars, sick of sneaking up to an empty bedroom at a party, or, when the weather had been good in the fall, having sex in someone's backyard after the game, where Lizzie and the football player du jour were often ineffectively hidden by the leaves of one tree or another. Because sex with those twenty-three guys was completely uninspiring, not to mention embarrassing, she was glad the act itself was quick. No one lingered around, before, during, or afterward. Of course, as a result of such hurried sex during high school, some of those boys would find themselves in a few years at a doctor's or therapist's office, dealing with issues of premature ejaculation. Still, Lizzie more or less sailed through the first few guys on offense with determination and a sense of triumph: she could do this, wasn't it larky, wasn't it going to be great to look back on it later, during the dull years of her forties and fifties (impossibly old), and brag about what she'd done as a high school senior? But as the weeks went by she felt increasingly aggrieved and sorry for herself and then mostly furious at Andrea, who was supposed to be here playing the Game at the same time. It wasn't fair that Andrea had simply opted out of it.

Offense or defense, Lizzie found nothing at all approaching pleasure in the sex. It was a chore, like slogging through *Vanity Fair* had been the previous year. Dull and boring and hard to figure out why anyone would choose to read Thackeray's novel, let alone name it as one of their favorite books of all time, as Mrs. Syllagi, her English teacher, told the class it was. She just knew, in both cases, that she had to get through it, check it off her to-do list. Chapter 17 done, done, done. Dusty Devins, done, done, done. On to the next. With every chapter read or player screwed, that much closer to the end. And she'd actually finished the assignments, although you couldn't say triumphantly, in both cases.

The Great Game officially ended on March 30, 1991, at 11:38 p.m., when Lizzie whispered good-bye to Leo deSica, strong safety, closed the front door behind him, and began walking back upstairs to her bedroom. Leo was generally regarded as the best-looking player on the team, and he didn't lack for brains. He was the kind of football player that college coaches drool over, and was courted by all the schools whose teams perennially ranked in the top twenty. But in addition to all those qualities, Leo was a thoroughly nice guy. Rumors abounded that he and his longtime girlfriend Gaby had never actually done it, and Lizzie had hoped that this was true, so that Leo would be extra interested in sex with her. She told herself that she deserved to have the Great Game end with a big bang. (This was a pun that George would have really appreciated, but of course there was no way that Lizzie would ever be able to share it with him.)

In light of her sizable hopes for the grand finale, Lizzie decided that they'd end the evening in her bedroom. Mendel and Lydia tended to go to sleep early, so it would be no problem to take Leo up to her room without their knowing. All this went according to plan. But once Lizzie steered him into her bed and they'd gotten down to business, it turned out not to matter how good-looking or smart or sexy Leo was, all Lizzie could think about while he was kissing her — with great expertise, it must be said — was what a mistake this all had been and that Maverick, not to mention Andrea, was right all along. This realization, which made her want to cry, came out instead as a loud and bitter laugh.

Leo, confused, immediately stopped what he was doing. "What's the matter? What's funny?"

"Nothing. It's nothing," Lizzie assured him. "Everything's fine. Don't stop." She was tempted to tell him that the joke had turned out to be on her, but decided that would confuse him even more than the laugh had, and she just needed this to be finished so that she could start trying to forget about it. And then, finally, Leo was done. The Great Game was over. Hallelujah.

As Lizzie walked Leo down to the front door, they were unexpectedly met by Lydia, who was on her way up the stairs. Mendel followed her, holding two mugs of the strong herbal tea they favored. Nobody spoke, although it was possible that Mendel nodded at them before continuing up. When Lizzie locked the door behind Leo, she wondered if she'd just imagined the meeting on the stairs. It was pretty much every teen's worst nightmare, wasn't it, to be discovered by your parents more or less in flagrante delicto?

Upstairs, she went into the bathroom and undressed for the second time that night. She turned on the shower to the hottest water that she could stand and stood there until the spray became lukewarm, and then reluctantly turned off the taps and got out. The mirror was so steamed up that she could see only the faintest outline of her body. It might have been anyone, actually, which Lizzie thought was a good thing. She didn't really want to look too closely at herself. Not because of what she imagined that she might see — maybe a scarlet *A* above her breast, the word "wanton" incised on her forehead, things like that — but because she was afraid she'd see no difference in herself at all. Aside from probably now resembling a boiled lobster, she knew that any stranger looking at her body would never be able to guess how she'd spent twenty-three Friday nights since September. But, oh, Lizzie knew, with a sinking feeling in the pit of her stomach, that everything had changed for her since she'd embarked on the Great Game.

The next morning, rather than ask her parents if she could use their car, Lizzie took the bus out to the mall and bought eight packages of the whitest and cheapest cotton underpants she could find. Size XL. She might have gotten the L's, but she didn't see them and was too embarrassed to ask a saleswoman. Two dozen pairs of humongous and ugly undies; they lasted Lizzie for decades. When she got home she changed into a pair, enjoying the fact that they barely touched her body. She put on her loosest and rattiest jeans and a T-shirt that Maverick gave her when they were dating. The front proclaimed, "This is Dick. Dick is an Ohio State Fan . . ." while the back said "Don't be a Dick." This outfit was basically what she wore for the rest of the spring and all through the summer.

On Sundays Mendel and Lydia generally went into campus for only a few hours, instead spending most of the day at home reading the papers and journals of psychology that piled up around the house. Lizzie ventured out of her room only twice, once to put her sheets in the washing machine and then again when she transferred them to the dryer. Unless she'd invented the incident on the stairs, she was pretty sure that her parents would have something to say to her, although she couldn't imagine what that would be. She found out at dinner.

Lizzie, who wasn't hungry, pushed a grayish piece of meat loaf around her plate and wished they had a dog she could surreptitiously slip the food to. Just as she was about to ask to be excused from the table, Mendel said, "So, I take it that was your boyfriend?"

Lizzie tried to think of what to say. She was certainly prepared to lie; she'd spent a good deal of her life lying to her parents. But if she agreed that Leo was, indeed, her boyfriend, would there be any follow-up questions? Maybe. Lizzie didn't think she had the energy to make up much more of a story and decided to tell the truth.

"Well, actually, no. He's not my boyfriend," she began. "He was part of an extracurricular assignment I've been involved in since school began, which was to have sex with a lot of guys on the football team. He was the last one, and now I'm done. There were twenty-three altogether. Andrea was supposed to do it with me, eleven each, with one extra that we'd flip a coin for. We thought it would be fun, but she changed her mind. So I went ahead and did it myself. That's why he was here."

Neither of her parents responded for what seemed like a long time to Lizzie, then Lydia said in an encouraging sort of tone, "Goodness. That's pretty adventurous of you. How did you come up with that idea?"

"Andrea did," Lizzie said shortly, already regretting her honesty. She was staring at her plate, which looked even less appetizing than it had before, but out of the corner of

97

her eye she saw her mother pick up the pen and pad of paper that were never far from either of her parents. "Don't write that down," she screamed at her mother. "Don't write anything about it down. Just don't."

"Of course we won't, Lizzie," Mendel said soothingly.

"I was just going to make a few notes about a paper I'm working on. Nothing to do with you," her mother said. And Lizzie chose to believe her.

LYDIA AND MENDEL

Lydia and Mendel were all and everything to each other. Perhaps if they'd been able or willing to share their lives with Lizzie, she might have better understood how they got to be who they were, and why they treated her as they did. But of course that was impossible, since they hardly talked to her at all, and certainly never about their pasts.

Lydia grew up in New York, in a small town not too far from Syracuse. Because the western boundary of Richland was Lake Ontario, the winter snows were monstrous, heavy and constant from October to February. The wind cut through her, no matter how many layers of clothes she wore, and her hands were always red and chapped.

Lydia's parents met and married each other in a displaced persons camp in Ebelsberg, in Austria, after the war. A distant relative of Lydia's father, perhaps the foster son of a sister-in-law's brother's second or third cousin, had come to America in 1935 before the trains started chugging with determination toward their grim destinations of Auschwitz-Birkenau, Belżec, Chełmno, Ravensbrück, Majdanek, Sobibór, Treblinka, and other points east and west. He had for some reason nobody quite understood settled in Richland (perhaps he thought that the name was prophetic, that the streets there really were paved with gold) and built up a thriving wastepaper company. By the time the war ended he was so successful (especially as compared to the remnants of the family who'd survived the war in Europe) that he needed additional help with the business, so he sponsored Lydia's parents, Moishe and Brona Levinetsky, which allowed them to join him in Richland, in America.

They arrived — Brona was pregnant with Lydia — exhausted and in immediate need of warm clothes, English lessons, and cosseting, in the fall of 1947; they were among the lucky ones who got out of the DP camps relatively soon after the war ended. Their distant relative found them an apartment to live in, scavenged up sweaters and coats and secondhand shoes. He figured they would pick up whatever English they needed, which they did. Outside of work, he ignored them. There was no cosseting. Possibly the concept was unfamiliar to him.

While some of the survivors clung desperately to the memories of their past lives and circumstances, Moishe and Brona determinedly discarded all evidence of the people they'd been. One of the first things they did when they got to Richland was to adopt American names. They went to the county clerk's office, where Moishe morphed into Mike and Brona Ronnie. They also legally changed their last name to LeVine. How young they were.

Their response to having survived when so many others did not was guilt, but guilt wrapped in layers upon layers of anger, until the kernel of shame and self-reproach was unrecognizable, or at least they didn't acknowledge it in themselves. All that was left was a deep and abiding rage. They were furious about the recent past and disgusted with the present, and didn't view the future with any sanguinity. They came to America determined to forget their religion, which they blamed for the disaster that had all but destroyed European Jewry, and quickly made the decision that their child would be raised with no religion at all. Ronnie and Mike never understood why anyone would bring Jewish children into a world that would never let them forget their Jewishness and that would likely reward them with suffering, pain, and a tragic death.

Their daughter was born just a few months after they'd settled in Richland. They called her Lydia Ellen, an American name that still paid secret homage to their (dead) mothers, Lyudmilla and Esther. They mistakenly believed that they'd wiped their hands of everything that came before their arrival in Richland, New York.

Mendel's grandfather Pinchas Bultmann arrived in the New World sometime during the first decade of the twentieth century. He was fed up with the anti-Semitism he'd lived with daily in the Ukrainian shtetl where he grew up, always fearful of being drafted into the czar's army, and may also have been tired of his wife, Raisa, whom he gladly left behind when he emigrated. No more Jew haters to harass him! No forced service in an army that despised all of his kind! No wife for him! He settled first in the Lower East Side of Manhattan, of course, working alongside other newcomers in a kosher pickle factory. His job was to fill the jars with pickles and then pour liquid over them. He didn't much care for the briny, dillish smell of the factory, and after he moved on he never ate another pickle in his life. He also worried that constantly submerging his hands in the brine would injure them. He'd been a tailor in Vinkovitz and looked forward to taking up that profession again. Plus he just didn't feel comfortable living and working around so many other people just like himself. He stayed in the city only long enough to meet and marry Perla, also a greenhorn, also from the Ukraine, whose family hailed from Minkovitz. Vinkovitz Minkovitz: none of their descendants believed that part of the story. Whether he ever gave another thought to Raisa, whether Perla knew about his previous marriage, or why he chose to marry (bigamously) again, nobody ever knew. Or if someone did, no one told his grandson Mendel.

Pinchas and Perla wandered up through the Hudson Valley but couldn't find a town that suited them. They stopped for a few years in Rome, but Pinchas's tailoring business couldn't quite support Perla and himself, let alone his baby son, Avram. In 1914, shortly after Avram was born, the family moved to Rochester, where business improved significantly. Indeed, after he finished high school Avram went to work for his father, first to learn the business and then to build on Pinchas's good-enough success as a tailor. Together they opened a series of dry-cleaning establishments in the city.

When he was twenty-six, and almost solely on the urgings of his parents, Avram married Mina, a very nice American-born Jewish girl he'd met at the Leopold Street shul, the Rochester synagogue his parents belonged to. What everyone who knew her was struck by was that Mina, who'd been raised in an orphanage and never knew the identity of her parents, enjoyed her life so much. She whistled when she was happy and hummed when she ate something she liked. She looked like the heroine of a fairy tale. She was an inventive and instinctive cook. She loved going to the movies. She was an excellent dancer. Her many kindnesses to elderly members of the congregation were legendary. Her father-in-law, Pinchas, adored her, and Perla was effusive in her affection for the young orphan. Having no known relatives of her own, Mina quickly developed a keen interest in Bultmann family history and lore. She spent a lot of time interviewing her in-laws, asking them about their childhoods in the Ukraine and their journeys to America. In pursuit of her new passion for her husband's genealogy, she bought large sheets of butcher paper and began inking in an elaborate family tree. Letters filled with requests for details of births, deaths, marriages, and other relevant or interesting details flew from Mina in Rochester to the large extended family of Bultmanns who were still in that part of eastern Europe that was variously Russia, Germany, Ukraine, and Poland, and to that much smaller group who'd left their homes for what they hoped would be greener pastures: the Fienbergs in Israel, the Coopersteins in Argentina, the Manns in London's East End (they'd shortened their name soon after arriving in the 1920s), the Bultmanns in Sydney, and the Litwaks in Johannesburg. There were so many letters going out that Mina had a separate line in her monthly household budget for stationery and stamps.

And the results of her queries were impressive. Mina had to allocate more money in her budget to purchase more supplies. She accumulated so much information that she began papering the walls of what would become Mendel's bedroom with the family tree. As the 1930s ended Mina started to notice that responses from the German/Russian/Polish/Ukrainian branch of the family slowed down to a trickle and then stopped altogether. This lack of communication became increasingly worrisome. From South Africa to Australia, from Palestine to Buenos Aires to London, the extended family, but especially Mina, the keeper of the genealogy, fretted.

When Avram and Mina read what little there was about the concentration camps in the Rochester *Democrat and Chronicle,* it seemed beyond belief that such things existed. Mendel was born on December 27, 1944; when he was a month old the Russian army liberated Auschwitz, and Mina and the rest of the Bultmann clan finally had to accept a new reality. She knew now why her letters hadn't been answered. The relatives left behind in the shtetls of Vinkovitz and Minkovitz, most of Pinchas's childhood friends, distant relatives he'd dredged out of his memory for Mina's butcher-paper family tree, seemingly even Raisa, his wife, his real wife, everyone he'd ever known, had most likely died in Janowska concentration camp. It appeared there were no more Bultmanns in eastern Europe.

The Rochester Bultmanns were in shock,

in denial. Pinchas and Perla died of it, Avram believed, one after another, before Mendel turned one. Mina and Avram's joy at the arrival of their son was overwhelmed by the tidal wave of grief and loss. Mina took a thick black crayon and obliterated the names of all the family members who were gone, something she greatly regretted doing in the years to come. The wall next to Mendel's crib was a record of a lot of death and the names of the few relatives who'd escaped eastern Europe before the war. Mina never took the sheets of butcher paper down. It was a far cry from the Mother Goose wallpaper a different sort of family might have chosen for a child's bedroom.

Mina went a little crazy. Though she'd never met any of the relatives who'd perished, she kept seeing pleading messages from them on license plates around Rochester. A billboard on the side of the road would signal a desperate account of starvation and hardship that only she could see. She believed that on page 27 of every book there was an encrypted description of the endless deaths of Bultmanns young and old. Finally, after she'd refused to eat, couldn't sleep, stopped washing herself or taking care of Mendel, Avram took her first to the rabbi, who told him to take her to Strong

Memorial Hospital, where the doctors treated her depression, somewhat successfully, with electric shock therapy. They couldn't, however, ameliorate her sadness, which seeped through the Bultmanns' house like a noxious odor. Nothing would ever cure that.

Mendel and Lydia met each other when they were twelve years old. Syracuse University implemented a summer program for "gifted and talented" kids, those who'd scored high on the standardized tests every seventh grader in the state of New York had to take. They spent two weeks living in a dorm, all expenses paid, taking introductory classes, and spending the evenings sitting around in seminars with real professors and real college students, talking about themselves and what they were studying, or else going to concerts, watching movies, and playing board games.

They met again almost a decade later, the first week of grad school at Columbia, at a reception to welcome new students. When the head of the psych department introduced them, Lydia looked at Mendel, who looked back at her. They spoke at the same time: "I know you. You're the one who talked all the time" (Mendel) and "I know you. You're the one who never said a word in the whole two weeks" (Lydia). It turned out, although they came to it from very different undergraduate majors (Mendel, statistics, and Lydia, biology), that they were both interested in studying behavioral psychology. From that moment on they were inseparable.

Their choice of careers was the right decision at the perfect time. Skinner boxes, teaching machines, programmed learning, behavior modification — they were all drifting down into the public's consciousness. The seminal paper by B. F. Skinner, "The Science of Learning and the Art of Teaching," was assigned in three of the four classes they took their first semester of grad school. They were stunned by his insights and believed that behaviorism was the answer to every problem, from education to relationships to combating Nazism to teaching rats to run through mazes. Mendel and Lydia started publishing papers in their second year of grad school, when Skinner's essay had sunk well and deeply into the marrow of their bones. They began with letters to the editor. Then on to op-eds in the *New York Times, Washington Post,* and *L.A. Times,* many dealing with improving teaching, others with suggestions for efficacious parenting techniques. "Efficacious" was one of their favorite words. Their first jointly written paper, "Schedules of Reinforcement and Classroom Management Strategies," appeared in the inaugural issue of the *Journal of Applied Behavior Analysis.* They were off to the races.

So it wasn't exactly happy news that a baby was on the way. Lizzie was an accident, the result, Lydia knew, of the way the birth-control pills made her feel and how she'd too frequently, as it turned out, "forget" to take them. Once Lizzie made her unfortunate presence known, Mendel and Lydia took a morning off from working on their dissertations and were married at the city clerk's office. They celebrated their wedding by going home to their apartment and getting back to work on their respective dissertations: Lydia's on appetites and aversion in young female rats and Mendel's on purposive behavior in maze-running rats. Lydia hated to take time off to see her obstetrician; she was now at the stage of analyzing her data and — finally! — writing up the results. She was forced to postpone the final revisions on her dissertation when the baby she hadn't particularly wanted decided to be born. Mendel was less unhappy about the whole situation, Lydia believed, not only because he hadn't been physically inconvenienced from the moment egg and sperm connected but also because his mind hadn't been compromised during delivery, when the doctor gave her scopolamine without fully explaining to her what its effects would be. She didn't like not being able to remember what went on while the drug played havoc with her mind.

After Lydia came home from the hospital, she realized just how tied down she'd be to this endlessly shitting, spitting-up, and crying baby. How would she ever get her work done? Mendel was fortunate in that he could go to the lab early in the morning and not come home until he'd written great sheaves of his thesis, which was often very late at night. Lydia found the whole situation unbearable. After some discussion, Mendel put signs up in all the dorms at Barnard, and they finally assembled a group of young women who'd rotate in and out of the apartment and Lizzie's young life, feeding her, changing her, and, depending on their own personalities, rocking her, cooing or singing to her, or ignoring her.

Mendel and Lydia were the stars of their class. They were wooed by Brown, Yale, Berkeley, and the Universities of Texas and Michigan. In May 1975, when Lizzie was not quite two, they moved to Ann Arbor and began the work that would bring them fame (at least among the other behavioral psychologists of their era).

Whenever she approached the front door of the house she grew up in, Lizzie often thought that when the real estate agent first saw Lydia and Mendel, she must have chortled in glee. Those years spent getting their PhDs from Columbia? Forget it. These were two small-town kids from the under-populated vastness of New York State who wouldn't know a copper pipe from a plumber's snake. Did she have a house for them? You just bet she did.

The place she sold them was a mess but presumably had, in real-estate speak, good bones. (Lizzie learned this terminology only later, when she and George were looking for their own house to buy.) It had been for sale for so long that every agent in town contributed fifty dollars every time they showed it to a potential buyer who didn't bite at the opportunities it afforded and declined to make an offer. By now the kitty had enough money to pay for a lavish vacation for some fast-talking and persuasive agent — which were the primary character-istics of the woman who showed it to Mendel and Lydia.

It was the only wood-frame house on the

block. The others were solid and substantial fraternity and sorority houses in their varying architectural styles. Directly behind it was the Kappa Kappa Gamma house. Next door on the right, if you faced the Bultmann home, were the Chi Omegas, all blondes from the better suburbs of Detroit and Cleveland. On the left was the Pi Beta Phi house, with girls smarter than the Kappas and less blond than the Chi Os, from different but equally affluent suburbs. Directly across the street the Sigma Alpha Mu brothers played endless games of HORSE, went through many kegs of beer, and threw Frisbees with abandon.

The house had been, and continued to be for all the years her parents lived there, a fixer-upper. Perhaps the agent had described it as "a handyman's dream." If she had, it was clear that Mendel and Lydia either didn't know what that phrase meant (highly unlikely, as its meaning was self-evident) or that they misheard and/or didn't pay any attention to the words. Pretty much everything was in terrible condition. Lizzie knew this because pretty much everything was still in terrible condition for the whole eighteen years that she lived there. The edges of the linoleum in the kitchen were peeling; Lizzie still remembers when, at age ten or so, she tripped, fell, and on the way down hit and chipped part of a front tooth on the edge of a counter. This was a tooth that George had been pleased to get his hands on and had done a wonderful job of repairing.

Against all the rules of their department and the university at large, Lydia and Mendel made good use of their students, particularly their PhD students, to attend to different parts of the house. When she was old enough to realize what was going on, Lizzie wondered whether her parents accepted these students as advisees every year based not on any academic qualifications or interests but solely on their household cleanup, paint, and fix-up capabilities. There was the student whose dissertation was on the optimal height of urinals in K–6 schools who happened, perhaps not so coincidentally, to be the son of a plumber in Waukesha, Wisconsin. He certainly knew the difference between a copper pipe and a plumber's snake. Over the years there were one or two frustrated fine arts majors who would happily paint the rooms, especially as Mendel and Lydia couldn't care less what color the walls were and thus left the choice up to them. Sometimes the interior of the house would be painted every year and sometimes a decade or more would go by before a student who'd majored in studio art as an undergrad showed up. Oh, there were amateur but capable carpenters, very occasionally a bricklayer, and once someone who actually knew about reroofing houses. It was amazing who ended up studying with Lydia and Mendel.

Still, the house suffered mightily from old age and neglect. It looked scary from the outside, and Lizzie knew that even kids her own age were loath to look at it as they walked by. Halloween brought very few trick-or-treaters, although Lizzie and her longtime babysitter Sheila had great treats for those who did make it up the uneven steps and across the sagging porch to the front door. Some years there were none. (The student/bricklayer hadn't been particularly good. Perhaps that was why he'd gone into psychology rather than become a mason.)

Whenever Lizzie made a new friend in school, she'd try to prepare them for the sight of the house, but it still came as a shock to many of them. She remembered the first time Andrea came home with her — they were in the second grade — and Andrea's astonished gasp at the sight of it.

Lizzie's bedroom, however, was a comfort

to her. When she was thirteen, a grad student chose to paint each of the four walls a different shade of pink. Despite the fact that Lizzie had never been particularly fond of pink, she loved the result. And her room was at the rear of the house, so its two windows faced the back of the Kappa Kappa Gamma sorority. The Kappas had a screened-in porch that ran the entire length of the house, and every fall and spring the new pledges would practice the sorority's theme song out there. Lizzie would lie in bed, year after year, listening to them harmonize.

"Kaaa pa, Kaaa pa, Kaaa pa Gaaa muh,

I aaaaammmm so haaapy thaat I aaaam uh

Kaaapa, Kaaapa, Kaaapa Gaaa muh," and so on.

During the nights of the Great Game, when the boys were otherwise involved with her body and Lizzie was tired of reciting poetry, she'd silently hum it to herself, over and over. It passed the time.

SHEILA

Sheila came into Lizzie's life this way: Dr. Lydia Bultmann, in a very bad mood, was grocery shopping. She was in a terrible mood for a couple of reasons. She hated shopping. She couldn't stand being lumped together with the unwashed masses wandering the aisles, and the manipulative marketing of the advertising agencies annoyed her intensely. Plus she just couldn't abide waiting in line. By this time in their lives, the Bultmanns had plenty of money, but Lydia had from the early years of their marriage (when she and Mendel really had very little money) always feared it would run out. She still only bought the store brands and whatever was on sale, which made for uneven meals. In the past she'd just ask one of her grad students to pick up the basics, which in Lydia's mind were milk, hamburger, coffee, cereal, cigarettes, and bread.

But she could no longer ask a grad student to run to the store and shop for her. The dean, who had perhaps received a complaint or two from one of the students who, over the years, had plumbed, painted, roofed, or otherwise worked on the Bultmann house, had sent out a strong message reminding the faculty that their grad students were not their personal servants; they were to lay off asking them to do anything that was not relevant to their schooling. Lydia took great offense at this. It meant she'd have to take even more time away from her research and find someone to take care of three-year-old

Lizzie while she and Mendel were at work.

She was standing behind a youngish woman who was very slowly paying for her groceries and at the same time conversing with the equally youngish woman who was manning the cash register. Despite herself, Lydia was listening to the conversation.

"So I need to find a job that will give me time during the day to take classes. I can't do these eight-hour daytime shifts and go to school at the same time."

"What kind of job?" said the slow payer. "How about waitressing?"

"No, I was thinking more about babysitting; that might be more flexible."

Lydia liked the look of the checker, but even if she hadn't, it probably wouldn't have mattered. It was as though the god she didn't believe in had answered the prayers she hadn't prayed.

"Excuse me," she said, "but I'm in need of a full-time nanny, someone who will live in. My daughter is three."

"Really?" said Sheila, for it was she.

Hard to believe unless you knew Lydia Bultmann well, but that constituted the whole hiring process, and Sheila moved in with the Bultmanns a week later.

She met Lizzie, who knew nothing of a new babysitter, the next morning. Mendel and Lydia were already at work and Sheila was sitting at the kitchen table, drinking coffee that was way, way too strong, when she heard a series of thumps. It was Lizzie, trying a new technique to get herself down the stairs. She could walk down them if someone held her hand, and she'd also taught herself to come down backward. But this morning she'd gotten herself out of her crib and had the idea of sitting on each stair and then carefully moving to the next stair down. This is what Sheila heard, the *bump bump bump* of Lizzie's behind as she went from stair to stair.

She hurried to the hall, and when Lizzie reached the bottom step, Sheila was kneeling, just at Lizzie's height, waiting for her. Lizzie didn't cry at the sight of a strange woman and she didn't ask where her parents were. She just stared intently at Sheila, who said, "Hello, Lizzie, I'm Sheila, your new babysitter. I'm going to live in your house, so we'll have lots of time to play. We'll have a lot of fun together." She held out her hand to Lizzie. "Let's go eat breakfast. How do pancakes sound to you?" Lizzie smiled and took Sheila's hand and they walked to the kitchen.

Lizzie loved Sheila from that moment on. She could climb onto Sheila's lap to listen to a story (Sheila was big on reading stories to her) and not be afraid that she'd be poked by a sharp hipbone or misplaced elbow. Sheila's body was like the coziest couch in the world; it was comforting and welcoming and homey. Even when Sheila had an exam she should be studying for, she'd put Lizzie first.

Every day after she picked Lizzie up from day care (later from elementary school) they'd do something special together. Sometimes they'd go to the park and Sheila would teach Lizzie how to weave flowers together into bracelets or tiaras. A tiara made of Queen Anne's lace! Who even knew it was possible? Sometimes they'd look for four-leaf clovers. Throughout her entire life, Lizzie never met anyone else who could find four-leaf clovers like Sheila could. Any patch of wild clover would yield one up the minute Sheila started looking. Sometimes they'd go to the library and Sheila would check out the books that she'd loved when she was Lizzie's age. Sometimes they'd go to Sheila's house and watch her father's model trains make their way over a complicated layout, and Sheila's mother always had cookies and milk waiting for them.

Or they'd stop at a crafts store and Sheila would buy yarn and big knitting needles and teach Lizzie to knit. She bought jars of finger paint in every color available and big sheets of paper so they could smear the colors together to their hearts' content. At Christmastime, Lizzie, with Sheila's help, wove potholders as presents for her teachers and Sheila's mother. It was no use giving one to Lydia. She didn't ever cook.

When they did go straight home it usually meant that Sheila had some idea that involved food. Sometimes they'd spread crackers with peanut butter and pile one on top of another to make a tower. Then they'd see how many peanut-buttery crackers they could eat at one time. Lizzie's record at age eight was eleven, which Sheila told her surely set a new record for her age group. Saltines were the best for this purpose, and Sheila made sure that the Bultmann pantry always had an almost full box of them. Sheila taught Lizzie how to make brownies in a mug using the microwave and how to pop popcorn from scratch.

Sheila brought her portable sewing machine over to the Bultmanns' and showed Lizzie how to use it. Sheila made most of her own clothes and she let Lizzie help with the easy seams. Once Lizzie got to put the zipper in. It's true that Sheila then had to carefully unstitch the zipper so that she could put it in again, correctly, but still she was very complimentary about Lizzie's first attempt at doing something that was really hard. (It should be noted that after Sheila went on to live the rest of her life, without Lizzie, Lizzie never touched a sewing machine again.)

For a very long time, the best day of Lizzie's life was the day that Sheila and her boyfriend, Lucas Apple, took Lizzie to the Michigan State Fair. They drove to Detroit early in the morning and spent the whole day there. Not only did they wander through the barns to see all the animals — and Lizzie got to pet a goat and a horse and a pig — but she also rode on the merry-go-round (three times), the Ferris wheel (twice), and an exciting ride called the Tilt-A-Whirl, which she only went on once because it was a little too scary. They had cotton candy and hot dogs and fried Jell-O and elephant ears. Lizzie was a little nervous when Lucas ordered the elephant ears, but when she saw they weren't really the ears of an elephant, and especially after she tasted one, she didn't want to eat anything else, ever. When Lizzie's legs got tired, Lucas put her up on his shoulders so she could see everything that was happening. They didn't leave for home until after it got dark, and

they stopped for dinner on the way home at
Bill Knapp's because Sheila wanted Lizzie
to have the fried chicken and biscuits and
then have the chocolate cake for dessert.

Sheila moved out when Lizzie was nine.
Because Lydia and Mendel were both at
home when she said good-bye to Lizzie, it
was a sadly formal occasion. Neither wanted
to cry in front of Lizzie's parents. All they
could do was hug each other for a long time.

That was Sheila.

MYSTERIES OF KINDERGARTEN

Lizzie and Andrea both went to Hally
School for kindergarten, but were in different classes. Lizzie's teacher, Miss Beadle,
was tall and stern and often cranky. It was
unclear if she really liked kids or not.
Andrea's teacher was short, plump, and
jolly. Could her name have actually been
Mrs. Jolly? That's what Lizzie remembers.
"You have to be jolly when you're short and
plump," Sheila told her once, darkly. "Otherwise it's intolerable."

Andrea's classroom was large — really the
length and width of two classrooms. It had
lots of windows. There were murals of
nursery-rhyme and fairy-tale characters on
the walls: Hansel and Gretel walking
through the woods on their way to the

witch's house, holding hands; Humpty-Dumpty on his wall, surveying the scenery; Sleeping Beauty at her christening; the Three Little Pigs whistling happily as they built their houses. You knew, when you looked at the pictures, that bad stuff was going to happen to them all, but not quite yet. There were trunks of clothes to use for dress-up, almost anything you could think of to be: pirate, princess, carpenter, bride, goblin, hobo, and spaceman.

At one of the long ends of the room there was a kitchen, with a miniature stove, sink, and refrigerator. The refrigerator door opened and water came out of the sink's faucet. The stove had four painted-on burners and an oven with a door you could open and pretend to bake your pies and cakes. There were pots and pans in the cupboard under the sink, and plastic dishes and silverware. At the other end of the room was a workshop, with a variety of pretend (but very realistic-looking) tools: saws and hammers, screws, nails, and pliers.

There was a grid painted on the floor, so that on rainy or cold days you could still play hopscotch. There was even a space large enough for a pretty good game of freeze tag inside Mrs. Jolly's room. There were shelves and shelves of dolls and doll clothes and puppets. Piles of games like Uncle Wiggly, Parcheesi, and Candy Land. A little library of books. Lizzie's whole class went there for an hour two mornings every week.

Miss Beadle's room, where Lizzie spent most of her time, couldn't have been more different. No windows. Big enough for the class to play Farmer in the Dell, but not much else. Shelves, yes, but fewer dolls and those in worse condition, with their arms or legs about to come off, or looking as though someone had tried to scalp them and almost succeeded. No clothes to change them into. Only one basic set of clothes to dress up in. A Raggedy Andy doll that smelled like cat pee. A checkers set with some of the pieces missing. Wooden puzzles with pieces missing. Wooden puzzles that a two-year-old could have solved in three seconds or so with pieces missing.

The murals on the wall in Lizzie's classroom were of the scary bits of stories: Jack and Jill tumbling dangerously down a steep and icy hill, the Wolf Granny clutching Red Riding Hood in her ferocious grasp, the troll reaching from underneath the bridge to grab an unwary walker.

Was this memory possibly true? Surely not. There couldn't have been one classroom with so much, and the other with so little, one so desirable and the other so desolate. And who decided which kids were assigned to which teacher? But that's what Lizzie remembers, that sour teacher and that awful room.

The only good part of Lizzie's whole year of kindergarten was that Maverick Brevard was also in her class. On one of the days they spent sixty minutes in Mrs. Jolly's room, Lizzie pretend-baked a beautiful cherry pie and gave Maverick a piece, which he pretended to think tasted delicious and then pretended to kiss her cheek.

Much later Lizzie asked her mother how she happened to end up in Miss Beadle's class. "I didn't trust that other woman's smile," Lydia said flatly. "Or her name. What was it, Gaiety? Gaiety Jolly. Almost certainly an alias."

THE QUARTERBACK

Of all the participants in the Great Game, the most worrisome for Lizzie to deal with was Ranger Brevard. Partly this was because he knew her as his older brother's girlfriend, and she thought that he might not be as willing — nay, eager — as the others to participate. But mostly it was because Maverick's depiction of her as the older-woman seductress of an innocent boy bothered her. A lot. So it was that on the Friday night of Ranger's week, while they were lying underneath the stands by the football field and heading toward the final activity in the game plan, Lizzie said, as she unbuttoned her shirt and Ranger started taking off his pants, "So, have you done any of this sort of thing before?" She knew it sounded ridiculous — there were surely more elegant ways of asking if he was a virgin without coming right out and asking him — but she felt she needed to know. "What, you mean sex? Are you kidding me? Of course. Freshman year. Violet Burnett." Lizzie was relieved. She wondered if knowing that would reassure Maverick (begone, O Lizzie the seductress!) or make him jealous as hell.

THE POST (GREAT) GAME SHOW

The postgame analyses began the very night the Great Game ended. There were two men in her head talking loudly to one another ostensibly about football, some random football game that they'd been the announcers for, but it seemed to Lizzie that she was the subject of the conversation. They were evaluating her, the quarterback of the Great Game. Some of the things the voices said made no sense. They commented on her throwing arm ("Her me-chanics are awful"). The way she read the defense ("So-so at best"). The condition of the field ("Hard to get the running game going with all this mud"). The size of the crowd ("Who'd ever want to see her play?"). They analyzed dropped balls and muffed handoffs. "She's a dead loss," one said. "Can't see how the team can win with her at quarterback. Thinks she's better than she is." They questioned incredulously why she'd juked left when there was a player open downfield on the right ("Throw the ball, you idiot. You're not the running back, remember?").

And often and often, she'd hear one analyst say casually to another, "She's always been a loser, you know."

"I do know. And I couldn't agree more," the other voice would reply. "It's been one bad decision after another. Who'd ever want a failure like that on their team?"

For the first few years Lizzie just wanted the voices to stop, or, if not stop, at least to let up, to talk about something else, to take a break from judging her, to advertise Chevy trucks or Budweiser. She thought she might have borne it better — it would have been easier for her — if they'd ever talked about another player in a similar Great

Game, but they concentrated solely on her. In her mind she saw a blackboard filled in with X's and O's in complicated patterns; the voices were charting plays in which she played some role that wasn't clear but that she knew was something she never should have taken part in. As she and Jack walked through the Law Quad holding hands or sat together in the UGLI, or went out for pizza, or played a killer game of Monopoly or dirty Scrabble — or, worse, even when she was trying to lose herself in making love — the voices in her head kept on with their relentless evaluation of who she was and what she'd done.

Over the years those voices diminished to a low-pitched hum, a deep buzzing in her head, so that she couldn't make sense of most of the words. But occasionally she'd clearly hear her name spoken. "Lizzie," someone would say. She'd turn around quickly to see who was talking to her and find nobody there.

But when the post Great Game show began, the voices were maddening. Crazymaking. Frightening. She couldn't imagine trying to describe them to a doctor, or really to anyone except Marla and James, who already knew she wasn't nuts. What was so strange, and so difficult for Lizzie to understand, was that when she (and Andrea) first conceived of the Great Game, they saw it as good fun, a prank, an escapade, a joke, a jape, a hoot and a holler, a conversation starter when they got old, and the ultimate showstopper. She (and Andrea) even wondered if the Great Game of their adolescence might have a place in *Ripley's Believe It or Not!*

Lizzie'd thought back then that they'd dine out on it for decades. She'd imagined that years later she'd be sitting around with her friends, having coffee, and she'd tell them about those twenty-three football players, and one of the women would say, "What a great idea," and everyone would express chagrin that they hadn't done the same thing themselves. Or at a dinner party far in the future, a fellow guest would ask her what she had done in high school and she'd reply casually, "Oh, I fucked the starters on the football team," and then everyone would laugh and laugh about her glorious past. What she hadn't realized was that once you got through with high school, nobody but you gave a damn — or even remembered — what happened to you there.

There was a moment, before Andrea turned traitor and withdrew from the Game before it even began, that Lizzie believed that all her other accomplishments would pale in comparison, become essentially unimportant if she fucked half the football team. Who cared if you had starred in the school play, been elected class president, gotten into a great college, or won a National Merit scholarship (none of which Lizzie actually had done)? Instead, you'd had all that sex; nobody else could say that. It turned out not to be like that at all; in the first place Lizzie had ended up fucking the whole football team (which was too much sex for any high school senior to deal with). And afterward, for months and months, she was so profoundly tired that she could barely get up in the morning; there were very many mornings she didn't get up at all. She had trouble doing her homework; she couldn't concentrate on anything for more than a few minutes. The voices never went away. There was no one she wanted to talk to, no one who would understand what she'd done and why and what happened as a result. This silence on her part seemed irreversible, possibly making it impossible to change.

For a long time she couldn't read anything but poetry. This was when she memorized all those poems by Millay, whose life was a great comfort to her. Vincent — as she was known to her friends — had been with so many men, and yet out of those experiences came all these poems that Lizzie loved so much.

And because for years and years the voices in her head never let Lizzie forget that the Great Game had been a stupid idea right from the beginning and that she'd been an idiot for participating in it, her past was always there, a living thing. It shaped her present and her future. There was no way that she could forgive herself because those two announcers in her head continually condemned her behavior in the Great Game. They condemned her. They hammered away at her, a constant reminder of what a terrible person she'd been and always would be. Someone so clearly undeserving of both friendship and love.

JACK AND LIZZIE HAVE SEX
Jack saw Lizzie's rather distinctive underpants on Lizzie quite soon after they met. The professed reason that they'd gone to his apartment after the second day of class was that Jack said he wanted to lend Lizzie a paper on Housman he'd written a few years ago, but both of them knew giving her the paper was just an excuse to spend time

together, which they both knew was just a euphemism for making love.

Lizzie waited nervously while Jack rummaged through the mess on his desk, which was covered with papers, magazines, and books. His search was unsuccessful. "Crap," he said. "I know it's here somewhere. All, right, forget it, I'll look for it tonight." He sat down next to her on the couch and abruptly changed the subject. "You'll skip your anthro class today, right?" he asked, and Lizzie assured him that that was the plan.

When Jack put his arm around her and pulled her toward him, there was a long moment when Lizzie resisted. Oh God, she thought, this isn't right. I'm not right. Why am I afraid about what's going to happen next, when it's exactly what I want to happen, what I've thought about happening ever since we sat in that filthy booth at Gilmore's talking about poetry, or even before that, when he started to defend me in Terrell's class?

"What's the matter?"

"Nothing," Lizzie said quickly. "I was just surprised."

"Really? I thought this was what we both expected would happen."

"It's . . . it's just that it seems so sudden.

No, that's not what I mean, it's not sudden; I mean, it is sudden in a way, but that's not what I meant." She floundered on. "I don't know what I mean. Never mind. Forget I said anything."

"It's more what you did than what you said, actually," Jack said.

"Okay," Lizzie said desperately. "Let's start again. You put your arm around me and start kissing me and I'll kiss you back, okay?"

Jack didn't move. "Look, are you a virgin?" he asked.

This was one question Lizzie could answer honestly. "No, of course not. Really, I just had a sort of minor freak-out for a second. Can we please forget it?"

They did, and after that it seemed a pretty natural progression that they'd wind up in bed.

They were just beginning to undress when Jack said, "Are you on the pill?"

Lizzie hesitated. "Why?"

"Because if you aren't, then I'll get a condom."

"Um, I'm not, actually."

"Okay, give me a minute to find one."

While Jack looked through the drawers in the bedside table, Lizzie tried to get her underpants off as unobtrusively as possible,

133

but Jack too quickly found what he was looking for and turned back to her while she was still in mid–panty removal.

He stared at them, stunned into silence. Finally he said, "Jesus, Lizzie, those are the most anticlimactic things I've ever seen. What sort of subliminal message are they supposed to project to people who encounter them? Where do you even buy them?"

Lizzie blushed. Why hadn't she thought to borrow a pair of Marla's?

"Actually, nobody else has ever seen them. Except my roommate."

"Really. Can I ask why you wear them?"

Lizzie fumbled for an answer. "They're comfortable, for one thing."

"Okay, I'll grant you that comfort's important, but it's like you're hiding yourself in granny underwear." No one could ever say that Jack McConaghey hadn't understood Lizzie from the get-go.

In between the kisses and caresses that followed, Jack promised her that he'd try to block her hideous underpants out of his mind, but the fact that they were so large and so white might distract him at critical moments during the next, say, hour or so. He hoped she'd understand.

Afterward, they lay next to one another in Jack's single bed, holding hands, until their breathing returned to normal.

"Well . . ." Lizzie spoke first. "I'm glad that in the end they weren't too terribly anticlimactic."

"It was touch and go for a while, but lust prevailed over aesthetics."

Lizzie didn't much like the word "lust," especially when applied to what had just happened between them.

"So, Ms. Bultmann," Jack began, but Lizzie interrupted him.

"Don't call me that. I hate it."

"Really? Why?"

It was obvious to Lizzie that Jack loved the question "Why?" but she wasn't going to explain her parents and her past to him. "I guess it's the double *n* at the end," she said. "It just seems so pretentious."

"Okay. I apologize," Jack said. "It'll be 'Lizzie' from here on out, but what I was going to ask you was —"

Before he could finish, Lizzie cut in again. "Are you thinking that you want to have the sexual-history talk now? Because I don't."

Jack sat up. "Wow, moving along quickly here, aren't we? That's not what I was going to ask, but if you want to remain a woman of mystery who wears enormous granny underpants, that's okay for now. I'll tell you about me instead. Okay?"

Lizzie nodded. "I'd like that."

"I'm twenty-two; I grew up in a tiny town in West Texas. My high school was so small that we could only play six-man football, but still people felt that if you weren't a football player you were a wimp. Only they used other words."

"And you didn't play, right?"

"Right," Jack said. "I think it's a sport for barbarians. It's like we're the ancient Romans watching the gladiators. But life was even worse if you didn't play football and your favorite class in school was English. Then you were in real trouble. But you know what's weird?"

Lizzie had no idea.

"I still go back there every summer, to the same job mowing lawns that I had all through high school. It's like I have to go home and mow lawns. Either it's the real world — the dust and dry air and the emptiness all around us — and I need to revisit it every year, or this is the real world, the books, and the libraries, and professors wearing cords and suede patches on their jackets — and sometimes I need to be done with it."

Lizzie got a peculiar pain in the general region of her heart. "What about this summer?"

"Oh, you mean because I'm graduating? Of course I'll go home."

Jack waited to see if she had any more questions, but Lizzie remained silent. "Do you still want to remain mysterious?" Lizzie nodded. "Okay, then the question I was going to ask, which started this whole detour, is this: If this" — he indicated their naked bodies — "is going to be repeated frequently, which I definitely hope it is, what would you think about making an appointment at Planned Parenthood to get a prescription for the pill? So there wouldn't be any possibility of babies in our near future? I'll go with you if you want."

"Really? Really?" She hugged Jack, the fact of his going home for the summer forgotten for the moment. "I love that question. Let's do it. Let's call right now and see if we can go in this afternoon."

THE OFFENSIVE TACKLES

The right and left offensive tackles were the cringe-worthy Cringebeck twins, and that was the best you could say about them. Lafe (rt) and Rafe (lt) were somewhat attractive in a hayseedy sort of way, especially if you were drawn to very large, loopy guys with freckles and dirty-blond hair. They were known for their weird sense of humor,

137

which had caused Lafe to have LT tattooed on the right side of his neck, while Rafe's tattoo, on the left side of his neck, said RT. They both thought this was hysterically funny and didn't understand why nobody else did. They sometimes were a little unhinged on the football field, which Maverick had assured her was fairly typical for tackles. But in bed they were perfect lambs. Rather than have sex with Lafe the week after Rafe (which seemed to Lizzie to be a little too kinky for comfort), she scheduled the kicker and wide receiver in between them.

JACK SENDS SOME POSTCARDS

The day after they visited Planned Parenthood, Jack sent Lizzie a dozen red roses, along with a postcard that read "Take your pill." Even more than the roses, Lizzie thought the card itself, which was a photo of Edna St. Vincent Millay, was wonderful. Marla, who hadn't yet met Jack but wondered aloud whether it was entirely wise for Lizzie to become so involved with him so quickly, agreed that it was a very romantic gesture.

For the next twenty-seven days that the doctor had said to wait before they could rely on Enovid for birth control, Lizzie got a postcard in the mail that said simply, "Take your pill. Love, Jack." Each card had a photo of a different writer, many of them poets. It was clear that Jack had spent a lot of time at the bookstore choosing cards that he knew Lizzie would like.

She saved every one of them until a few days before she and George got married. Afraid that he might discover them and ask her about Jack, she cut them into strips and ceremoniously burned each one of them in a large ashtray she'd taken from her parents' house. Photos of T. S. Eliot, Ezra Pound, Marianne Moore, and others quickly disappeared in the flames. More quickly, much more quickly, than her memories of Jack.

THE TIGHT END

The tight end Dylan Mosier also ran track. His goal was to compete in the 1998 Summer Olympics in Tokyo in the long jump. He worried constantly about potential injuries, that he'd tear his ACL or wreck a shoulder in a game. He'd just as soon not have played football at all but he didn't want to disappoint his father, who had been Ann Arbor High's tight end back in the day. Dylan was killed when his motorcycle skidded on a dry road late on the night of the senior prom. It was still not clear what hap-

pened or whose fault it was, if anyone's.
That was a sad story.

SPRING QUARTER, 1992

The only times Lizzie didn't think about
Jack was when she was with him. She
wanted to be with him all the time. She
hated that the day contained so many
minutes without him. She hated that he
couldn't come up to her room in the dorm,
that she ate breakfast without him, hated
that she had four classes without him, hated
the random chitchat with other students.
She especially hated that there were times
when he told her that he needed to concentrate on some work he was doing and didn't
want her around to distract him. She hated
that for some strange reason he didn't want
her to stay overnight in his apartment. (She
would have moved all her stuff over there if
he'd let her.) All that mattered to her was
being with Jack, although, looking back, it
wasn't totally clear to her what they actually
did with the time they spent together.

Well, sex, of course. Sometimes it seemed
as though they were constantly ditching
whatever else they were doing to have sex.
They walked out in the middle of movies.
(Lizzie figured that in the time they'd been
together they'd only seen one movie from

start to finish. It was a revival of *Chinatown,* and they almost made it through the credits because Jack loved knowing who catered every film he saw, but gave it up and got back to Jack's as fast as they could.) They snuck out of birthday parties for their friends. They left dinners half-eaten, all so they could go to Jack's apartment and make love. And Lizzie and Jack didn't bother getting to the bedroom before they began pulling off each other's clothes. They'd made the sensible decision to sit several rows apart in Terrell's poetry class so they wouldn't be tempted to hold hands or worse. One day she passed him a note — altogether it went through the hands of the eight people sitting between them — that said, "shall love you always," a line from one of her favorite Millay poems. After he read it, Jack turned and smiled at her. Then a few minutes later he piled up his books and left, and a few minutes after that Lizzie walked out of the room too. Terrell was still droning on, punctuating his lecture by pounding his fist on the table. Outside the classroom, now frantic with desire, they found the nearest place where they could have some expectation of privacy. It was the girls' bathroom, where the tile was cold and not particularly clean, but of course none of that mattered. Afterward Lizzie thought with a malicious kind of pleasure how displeased Mendel would have been had he seen how dirty the floor was.

Or they'd be studying together at the UGLI, sitting side by side at a long table, Jack reading and making notes on some important English-major classic like *The Castle of Otranto* and Lizzie trying to memorize bits of information for her Introduction to Anthropology course. Years later, all she remembered from the class was that East St. Louis was not, as one might think, in Missouri, but actually in Illinois. Why this was important has escaped her, if she'd ever known. She had a vague memory it had something to do with mounds, but wasn't sure anymore what mounds were in an anthropological or historical context. Anyway, Jack would run his thumb over her palm, making her shiver, or she'd stop underlining in the textbook and reach under the table and touch his thigh. They never got much studying done when they were together. This didn't matter to Jack, who'd already been accepted into several MFA programs for the autumn and was trying to decide among them, and Lizzie knew she could eke out passing grades with the barest minimum of studying.

They had lots of sex.

THE OUIJA BOARD PREDICTS LIZZIE'S FUTURE

Lizzie came home late after a date with Jack (which both began and ended up in bed). She found Marla and James sitting in one of the public rooms in the dorm. They'd been studying but were delighted to take a break and listen to Lizzie talk about how wonderful Jack was. "Oh, I know what let's do," she said. "Let's get the Ouija board out so we can ask it about our futures." The Ouija board was kept in a closet with all the other games; Lizzie had noticed other girls using it, but had never done it herself. Marla categorically refused to take part, but James, after some coaxing and then determined pleading by Lizzie, finally agreed.

They warmed the board up by asking it simple questions that could be answered by a yes or no. "Are you in Ann Arbor, Michigan?" "Is George Bush the president?" "Is four plus four nine?" Once they were satisfied that the board was working well, Lizzie asked, "Who am I going to marry?"

She and James both kept their hands on the planchette. James promised her that he wouldn't try to influence its answer by a well-camouflaged nudge toward any particular letter. Lizzie held her breath as it took off on its own almost immediately, darting around the board to spell out *J-A-C-K-M* and then refusing to move again.

"Oh, wow," Lizzie said, delighted and impressed with the results. "Look, Marla, that's what I hoped it would say. You guys should definitely do it."

"We know who we're going to marry," Marla said. Her tone was a bit tart but Lizzie didn't notice. She was floaty with bliss.

JACK LEARNS ABOUT THE GREAT GAME

Lizzie came by Jack's apartment one afternoon to study with him before they went out for a celebratory dinner; it was June 1, two months since they'd met. She expected to find him at his desk, working on one of his senior papers, but instead he was sitting on the couch, immersed in an issue of *Psychology Today*. "Hey," he said, holding up the magazine. "I picked this up at Shaman Drum because the cover story is about poets and depression, but then I saw this article." He gestured to the piece he was reading. "These must be your parents, right? I mean, Bultmann, at the University of Michigan."

A ghost walked over Lizzie's grave, and

she shivered. There didn't seem to be a way to deny that her parents were her parents, however much she'd like to. The title of the article was "What College Students Think About Adolescent Sexual Behavior." Another ghost started pacing.

"I guess it's about sex, then," Lizzie said.

"Yeah, and it's pretty interesting," Jack said. "Why didn't you tell me your folks were on the faculty?" He didn't wait for Lizzie's answer. "Anyway, they asked a bunch of undergraduates what they thought about all sorts of different sexual behaviors, ranging from a couple who made a commitment to chastity until marriage at one end to a high school senior who slept with her school's entire football team on the other."

Could this be happening? Was it possible that Mendel and Lydia had lied to her when they promised they wouldn't write about it? Well, yes, it seems they did. Why had she ever believed they wouldn't make use what she'd told them? Now they had another publication, plus they'd gotten their names before a larger audience than any academic journal possibly could have. And if, as a result of discovering their perfidy, their daughter was devastated, unable to breathe, what did that matter to them? It mattered exactly nothing to them. Zip. Nada. Nothing. Zero. Lizzie walked carefully to the couch and sat down next to Jack.

"I'm not sure I buy any of it," Jack went on. "Do you think they just invented their examples? I can't imagine marrying someone without ever having sex with them, can you? I mean, wouldn't you want to find out if you were compatible or not?"

"Yeah, I guess I'd want to sleep with someone before I married him." We are sleeping together, Jack, she wanted to say to him. Let's get married and never talk about my parents again.

"But I don't think that other one could be a real case either. Why would a girl fuck an entire football team? Do you think anyone could be that insecure? Or pathetic?"

The two announcers in Lizzie's head were gleeful. "He's nailed her," one said. "Pathetic and insecure: couldn't have done better myself." "Absolutely," said the other. "Describes her to a T." Lizzie shook her head, trying to dislodge the voices. She wanted to say something but wasn't sure what. She just wanted Jack to stop talking.

"It's not the sex part of it," he continued, "that's just sex, but . . . I don't know, I guess every school has a slut or two. There was a girl in my class that might have done something like that. Everybody felt sorry for her,

146

but it was hard not to laugh at her too. She was so damn desperate. A lot of the guys were happy to sleep with her, but nobody wanted to date her."

Lizzie started to cry. She reached over and grabbed the magazine, trying to tear it in half. Jack stared at her in confusion. "What's wrong? What did I say?"

Lizzie ignored him. Trying to tear the magazine in half wasn't working, so she began pulling out handfuls of pages and ripping them into shreds. When the magazine was no longer intact and she was surrounded by tattered and torn bits of paper, she said through her tears, "First of all, it wasn't the whole team, just the starters. That's a huge difference. And I don't think that I was pathetic at all. I think I was pretty popular. At least before."

"Wait a second," Jack said. "This is you? That part is about you? You did that?"

He walked over to his desk and started rearranging the piles of books there. Without turning around to face her, he said, "God, Lizzie, I never would've said those things if I'd known it was you. What I said, I know you're not like that girl at all. Honestly."

Lizzie got up and went over to him. "Will you hug me?" When his arms were around her, she muttered into his shirt, "I just have one question and then I don't want to talk about it anymore. Does knowing I did that change the way you feel about me? Are you, like, shocked? Or disgusted?"

"No, of course not," he assured her (but it didn't assure her). "I'm just surprised, that's all. If you don't want to talk about it, we won't; but if you ever want to tell me about it, I'm here for you." He pulled away but kept his hands on her shoulders. "Now, on to the important stuff. When are you going to pay me the ten bucks for the magazine you've just destroyed? Should I put it on your tab?"

They both laughed (although the laughter sounded false). Lizzie took a collection of Philip Larkin's poetry off Jack's bookshelves and sat down to reread some of her favorites, and Jack sat down at his desk and began making notes on *Clarissa.* It could have been any evening at all.

But when they got back from a depressing dinner — neither Lizzie nor Jack had much to say — and had sex, Lizzie felt disengaged from her body, as though she were floating above it, watching but not participating in what was going on. She understood that Jack was trying to please her, doing everything he knew she liked, but she wasn't any longer inside the experience with him. Her mind, racing madly along a circuitous path that always ended up where it began, and then beginning again, kept her so tense that she couldn't feel Jack's touches. That feeling — or lack of feeling — was all too familiar to Lizzie. It reeked of the Great Game. It was exactly how she'd felt with Rafe and Lafe and Leo and with Billy Jim and Loren and all the rest of the team.

Lizzie was panicked now by the thought that, even loving Jack, sex with him was reduced to something much less than pleasure and much more like an onerous task. "Stop," she said.

"What's the matter?"

"I want to ask you something."

"Right now? This isn't such a good time. Maybe we could find a better time to talk." He started to stroke her breast again.

Lizzie pushed his hand away. "Jack, do you promise that knowing what happened with the football team won't change anything about us being together? Do you absolutely promise me that?"

Of everything that was terrible about that afternoon and evening, Jack's hesitation before he answered her was perhaps the hardest for Lizzie to bear. He finally spoke, very slowly, searching for the right words. "No, I don't think it changes my feelings for you, but I guess I wonder why you did it. It just doesn't seem like you."

"For fun," Lizzie answered shortly. "I did it for fun."

"But it's an odd sort of fun, isn't it? And then what about everything else? Does that mean that something like this" — indicating the rumpled sheets — "isn't fun? Or what about going to a poetry reading? Or some movie, or to Gilmore's for breakfast with me? Are those fun too? How do they compare?"

Lizzie bit down hard on the inside of her cheek, forcing herself not to tear up again but perhaps making her words difficult to understand. "It's too complicated to explain," she said, "but, yes, of course all those things we do together are fun. What I did, it was a huge mistake."

"Okay, I can accept that it was a mistake. Everyone makes mistakes, right? Maybe we can just forget that article. I promise that it doesn't change anything about you and me."

But it does, Lizzie thought with sadness. Everything is different now.

A CONFRONTATION, OR NOT

When Lizzie got back to the dorm later that night, Marla was drinking tea and listening to an old Lyle Lovett tape. She took one look at Lizzie, though, and immediately turned off the music. "What's wrong?" she asked.

"Jack found out about the Great Game," Lizzie said, giving in to the tears she didn't cry during her last discussion with Jack. "And now he despises me."

"He said that to you? Really? That he despises you? That doesn't sound like the Jack I don't really know."

"Well, no," Lizzie admitted. "He didn't exactly say that, but it's how he acted after he found out. Like I was all of a sudden not who he thought I was."

"Go back — I still don't understand how he found out about it."

"It's my parents — it's always my parents who ruin anything good that happens to me."

"They told Jack?"

"No, of course not, I'd never let them meet Jack. He read an article they wrote in *Psychology Today* that was partly about that and sort of put two and two together and came up with me. But it was really my fault."

"Why?"

"I told him the truth, because I was so upset by something he said. It's my fault," Lizzie said gloomily. "If I learned anything from my parents, it's that I can never do anything right."

Those ever-present voices in her head, always alert to any weakness she showed, agreed with one another that it was about time to take her out of the game, maybe for good. "She's a loser, pure and simple," one of them said. "Hardly pure," the other replied. "But definitely simple." They mimicked cheerleaders and chanted, "Loser, loser, loser, loser."

Lizzie cried harder.

"Lizzie, try to stop crying now and tell me exactly what happened so we can figure out what to do."

Lizzie tried. She went into the bathroom and blew her nose and splashed her eyes with cold water. Coming out, she said, "If I'd just kept quiet and not reacted to what he said, everything would be okay. I ruined everything."

"I have no idea what happened or what you're talking about. You need to start at the beginning. You went to Jack's apartment and . . ."

After Lizzie recited what she hoped was an accurate record of the events in the right order, Marla thought for several minutes before she spoke. "Forget what happened with Jack for a second. The important part is what your parents did to you, which was just awful. They'd really promised not to?"

"I don't think they promised, I don't remember anyone using that word, but I know they told me they wouldn't write about it."

"Wow. You need to talk to them, Lizzie. You need to make it clear how much it hurt you, what a betrayal it was."

Lizzie was aghast. "Are you kidding? I can't talk to them about what they did. I can't talk to them about anything. I've told you how they are. They've never cared about my feelings. My feeling bad wouldn't interest them in the slightest."

"If it was my parents and they lived a mile away, I'd go over there right now. I'd wake them up and tell them exactly what they did to me. They need to know that."

"But, Marla, don't you see, that's your parents. They're normal. They care about you. Mendel and Lydia would just figure out a way to make it seem as though I was the one who was wrong. But I'm not. I know I'm not. They shouldn't have included me in the article."

"No," Marla said slowly. "You're not wrong. They are. I really wish you could confront them about what happened."

"It'd be totally useless. It's done, and I

can't think about it anymore tonight. All I hope now is that Jack was serious when he said that what I did didn't matter to him. But I know it did."

That night the voices had the final words. "Know it did, know it did, know it did," they sang. It was the last thing Lizzie heard before she fell asleep.

JACK LEAVES FOR HOME

The night before Jack left, they walked to Island Park and sat on a bench and watched the sky turn a deep dark blue, become nearly indistinguishable from black, and then turn really black. Stars slowly became visible, and Lizzie began quoting one of their favorite Housman poems:

Stars, I have seen them fall,
But when they drop and die
No star is lost at all
From all the star-sown sky.

The toil of all that be
Helps not the primal fault
It rains into the sea,
And still the sea is salt.

Jack let her finish before he spoke. "Nice."

154

"Nice? I don't think it's nice at all. It's scary, that nothing really changes, no matter what happens. 'It rains into the sea, and still the sea is salt.' That means that change is impossible — terrifying."

"Yeah, I guess you're right," he began, clearly not paying much attention to what she'd said. "Listen, Lizzie, let's head back. I'm leaving really early in the morning and haven't packed or anything. I need to box up my stuff and put it in the storage locker because I've sublet my apartment for the summer."

"Can I help?"

"No, I think it'll go faster if I do it myself. I need to figure out what I should take with me."

They walked back to the dorm in the dark, their arms around each other's waist. At the door they kissed, most unsatisfactorily from Lizzie's point of view. She didn't want to let him go. She didn't want to let go of him. Jack gently untangled himself from her and said, "I'll see you at the end of August."

"Will you write me lots and lots of letters?"

"Sure," he said, giving her one last kiss.

"Don't go," Lizzie whispered to herself, trying not to cry as she watched him leave. "Please, please don't go."

Marla was sitting on the floor of the common room, paging through some art books; James was playing solitaire. They both looked up when Lizzie came in. "Gone?" Marla asked sympathetically. Lizzie nodded. "It's only three months till he's back," she reminded Lizzie. Lizzie nodded again, not trusting herself to speak.

James said, in a declaiming sort of tone, " 'And when it was all over, Arthur said, Well, it's all over.' "

Marla looked as though she were going to throw one of those heavy art history books at her boyfriend. "James, you idiot, what's wrong with you? That's a terrible thing to say to Lizzie. Besides, it's not all over, it's just for the summer."

Lizzie knew that as much as Marla and James loved her, they weren't necessarily huge fans of Jack's. They tolerated him for Lizzie's sake, but Lizzie could always hear an undertone of disapproval in their voices when they talked about him.

James shrugged. "I don't know. It seemed appropriate."

"Well, it's not. It's rude and hurtful."

"It's okay," Lizzie managed to say. "This part of it is over, so it does fit in a way."

The days went by slowly. She and Marla moved to an apartment. Summer-school classes wouldn't begin for another three weeks. Lizzie worked extra hours at the library shelving books, all of which looked frighteningly uninteresting. Nothing she did managed to keep her from brooding over Jack's absence from her life. It was a lousy time.

THE FULLBACK

Dustin Devins, the fullback, was also the kick-return specialist; he ran back five (five!) kickoffs for touchdowns in one game, an achievement that no one before or since had ever come close to duplicating. (When she was bored, Lizzie periodically checked that his record was intact. Last time she looked it was.) Dusty read compulsively, and often quoted Schopenhauer and Heisenberg to the rest of the team, who listened (according to Maverick) in mystification. Everyone thought he'd go to Harvard, but he didn't. He got a free and full ride to Earlham, in Indiana, where he became a Quaker, majored in sociology, and wrote forcefully in alternative newspapers about the intertwining of football and violence, to the great detriment of football. He'd grown to hate the game.

That summer — the summer after Lizzie's freshman year, the summer Jack went home but was supposed to come back to Ann Arbor in the fall to start his PhD program — was the beginning of Lizzie's antagonistic relationship with sleep.

Growing up, Lizzie loved going upstairs to bed. She greeted sleep with relief. Mendel and Lydia insisted that her door be open all the time, except when she was sleeping, so bedtime was her only time for privacy. Those relatively few nights when she couldn't fall asleep, because she was worried about school, or something Andrea said, or her stomach ached or her head pounded with pain, she'd get up quietly and take two aspirins (for the headache) and then read until her eyes felt too heavy to keep open and then she'd sleep.

She'd decided to take two classes that summer, Political Geography and Transformational Grammar. The geography class met at seven a.m. on Tuesdays, Thursdays, and Saturdays. Lizzie figured that because there would be so few students in attendance (because who in their right mind would want to study geography at such an ungodly hour?) she'd be forced to focus her mind on something besides Jack in order to get a decent grade. The grammar course met at a much more conventional time, but since Lizzie had only the foggiest notion of what transformational grammar was, and suspected that just a handful of other undergrads might actually understand it, and even fewer find the subject interesting enough to spend their summer hours (usually the most beautiful time in Ann Arbor) studying, the class would be small enough, and the subject difficult enough, that she'd have to pay close attention to what was going on. She was correct on all counts. For a brief six hours a week she had a respite from her obsessive thinking about where Jack was, what Jack was doing, and why he hadn't written her.

After a week, and then another week, had passed without hearing from Jack, Lizzie began to yearn for sleep. She'd walk home from class or the library as slowly as she could, in order to give the letter from Jack, because surely this day there would be one, more time to arrive at her apartment. If only there'd be a letter there, waiting for her. It could be as prosaic and dull and short and unforthcoming as "See you in August." Please, Lizzie prayed to Jack, please write me.

She and Marla never got much mail. It

was easy to riffle through the credit-card offers, the ads, and the requests from various charities and immediately see there was nothing from Jack. But Lizzie was unable to go through the envelopes only once. She'd compulsively examine them again, and then a third time, giving each envelope a shake just in case another was stuck to it. Then she'd begin the wait for another chance to hear from him. She hated Sundays, when no mail came. Lizzie wondered whether it would be better or worse to have lived in England during the nineteenth century, when mail was delivered twice or three times a day, and still there'd be nothing from Jack. Would that have increased or decreased her sadness? She didn't know. She did know how much more miserable she felt every day.

When she finally crawled into bed at night, she couldn't fall asleep. She wanted to sleep. She thought that sleep would not only "knit up the raveled sleeve of care" (see, she had paid attention once in a while in her Shakespeare class) but also speed up time until the mail came again. Every day she finished working at the library around four and walked home to the apartment she and Marla and James had rented for the summer, only to find there was no letter

160

from Jack. Then, in desperation, she'd begin counting down the minutes, carelessly doing her homework until she felt it was late enough to go to sleep as though she were a normal college student and not some quivering Jell-O-y mass of misery. Most evenings she was alone. Marla was in the art building looking at slides. James was at the library studying.

She couldn't eat. Her stomach had a hollow anticipatory feeling that led her to believe (rightly, it turned out) that eating anything would lead to a disastrous outcome. The lack of sleep made her even more vulnerable to tears. She wasted hours at the end of the day walking around the three rooms of the apartment, hugging herself, repeating "Don't cry, don't cry, don't cry" until the words lost their meaning and became merely sounds. She lost a lot of weight very quickly and avoided looking at herself in any mirror she encountered. Whenever she did fleetingly glimpse her reflection, she didn't immediately recognize herself. One night when James and Marla were home for dinner and Lizzie was pushing food around her plate, James told her that she was way too thin.

"You're making yourself sick. Eat something, Lizzie, please," Marla begged.

161

But she couldn't eat.

And she couldn't fall asleep. Though her desire for oblivion, even temporary oblivion, was strong, sleep would not come, declining to accommodate her yearning for its appearance.

Oh, she tried all the usual measures. First, a cup of warm milk, to which — because she was now an adult — she added a good measure of brandy, purchased specially for this purpose, but later in the summer used it the way it was intended: straight. She didn't sip it either. She ate saltines, sometimes with peanut butter, if her stomach felt up to it. She took long bubble baths.

James told her that he'd heard that a good technique for falling asleep was to take each worry you had and dump it into a trash container, one by one, until all your worries were disposed of and you were asleep. She tried it one night, taking her many-claused worry that Jack didn't love her, had never loved her, would never come back, would never be seen by her again, maybe he was dead and nobody thought to tell her, maybe he'd never taken their relationship seriously, maybe she was just like the girl in his high school who nobody would date, maybe the Great Game had ruined any chance she had at being with Jack, maybe he was gone forever. She ceremoniously emptied all those fears into a large silver trash can. But they refused to stay there, jumping up like magic beans and relodging themselves in her mind. She reported to James that, regretfully, it hadn't worked.

She played "A . . . My Name Is Alice" but made it harder for herself by adding an adjective to whatever the carload was and the car had to be filled with people, not things, so instead of organic oranges and boring books, she had carloads of dastardly Danes, eager electricians, cowardly criminologists, and nasty neurosurgeons. Q, Z, and X were always difficult, but her years of reading made them easier to do. "Q my name is Queenie / And my husband's name is Quentin / And we come from Queens / With a carload of questionable quislings."

That sort of thing. She was bothered a little by the use of Queenie and Queens, so substituted Quebec for the location, which made her feel a bit triumphant but didn't help with falling asleep. Perhaps this game had never been a particularly good sleep magnet. There was too much concentration involved. Maybe she needed something easier.

She recited all the Housman poems she knew but had to stop when she got to

"Stars, I Have Seen Them Fall" because it took her thoughts back to the last night with Jack, which was disastrous. When that happened she'd get up and smoke some of James's ample supply of pot, but at the beginning of the summer it did ruinous things to her, it made her paranoid, made her heart beat erratically. Her eyes, already red from crying, became even redder.

Those summer nights nothing helped. The minute she got into bed her sadness began to smother her. She'd toss and turn, trying not to panic at the thought of a Jack-less future.

Much later, when Marla got home, she'd peek into Lizzie's room and, seeing that Lizzie was still awake, she'd come sit next to her and hold her hand, and quietly say, "Come on, now, breathe with me," and, holding Marla's hand, breathing along with Marla's breaths, Lizzie could finally let go of another day without Jack and sleep.

When Marla couldn't be there, James sat at the side of her bed, breathing her to sleep. When he took her hand one night, he said, "Lizzie, listen. Jack is an asshole. I never liked him and I thought he was totally wrong for you. You're better off without him."

Lizzie wanted to insist James didn't know

what he was talking about, but she couldn't formulate the right words to contradict him. It was extraordinarily comforting to have James and Marla with her, knowing they loved her. Even at the time, and more so as the years went by and she looked back on those summer months of Jack's inexplicable silence, Lizzie knew that this was a great kindness Marla and James were doing her.

"Lizzie, why don't you just write Jack? Or even better, pick up the phone and call him," Marla asked one night in July. And then Lizzie had to admit to her that they'd never really talked about things like what town in Texas he grew up in, or what his father did, or if he had brothers or sisters. Lizzie realized that she really didn't know much about him, except that he loved poetry and hated football. She knew it was a small town in Texas, near nowhere in particular, and that was about it. Marla sighed. You could eliminate Dallas and Austin and Fort Worth and Waco and San Antonio and Lubbock and Houston and there were still a lot of places in Texas fitting that description.

"How could you not know where he's from? Surely that would come up in the conversation one time or another. You were inseparable for the whole quarter."

Lizzie felt obscurely ashamed. "I don't know, James. We didn't talk about things like that. I didn't ask him about it, I guess. I don't know why. We were too busy doing other things."

"So now he's back home in Podunk, Texas, about to marry his high school sweetheart, who waited four years for him to graduate and come back to her and make babies together."

Marla wasn't happy with this. "God, James, shut up, that's really cruel and you're totally not helping, you know," but Lizzie only shook her head, defeated. What was there to say? That was as likely a scenario as anything she could think of. And she had thought of it.

By the middle of August, when they felt they'd taught Lizzie how to breathe herself to sleep, Marla and James asked if she would be okay staying by herself so that they could go home for a couple of weeks. Although Lizzie dreaded being alone, she felt she could hardly tell them not to go. Final exams began later in the week, and maybe the concentrated study she'd need to do would either exhaust her into sleep or at least keep her mind on a non-Jack track.

The first night they were gone was the worst night she'd so far had that summer.

Her eyes felt too gritty to close and she felt too jumpy to settle down. She got up and drank a cup of warm milk with brandy and went back to bed. An hour or so later she got up and had a cup of chamomile tea and went back to bed. An hour or so after that she got up to pee and came back to bed, straightening her pillows so she could sit up and reread her favorite sections of *I Capture the Castle,* which she normally found extraordinarily comforting. Then she turned out the light and played the easiest variant of "*A . . .* My Name Is Alice." Then she started reciting all the Housman poems she knew. Then she got up again to check on some verses in "Shot? So Quick, So Clean an Ending?" that she'd forgotten, probably because they were too sad. Then she got back in bed and recited the corrected verses to herself. Then she got up to pee again. Then it was morning and Lizzie had to get up for good and go to her geography class.

As she sat down and took out the textbook, the girl sitting next to her said, "You look terrible."

"I know," Lizzie said, appreciating the frank assessment. "I can't fall asleep anymore. It's been like that for months."

"You should go to Health Service. I hear they'll give you sleeping pills if they think you really need them."

Okay, Lizzie thought, I can do that.

The nurse took Lizzie into an exam room. "Dr. Teacher will be in soon," she said as she closed the door. There was no chair, so Lizzie perched somewhat precariously at the edge of the examination table while she waited. She was all ready to have a light introductory exchange with him about what it was like being named Teacher and choosing to be a doctor, but it was clear as soon as he came into the room that there wouldn't be any light conversation forthcoming. He studied her chart for a few minutes, although what there was to study on it was a mystery to Lizzie; it was the first time she'd ever gone to the clinic.

Finally he looked up at her. "Bultmann," he began. "Any relation to —"

Lizzie didn't let him finish. "My parents," she said shortly.

He looked a shade more interested in her. "Lovely people," he said. "Simply brilliant, both of them. You're very lucky, you know. They've both made significant contributions to the field."

Lizzie's heart sank. This was already not going well.

"The nurse says you're interested in some medication for sleeping."

"Yeah," she began. "It's just that finals are coming up and I haven't been able to sleep and if I could just get some sleep . . ."

"Ah, you're taking some advanced psychology courses, I presume, to follow in your parents' footsteps?"

"No, no." Lizzie knew she sounded horrified but couldn't help herself.

"If not psychology, then what?"

"Uh, a grammar class, and another one in, you know, geography."

"Those must be fascinating," Dr. Teacher said in a tone of voice that made it clear he didn't think it was fascinating at all. "By the way, I've always wondered what your mother's maiden name was."

Lizzie was bewildered but still game. "LeVine."

"Ah," he said triumphantly, making a note in the chart. "Well," he went on, "do we have any idea of what's causing this inability to sleep?"

At this point the last thing Lizzie wanted to do was talk to Dr. Teacher any more than she absolutely had to.

"No, not really. It's just become a lot harder to fall asleep recently."

"Ah. Do you have a boyfriend?"

"A boyfriend? Um, I guess not, no, not currently."

"But you did have a boyfriend?"

"Well, yes, I guess so."

"Recently?"

"Sort of recently. Sure."

"But you don't any longer. What happened?"

Lizzie stopped to think. How could she answer that? She didn't know what had happened.

"He graduated."

"This past May?"

Lizzie nodded.

"So you broke up?"

Yes, she admitted, they'd broken up.

"He with you or you with him?"

Would this never end? Why did he need to know this? She felt she was entitled to some tactical lying.

"Mutual. It was a mutual breakup. Look, all I want is, like, five sleeping pills, just so I can sleep the nights before the exams."

"How about if I give you three?" he offered.

This was insane. Were they actually bargaining over the number of sleeping pills he'd prescribe for her? Maybe they'd split the difference and he'd give her four.

"Sure," Lizzie answered wearily. "Three is fine."

Dr. Teacher stared at her stonily. "I'm going to give you a prescription for five pills," he said sternly, "but I'm going to put down on your permanent record . . . your permanent record," he emphasized, "that you're suffering from insomnia due to an unsuccessful love affair."

Lizzie left the clinic with five sleeping pills and what, even in her misery, she recognized was a terrific and endlessly reusable sentence.

"Where is your permanent record, anyway?" James asked when they'd returned from Cleveland and she told him and Marla about the visit to Dr. Teacher. "Do you think it's what Saint Peter looks over when he decides whether you're fit for heaven or bound for hell?"

Or Marla's mother would send her a particularly unattractive sweater as a gift, one with, say, reindeer on it. Obviously this fashion blooper on Mrs. Cantor's part would end up on her permanent record.

James wondered if good things also went on your permanent record. "I won the fourth-grade spelling bee. Do you think that's on it?"

"Gosh," Marla said, "I think that's the year I lost because I couldn't figure out how to spell 'niece.' I remember asking myself if the i-before-e rule worked in this case, or if niece was an exception, like in 'neighbor.' Not, as I came to find out, an exception. Do you think that's on my permanent record?"

"Do you think the permanent records are kept in a huge bank vault in Washington? Who has the key? What if they lost it? Would that go on their permanent record? Would they have to start setting up all-new permanent records, sort of a clean slate for everyone?" Lizzie wondered.

They could go on for hours like this. And frequently did.

A LETTER FROM JACK

It was December 8, and Lizzie's last class on the last day of classes before finals week was just ending. It was also, if anyone was counting (and Lizzie was), six months to the day since Jack kissed her good-bye and vanished from her life. After the bowling debacle, she had tried to cut back on her marijuana intake, but wasn't quite as successful as she might have wanted. Weed was a blessing and a curse, Lizzie thought, stoned, as she stood up from her desk and stuffed the *Collected Chaucer* into her backpack. Pot took away the immediate pain of Jack's absence because all that she experienced in the present moment seemed so

172

compelling that the fact of the loss of Jack was much less interesting than seeing the shape and shifting colors of the emptiness that surrounded that fact. And pot gave her so much more: she saw, for example, the scaffolding of crossword-puzzle grids. Certain words, like "ontogeny," "regency," and "exculpation," delighted her, and despite having no idea when or even if she'd heard them before, she knew their meanings because of the sounds they made as they sang in her mind. When she was stoned she could study her toes, which she normally hated, for hours, and realize, as she wiggled them appreciatively, that in fact they weren't any uglier than anyone else's. They were just toes, and hers, and, in their own specific way, were quite lovely. When she was high she could tune out the voices in her head more easily, although one terrible night when she sat around with James and Marla, all of them high, the announcers started speaking in a slow, deadly voice. Every criticism was enunciated clearly: Horrible. Ugly. Stupid. Crazy. Inept. Selfish. Clumsy. Evil. It felt as though they were pelting her with bits of ice that had been sharpened to a point at one end.

Lizzie also knew that when you were stoned, all you could do was be stoned. You couldn't study because you were hyperalert to every sight or sound. Classes were a joke because there were too many distractions. Being so stoned all the time didn't have a salutary effect on her grades. She was perilously close to failing all her courses. She'd managed to eke out a C in her geography and grammar classes in the summer (blessed be the sleeping pills), but this quarter she'd taken a full load of five courses. Even the Chaucer, which she'd looked forward to because Jack had once told her how much he admired the teacher, didn't hold her interest, whether she was stoned or unstoned. She'd tried it both ways. And without the pot the pain came back two- and threefold, a dreadful rebound effect from exiting the stoned world.

It was going to be a long weekend, trying to catch up with the readings so that she had a decent chance of passing an exam in anything but sadness. Already, most of what the teacher had said about Chaucer, his life and times, and his poems had faded away. She could remember only the first three or four lines from the Prologue (although she could recite them in a credible if midwestern-inflected Middle English). Her major takeaway from Chaucer's life was his peccadilloes (or worse) with Cecily Champaign, whom Dr. Ragland referred to cheerfully as "Bubbles." Bubbles Champaign. Lizzie did love that, stoned and unstoned. Her Literary Theory and second-year French classes had both become a blank. Did the semioticians have a theory of despair? Could she say it in French? Worse, she couldn't at this moment even bring to mind the two other classes she was taking fall quarter.

Lizzie found herself outside, although she had no actual memory of leaving the classroom building. Indian summer had made an appearance after a chilly fall in Ann Arbor, and the brownish-colored leaves of the maples were still drifting off the trees. They made a satisfying crunch as she walked back to her apartment. It was warm enough for people to open their windows; she could hear music coming from the dorms. Lizzie stopped and listened to a woman singing a lightly jazzed-up version of "I'm Going to Sit Right Down and Write Myself a Letter." She suddenly got a dazzling idea. Lizzie decided she was going to go home, sit right down at her desk, write herself a letter, and make believe it came from Jack. Reading it, she'd learn why, exactly, he never came back. Brilliant.

She dumped her backpack and jacket on

the couch and sat down at her desk and began writing.

Dearest Lizzie (because you are):
I'm writing to apologize and explain — or try to explain — why 1) I didn't come back to Ann Arbor this fall and 2) I haven't written before.

I think that perhaps I gave you the wrong impression about me. Not the wrong impression about the way I felt about you. I loved you. I really did. I just realized, slowly and with difficulty over the quarter, that I simply couldn't do it. I don't even know if I can make you understand what it is I couldn't do. I could love you (I do love you), most likely shall, as Millay says, love you always. I can write you love poems forever. But, Lizzie, oh, Lizzie, I don't want — I can't have — a relationship that's so confining that I can't breathe. I don't want someone who's everything to me and I don't want to be everything to someone else, even you. I don't want to be part of a great love story. It sort of reminds me of those lines by Auden that we read in Terrell's class about not wanting everyone's love but to be the only love of someone, that the person who

176

loves you loves only you. Isn't that how you feel? But I don't. That's not me. The thought of that makes me physically sick. And it was happening, Lizzie, it was. You know it was. We were just too entangled with one another. Every day, every hour, it was harder and harder to see where I ended and you began. I still feel like slitting my wrists when I even think about what was happening to us.

Will you forgive me for being unable to talk to you about how I was feeling and just leaving? Can you forgive me for being the way I am? I hope so. I hope that we run into each other somewhere someday — leaving a movie, or more likely it'll be at a poetry reading — and smile and remember how wonderful it could be when we were together, and not think about how it ended. I hope we can someday be friends.

With all the (imperfect) love I'm capable of, Jack

After she finished writing the letter, she folded it up and put it in an envelope and addressed it to herself. For the sake of verisimilitude (verisimilitude! great word!), she supposed that she should actually put a stamp on it and drop it into a mailbox so that she'd get it in a day or two, but that seemed, even for her, a bit too much. Sealing and addressing the envelope would just have to be enough.

She walked around the apartment for a while, unpacking her book bag, getting a can of Diet Pepsi, and grabbing a handful of pretzels. She arranged her books on her desk in the order she'd need them for studying for her finals, which began on Monday and ended (for her) on Wednesday. Who makes up the finals schedule, anyway? She went into Marla's room and felt her familiar awe at how neat Marla was. It looked as though no one had lived there for weeks or months. She walked around the apartment a few more times. She wished she had stocked up on champagne, just in case this moment — a letter from Jack — actually ever arrived. And now it had. She sat down on the couch and took a deep breath. Then she opened the envelope and started reading the letter. After encountering the first word, she got up, rummaged through her desk for a pen, which happened to be red, and sat down to finish it.

Dearest Lizzie (because you are): NO!!! YOU DON'T GET TO USE THIS WORD NEXT TO MY NAME. WHAT

A LIAR YOU ARE.

I'm writing to apologize and explain — or try to explain — why 1) I didn't come back to Ann Arbor in the fall and 2) why I didn't write before this.

I think that perhaps I gave you the wrong impression about me. IT'S ALL TOO LATE NOW. CAN'T YOU SEE THAT? Not the wrong impression about the way I felt about you. I loved you. I really did. BULLSHIT. BULLSHIT. BULLSHIT. THEN WHY DID YOU WAIT SO LONG TO WRITE ME? WHY DIDN'T YOU CALL? HOW COULD YOU JUST LEAVE ME LIKE YOU DID??!!??? I just realized, slowly and with difficulty over the quarter, that I simply couldn't do it. I don't even know if I can make you understand what it is I couldn't do. I could love you (I do love you), most likely shall, as Millay says, love you always. GOD, WHAT A BASTARD YOU ARE, JACK. I can write you love poems forever. I DON'T WANT THEM, NOT FROM YOU. But, Lizzie, oh, Lizzie, I don't want — I can't have — a relationship that's so confining that I can't breathe. I don't want someone who's everything to me and I don't want to be everything to someone else, even you. I don't want to be part of a great love story. YOU WERE NEVER EVERYTHING TO ME. NEVER NEVER NEVER. DON'T FLATTER YOURSELF, YOU ASS-HOLE. It sort of reminds me of those lines by Auden that we read in Terrell's class about not wanting everyone's love but to be the only love of someone, that the person who loves you loves only you. Isn't that how you feel? WHAT DO YOU CARE WHAT I FEEL? YOU KNOW, YOU'VE JUST RUINED AUDEN FOR ME FOREVER. But I don't. That's not me. The thought of that makes me physically sick. And it was happening, Lizzie, it was. You know it was. I DON'T KNOW THAT AT ALL. WE LOVED EACH OTHER. ISN'T THAT WHAT LOVE IS SUPPOSED TO BE? We were just too entangled with one another. Every day, every hour, it was harder and harder to see where I ended and you began. I still feel like slit-ting my wrists when I even think about what was happening to us. I WISH YOU HAD. I WISH YOU WERE DEAD. IT WOULD HAVE BEEN EASIER FOR ME IF YOU WERE DEAD.

Will you forgive me for being unable to talk to you about how I was feeling and just leaving? NO NO NO NO NO NO. YES, JACK, THAT'S A NO. NEVER. Can you forgive me for being the way I am? I hope so. NOT GONNA HAPPEN, DIPSHIT. I hope that we run into each other somewhere someday — leaving a movie, or more likely it'll be at a poetry reading — and smile and remember how wonderful it could be when we were together, and not think about how it ended. AS SOMEONE FAMOUS ONCE SAID, NOT IF I SEE YOU FIRST. I hope we can someday be friends. CAN YOU REALLY THINK THAT? AIN'T EVER GOING TO HAPPEN EVER EVER EVER EVER.

With all the (imperfect) love I'm capable of, Jack I'M TOTALLY NOT INTERESTED IN YOUR (IMPERFECT) FUCKING LOVE. STICK A FORK IN ME — WE ARE DONE DONE DONE DONE DONE. AND YOUR PARENTHESES MAKE ME FEEL LIKE SLITTING MY WRISTS. HOW FUCKING PRETENTIOUS YOU ARE, JACK. AND THAT'S THE LAST WORD.

181

Lizzie put down the red pen and went into the kitchen. She got another can of soda. When she closed the refrigerator door she searched among the pictures, the long-outdated invitations, the cartoons and notes all stuck on with magnets, and finally found what she was looking for. She studied it for a few silent minutes, smiling as she remembered the bowling debacle, and then she picked up the phone and called George.

THE KICKER

The kicker Steve Wender had an extreme outie belly button. It seemed awfully petty of her to find it so off-putting, but that's what Lizzie felt. Her time with Steve was highly educational if you were majoring in football. During his five days of the Great Game, Steve talked about nothing but that, focusing on his great hero, fellow kicker George Blanda, who, Lizzie learned, played in the NFL for an unbelievable twenty-six seasons, first as a quarterback and then, in the last eight years of his career, as the kicker for the Oakland Raiders. Steve's ambition was to play twenty-seven seasons in the NFL, but admitted to Lizzie that it wasn't likely. Blanda retired in 1975 when he was forty-eight but that was a different era entirely.

GEORGE AND LIZZIE'S FIRST DATE

George and Lizzie met for lunch at Drake's Sandwich Shop. As they sat down, Lizzie could hear the Baird Carillon chiming the quarter hour and murmured, " 'Oh, noisy bells, be dumb.' "

"What?"

But Lizzie knew that if she began explaining to George that it was a line from a particularly depressing Housman poem that was one of Jack's absolute favorites, it would open up the conversation in ways she wasn't prepared to follow through on.

"Oh, nothing, really. I was just mumbling."

Lizzie ordered a grilled cheese on rye bread sandwich. It was her go-to choice for stressful times, and George, seemingly unfazed by her prevailing winds of tension and anxiety, a BLT. They both had iced tea, which seemed counterintuitive, since it was the coldest Ann Arbor January since 1908. Lizzie apologized again for the bowling fiasco and ruining George's game, and after George gallantly said that it was unimportant, in fact he'd totally forgotten about it until she mentioned it, and that he was sorry they hadn't been able to get together in December after she called but he'd been swamped with assignments because it seemed that the second year of dental school was much more demanding than the first, and then he always went home for Christmas, so this was his first chance to see her, a silence fell. They chewed companionably. It made Lizzie happy that George was also drinking iced tea. She'd always been the only one she knew who ordered it no matter how cold it was outside.

Lizzie felt pressured to say something in return. The bells, thank God, were quiet. She had about ten minutes before they rang again. Why had she agreed to come here, anyway? Okay, here goes. "Where's home?"

"Tulsa. I'm pretty sure I'm the only Oklahoman in the dental school. At least, I've never met anyone else from home."

"Me either," Lizzie said. "I mean, you're the first person from Oklahoma that I've ever met. I did know someone from Texas, though. Does that count?"

"Absolutely not," George said. "We hate Texas, except maybe for the Cowboys. You know, the football team from Dallas. Are you a football fan?"

Lizzie hesitated, thinking about Maverick and the Great Game. "I kind of have a love-hate relationship with it, actually."

"That sounds pretty mysterious."

"Yeah, well, maybe we can talk about it

184

another time," Lizzie said. "So tell me, what's it like there in Oklahoma?"

"Hot and dusty and lots of tornadoes. We had a dog when I was a kid, and we could always tell when bad weather was on the way because he would start shaking and whining and immediately go hide in the front closet, where we could hear him whimpering. Even though I was always really scared, Doodle made me look good by comparison."

"Doodle's a great name."

"Doodle the Poodle," George said happily. "He was my mom's dog from before she and my dad got married. His formal name was Drummer Boy the Fourth, but we called him Doodle."

"I always wanted a dog, but my parents aren't pet people," Lizzie told him. "So I always envied my dog-owning friends here."

"Here?" George asked. "You mean you grew up in Ann Arbor? Do your parents work at the university?"

Lizzie delayed answering until she'd gotten the waitress's attention and requested a refill on her iced tea. Then she tried to change the subject. "Do you want to hear something funny? I always thought that only women drink iced tea. You're the first guy I've ever met that drinks it too. Even the

185

words 'iced tea' seem kind of quaint and southern somehow. You know, big houses, wraparound porches, ladies with their fans, rocking chairs, the Union Army rumored to be on its way."

George laughed. "And now you know at least one man who's pro–iced tea. Plus, as my mom would tell you, Oklahoma is definitely a southern state. She's a real tea drinker, and I got in the habit from her, I guess. Plus I think it's a lot healthier than soda is, although tea can really stain your teeth."

Lizzie, who also drank a lot of tea, both hot and iced, immediately resolved not to open her mouth again just in case her teeth were stained.

"So you didn't say where you grew up," George reminded her.

By now Lizzie was ready with her answer. "Oh, I grew up here, a faculty brat. Both my parents teach here."

"What do they teach?"

"Psychology. They're pretty weird."

"Weird how?"

"When I was little," Lizzie began, "maybe about three, I was in the lab preschool that the School of Education runs here. One night at dinner I asked my father if I could aim his penis when he was urinating. In our house we always used the correct word for body parts — no wee-wees or pee-pees for us."

George smiled. "What did he say?"

"He put down the book he was reading, probably something about school testing, then looked over at my mother, who was also doing something else at the table at that moment, probably making notes on an upcoming lecture. I'm sure that he was hoping for some help from her as to what to say to me, and just as clearly, at least to me, was the fact that he wasn't going to get any.

"He finally said, very kindly, 'No, Lizzie, I have to aim my own penis, to keep things neat in the bathroom.' And I said, 'But, Mendel, I always aim Sanjay's at school.'"

"You called your father by his first name when you were three?" George asked incredulously.

"Yes, both of them, Mendel and Lydia. I used to think that everyone did." She paused. "This is a weird conversation to have."

"I think it's nice. So don't stop now. What happened next?"

"Mendel started chuckling. Lydia put down the pen she was using and began laughing too. It was actually quite wonderful for a moment or two. Then they both went back to what they were doing."

"Well," George admitted comfortably, "we were definitely a wee-wee or pee-pee and poop family. But here's a story you'd like, I think. We were all sitting down together, eating dinner — my mother's big on meal-togetherness. My dad always began by asking us what we had learned in school that day, or from the newspaper, or if we had any questions. I must have been a bit older than you, maybe six or so, and Todd, my older brother, was seven.

"I said that one of the boys at school told me babies are made when a man and a woman stand on opposite sides of a room and then the man holds his penis out and runs at the woman yelling 'Charge.' And my dad, very seriously, said, 'No, George, that's not usually the way it's done, although it does sound like a compelling idea. Would you like me to explain how and where babies come from?'

"Well, by now I was really embarrassed, and I told him no, not right then, maybe later, but Todd said that, yes, he really wanted to know, that he had a lot of theories about it but was interested in the truth."

"The truth," said Lizzie, giggling. "So were you there when your dad explained it to your brother?"

"No, I didn't want to be there," George said. "I waited another year or two before I got my own sex-ed talk. What about you?"

"When I was six, Lydia gave me a book called *From Egg to Chick*. That was her way of eliminating any chance of a discussion. I think maybe one of her grad students told her about it. I must have lost it or something. I'd love to know now what it really said."

"When you got older, did you think that's why girls were sometimes called chicks?" George asked.

"I did! How'd you know that?"

"A wild guess," George said. They smiled at each other.

GEORGE CALLS HIS MOTHER

George called his mother. "Hey, Mom," he began.

"Georgie," she answered, her voice delighted. "Drill any producing wells recently?" She chuckled; chortled, really. He felt the reality of her, warm and loving and so solidly there, although there were almost a thousand miles between them.

Her joking question referred to one of a number of possibly apocryphal stories she'd recounted over and over when George and Todd were children, stories of her own experiences as a kid going to Dr. Ted Gratz, her family's dentist in Montreal. He was, Elaine said, probably the nicest man she'd ever known, hands down, although this was not always a good thing. He was so nice that he was unable to turn anyone away who needed him, so making an appointment for a cleaning, say, was pretty useless, because when you arrived at the office, it would already be filled with people waiting patiently to see him too, whether they had an appointment or not. Here she'd pause and say with a wink and a smile, "Do you get it: they were waiting 'patiently'?" When Todd and George nodded that, yes, they got it, they got it, Ma, they always got it, every single time she retold the story, she went on. "And then there were those who weren't waiting patiently, so that there were always muffled and sometimes not-so-quiet cries of pain echoing throughout the waiting room. But we got used to that sort of thing. We'd pack lunches and get ready to spend the whole day there.

"Occasionally," Elaine went on, "there would be people kneeling on the floor, praying to God to deal with their aching tooth before the dentist could get his hands on it."

Evidently Dr. Gratz was also unable to

keep any staff for very long. "Despite his niceness?" George asked Elaine once.

"Probably because of it," she said, an answer that George didn't understand until he became a dentist himself. This meant that while Novocain injections were taking effect, or X-rays were developing, Dr. Gratz would grab a broom and energetically sweep the floor. Or answer the phone, or whatever else needed to be done, depending on which employee had quit or hadn't shown up that day.

There was never any privacy in Dr. Gratz's dental offices: his was a booming voice and he never tried to modulate it to hide what he was saying to his patients. "You call those teeth?" Elaine once heard him say, admonishing the poor patient in the adjoining room. "They look like cigarette butts to me." This, Elaine added to her sons, was the major reason she never smoked and wanted them to swear they'd never take up smoking either. Plus, the cigarette-butts comment was also an incentive to brush morning and night. Sometimes at noon too.

But the neatest thing about Dr. Gratz, she told them, was that he always inscribed the silver fillings he used with "Ted drilled here" and the date. This just had to be something Elaine invented, George felt. How could someone do that, write so small? But wasn't it true that there was a whole industry of people who wrote on tiny grains of rice?

"Let me see your teeth," he demanded of his mother when he was seven and she'd finished telling him the story for the bazillionth time. "Oh, Georgie, I'm happy to, but I'm afraid it won't do any good to look at my teeth, because all those old silver fillings that Dr. Gratz did have been replaced with composite ones."

"Let me see," he repeated, and she obediently opened her mouth and allowed him to peer in. "There's a silver one," he told her, "way in the back."

"Oh, that one," she replied quickly. "I didn't have that filling done until after Dr. Gratz had retired and I was in college. That was done by this young guy, Dr. Sidlowski. He didn't ascribe to the inscribing that Dr. Gratz did."

George was still suspicious but couldn't think of what to ask next.

"Oh," Elaine would continue, nostalgic, "those were the days when going to the dentist was a real test of courage. And the spit-sinks. Did I ever tell you two boys about the spit-sinks?"

"Yeah, Ma, you did," Todd would say, already way past boredom into desperation to get away.

"You did, but tell us again," George amended his brother's statement.

"Well, these days, the dentist drills or the hygienist cleans, and they spritz water in your mouth and then they use a suction tube, so you can never see what they're vacuuming up. In the olden days, when I was a child in Montreal," she'd say dreamily, "Dr. Gratz would work for a while, drilling away, and then he'd stop, thank goodness, and say, 'Spit now.'"

"Why'd he stop drilling then?" George asked.

"His hand got tired," Todd responded before Elaine could.

"Oh, I imagine that he felt you needed to have a rest from opening your mouth so much," Elaine speculated. "You'd take a sip of water from this teeny tiny paper cup and then you'd spit, and out would come bits of tooth, and blood, and sometimes pieces of popcorn. And there was water running around the sides of the sink, so you'd see all that stuff be washed away. Dr. Gratz's spit-sink was green, I remember. Those spit-sinks certainly made you feel brave. Now I feel as though I'm missing out on the best part of going to the dentist."

George, at nine, already suspected he

wanted to be a dentist, although not at all like Dr. Gratz, and his mother's stories always gave him much to ponder. "Why were there pieces of popcorn in your teeth? Didn't you floss enough?"

"Georgie, you ask the best questions. It's because they didn't have floss when I was a little girl. Dr. Mordecai Floss hadn't invented it yet."

Todd, the (young) man of the world, rolled his eyes. "That cannot be his name, Ma. You're making it up."

"Maybe, maybe not. I might be mistaken in thinking his name was Mordecai. It may have been Milton."

Todd stalked out, highly insulted at not being taken seriously, but George always hung around, waiting for more of his mother's stories.

George adored his mother, always had and always would, but he felt that as a loyal son he needed to curb her tendency for puns and bad jokes, especially when he knew for a fact that she'd told those same stories to his father back in the years before Allan left dentistry and returned to school to become an orthodontist, and tightening braces became his stock-in-trade.

"Way not funny, Mom. As I'm sure Dad told you once upon a time. And for that matter, it's unseemly to mock your son's profession. Plus your jokes would be a lot funnier if you didn't laugh at them yourself before anyone else has a chance to respond to them. I might have laughed," he went on, "if you'd given me the chance."

"Oh, Georgie, don't be such a stick-in-the-mud. Laugh now. Make me happy."

"Ha ha," George responded obediently. "Mom, I'm not coming home for Thanksgiving."

Her voice lost some of its timbre of happiness; a stranger wouldn't have noticed, but George, who was so attuned to his mother's feelings, did. "Oh, what a shame. Do you have to work?"

"Yeah, I'm on call Saturday, so it would have been hard anyway, but it's mostly that this girl invited me to have dinner with her family."

"A girl?" The lightheartedness was back in her voice. "Someone new? Is she in school with you? Where did you meet her? *When* did you meet her? What's her name?"

George answered her in order. "I met her a while ago, bowling. She grew up here, and her parents are professors. She's still an undergrad, a junior. Her name's Lizzie. We've been dating since January, I guess."

"Since January?" Elaine was incredulous.

"It's October now. How come this is the first time I've heard about her?"

He imagined his mother sitting down at the kitchen table, winding the telephone cord around her wrist, and settling in for a long talk with her younger son. "Because I knew if I told you that you'd respond just like you're doing. And besides, I can't really tell how serious it is yet. I sort of wonder if she thinks it's serious at all. Are you in the kitchen?" he went on, in an attempt to derail the next set of questions he was sure were coming. "Did I interrupt anything? How's Todd doing? Still surfing away in Oz?"

"Don't distract me," she said, effectively closing off that avenue of verbal escape. "Have you thought about what you're going to bring? What time do they eat?"

"Oh, Mom," George groaned. "She just invited me. We haven't gone into a time schedule or menu options."

"Wine for sure," Elaine went on, unheeding. "A couple of bottles, one each of red and white. How about if I send you a loaf of my cranberry bread, and maybe a zucchini or pumpkin bread too? It's too bad I can't send my wild-rice casserole. Would you make it, if I sent you the recipe?"

"Don't send anything. I'm sure they'll have enough food to feed me without any

196

additions from the Goldrosen family. I'll bring wine, though. How's Dad? Is he home? I'd like to say hi to him too."

"Oh, I wish you'd bring Lizzie home for Christmas, especially since Todd won't be here. It's been so long since we were all together. Do you think you might?"

"Probably not," George said. "But I'll see. Maybe I'll ask her."

"That would be wonderful if you would. I'd love to meet her."

"Let me see how Thanksgiving goes, okay?"

"All right, but just remember that I'd be so happy if you brought her to Tulsa for Christmas. And if she asked you to spend Thanksgiving with her family, that's surely a sign that she thinks it's some sort of serious."

"It's hard to tell with Lizzie what's serious and what isn't," George said a bit glumly. "Sort of like with you."

Elaine laughed. "I'll get your father."

THE RUNNING BACK

It was generally believed that Ranger was the best player on the team, but the running back Mickey Coppel had many supporters who thought that he should be considered numero uno. During Lizzie and

197

Maverick's junior year, Mickey was a wonder. There was no other word for it. He was a solidly built five feet ten inches and had an intuitive sense of what was happening on the rest of the field. Plus he was a devilishly fast runner who always seemed to be moving at top speed and yet could come up with another, faster gear when he needed it. His career rushing total was 11,232 yards, which made him the number seven high school running back ever, according to *The National Federation of High Schools Record Book.* Although he had an excellent college career playing for Florida State, his Ann Arbor fans always wished he'd stayed at home for college. He was drafted in the second round by the Buffalo Bills to back up Thurman Thomas, which was a mixed blessing. Because Thomas was one of those suck-it-up players when it came to playing hurt, Mickey never saw much playing time. On the other hand, he was on the team during the period they won four consecutive NFC titles and went on to lose four consecutive Super Bowls. After he retired from the Bills, Mickey had a great career as a color analyst on ESPN and was a familiar face to millions of football fans. But during his participation in the Great Game, Lizzie found his front teeth so prominent that it made kissing uncomfortable. Naturally he'd gotten them fixed once he hit the big time, and it was now difficult to imagine how he looked in high school.

THE FIRST THANKSGIVING (WITH GEORGE)

Since neither Mendel nor Lydia cared much about food or drink, Lizzie was always surprised at how they chose to celebrate Thanksgiving. For as long as she could remember, every year Lydia and Mendel invited all of their advisees and friends of the advisees who weren't going home for the holiday, as well as stray faculty members, to come for dinner. This added up to a lot of people, and the year George came was no exception. Many of the faculty members brought along their own folding tables, which were set up all over the first floor of the house. Everyone also brought food of some sort, which could range from baked ham to lasagna, stuffed dates to shredded carrot salad. You never knew what the final meal would look like. Mendel and Lydia always assigned their most favored students to various shopping and cooking tasks. The chefs showed up promptly at nine a.m. on Thanksgiving morning, arms full of groceries, and took over the kitchen. One stuffed the turkey, another made pies, and the third was in charge of everything else, which included a sweet-potato casserole as well as green beans made with cream of mushroom soup with fried onion rings on top. To give the impression that she was interested in what her students were doing, Lydia sat at the kitchen table and chain-smoked while she proofed an article or read a book. Mendel futzed around the cooks, a cigarette in one hand, a bottle in the other, pouring generous glasses of wine for everyone. The wine was accepted, but his offers of help were always refused.

After the cooking and baking began, Lizzie kept well out of the way. For many years this was when she and Andrea used to meet at Island Park and sit on the swings and compare notes about their horrible parents. Freshman year she'd gone home with Marla for the Thanksgiving holiday, and last year James and Marla had been at the Bultmanns'. This year she was upstairs in her bedroom, trying to write something meaningful about Stephen Crane's *Red Badge of Courage* for her American lit class, but failing badly. What she wanted to do was sit on her bed and wring her hands. She already regretted her rash decision to invite George to come for dinner.

They had been sitting around George's apartment, competing in a game of *Jeopardy!* James was Alex Trebek and Lizzie, Marla, and George were each holding a buzzer. Before George's arrival in Lizzie's life, the other three had devised a three-person version of it and played regularly. James usually won, Marla came in second, and Lizzie was almost always a distant third. All she knew about was literature, and questions she was sure of didn't come up nearly often enough. This was the first time George had played with them, and halfway through the game he had a comfortable lead over Marla, while Lizzie, as usual, lagged far behind them.

"Okay, here's a difficult question that I somehow doubt any of you will get," James said. "I sure wouldn't. 'A movie title from the 1980s that also describes a kind of carpet.' "

"I know this!" Lizzie yelled as James finished reading the clue, and smashed her hand onto her buzzer just as George was saying "I got this!" and hitting his buzzer.

"Lizzie, you were a nanosecond faster," James said. "What's the answer?"

"What is *Shag*?" Lizzie said proudly. She knew it was the right answer. "I love that movie. Is that what you were going to say,

201

George?"

"Uh-huh, it's my mother's favorite film, and she made my brother and me watch it with her. It's pretty good."

"Wow, nobody else I know has even heard of it. And I'm shocked that you like it, George, since it's such a girlie sort of movie. You know, it's so sweet — the whole romance subplot with Annabeth Gish."

"Sweet's the right description of it, but it's not so sweet that it makes your teeth ache."

Lizzie laughed. "Only a dentist would make a comment like that."

"Well, I've never even heard of it," James admitted. "Have you, Marla?"

"Nope," Marla said. "But I'm not fond of sweet movies and usually Lizzie isn't either. But you know, George, you've found the road into our finicky Lizzie's heart: not only do you like a movie she likes, but you said 'made my brother and me watch it.' If you'd said, 'my brother and I' you'd have no chance with her. You've now passed two of her secret boyfriend tests. Oh, wait, I forgot one, you both like iced tea in any weather. That's three tests you've aced. It's a match made in heaven."

George smiled and Lizzie frowned. "Shut up, Marla," she muttered. But it was true.

The more time she spent with George the better she liked him. At least he wasn't boring. And he was doing awfully well at *Jeopardy!* She turned to him. "Marla and James go home for Thanksgiving, but if you're around and don't have anything to do, would you like to come to my parents' house for dinner?"

"Is that another test?" George asked Marla. "I'd love to come to Thanksgiving," he told Lizzie, without waiting for Marla's answer.

"It'll be different, that's for sure," James warned him. "We were there last year."

George arrived in a scrum of other guests, doddering professors and their doddering wives, widows and widowers of doddering professors, and all of Mendel's and Lydia's students who had no other place to go. George was laden with packages. Even though he'd specifically told her not to, Elaine had FedExed several loaves of cranberry and zucchini breads. For some weird reason she'd also sent a challah, along with some jars of homemade jams, a large box of Frango chocolates, and several bags of gourmet popcorn. He wasn't sure whether the popcorn was intended for the Bultmanns or not, but he brought it with him anyway. All that, along with the wine (he'd bought two bottles of white and one of red), wasn't easy to carry. He didn't want to drop anything but was equally worried about bumping into one of the many elderly guests who probably couldn't keep upright if someone tapped their arm. Everyone was carrying food, but nobody was as weighed down with packages as George.

He'd been counting on Lizzie answering the door, but instead it was an older man who first greeted the other guests and then looked at George. George assumed it was Mendel.

"You are?" the man asked, raising an eyebrow.

George attempted to transfer all his packages to his left arm so he could shake hands, but was unsuccessful. He resorted to nodding politely. "I'm Lizzie's friend George."

The man didn't look any more enlightened as to George's identity. George went on, "She, um, Lizzie invited me for Thanksgiving dinner." He looked around. Why wasn't Lizzie coming to his rescue, either by assuring her father that George was who he said he was or by unburdening him of Elaine's gifts and the wine, which together were growing increasingly heavy?

Ah, there she was, dashing down the stairs. "Mendel, this is George," she said.

"George, Mendel." Mendel finally nodded, and George nodded back, feeling ridiculous. Lizzie took him into the kitchen and lined up everything he'd brought on a counter.

"Wow, this is all from you?"

"Well, my mom sent it for you and your parents."

Lizzie shook her head. "Totally unnecessary. But awfully nice of your mom."

She poured them each a glass of wine. "Listen," she began. "About the food . . ." but he didn't hear what she said next because — at no signal that George detected — everyone around them suddenly rushed into the dining room, took a plate, and lined up at the buffet tables, which were crowded with an array of food. George was swept along with the crowd. He lost sight of Lizzie momentarily.

It was hard to know what to choose. He wished he knew what Lizzie was going to say. What was it about the food that she wanted to tell him? He wished he'd grabbed hold of Lizzie's hand and held on tight. She was still nowhere to be seen. George sighed. He took a piece of turkey and ladled some stuffing on top of it, then poured gravy over it all. His plate still looked pretty barren. He added some mashed potatoes and then couldn't resist taking a square of lasagna as well. The lemon-yellow Jell-O salad filled with miniature marshmallows and canned fruit cocktail precipitated a wave of nostalgia for his childhood. When he visited his grandparents in Stillwater the dinners would always include Jell-O salad of one flavor or another. But whatever the flavor, the Jell-O would be filled with miniature marshmallows and canned fruit cocktail. He hadn't had it for years. He took a large helping.

While he was scoping out the dessert table, there, finally, was Lizzie, making her way toward him, carrying a plate that was empty except for a few carrot sticks and pieces of celery.

"Is that all you're eating?"

"Didn't you hear what I said about the food?"

"No, I was dragged away by the screaming starving hordes of your parents' friends."

"What I said was that the food's basically inedible, no matter who made it or what it is."

"All of it? Really?" He indicated the Jell-O, which he was dying to sample. "And what about the desserts?"

"All of it," she said firmly, "except maybe the desserts."

"Okay, can we go check out the desserts?

And can I just taste the Jell-O? I'm pretty sure nobody could possibly ruin that."

"With this crowd you can never be sure of anything. You should hear some of my Bultmann family Thanksgiving food stories. The trips to the emergency room at St. Joseph's, the failed Heimlich maneuvers to dislodge an errant turkey bone. The fight to the death over the last chocolate brownie on the tray."

"You're very funny, Lizzie," George said.

"I am, it's true. Not many people know that about me, though."

"Despite your warnings, I'm going to try some of the desserts."

"I suppose lots of people have remarked on what a good eater you are," Lizzie surmised.

"My Montreal grandmother loved it when we visited because between me and Todd she didn't have leftovers. The human garbage disposals, she called us." George laughed.

Rather than share a table with other people, they ended up sitting on the stairs. Lizzie crunched on her carrots moodily, and George carefully tried little bits of everything he'd taken. The Jell-O was disappointingly, cloyingly sweet. And the fruit cocktail didn't really taste like fruit. It didn't taste like anything at all. How disillusioning. Was this what becoming an adult meant? That you pulled aside a curtain and saw a sad truth you hadn't understood before? He was grateful that the brownie was delicious, though. He moved up a stair to sit next to Lizzie and put his arm around her.

They left right after dinner. George wanted to say good-bye to the Bultmanns but they seemed to have disappeared. "Don't worry about it, George," Lizzie said. "Let's just go. They wouldn't care either way."

George was unconvinced but tried not to worry about it.

"Awful, wasn't it," Lizzie said, not as a question.

"Yeah, it was a little odd, I guess. Just like James said."

"You're too nice, George, do you know that?"

"My brother once accused me of the same thing, actually. But I didn't agree with him. I like being nice. So, no, it wasn't awful, it was just . . . weird."

Lizzie sighed. "They're just not normal, you know. All they care about is their work. I don't know why they put on this charade of celebration. Did you notice how all the hot food was actually cold?"

"Well, I guess that if it's a buffet and you

get your food and then sit down, things are often cold by the time you're ready to eat it."

"Marla's mother has warming trays."

"So does mine, actually," George reluctantly admitted. "The desserts were good. But the turkey looked really undercooked."

"Yeah, it was raw. It always is. I tried to warn you. I always pretend I'm a vegetarian at Thanksgiving. I wonder who brought the macaroni and cheese this year. It looked okay. God, I'm starving now. Are you hungry? I rescued the popcorn, the chocolates, a bottle of wine, and the cranberry bread. We can have a feast tonight."

George laughed. "Do you think your father would even recognize me if he saw me again? And I never even met your mother. Damn, I really wanted to make a good impression on them. Aren't they interested in who you're dating?"

"Nope, never have been and never will. Sometimes that's good and sometimes that's bad."

"My folks are so different," George said. "If I brought a girl home for Thanksgiving, my mother would be all over her, grilling her, asking her what her parents did, what's she studying, if she has brothers and sisters, her favorite books and movies —"

Lizzie interrupted him. "Your mother and I would have at least one thing in common: that we both love the movie *Shag*."

"My mother would love you, Lizzie."

"Really? Are you sure? Nobody's mother loves me."

George took her hand. "Elaine would be the exception that proves that rule."

AN INVITATION

George was on call on Saturday after Thanksgiving, but he and Lizzie decided to take a chance and go see the Coen brothers' new film, *Barton Fink*. As they walked back to George's apartment, Lizzie congratulated him on not having to leave the theater and attend to someone's emergency tooth issue.

"I would have thought that Thanksgiving was a prime time for disaster, especially with food like pecan pie."

"You'd think so," George agreed happily. "But maybe the dental gods knew that we wanted to spend the day together and planned accordingly."

They were in general accord about how much they'd enjoyed the film (George perhaps a tad more than Lizzie), how great the casting was, how they couldn't think of anyone better to play those roles than John

Turturro and John Goodman. Lizzie had read in the newspaper that morning about all the literary allusions in the film, but she and George could only name one: Shakespeare.

"That doesn't say much," George said. "It's probably hard to find anything written after 1600 and probably even earlier that doesn't have some allusion to his plays."

Lizzie agreed. "I remember reading a novel in which one of the characters, a college professor, was writing a book on the influence of Emily Dickinson on Shakespeare and how his colleagues always misheard it and thought it was the other way around. I wish I could remember the title, because talking about it now makes me want to read it again. It's so interesting to think about. Do you think we read Shakespeare differently because of Dickinson's poems?"

"I don't know," George said. "You'll have to read me some of her poems. I haven't read anything by Dickinson since high school, and that was the poem about death, the one that's always included in anthologies. Maybe I'd understand it better now. Anyway, how would you even demonstrate that it was true, though?"

"I guess you'd study a lot of Shakespeare

criticism written before and after Dickinson and compare them."

"I don't see how that would work," George argued. "There's no real way to know in any case. It's all down to interpretation, anyway."

"All I was saying is that I think it's such a cool idea. Pascal's influence on Sappho; Saint Aquinas's influence on Homer. Gosh, the possibilities are endless." Lizzie untucked her arm from George's and moved away a few inches so they were no longer touching. "You're no fun, George. I really hate it when you have to have all the facts before you can even wonder about something."

George was deep in thought and gave no indication that he'd heard Lizzie. He didn't seem to notice they were now walking separately.

Finally Lizzie couldn't stand it any longer. "Are you *still* thinking about what facts you'd need to in order to prove influence works backward in time?"

He took her arm and firmly tucked it back in his. "No, actually. I was wondering if you'd like to come home with me for Christmas."

Lizzie was flabbergasted. "Go with you to Tulsa for Christmas? Really? Tulsa, with you? Why?"

He stood so that they were facing one another. "Because we've been going out for almost a year, which is longer than I've ever dated anyone, and because I'd very much like to have my parents meet you. And you to meet them. Will you think about it? We probably have a few days before we need to get our airline tickets."

When they got back to the apartment, they turned on the television to watch the Eagles beat the Giants in a meaningless game. George didn't care who won — he suspected that nobody but the coaches and probably some of the players on both teams did either — but he always got a kick out of telling Lizzie about what OSU players were on which team and how high they were drafted and whether he'd seen them play. Lizzie wasn't really listening. She was worrying up a storm. What did this potential visit mean? Did she even want to meet his parents? Was this going to be like the thin edge of the wedge, *après lequel, le commitment*? And, gosh, she had begun it, really, hadn't she? She'd initiated every forward movement in their relationship. They wouldn't be together if she hadn't called him way back in December or agreed to go out with him all year. And, true, she had brought him to her family's disastrous Thanksgiving (which in retrospect had somehow brought them closer together), but that wasn't because she wanted her parents to meet him or vice versa. She'd invited him because she couldn't stand being home and hoped his being there would help her get through the day. Maybe the role George played in her life was to distract her from the voices in her head and all her despair about Jack.

Ugh, Lizzie, she said to herself, that is a terrible thing to think. Unfortunately, it sounded very true. Maybe she needed someone in her life besides Marla and James, another person who didn't despise her or think she was an awful human being. Maybe that someone was George. It was quite possible that George had unaccountably fallen for her, and fallen hard. He didn't know about Jack or that biggest, stupidest, most awful mistake, the Great Game. He had no idea of all her many sorrows and her multitude of flaws. She remembered a line from a poem by Stephen Dunn, one of Jack's favorite poets, about wanting to be loved beyond deserving. That's what she wanted. And Jack couldn't. Or wouldn't. But maybe George could, and would.

Still, the decision to go to Tulsa had big stakes and lots of possible repercussions.

"It's such a family holiday, maybe your folks wouldn't want you to bring me."

"Are you kidding? My mother loves company. Really. She begged me to invite you. Please come."

Lizzie hesitated. "I don't know. Let me think about it, okay?"

That evening, in a panic, she asked Marla whether, if she went to Tulsa, she needed to bring presents for George's parents and, if so, what she should bring. Marla loved buying presents and did it brilliantly. She had an instinctive sense of what someone would enjoy receiving and didn't mind shopping until she found exactly what it was she was looking for. Lizzie knew from firsthand experience that Marla could figure out what you really wanted even before you knew it was what you wanted. Marla's talent was how Lizzie now had a supply of bath accoutrements, salts and oils and nice-smelling soaps, none of which Lizzie had ever thought she wanted and would certainly never purchase for herself. Lizzie, on the other hand, had no facility for either part of the process. She tended to be so overwhelmed by the quantity of choices available that she left the store empty-handed, feeling both guilt and relief. Plus there was no way she could ever fathom what someone else would want.

Marla's firm opinion was that, yes, Lizzie needed to bring George's parents a gift. At the very least, a hostess gift, to thank them for their hospitality. She ruled out candy and liquor. Too much of a stereotype: the new girlfriend arriving with candy and liquor in hand. Marla favored the dramatic and inventive. She instructed Lizzie to ask George some questions about his parents.

The next day she reported the answers back to Marla. Yes, they both liked to read. Yes, they liked to travel, or at least George's mother did. His father was a hug-the-hearth. "George didn't put it in those words, but it's what he meant. You know, I've always wanted to say 'hug-the-hearth' and never thought I could find a way to use it in a sentence. It's from a poem by the oh-God-the-pain girl."

"Move on, Lizzie, time's a-wastin' and James is awaitin' for me."

"Okay, okay, but how come nobody except Jack ever likes it when I quote poetry to them?"

"Shouldn't you be putting the verb in that sentence in the past tense? For your own sake? True, Jack let you quote poetry, many months ago now. False, Jack is still here. He is not here. He left you and didn't come back," she ended astringently. And partially made up for what she'd said by adding lovingly, "And I'm happy, and James is happy, and I bet George would be over the moon to have you read poems to us. But, Lizzie, that particular Jack McConaghey train left the station months ago. It's done gone."

Lizzie went on relaying George's answers, now feeling a little chastened and somewhat depressed. She wished Marla hadn't been so definite about Jack's absence. Yes, both Goldrosens were interested in politics. They had both marched on Washington and volunteered at the local Gene McCarthy for President campaign in the 1960s when they were young. Yes, they listened to music. Allan preferred jazz and Elaine was still addicted to the music she'd listened to in her twenties and thirties, which included all those now iconic singers like Joan Baez and Joni Mitchell. No, Elaine didn't particularly enjoy cooking, but loved baking and reading about food. No, they weren't both sports fans. Only Allan was. No, they weren't particularly collectors of anything. Yes, they liked the theater. They went to New York three or four times a year to see the latest plays, and saw whatever plays were offered in Tulsa. Yes, they had a lot of family photographs around the house.

"You can stop there," Marla told Lizzie. "That gives me enough to go on. I'll have a list for you by this afternoon."

"Don't hurry. In fact, don't work too hard on it. I haven't decided yet whether I'm going to go or not."

"You're going," Marla said, either encouragingly or forebodingly or perhaps a mixture of both. Lizzie couldn't tell for sure.

A few days later at breakfast before they left for class, Marla asked, "Have you decided yet?"

Lizzie swallowed the piece of toast she'd been chewing. "Nope."

"Well, get cracking, girl. I assume George is waiting for you before he buys a ticket."

"Do you think I should go?"

Marla sighed. "Of course. Why wouldn't you? It's not like you're committing yourself to anything. You're just going for a visit. What's the worst that could happen? You might be a little uncomfortable or bored, but you'll be more bored here. James and I will be gone and Mendel and Lydia are hopeless, as you never tire of telling anyone who'll listen. Of course you should go, especially because I have some great ideas about what presents to give. But before you actually buy anything, don't forget to check with George to make sure he thinks it'll go over well and that they don't already have it."

"Yes, Mother, I won't forget. And will you come shopping with me?"

Marla sighed dramatically. "Yes, dear daughter, I guess I will come shopping with you. I can get started on my own Hanukkah stuff. Maybe I'll buy the same presents for my parents and James's. Now go call George to tell him you're going. I mean it. Do it."

"Yes, Mother, I will."

"Now. Go call him now."

Lizzie stood up and then sat down again. "Do you think I need to get George a present?"

"I'm not sure what the etiquette books would say, but I'd say no, it's not necessary. Your going with him is his present."

"That would be really good, because I have no idea what I'd buy for him."

So the die was cast, the decision taken, the tickets bought. Needless to say, George was thrilled. His mother, when he called sounded — was it possible? — even happier than George was to hear the news. George knew better than to tell Lizzie that.

She studied the list Marla gave her. She had a lot to choose from. There were many suggestions of books, and Marla had starred the ones she thought would be especially appropriate, which included *Wild Swans: Three Daughters of China* by Jung Chang (biography and history); David Simon's *Homicide: A Year on the Killing Streets* (sociology and crime); Beryl Bainbridge's *The Birthday Boys* (fictional biography of Scott's journey to the South Pole); *Savage Inequalities* by Jonathan Kozol (sociology and education); James Stewart's *Den of Thieves* (financial chicanery); books by the food writers M.F.K. Fisher and Elizabeth David. If none of the books met her approval, Marla had added a CD of the original soundtrack from the Broadway version of *Evita* (which encompassed, conveniently, politics plus music); unusual picture frames; and a subscription to Harry & David's fruit-of-the-month club.

Lizzie went over the list with George, whose already high opinion of Marla increased tenfold. What a terrific job she'd done, he told Lizzie. He could swear, looking at the list, that she'd spent a lot of time with Elaine and Allan and knew them well. Lizzie relayed this to Marla, who was very pleased with herself. Lizzie ended up buying books: for Allan, *Den of Thieves,* and

Elaine, *The Art of Eating.* George decided he'd get his dad *Savage Inequalities* and his mother *Evita,* since he knew they'd seen it and didn't think they'd ever gotten the CD.

Lizzie's Christmas shopping was done. Of course the Bultmanns never exchanged presents. Lydia was on principle violently against any religious holidays and Mendel simply wasn't interested in celebrations. When Sheila was Lizzie's babysitter, she'd always bring her a holiday gift or two. Lizzie recalled with much embarrassment the presents she'd foisted upon her beloved Sheila in return: one year there were guppies in a fishbowl; another year (a particularly painful memory) a set of oversize jacks that she'd coveted for herself. Stop thinking about the past, Lizzie!

WHAT YOU REMEMBER
AND WHAT YOU FORGET

Lizzie well knows that what you remember and what you forget is surpassingly strange. She can recall some things from the past with an almost eerie clarity. She can, for example, still remember the chalky taste of the powdered milk Mendel and Lydia favored and the socks Cornball Cornish wore the night they fucked in the Great Game (he never took them off; she remembers that too). And yet there's so much she's forgotten: the exact shade of Jack's blue eyes; the name of the woman that Todd almost married; Andrea's mother's first name; the plot of Umberto Eco's *Name of the Rose,* a novel she'd actually liked quite a lot; the name of the girl she'd won a double-Dutch jump-rope contest with in eighth grade; the sound of Jack's voice when he said good-bye to her for what she didn't realize was the last time — oh, the list of what she's forgotten goes on and on and on.

But here's what she does remember:

1. Sheila telling her that Lizzie should never ever learn how sausages or laws were made. And if she happened to find out, she most definitely shouldn't tell Sheila about it.
2. The crackly, sticky, generally uncomfortable feel of the torn leather booths at Gilmore's, which, regardless, is her second favorite coffee shop, because it's where she and Jack used to go.
3. Being at a family Hanukkah party at Andrea's house when she was about ten and hearing Andrea's married cousin Ginger saying to

someone (but who?), "I have to sleep under the bed if I don't want to get pregnant."

4. The painting of a naked woman on the wall by the stairs at Andrea's house, and how embarrassed she was each time she saw it.

5. Finding the rhyme "Monday's child is fair of face" in some book from the library and, after figuring out that she was born on a Wednesday, realizing that it was why she was filled with woe. Too bad she hadn't been born on a Tuesday, full of grace, or, even better, on a Friday, since then she'd be both loving and giving.

6. Taking a chance by telling a Health Service doctor that she felt awfully blue much of the time only to have him respond by telling her that she had an unreasonable expectation of happiness. Lizzie wonders whether her desire for happiness, as opposed to an expectation of it, is unreasonable as well.

7. The smell of Wind Song, the cologne Sheila always wore.

8. Her father telling her angrily that there were more important things

to cry over than the fate of a fictional horse and being shocked that he knew that Black Beauty was a horse.

9. Her Halloween costume when she was seven: a traffic light, which Sheila created.

10. Naomi Abrams telling Lizzie (in third grade) that her mother looked like a witch. The thing was, Lydia's appearance was somewhat witchy.

11. Her first-grade teacher announcing that the next person who talked out of turn would have to stand in the corner for five minutes, and, wouldn't you know it, Lizzie was that person. She spent a significant amount of time in the first grade standing in that same corner.

12. How, when she was nine, in third grade, right before Sheila stopped working for the Bultmanns, Lizzie told her parents at dinner — it was dispirited pork chops and under-cooked scalloped potatoes (although she knows full well that "dispirited" is not a word she'd have ever said back then) — that her homework was to draw a family tree and present it to the class, with

stories about her ancestors. Mendel looked down at his plate and took a small bite of potato. Lizzie could almost hear it crunching between his teeth. Lydia said grimly, "Ah, the family genealogy. I wondered when that would rear its ugly head. You'd think the Holocaust would have put paid to that particular assignment." (Lizzie also knew that she had never heard the word "genealogy" before Lydia said it. Or what "put paid" meant.)

Lydia continued, "A study of genealogy does not work for such happy few as we, since we have no ancestors." (It was many years before Lizzie realized that Lydia's "happy" was to be understood as ironic.)

"But," began Lizzie just as Mendel shook his head.

"No. Your mother is right. Use Sheila's family instead. Pretend they're your own. She'll be happy to help you draw a family tree and you can ask her if you can meet her grandparents. They'll tell you all the stories you need to make a presentation."

Which is how for a while Lizzie's father (Warren) was a man who worked at the Bendix factory outside Ann Arbor and her mother (Adele) was a secretary at the university. Warren's parents were a minister (Jacob) and a housewife (Lorene). Lizzie's pretend paternal grandparents met when Irv was working as a chassis assembly-line supervisor at the Ford River Rouge plant in Dearborn and Mary was the waitress at a restaurant where he went on his union-authorized breaks to drink coffee and smoke. The minister collected model trains (HO gauge), which he bequeathed to his son Warren, who turned his garage over to the collection and enthusiastically built it up to an impressive degree. The garage was filled with several Ping-Pong tables that had been pushed together to display the complete setup. During her oral report to the class, Lizzie noted that it was almost time for him to find another, much bigger place to keep his trains, because the collection was rapidly outgrowing the garage. "My dad," Lizzie continued, "loves trestles, so there are lots of them that the train has to go over as it makes its way through the big towns and small cities. There are farms and schools and lots of houses. There are even people living in those places, and they have dogs and cats and one of the houses even has a tiny rabbit on the front lawn. Kids stand on the steps of their house and wave at the conductor and engineer when the train goes by.

"My dad," Lizzie went on, "was sorry he didn't have a boy to share his hobby with." Her mom, she said, wasn't much interested in the trains. But she, her father's daughter, loved them, although she was forbidden to play with the trains unless her dad was there.

Lizzie passed some pictures around for the class to see: a Polaroid of the railroad's layout. Another one of her grandfather Jacob's first church, in Milan, Ohio. And another taken at her parents' wedding, which was at Greenfield Village, the indoor-outdoor museum that housed Henry Ford's collections of cars.

Nobody challenged her, not even the teacher, whose name Lizzie didn't remember, and who definitely knew who her real parents were. She might even have gotten an A on the assignment.

THE CORNERBACKS

The boys who played defense were much less interesting to Lizzie than the offense had been. After all, defense had originally been Andrea's bailiwick, and Lizzie had decided to go on with the Great Game only after finishing with the offense in a badly mistaken desire to complete what she'd started. Honestly, those eleven defensive players are mostly blurred together in her mind.

The two cornerbacks were Micah Delavan and Mitchell Oberski. They were inseparable and together known as the M&M's. Micah only had four fingers on his left hand, while Mitchell had a large birthmark the shape of Wyoming on his back. The two of them went off to college together and as far as Lizzie knew they were together still.

WHAT LIZZIE HATES
ABOUT HERSELF

That she can't bring herself to tell George about Jack.

That she can't bring herself to tell George about the shame of the Great Game.

That she never should have told Jack she was the girl in the *Psychology Today* article, because that was why he left her and never came back.

That she is a too-easy weeper. Lizzie understands this to be a reaction to the fact that Mendel and Lydia became furious when, as a child, she cried. What sort of parents refuse to let their child cry? Unfortunately, the sort that gave birth to, and raised, Elizabeth Frieda Bultmann Goldrosen, that's who.

That she always, always either loses one of a pair of earrings or gets an ineradicable stain on a white shirt.

That she looks exactly like Mendel, if Mendel were female, although she supposes that it's better than looking like the witch Lydia.

That she's failed so miserably in so many different parts of her life.

That she is the same rotten housekeeper that her mother was. George was the total opposite. He could walk into a room, give it a stern glance, and it immediately resolved itself into neatness: the books lie attractively on the coffee table, the magazines arrange themselves in a pile from oldest down to newest; and the dust bunnies cast themselves into the air and disappear. On the other hand, when Lizzie walks into a room, chaos ensues. No matter how hard she tries, the room remains a mess. George counseled patience (he pretty much always counseled patience), advising her to vacuum more carefully, to take her time and do one thing to completion at a time. This was very hard, not to say impossible, for Lizzie to accomplish. She hated herself for this thought but secretly wished that George had some grad students that she could co-opt to clean their house.

CHRISTMAS CHEZ GOLDROSENS, 1992

December 21

Part of the Goldrosen tradition was that George always came home on the twenty-first of December and flew back early on the twenty-sixth. For Lizzie, the day they left Ann Arbor proved frustrating in the extreme. Already nervous and regretting her decision to accompany George home, she twice came close to bolting from her seat while they were waiting for their flight and finding her own way home. Nothing that happened on the trip down to Tulsa boded well, in her opinion, for future trips to Tulsa (and she was right; their Christmas flights never went particularly smoothly). Their plane out of Metro Airport departed late because a fierce storm over Lake Michigan caused whiteout conditions at O'Hare, so they missed their connection in Chicago and were rerouted via Salt Lake City, which involved an endless stay in a terminal that Lizzie thought resembled a waiting room for long-haul buses. Of course George was perfectly content. He read old issues of the *Journal of the American Dental Association,* fascinated by the intricacies of veneers, tooth decay, implants, and whether or not a dentist had a moral, if not legal, obligation to report suspected child abuse. Although Lizzie'd brought a novel with her (Barbara Kingsolver's *The Bean Trees*), she couldn't sit still long enough to open it and begin reading. Instead she paced.

Lizzie hated waiting for anything: she became bored and edgy, inclined to snap at everyone around, even strangers. She walked around the terminal, growing more upset by the minute. At first she tried to decide if she'd made the right decision by coming

231

with George. She wondered what Jack would say if he knew what she was doing. She wondered if *she* knew what she was doing. Meeting Mendel and not meeting Lydia at Thanksgiving hadn't sent George scurrying out of her life. He didn't exactly enjoy Thanksgiving dinner with the Bultmann family (what sane person would?), but he didn't give up on Lizzie as a result. She sort of wished that Jack had come home with her sometime that spring they were together; maybe that would have helped him understand her better.

All this thinking about the present, the past, and the future was exhausting. By the time they finally landed in Tulsa, Lizzie was worn-out, hungry, wired from drinking too many Cokes in the Salt Lake airport and too much coffee on the plane. She'd had it with the weather gods and (unfairly — it was mostly unfair to blame George for much of anything; Lizzie knew this, but it didn't prevent her from doing so) with George for dragging her to Oklahoma. George was simply glad they'd finally arrived. Now his parents could meet Lizzie.

Elaine and Allan were waiting for them at the gate. They took turns hugging George and Lizzie. "We're so happy you're here," Allan told them.

Lizzie tried not to smile too widely, wondering if either of George's parents noticed that one of her incisors was slightly crooked.

"Lizzie," Elaine said, hugging her again, "we're just thrilled to finally meet you. It's lovely that you came home with George. He's told us so much about you." Lizzie tried not to pull away from Elaine too quickly, but she was, sadly, too much of a Bultmann, used to Bultmann pseudo-hugs, to feel comfortable in Elaine's embrace.

"I'm glad to be here too," she managed to say.

"George, you and Dad wait for the suitcases in baggage claim, and we'll meet you at the car."

"George's told me a lot about your family's Christmases," Lizzie said as they walked. Walking to the car! This was like a toy airport compared to Detroit's.

"We do have a ton of family traditions," Elaine admitted. "Some of them go back to my childhood, but mostly they're things we've just come up with since the boys were babies. I love this time of year. You'll see. It's sort of sad that the days just whiz by."

Just at the moment, days whizzing by sounded good to Lizzie.

"Oh, here they come. Good. You both

233

must be starving. Let's hurry and get you home."

The Goldrosens' house was at the end of a cul-de-sac. It was redbrick, two-storied, stately, and serene. It looked only a little smaller than the Kappa house in Ann Arbor. It looked nothing at all like the house where Lizzie grew up. "I've put you in the bedroom that's directly across the hall from George," Elaine said. "Let's get your luggage upstairs, and as soon as you come down we can eat. It's just so lovely that you're here," she repeated. "I wish Todd had come home. Australia's so far away. It's always so nice to be together on holidays, especially Christmas."

The Goldrosen traditions turned out to be many and various. Throughout them all, Lizzie tried to look happy and as though she were enjoying everything. This was mostly not very difficult, although at night her jaw ached from smiling. She would recall that first Christmas visit much later, when she'd go to parties honoring George and have to appear to be having a good time in that same determined way in front of his devoted fans and avid followers.

December 22
Right after a sumptuous breakfast that

included bagels (which arrived via FedEx, every week, from the St. Viateur Bagel Shop in Montreal. "These are the bagels I grew up with," Elaine told Lizzie. "I think they're so much better than the ones everyone raves about in New York"), cream cheese, lox, tomatoes, Swiss cheese, and red onions, George and his father left to go to Allan's office so he could show George all the latest equipment and generally talk teeth.

Lizzie and Elaine sat down at the kitchen table and began blowing out the insides of twenty-four eggs. Lizzie discovered that it was much more difficult than it sounded. First Elaine showed her how to poke a hole in each end of the egg. "You have to begin with a sharp needle to pierce the shell, then gradually make the holes a little larger. Sometimes a darning needle works better for that part, but you have to be careful not to break the egg."

It took her about half an hour, from first tentative needle jab to the empty shell, per egg. Elaine, with her years of practice behind her, was much faster. Somehow she'd never thought of the insides of eggs before, or at least not in quite the same way as she saw them now.

She felt embarrassed and clumsy because she'd smashed three eggs in the process, but Elaine didn't seem to notice, or in any event, didn't comment on it. The resulting mixture — a bowl of egg whites and yolks — looked so disgusting that Lizzie decided she might have to give up eating eggs until the memory of the contents of that bowl blurred a lot.

Once the eggs were empty, Elaine brought out a big cardboard box filled with ribbons, crepe paper, scraps of felt and other material, construction paper, Magic Markers, and glue sticks, along with several large jars of paste. It was everything they might need or want to use to decorate the eggs. They gave them faces, pasting on bits of felt that they cut into shapes for the eyes, nose, mouth, and eyebrows, and followed that up by attaching yellow, red, black, or brown yarn for hair. Sometimes they braided the yarn, and sometimes put it into a ponytail using a contrasting piece of yarn to tie it up. Despite her feeling she was doing something wrong, or not living up to Elaine's expectations, Lizzie felt pretty relaxed. "I was awful in art in elementary school," Lizzie told her. "But this is really fun."

They attached pipe cleaners to make arms and legs (another job that required a very light touch; Lizzie broke three more eggs and Elaine one) and finally they concocted dresses made out of the crepe paper.

"This is a paste-intensive job, isn't it," she commented to Elaine, looking at her encrusted nails.

"You bet. I think this whole holiday season is the only thing that keeps Elmer's in business. Oh, and nursery schools, of course. But wait until tomorrow: there's lots more paste still to come."

Later in the day Elaine and Lizzie carefully unwrapped from layers of tissue paper the almost two dozen dolls that Elaine had created in Christmases past. "I mostly give the dolls away, but I always keep my favorite for the top of the tree. I'm saving them for my granddaughters, if Todd or George ever gets married and produces female children."

They then began baking dozens and dozens of cookies for the family to eat and to give as gifts to friends. The word "friends" encompassed Wade, the FedEx driver, the mailman (despite his obvious and obnoxious support of the archrival Sooners from the University of Oklahoma), and the guy who delivered the paper every morning, as well as those of Allan's patients lucky (or perhaps unlucky) enough to have a late December appointment with him. They made gingerbread persons ("I refuse to call them men,"

Elaine told Lizzie. "After all, they could be women wearing pants") as well as chocolate and peppermint thumbprints. Elaine had a large collection of cookie cutters, and they used these to make sugar cookies: bells, reindeer, wreaths, and plain old circles. They added small holes at the tops of one batch of assorted shapes so that later they could be hung on the tree.

"It's easier to roll out cookies if you refrigerate the dough for an hour or so. A lot of people don't know that, and they try to do it all right away. Not a good idea. And that gives you time to start straightening up the kitchen or, even better, to sit and have a cup of tea."

When the cookies were cool, Lizzie helped decorate them. Lizzie had extensive past experience with frosting — she and Sheila used to spend many hours of their time together baking and frosting cookies and cakes. Perhaps applying frosting was a talent, like bicycling, that once learned is impossible to forget. And anyone can shake sparkles onto a cookie. You can be clumsy and ill at ease and still do a good enough job. Although maybe she was putting on too much? No, and so what if she were? She knew that Elaine wouldn't care. She started to feel a little better.

Finally, Elaine made mandel bread, "the Jewish biscotti," Elaine told her. "They're Allan's favorite, and George and Todd love them too. We'll probably have to make more tomorrow or the next day. They're pretty labor-intensive — you have to bake them twice, so we don't have them very often. Have you ever had one?"

"No, I don't think so. I mean, biscotti, yes, every coffee shop in Ann Arbor has them, but not mandel bread."

"Ah, coffee shops," Elaine said ruefully. "You'll find that they're few and far between in Tulsa. Not like Montreal, where there's one on every corner. I think that sort of really urban lifestyle is what I miss most about living here." Lizzie nodded but couldn't decide if she needed to respond, or if she even had anything to add to the discussion.

"Two things to know about mandel bread, though, besides how delicious they are. They eat up" — and here she glanced at Lizzie meaningfully as if to say, " 'Eat': Do you get it?" looking for all the world like George when he made a joke — "an inordinate amount of time. Plus, if it's finger-licking-good cookie dough that you're after, they're not what you want to make. When I'm in a wanting-to-eat-lots-of-dough sort

239

of mood, I make banana-oatmeal cookies. That dough is unbeatable. But once they're baked, mandel bread is pretty irresistible. We'll bake some extra so that I can send a couple of tins back to Michigan."

Lizzie enjoyed playing sous-chef to Elaine, rummaging through the kitchen cupboards for whatever was needed for each recipe. They spent a companionable day together, mixing, tasting, rolling, baking, nibbling, washing up, and eating. Lizzie discovered that Elaine also dunked her cookies into her tea. The winter sun shone through the six-pointed mosaic star hanging in the window. It cut the light into straight-edged patches of color that landed on the table, the stove, and even Lizzie's arm as she moved around the kitchen. By the time they finished drying the last of the baking sheets, measuring spoons and cups, cooling racks, and multiple spatulas, Lizzie, calmed down and almost happy, felt that all she wanted to do from this day on was to follow Elaine through the rest of her life. Suddenly she badly wanted to tell Elaine about the Great Game, about Jack, about how she didn't really know how she felt about George, but she also knew that, for a number of reasons, both obvious and not, it most likely wasn't the best thing to do.

"Do it, do it, do it. Ruin everything right now," the voices in her head chorused. "Tell her all about it. Do it, do it, do it." But Lizzie refused to listen to them.

Right after dinner, they all went together to choose a Christmas tree. Elaine, Allan told Lizzie, was always inclined to take the first really tall and bushy one she saw; it was how she shopped for everything: quickly and decisively. Allan insisted on walking through the entire lot before he'd finally reach a decision on what tree he wanted. Elaine pointed out to Lizzie that the tree they finally bought was exactly the one that she'd chosen in the first five minutes of arriving at the tree lot. Everyone laughed, including Allan. By the time they got home and George and Allan had the tree set up in the living room, there was just time for more cookies and hot chocolate before they all trooped upstairs to bed. Lizzie thought that this was close to a perfect day, certainly the best since Jack left.

December 23
The morning and most of the afternoon were devoted to decorating the tree. Lizzie expected Elaine to bring out boxes of ornaments — family heirlooms, perhaps — but learned that each year the Goldrosens made

241

everything that went on the tree. Allan left for work, weighted down with many bags of cookies for the staff and patients, but George, Elaine, and Lizzie sat around the kitchen table — there was still a lovely tinge of cookie in the air — cutting Christmas wrapping paper into strips so they could put together chains to hang on the tree. Lizzie remembered making chains in elementary school using construction paper, which had been much harder to work with.

Elaine said, "You know, Lizzie, George will tell you that I'm terrible at arts-and-crafts projects. And he's right. I don't do this sort of thing at all the rest of the year. It's just that I love all the ephemera of Christmas, and I've always liked the idea of having a do-it-yourself holiday, or at least as much as we can do ourselves."

"She's not kidding about her craft skills," George added. "Her favorite book when we were growing up was *Easy Halloween Costumes You Don't Have to Sew.*"

Elaine chuckled. "I always thought I should buy dozens of copies of it and give them out at baby showers. I am very adept at stapling, if I do say so myself."

"You were the best, Mom. Too bad there wasn't a stapling contest you could enter."

"Did you and Todd help make decorations

when you were little, George?"

"Oh, absolutely." George started laughing. "One year, when Todd was seven and I was five, Mom left us alone when the doorbell rang — who was it, some delivery guy? Or was it a phone call? — and we had a paste fight while she was gone. We covered our hands with it and then chased each around the house trying to smear it on each other. There was paste absolutely everywhere — the walls, toys, our faces, clothes, beds, refrigerator. Mom was not happy with us. I remember that too."

"It was a call from your grandmother, wondering what time we'd get to Stillwater the next day, and then she went on and on about the jewelry store and did I want this necklace that they'd special ordered for someone who never picked it up? I couldn't get off the phone. I kept trying to tell her I had to go and she kept talking over me. I knew something was going on with you two boys. And all these years later, I sometimes still find dried blobs of paste around, stuck to something totally unexpected, like the bottom of the waffle iron. I guess it's also a sign that I never clean thoroughly enough either."

"And even after that, Mom was so desperate for help that she put up with us."

"It's more that it's no fun doing this alone. The fun is being together, like we are now." Later they strung popcorn and cranberries into more chains to loop around the tree and on the mantel. George was quite deft at this part of the work. (It was why he would go on to be such a good dentist: patience and skill.) Lizzie could imagine him and Todd poking at each other with their needles, with much popcorn being eaten and/or spilled, and fresh cranberries rolling across the kitchen floor, waiting to be squashed by sock-clad feet.

On that first visit, when all the chain making and stringing was done, George took Lizzie on a short tour of his past. The bowling alley in West Tulsa, he said, which was ultimately the reason they were together, here, now, at this very moment, went out of business long ago, but they drove to the strip mall where it used to be. "Look — I think that's the same gaming store where Todd used to skip out on bowling to play Dungeons and Dragons," he said. "Who'd have thought that it'd still be around?" His high school was closed for vacation, so they couldn't go in, but Lizzie couldn't help comparing the spaciousness of the large campus — with its lower, middle, and upper schools spread out over several acres of well-manicured lawn — to the cramped, creaky, and much older building where she'd spent her high school years. They went for a walk along the Arkansas River. It didn't, Lizzie told George somewhat belligerently, even compare with the Huron. George readily agreed.

"But it's pretty neat that we both grew up with rivers in our lives, isn't it?"

All this "we"-ness with George was making Lizzie uncomfortable. She tried to find a neutral subject.

"Your mother's great."

"Yes," George answered immediately, "she is. She thinks you're pretty wonderful too," he added.

The voices in Lizzie's head jumped in quickly, as though they'd been waiting for just this opportunity: "And here I thought George's mother was a lot smarter than that. If she really knew this kid she wouldn't like her at all."

"Really?" Lizzie said, obscurely pleased but wondering if the voices didn't know better than George. "She doesn't really know me."

"C'mon, Lizzie. I know you and I think you're entirely wonderful. Really."

Oh, George, Lizzie said to herself. You don't know me at all. If you did, you would never use the adjective "wonderful" to describe me.

That night they went to see *Back to the Future* and then out for pizza and beer with Blake, who was George's best friend ever since they were kids, and Alicia, his fiancée. They were both teachers — Alicia in elementary school (kindergarten) and Blake in high school (history and football coach) — and they spent the entire evening talking about Blake and Alicia's upcoming wedding, save for the two hours and six minutes that the four of them watched the movie. Everyone except Lizzie had already seen it (Blake and Alicia twice before), but they agreed that it was worth watching any number of times. Lizzie thought perhaps once was enough for her. Afterward, they drifted into a bar around the corner.

While they drank their second pitcher of beer, Blake and Alicia took turns telling Lizzie and George in almost minute-by-minute detail how they had arrived at a wedding date (in Lizzie's view a particularly pointless account that ended with the decision being made via a flip of a coin) and had chosen a caterer — lots of taste testing, which was great (Blake), and too fattening (Alicia). They shared the pros and cons of getting married in a church and having the reception there rather than at, say, a hotel. Alicia took out Polaroids of her four bridesmaids trying on their dresses. "We found them at Miss Jackson's and thank goodness everyone's pretty much a standard size, because I don't know what we'd have done otherwise. It's almost impossible to find a dress and a color that looks good on everyone, don't you think, Lizzie?"

"Sure. Absolutely," she automatically responded. Do I care, Lizzie wondered, if Alicia and Blake like me? What are the chances that I'll never see them again, which would be just fine with me? Does George care if I like them? I hope not but I just bet he does.

In light of that belief, Lizzie opted not to point out to Alicia that she and her bridesmaids were all blond and about size six, so how hard, honestly, could finding the right color be? Instead she tried, for George's sake, to look interested.

"Oh," Alicia said suddenly to Lizzie, who was now peering intently into her beer, hoping it would reveal a future that included Jack. "Did George tell you that he's the best man? And, Lizzie, you should totally come too. It'll be so much fun."

"Best party of the year, Lizzie," Blake promised. "And you'll get to meet all

George's friends at one go."

"I'll see," she told them. "I'm not really sure where I'll be in June. I might be traveling."

George looked at her quizzically but didn't say anything, which was good, because the voices were having a field day attacking her. "Traveling. I might be traveling," one mimicked her. "Couldn't she even come up with a better excuse? Please tell me where on earth she could be traveling."

"Just tell them the truth," the other voice advised. "Make it clear how stupid you think they are." Lizzie tried not to listen, but it was hard.

"We'll get your address from George," Alicia called out as George and Lizzie walked to their car. "For the invitation. But we're counting on you being there."

"Aren't they a great couple?" George asked cheerfully as he opened the car door. He was looking forward to parking somewhere and fooling around with Lizzie in the backseat of Allan's big Buick. "You liked them, right?"

Lizzie's fallback position was almost always to lie, and she tried out a few different sentences she could use with George. "What the hell," she said to herself, and spoke. "Truthfully, George, I found them

248

pretty boring. If you must know, I'd rather have stayed home and talked to your mother. Tell me again why we had to go out with them tonight?"

"Mom's great, so I get that, but Blake's my best friend," George protested. "I always see him when I come home."

"Too bad," Lizzie said, the voices in her head going wild. "Was he always so uninteresting?"

"Uninteresting? Are you kidding?"

I'm pretty sure that lying would have been the smarter thing to do, thought Lizzie. But it's too late now. "No, I'm not kidding. As I'm positive Alicia and her blond friends would put it, I think they're BORR-innnggg."

"That's not how she'd describe herself and Blake."

"Oh, George, you know what I mean. That's definitely how she'd say the word 'boring.' That's *b-o-r-i-n-g,* in case you're wondering how to spell it. BORR-innnggg."

"Lizzie —"

"No, wait, George, listen, what did we talk about all night? Their wedding."

"What did you want to talk about that we didn't?"

"Anything. Politics, science fiction, the Super Bowl, China. The breakup of the

249

Soviet Union. Poetry. Whether Britain should abolish the monarchy. The future of Africa. Whether pot should be legalized. The price of eggs."

"Is that what you and Marla and James talk about? How much eggs cost these days?"

Against her will, Lizzie laughed. "Well, not about legalizing pot, at least not when James is there, because legalization would ruin his business. But do you see what I mean? I think hearing about someone else's wedding is the definition of tedium. And she's so blond."

The first of Lizzie and George's many many Difficult Conversations might have ended there and the evening salvaged, except that Lizzie refused to let it drop.

"They just went on and on about the color of the bridesmaids' dresses and cake tastings. Do they even read?"

"Lizzie, Blake has a master's degree in history. And he's not stupid. I mean, he's not going to win the Nobel Prize for Physics, but, hey, are you? He was captain of our Lincoln-Douglas debate team in high school. And I bet he's a good enough history teacher. I know he's a great football coach. The team worships him. I don't know Alicia very well yet, but I do know lots of the girls that Blake dated before he met her, and they weren't stupid either. Oh, yeah, and he graduated magna cum laude. That's more than I did."

"Sure, from some third-rate A-and-M college."

This was more than even George could take. "Hey," he said, sadly coming to the conclusion that his deep desire for a make-out session ending with sex with Lizzie was not going to be fulfilled. "I went to that third-rate school too, you know. And it's a university. It stopped being Oklahoma A and M years ago. In the 1950s. And my dad went there. And he's no dummy."

"But you eventually left," Lizzie pointed out.

"After I graduated. Because it doesn't have a dental school."

"And Todd didn't go there."

"He didn't go anywhere. He was in Sydney."

Lizzie realized the particular thrust of that argument had run its course, and she shifted topics. "So tell me, where'd little Miss Perky go, again? I know you told me, but I forgot."

"Oral Roberts University," George said stolidly. He'd known that was coming.

Lizzie sniggered evilly. "I read about that college. You know, don't you, that they have spirit monitors on every floor in the dorms, so that someone can tattle to someone else if you're breaking a rule or even edging close to it. I bet your precious Alicia was a spirit monitor. Maybe she can give you some spiritual guidance. Besides, neither of them asked anything about me, like what I was studying, or how we met."

"Blake knows how we met. I told him and I'm sure he told Alicia." George paused awhile before going on. When Lizzie started to speak he stopped her.

"Listen, Lizzie, I don't know how we got into this . . . well, I do know how we got into this, but I just want to say something, and maybe this is an awful time to say it, and maybe I shouldn't, but listen, Lizzie, do you even care about what's going on in my life when we're not together, or what my life was like before we met? You don't ever ask. Do you ever tell me anything important about your own life? No. You never share anything. I'm amazed you invited me to Thanksgiving dinner. You're probably one of the most self-centered people I've ever met. And, oh, yeah, I'm pretty sure that I'm in love with you, although I can't imagine why."

He started the car, ignoring the tears that were now rolling down Lizzie's cheeks.

Neither spoke until they arrived back at Allan and Elaine's. Lizzie, still crying, started to open the car door, but stopped when George put his hand on her arm.

"You're a real snob, Lizzie Bultmann, did you know that? It's their big day, and I'm going to be the best man. Why shouldn't they talk about it to me and expect me to be interested?"

"Well, were you?"

"No, not particularly," George admitted. "It did get boring, I agree. But if it were our wedding, I'd expect Blake to let us talk about it too."

Lizzie groaned. "But cake tastings and bridesmaids?"

"Even that. It's what friends do."

"But they're not my friends."

"Not yet, no."

"Not ever."

It was George's turn to groan, which he did, loudly. "Look, you've just met them once. Can't you cut them some slack? Surprise, surprise, they might grow on you."

She sniffed. "I'm not too enthusiastic about slack."

"Then you have a difficult road ahead of you."

"I guess. But that's so not-new news to me."

Finally he turned to look at her. "I don't want us to fight; I really want you to have a good time here. We don't have to agree on everything. I love you, I just wanted you to know that."

Lizzie shook her head, but didn't say anything, whether from sadness, or pity, or frustration, George couldn't tell.

December 24

When Lizzie came downstairs the next morning, Elaine was sitting at the kitchen table with a mug of tea and the newspaper. Lizzie poured herself some tea from the pot and sat down with her.

"George went to pick up some stuff for his grandparents. He should be home soon, but I'm glad we have this time to ourselves. I wanted to tell you something."

Lizzie put down the cup, but not before the tea sloshed on the table. How had she so quickly come to this point of being afraid that Elaine might have realized that she was just pretending to be the nice girl that her son was dating? Oh, right, that her son was in love with. With whom her son was in love.

Elaine got a sponge and wiped up the spill, not noticing, or deliberately overlooking, Lizzie's discomfort. "I wanted to tell you, so you're not surprised when you meet her, that my mother-in-law can be a real terror. She loved — still loves, of course — Allan, to the point of distraction, and Todd and George even more than that. She worships them. It was lovely when the boys were growing up because she'd always be so happy to listen to my stories about them over and over. She's always been forthright, but now I think she's deliberately modeled herself on Maggie Smith, the British actress. If there's a tart remark to be made, Gertie will undoubtedly make it.

"It took her a long time to warm up to me. She was furious that Allan wanted to marry me and terrified we'd live in Canada near my folks rather than in Oklahoma. Over the years we've become closer, but I wanted to warn you about how difficult she can be. On the other hand, Sam is uncomplicated and totally likable. Allan's just like him, and you know how nice he is. There. That's done. I haven't offered you breakfast because you'll stop at the Pancake House in Sand Springs, which is yet another of the Goldrosen traditions you'll get to experience."

"You're not coming with us?" asked Lizzie, a bit dismayed.

"We'll see them next week, after the Christmas tree comes down."

"I wish you were going to be there," Lizzie allowed herself to say.

"No, no, you and George will have a nice day by yourselves with Gertie and Sam. And one more piece of advice: Don't eat a lot at the Pancake House, because Gertie will have cooked up a storm in anticipation of your visit. And unlike me she's an excellent cook. Plus, and most importantly, her feelings will be hurt if you turn down her offers of second and third helpings."

George heard the last sentence as he came in the door. "Just wait, Lizzie. Grandma's company meals are amazing. You won't be able to see the table because there'll be so many dishes on it."

They stopped at the Pancake House in Sand Springs and then drove through Mannford, along the edge of Oilton, and from one side of Yale to the other before they finally got to the outskirts of Stillwater. Neither brought up what had happened the evening before. George told Lizzie about his grandparents; she didn't mention what his mother had said, although Elaine hadn't indicated that it was a secret.

"After they realized that neither their son or either of their grandsons would ever want to move back to Stillwater and manage Goldrosen's Fine Jewelry, Gertie and Sam decided to sell the store to one of their employees," George began. "The guy who bought it immediately changed the name to Bling It On. There's no way that Sam and Gertie would get the joke, and they were terribly distressed that he felt he needed to rename a business that had been successful for a long time.

"Even the decision to sell the store had been very hard, because my great-grandpa began it almost seventy-five years ago. Family history says that his boat docked in Houston and he walked all the way to Tulsa with a peddler's cart that he picked up somewhere. He didn't speak much English and didn't have any relatives here because the older brother who'd sponsored him unceremoniously died before the boat even made it to Houston. Sam told me that his father once described the long slog from the Gulf of Mexico to Stillwater as moving from the wet heat to the not-quite-so-wet heat. Once he got to Stillwater it felt like he was home for good. And that's how Gertie and Sam feel. They still live in the house that my dad grew up in. And," George concluded, "Goldrosen tradition mandates that the grandsons, if they happen to be in Oklahoma, celebrate Gertie's December twenty-fourth birthday in Stillwater. That's partly why I come home every Christmas."

"So why aren't your folks coming with us? Or why don't your grandparents come to Tulsa to celebrate?"

"Well, Grandma absolutely refuses to set foot in our house as long as Mom has all the Christmas stuff up. And Pop, which is what we've always called my grandfather, goes along with her. You'll see, she's the one in charge."

They drove some more. Lizzie looked out the window at mostly different shades of brown, in a mostly unchanging landscape. She couldn't understand why anyone would want to live here. "How come you decided to go to OSU for college? Didn't you want to go further away from home?"

He turned the question back at her. "How come you decided to stay in Ann Arbor and go to college there? Didn't you want to get further away from home?"

"That was different." Even to herself Lizzie sounded defensive.

George asked the obvious follow-up question. "Different how?"

If diversion were an Olympic sport, Lizzie would most definitely medal.

"But obviously Todd left Oklahoma, so people do leave."

George, then and nearly always, was willing to indulge Lizzie, and didn't pursue his own question. "Yeah, Todd went about as far away as he could, but I knew that I'd probably go out of state for graduate school, so it seemed silly to leave before I really had to. Besides, from the time I was a little boy, we had season tickets for all the Cowboys' basketball and football games. I loved coming to Stillwater to watch the games with my dad and Pop. It wasn't ever a big deal to Todd, but I hated to think about the two of them going to the games alone, without me. It would have broken their hearts if I left too, just a few years after Todd did. I still feel guilty that I'm in Ann Arbor and not here on football Saturdays."

"What did your mom want you to do?"

"Oh, I think she really wanted me to go east to school. It's an understatement to say that she's never loved Tulsa. A few years ago she told me that she still spends her days kicking and screaming against the circumstance of living here. When Dad proposed to her she made him promise that they'd never move back to Oklahoma."

"What'd he say to that?" Lizzie asked, fascinated.

"That it was only sons whose fathers owned oil companies who come home to Oklahoma to run the family business, that he wasn't interested in living in Stillwater and working in the jewelry store. He basically promised that it wouldn't ever happen. And then he added something about orthodontists pretty much having the whole country to choose from."

"What'd she say then?"

"That, yes, she'd marry him."

Lizzie thought for a few minutes. "So what happened when your dad decided to come back?"

"He didn't tell her until he'd almost finished his residency, so they'd been married a few years by then. I think they argued a lot and for a long time. Mom never talks about that part. But Dad tried to convince her that, because they weren't moving to Stillwater, he wasn't exactly breaking his promise to her. She hates that kind of quibbling, so that made it even worse.

"When Mom's telling the story, she says that she just decided to be a grown-up and a good sport about it and come here because she loved him and because she saw how important it was to Dad. But Dad says that she wept and raged and told him she was pregnant and didn't want to be a single mother and that since he made the decision about where they'd live and bring up their kids, she could decide everything else from then on until they died."

Lizzie was becoming by the moment ever more infatuated with Elaine.

"Gosh, has she? Made all the other decisions? Or was it just an idle threat?"

"They agree about most things. I don't think Dad has ever been thrilled about all this Christmas stuff, but he goes along with it, even if he knows it upsets his parents."

George changed the subject. "Did either of your grandparents live near you when you were a kid?"

"Oh, George." Lizzie sighed. "You met Mendel, and Lydia's even worse, if that's possible to imagine. You know they're automatons, constructed out of coat hangers, powdered milk cartons, and a heart cut from a piece of graph paper. Nobody could possibly have given birth to them. I don't have grandparents."

George sighed. What could he say?

Gertie and Sam were sitting on the front porch, waiting for them. George enveloped his grandmother in his arms, loudly kissed her cheek, and told her happy birthday, then shook his grandfather's hand and pulled him in for a hug too. Only then did he put an arm around Lizzie and introduce her to his grandparents.

"This is Lizzie," he said proudly.

"It's so nice to meet you both."

The elder Goldrosens gave Lizzie identical tight smiles. They'd met several of George's girlfriends in the past and didn't have high hopes for this one either.

"Can we go inside?" Sam asked plaintively. "I'm freezing. And starving."

Lizzie handed Gertie the bouquet of flowers they'd bought that morning on their way out of Tulsa. "Happy birthday," she said.

"Whose idea was it to buy me flowers?" Gertie asked sharply. "Georgie? Why would you waste your money?"

"But they smell beautiful," Lizzie protested. Gertie gave her a look of such scorn that it brought back vivid memories of Terrell the Terrible and that awful poetry class where she'd met Jack. Jack. What was he doing this very moment? Did he ever think about her? Why had he really left her? Where was he? Not in Stillwater, Oklahoma, for sure. But why couldn't he be here? Lizzie decided that she needed to find a phone book to check if against all the odds he was now in the exact same (small) city that she herself was.

That progression of questions she'd directed at herself sidetracked Lizzie enough that she almost missed Gertie saying dismissively, "None of the flowers you buy from florists ever smell as good as the ones you pick yourself. These probably began the day in some New York hothouse. Ha! You know, Georgie, come spring, my wisteria perfumes the whole house."

"It does indeed, Grandma," George said, winking at Lizzie.

"Of course, the downside of that smell is that the wisteria is threatening to take over the whole backyard, not to mention the house, but Gertie can't bear to cut it down," Sam said. "If she ever decides that she wants to get rid of it, George, you and Allan will have to come dig it out. Those roots are more aggressive than telemarketers. We might have to bring Todd back from Australia to help us."

"Well, I suppose it was sweet of you to bring me these, Lizzie, although I'd have thought that Georgie might have mentioned my feelings to you, but no matter. The damage is done."

George was laughing as they walked into the living room. "Grandma, I had no idea you felt so strongly about florists and flowers. We'll do better next time. Here, sit down and open the rest of your presents. Here's a little something from Mom."

"Is it my mandel bread?" she asked eagerly as she opened the cookie tin. It was. She bit off a corner of one. "Not bad. I do have to give Elaine some credit: for a terrible cook she makes the best mandel bread I've ever tasted. Even better than mine. Perfect for dunking."

"And you've dunked plenty of them in your lifetime, Grandma, right?"

"She'd get a blue ribbon at the fair if they had a dunking-and-eating-mandel-bread category," Sam said proudly. "That's my wife."

George gave her the last package. It was smallish and rather lumpy, wrapped in paper with "Happy Birthday" written on it in different languages.

"Oh," Gertie said delightedly as she opened it. "What a surprise. Socks." She turned to Lizzie. "Every year since he was six I've gotten a pair of socks from Georgie for my birthday."

This particular year's were blue, with a blotch of maize at the toes and heels and a tasteful maize *M* at the top.

"Thank you, Georgie. These are very nice, but a little tame for my taste, don't you think? Not like those orange knee socks with Pistol Petes all over them that you once gave me."

"Pistol Pete is OSU's mascot," George explained in an aside to Lizzie.

"I loved those socks. I wore them till they disintegrated in the wash. I wish you'd find me another pair," Gertie said wistfully.

"What can I say, Grandma? This was pretty much all I could find in Ann Arbor, except for some plain white ones, which I knew you'd hate. And I thought you'd like the colors."

"I do, I do. You're such a sweet boy, Georgie." By stepping back, George successfully deflected her attempt to pinch his cheeks.

"Come on," Sam urged them. "Let's eat lunch. Are you kids hungry? I feel like I might faint from hunger."

While his grandparents were getting the food on the table, George showed Lizzie the framed class photos of him and Todd, beginning in kindergarten and ending with George's photo from his senior year in high school. "You were a pretty cute kid," Lizzie said. "Did you break a lot of hearts?"

George started to answer but was interrupted by Sam's insistence that they sit down at the table now, this minute, before the food got cold. Lizzie imagined that George might have said that he was constitutionally unable to break anyone's heart. Or he would have said something about not if you compared him to Todd. Yes, she already knew those things about him.

"Soup's on," Sam called again.

Literally, in fact: on their plates was a bowl of chicken soup with matzoh balls. That was followed by sweet-and-sour braised brisket. There were also latkes with a choice of applesauce or sour cream (or both), and kasha knishes. There were both meat and cheese blintzes. There was a loaf of challah still warm from the oven. Lizzie didn't think she had ever seen a table so crowded with food.

"Good Lord, Gertie, how much of this do you think we'll eat?"

"Stop, Sam. I wanted George to have a taste of Hanukkah. I know he doesn't get this kind of food from his mother. And save room for dessert," Gertie warned them. "I want to get rid of the birthday cake Sam got me from Safeway. Chocolate. Waste of money, of course. It won't be good. Those store-bought cakes become stale the minute you get them home. It's just like how new cars lose most of their value as soon as you drive them off the lot. So I made some of your old favorites, Georgie, just in case it's really inedible. And don't anyone spill their coffee. It's impossible to get those stains out of the tablecloth."

Of course the cake was absolutely fine,

but Gertie didn't care for it. The chocolate frosting was too sweet. She thought they'd used inferior ingredients. To clear their palates of the bad taste, she insisted that they each take a generously sized brownie and several miniature cream puffs filled with vanilla pudding and drizzled with chocolate sauce. No one wanted ice cream, although she offered to get it from the freezer. Twice.

By the time Lizzie finished eating everything Gertie had insisted on serving her, all she wanted to do was crawl into bed and sleep. It's possible she dozed off for a moment. Gertie and Sam were carrying platters of food back into the kitchen, and George was clearing the table. With some difficulty, Lizzie rose to her feet and made a move to help, but Gertie said, "No. Just sit. You can help another time."

"Are you sure, Mrs. Goldrosen?"

"Absolutely sure. I'm very particular about how I load the dishwasher. Don't you find everyone is? I'm sure your mother has her own thoughts on the subject."

Lizzie, not being sure whose mother was being referred to, didn't answer. As far as she could remember, Lydia hadn't ever expressed an interest in, or opinion about, their dishwasher. She'd certainly never put a single dish in it. Come to think of it, she might not even know the Bultmann family owned one.

Later, they showed Lizzie the sights of Stillwater. George drove and his grandparents narrated the journey. They pointed out George's freshman dorm, the fraternity where he lived for the next three years, the football stadium, the basketball arena, the first McDonald's ("We watched it being built, early in the 1970s"), Baskin-Robbins ("Ditto"), the house where Allan's best friend used to live when they were kids and the house where he and his family lived now ("He came home, you know, to teach at the vet school. I don't know why your father didn't bring your mother here. We needed an orthodontist more than Tulsa did."), Allan's dorm, Allan's fraternity (the same as George's) and his elementary, middle, and high schools ("He was president of his junior and senior classes, you know, George."). George slowed down in front of Bling It On, but Gertie told him not to stop. "Let's just go home, George. I'm getting tired."

When they got back to the house, Gertie announced that it was time for a little something to nibble on before George and Lizzie left. Rather than the brownies and cream puffs (the chocolate cake had been discarded), she brought out a banana cream pie ("I made Allan's favorite, even though he's not here") and an angel food cake, with strawberries and whipped cream ("Sam's favorite; I froze the strawberries myself."). "And it's real whipped cream, not that stuff Elaine serves," she announced.

While George and Lizzie were getting ready to go, Gertie disappeared into the kitchen and returned with Tupperware containers full of food to take back to Tulsa. "I kept the brisket," she apologized, "because Sam will want more meat blintzes. But I packed up everything else. It's a care package for Allan, like I used to send you boys when you went to camp. I know Allan misses my cooking, even though he probably never complains.

"And here're your Hanukkah presents. Open them now," she commanded. George waited while Lizzie unwrapped hers, trying to be as careful as Gertie had been with the gift from George. They'd given her a box of assorted Twining's teas.

"Oh, thank you," she said sincerely. "I can't wait to try all the different flavors."

Gertie nodded. "George told us you were a tea drinker. Like Elaine." Lizzie wasn't quite sure how to take this statement. Being like Elaine in this house was evidently a mixed blessing.

George's package was lumpy, a much larger version of the wrapped pair of socks he'd given to his grandmother earlier. He examined the wrapping paper. "This looks familiar," he commented, and asked her if it was the same paper she'd used on his gift last year. He took the absence of any response as a somewhat guilty yes. "Well, then," he said breezily, "there's no need to save it for another year," and tore it open.

"Oh my gosh. You guys shouldn't have. Look, Lizzie." This last was unnecessary, since where else would Lizzie be looking but at George's gift? It was a hooded orange sweatshirt emblazoned with a large Pistol Pete outlined in black on the front and COWBOYS written on the back. "Wow. I'll be especially sure not to wear this on game days in Ann Arbor; it isn't safe to acknowledge there are any other college teams. But here I can wear it all the time." He put it on over his flannel shirt.

Gertie and Sam looked pleased. "Wear it in good health, sweetheart," Gertie said. "You'd better get going. We don't like to think of you driving home in the dark."

They all stood around the car saying their last good-byes. Lizzie went back into the house, ostensibly to use the bathroom, but really to check the phone book in the kitchen. She opened it to the *M*'s. She could never remember if the *Mc*'s came before or after the *Mac*'s or if they were just in their normal place in the alphabet, but after looking carefully she saw there was no Jack McConaghey. No Jack. She'd been right. He'd never live in Stillwater, Oklahoma.

Sam hugged them both, and Gertie kissed Lizzie and then threw her arms around George. "You're always the best part of my birthday every year, Georgie," she told him. "You and Todd."

As George backed the car out of the driveway Lizzie turned around and saw Gertie standing on the sidewalk, waving to them. "She's crying," she said to George.

"I know, I know, I hate it, but she always does when we leave." He sighed. "I should really try to come here more often."

"What are you going to do with that hideous sweatshirt? 'Oh my gosh. You shouldn't have,' " she imitated him.

"Hey, I was being honest. They absolutely shouldn't have."

They laughed together.

"It was probably on sale," George said.

"Oh, for sure," Lizzie agreed. "Otherwise why would you ever buy it, even given your deep love for Pistol Pete? That's got to be the brightest orange I ever hope to see. It'll give most people a headache."

"Or blind them. Maybe it's like looking directly at an eclipse of the sun. How about if I leave it at home and only wear it when I'm visiting them in Stillwater? That'll satisfy everyone."

"But they're sweet," she continued. "At least Sam is sweet. I'm not sure how to describe Gertie. I wish I knew my grandparents. Maybe my life would have been totally different."

"Not so totally, I hope. I'd still like us to have met."

Why did George have to say things like that? What did he want her to say? That she felt the same way? They still hadn't talked about what had occurred the night before. Maybe George would forget that he said he loved her.

She spoke quickly. "And all that food. I don't think I've ever eaten so much. I can't believe she did all that cooking."

"Cooking for us makes Grandma happy. The thought of anyone she loves going hungry is anathema to her."

"Your mother's sort of the same way, isn't she?"

"She is, but not to that extent. I think if we hadn't eaten the cream puffs Grandma

272

would have been really annoyed with us."

"I wish I *hadn't* eaten them," Lizzie admitted. "I've probably gained ten pounds on this visit."

George reached over and took her hand. "You don't have to worry," he said.

Just before they got back to Elaine and Allan's, Lizzie said a little timidly, "Do you want to talk about last night, George?"

"No, not right now. We can wait at least until all that food's been digested."

"I just thought," Lizzie began, "because I just want to say I'm sorry I was such a pill about Blake and Alicia. It was probably uncalled-for. For some reason I was really uncomfortable with them."

George nodded. "Okay, that's fair. Though I did wonder about where you might be traveling in June, since you never mentioned it before."

"Right," Lizzie said, trying to pretend she hadn't said anything of the kind. "I did say traveling, didn't I. Maybe I meant to Marla's, I don't know. It's all I could think of at the time."

"Hold that thought, Lizzie. We're home."

December 25
After breakfast on Christmas day, the Goldrosens gathered around the tree to open

273

presents. It was almost as though Lizzie had always been part of the family. There was even a stocking with her name on it, hung on the mantel next to the other three. Elaine saw her looking at it and misread her thoughts, one of the rare blunders Elaine would ever make in understanding Lizzie. Which was pretty amazing, given that she'd never learn what Lizzie considered to be the defining events of her life.

"I'm so sorry your stocking's not like the rest of ours. By the time George told us you were coming, it was too late to order one. But we'll have one here for you next year. And maybe Todd will be here too," she said, a bit wistfully.

Once again Lizzie wasn't sure what to say, although she was pretty sure she should say something. George fidgeted and didn't look at either his mother or Lizzie. Oh God, Lizzie thought. What the fuck is going on? First George says he loves me and now this. If I were living in a horror novel, that would be the first vaguely ominous sign that I'll never get untethered from this family. Maybe Elaine can predict the future. Or maybe she's just insanely optimistic.

George felt, for what was perhaps the first time in his entire life, a tinge of annoyance at his mother. It was one thing for Alicia to invite Lizzie to the wedding and quite another for his mother to blithely assume — blithely assume! — that she'd be here next Christmas and forever after, even if that was exactly what George wanted.

They opened their gifts in turn, accompanied by a significant amount of oohing and aahing. Lizzie's presents were unexpectedly many and lavish: a very pale green bathrobe made out of the softest cotton she'd ever felt, sheepskin slippers, a rather large gift certificate to Shaman Drum bookstore, several bars of French milled soap (Marla would approve of that, Lizzie thought), an alarm clock from the Museum of Modern Art, and two mismatched china teacups and saucers.

George's presents included a cashmere scarf, a pair of sheepskin slippers, a bottle of Italian wine, four Riedel wineglasses, a lamb's-wool sweater, and a mug inscribed MY FAVORITE DENTIST.

Todd had sent his father a silk tie, his mother a boxed set of *Upstairs, Downstairs*, George a furry hat with earflaps, just like the kind they used to wear as kids, and Lizzie a pair of suede gloves.

"Oh," Lizzie said, stricken with guilt. "I didn't get Todd anything."

"I did," George assured her. "A Dallas

Cowboys warm-up jacket. That should confound the Aussies when he wears it."

Elaine and Allan were beaming. It finally occurred to Lizzie to wonder if George had ever brought another girl home for Christmas with his family, and, if so, what happened to her. Could it have been the girl he was with the night they met? What was her name? Lizzie thought she might ask George about it on the plane ride home.

George surveyed the stacks of gifts he and Lizzie had gotten. "We'll need another suitcase to carry all this back to Ann Arbor, Mom."

"Easily solved. You can take one of ours and just bring it back next time."

Allan looked at his watch. "We'd better get over to the shelter. They'll be serving lunch soon. Who's going with me? George? Elaine? Lizzie?"

Elaine spoke first. "I've got lots and lots of cookies and a couple of casseroles for you to take, but perhaps Lizzie and I will stay home. Is that okay with you, Lizzie, or do you especially want to go?"

"No, staying here is fine. We can eat cookies and try some of the teas from Mr. and Mrs. Goldrosen in my new teacups."

"Lovely," Elaine said, "and listen, I'm sure they'd be happy to have you call them Gertie and Sam."

"Of course they would," Allan added.

Sam, maybe, Lizzie thought. Not Gertie.

"I'm devoted to mismatched china," Elaine said as they were sitting at the kitchen table, drinking their tea — Elaine, Earl Grey, and Lizzie, Assam. "It just seems more festive to me. I don't mean to inflict my taste on you, though. It's too late to return these, now that we've drunk from them, but if you'd rather have two sets that match, I'll keep these and send you some others."

"No, no," Lizzie assured her. "I just never thought about it before. They're lovely."

They sat in companionable silence while they sipped their tea.

"So, Lizzie," Elaine began. "George told us your parents are important psychology professors at U of M?"

"Um, yeah, I guess so. A lot of people think they're important, anyway."

"I was a French major as an undergraduate, but I once considered going into psychology. I always thought I might be a good social worker or school counselor."

"I bet you'd be wonderful at that. Do you ever think about going back to school to get a degree?"

"Oh, I'm not sure I even want to at this

point. I think I'd rather be lazy and eat cookies and drink tea. What area of psychology are your parents in?"

"They're behaviorists, so they don't do counseling or therapy."

"What are they like? Are you close to them? Were they okay with you spending the holidays here?"

Lizzie paused. How to explain? How much should she tell Elaine? ("You're probably one of the most self-centered people I've ever met," George had said.)

"I'm so sorry," Elaine said instantly. "Is that too personal? You don't need to answer. I'm just always curious about people's lives."

"No, it's okay. I just need to figure out how to explain them to you. It's like" — she fumbled with her words — "they're just not the sort of people anyone could be close to."

"That must be sad for you. And difficult."

"Not really. Not anymore. It was harder when I was a kid. See, not only would they never do counseling, but they think psychologists who do do that are a joke. Or they would think it's a joke if either one of them had a sense of humor. Psychologists like them, behaviorists, don't believe in an 'inner self.' There's actually a famous joke, or at least famous in behaviorist circles and of course those who dislike behaviorists, that goes like this: Two behaviorists meet on the street and each one asks the other, 'How am I?' "

Elaine smiled. Lizzie wondered if she should go on. "Is this more than you want to know?"

"No, no, don't stop. I'm fascinated. Do they really not believe in an inner self?"

"Well, at least they don't believe that the notion of an inner self — or inner life — is useful for what they call the science of psychology." Lizzie emphasized the last three words and added air quotes around them. "And it's really important for my parents to think of themselves as real scientists." More air quotes. "Just like physicists, or biologists."

"How curious," Elaine said as she stood up. "Let's make another pot of tea — I want to hear more."

While the water was boiling Lizzie said, "I think George is terrifically lucky to have you and Allan as parents. It's just so nice here."

Being in Tulsa at his parents' house with George made Lizzie anxious (how did she feel about him, anyway?), but spending time alone with Elaine was calming and comforting and gave her some idea of what her life might have been like if someone besides

Lydia had been her mother.

Elaine gave her a quick hug and then said, "You're sweet. I see why George likes you so much. Okay, finish what you were saying before. I feel as though I should be taking notes. Are you going to give me an exam at the end?"

"Of course," Lizzie said. "And I should warn you that I'm a very hard grader. Anyway," she went on, "all those early behaviorists saw that real scientists, like biologists, only studied things that they could see, and you couldn't ever see the mind. Except perhaps your own. And that might be enough to write poetry, but it wouldn't pass muster as a scientific study. They believed that all that you *could* see was behavior. So they gave up any examination of the mind or the inner self, and just studied how people behaved. And if people insisted on talking about their 'inner experience,' well, that was just considered verbal behavior. Kind of embarrassingly bad behavior, in fact. Problem solved.

"I think it's all bullshit," Lizzie went on, "what my parents and their friends believe, and not just because they're my parents and I'm rebelling against them. Everyone knows they have a mind. And I'd hate a life without poetry in it."

Elaine nodded, a clear encouragement to continue.

"My parents think that people are like animals, and they'll do what they're rewarded for and won't do what they're punished for doing. And they think that's a great insight."

"Maybe some behaviorists should become animal trainers," Elaine joked.

"Actually, a lot of them did go on to become pretty good animal trainers. And people trainers too. My father spends his days running lab rats to try to shape their behavior in particular ways. And because of that, he's discovered some pretty effective ways of controlling people's behavior too."

"I've read about behavior modification. It's all the rage in pop psychology books these days, isn't it?"

"Yeah, but Mendel and Lydia usually publish only in academic journals that only their friends read. They're not at all interested in dumbing down their theories for a mass audience." Lizzie had a sudden flashback to the terrible afternoon that Jack showed her the article in *Psychology Today*. That hadn't dumbed down anything at all. "They used to try their theories out on me, though, all the time. Once, when I was almost three, and my father was training rats to press bars in their cages in order to get food, they decided to see if they could train me to stand up whenever they entered the room, so if I was sitting down and reading or playing with a toy when they came in, they'd be all cold and ignore me, but the minute I got up they started paying attention to me and acting loving. And sure enough, just like a rat, I learned what to do. It was like turning the handle on a jack-in-the-box. As soon as either one of them came into the room I, I'd pop right up. Things like that went on all the time. It didn't end until I left for college."

Lizzie shuddered. She hadn't realized before how much she actually knew about her parents' work and how awful it still was to remember when she was compelled to jump to attention without ever really knowing why. She hadn't ever told anyone else all about her parents. Oh, Marla knew quite a bit, but here she'd poured it all out to George's mother. Gosh, she thought, Elaine would have been a great therapist.

"That must have been very hard for you."

"Well, I had Sheila, my babysitter. She was wonderful. And I actually learned a lot from Lydia and Mendel. When I got to be a teenager, I manipulated them like crazy, and they were positively clueless. That was fun."

282

"Did they like George?" Elaine asked, unable to imagine any parent not approving of George as a date for their daughter.

"Like George?" Lizzie repeated stupidly, not understanding.

"Yes, when he came with you at Thanksgiving."

Lizzie thought for a moment. She'd never considered that before, what her parents might think of George. "I know it sounds weird, but Lydia was never around that day to introduce to George. And Mendel's simply pathetic. He's indifferent to everything but Lydia and his rats. Lydia's much more critical, so maybe it's better that she didn't meet George. Anyway, he was my first boyfriend to darken their door since I started dating."

"You didn't bring any of the boys you dated home? I would have hated it if I'd never met any of George's girlfriends."

Lizzie suddenly wanted to know more about George's other girlfriends, but didn't know if she should ask Elaine about them. "Well, my parents didn't care about anything I did, unless they planned to modify my behavior, so I tried never to do anything in front of them. I was always so careful. But here's the kind of thing they did care about. Or at least Lydia did. When I was a freshman a boy named Dane Engel called me. According to Lydia, who answered the phone, he asked to speak with me. And that did it for him."

"But why? I don't get it."

"Because one of Lydia's pet peeves is that you should never say 'talk with' someone, it should be 'talk to' someone. She refused to let him talk to me and when she'd hung up, after basically saying he wasn't welcome to call again, she told me why she'd done what she did. For my own good. My own good! Give me a fucking break. Oh, gosh, sorry — I guess it still bothers me."

"No, no, no, that's fine, don't be sorry."

"I think that's one of the reasons I like George," Lizzie told her. "He's smart but not a snob. I get the feeling that even if I did something stupid, like say 'between you and I,' George might flinch but he wouldn't kick me out of his life."

"You're absolutely right," Elaine responded. "George seems to be endlessly forgiving. I could tell you horror stories about the mistakes Allan and I made as parents, but nothing seemed to rattle George enough to make him give up on us."

Elaine changed the subject back to Mendel and Lydia. "Do you think your parents wanted you to be a psychologist too? Did

284

they mind when you told them you were planning to major in English instead?"

"God, no. I think they probably feel that as long as they're psychologists, nobody else needs to be."

Elaine shook her head, but whether it was in disbelief or sympathy, Lizzie couldn't tell. She was about to share some of her mother's other strong dislikes with Elaine — *Roget's Thesaurus* and fantasy trilogies were high on the list — but stopped when they heard Allan and George at the door.

That night they went out to a Chinese restaurant for dinner. This was the culminating tradition of the Goldrosens' Christmases. "Our last meal," Allan joked.

After the waiter left with their orders, Elaine picked up her bottle of Tsingtao beer. "I propose our first toast: to a wonderful time together this year and to us all being together next year, same time, same place. Only with the addition of Todd, because we miss him dreadfully."

They clinked glasses and drank.

"Who's next?"

"I am," Allan said. "To Lizzie, who was a good sport and a wonderful guest. We're so happy George brought you home for Christmas."

"Hear, hear," George and Elaine chorused.

"Well," George said, "I was going to propose a toast to Lizzie too, Dad, so how about this: to Allan and Elaine, the best parents anyone could have."

"Oh, Georgie, that's wonderful you feel that way," Elaine said, tearing up slightly. Allan took out his handkerchief and blew his nose.

"Can I do one?" Lizzie asked. "Or do you have to be a Goldrosen to participate?"

"You're an honorary Goldrosen, so have at it," George said.

"Okay." She raised her glass. "First, George, I'm so glad you invited me. You can't imagine how nervous I was about coming." She turned to smile at Allan and Elaine. "Thank you both so much for everything. I can see why George is such a nice guy, having you both as parents."

George thought that being a nice guy wasn't exactly the ringing endorsement you want from your own true love, but Lizzie was so stingy with saying, or maybe fearful of saying, anything positive that George knew he had to be grateful for even that crumb.

Allan blew his nose again. Elaine reached out and took Lizzie's hand. "You should have seen me the first time I met Gertie and Sam. I couldn't even talk because my teeth were chattering and I was sure I was going to vomit all over their shoes." Everyone laughed and Elaine went on, "I hope you'll come back soon, Lizzie."

Later, when they were maneuvering their chopsticks with varying degrees of facility (Lizzie was the most inept), Elaine started telling dentist stories.

"Now, Lizzie, I know you've never heard this story, but, George, I'm sure I've told you about Dr. Sidlowski before." She turned to Lizzie and said, "He was my regular dentist's partner. I went to him once, right before I left Montreal for Bryn Mawr because Dr. Gratz was on vacation or something. I'd broken a tooth after eating too many pieces of this really crusty sour-dough bread at lunch. I was just beside myself — who breaks a tooth at age eighteen? Don't answer that, George," she said hastily as he started to speak. "It was a rhetorical question. Anyway, they took me in right away, and when Dr. Sidlowski asked me how it happened, of course I blamed the bread. But then he asked how many pieces of bread I'd had, and I told him three, which was agonizingly embarrassing. And then he said in this critical voice, 'Well, clearly the first piece sensitized it, the second piece loosened it, and the third piece cracked it. Perhaps you should take a lesson from this.' And I have. I almost never have three pieces of bread right in a row, and I certainly don't when it's that crusty sort of sourdough. I'm glad I never had to go back to him again.

"I wonder if any of his patients ever complained about the way he talked to them. I suspect there's a way to find out. It's that sort of question that keeps me up at night."

"Nothing keeps you up at night, darling," Allan said.

Elaine chuckled. "You're right. But if I were the kind of person who did lie awake at night and ponder various questions, that's what I would ponder. If Dr. Sidlowski was ever made aware of what an awful person he was. There I was, already suffering from guilt and shame, and look how he treated me, with more guilt and shame. Don't ever be like that, George," she ordered, but it was unnecessary to say that, because everyone at the table knew there was no way that George would ever commit the sin that Dr. Sidlowski had.

"There's a book I really enjoyed that has a dentist in it," Lizzie began, "called *Do the*

Windows Open? Have you read it, Elaine? It's by Julie Hecht. It's a collection of linked short stories about this really neurotic woman. In one of the stories she's at her dentist's and . . ."

She paused. Should she continue? Okay, why not? she thought. It's probably inappropriate but also really funny. Okay, whatever. I'm going to go for it. George loves me, right? Isn't that what he said? I'll think about what I'm going to do with that piece of information tomorrow or the next day. In any case, let him see the real me. Let them all see the kind of person I really am.

She began again. "So the dentist is drilling away, and, I can't remember her exact words, but she's musing to herself something like 'Dentists have the highest suicide rate of everyone in the medical professions,' and then she goes on to say, 'Not high enough, in my opinion.' For some reason I think that's really funny."

For several minutes after she finished, no one spoke. Finally Allan coughed. Elaine looked up from studying the remains of the Chinese food on her plate. "Are you getting a cold, Allan?"

George interrupted before his father could answer. "Hmm, I can see how people who hate going to the dentist might find that funny. And you know, it very subtly makes an excellent point: people with depressive personalities shouldn't go into dentistry. Think about it: people come to you in extraordinary pain, you have to inflict pain to cure the original pain, and you're working on something that's only a bit bigger than a grain of rice, with little or no margin for error. I remember one of my teachers saying that what a dentist needed most was a steady hand, steady nerves, and an untroubled heart."

Lizzie looked at him gratefully.

"That's why we love George, isn't it, Lizzie?" Elaine said somewhat mysteriously.

"Yes," Lizzie said slowly. "I suppose it is."

THE DEFENSIVE TACKLES

M'Ardon "Mardy" Preatty, built like a fire hydrant, was undrafted and later signed by the Lions after a so-so career at Clemson. Although he never became the game-changing pro player that his high school coach had predicted he'd be, season after season he managed to hold on to a spot on the team. Of course, the team as a whole wasn't very good in any of the years he played for them. Lizzie occasionally saw him on television at the end of a lopsided game and she never failed to point him out to

George, although she never went on to mention under what circumstances they'd met.

The other tackle suffered in comparison with Mardy Preatty, but then, almost any tackle playing on the same team as Mardy would. Leon Daly chose not to go to college, or perhaps he dropped out before graduation, and was last seen by Lizzie working at the local Toyota dealership, where he was a highly skilled and much-valued mechanic.

LIZZIE MAKES GEORGE LAUGH

When Lizzie was little, Sheila used to tell her about watching the submarine races at Island Park with her boyfriend. It sounded really exciting to Lizzie: submarine races! Whoa! What submarine races were didn't become clear to her until one morning in Tulsa when she and George were walking on the River Parks Trail and she wondered aloud if they had submarine races on the Arkansas River too. George looked at her and gulped loudly. At first Lizzie thought he was choking and regretted that she'd never learned how to do CPR, but then he started laughing. George was a laugher, all right — it was one of the things Lizzie loved about him. His was the sort of laugh that had people who heard him rolling on the floor, joined in a fellowship of mirth. Lizzie had obviously missed the joke, if a joke there was. In any event, George was bent over, chest heaving, hands on his knees. Every time his laughter seemed to be slowing down, he would gurgle something mostly indistinguishable that sounded to her like "submarines, Arkansas" and go off again. Finally, when he got himself more or less under control, he explained as you might explain to a young child.

"Lizzie, honey," he began. "I have some breaking news for you. Submarines are underwater, right? So you can't see them. Saying you're watching a submarine race is a euphemism for making out."

Oh, how embarrassing, Lizzie thought then, her face reddening. I am so glad I never told Jack about those stupid submarine races.

George was constantly surprised at how naive Lizzie was, how easy it was to tease her. His favorite Lizzie story, which he tried not to remind her of too often, had to do with IGA grocery stores. Passing one on their way home in Ann Arbor, Lizzie wondered aloud what the initials stood for.

"You know about the International Geophysical Association, right?" George asked, in the tone of voice that indicated that absolutely everyone knew and anyone who didn't was impossibly lacking in smarts.

"I guess," Lizzie said. "I mean, I sort of know what the words mean, especially 'international' and 'association.' Those I'm sure about. Why?"

"Their hundredth anniversary was about ten years ago, and they decided to start a chain of grocery stores to make some money for the group."

George thought that Lizzie must know that he was joking — that his explanation was so ridiculous it had to be invented — but had chosen not to laugh because she knew he wanted her to. He believed that until several years later, when they were in Sheridan, Wyoming, for a dental convention and saw another IGA store.

"Oh, look," Lizzie exclaimed. "There's another one of those Geophysical stores. They're everywhere, aren't they?"

Her gullibility was only one of the many reasons that George adored Lizzie. And the fact that she usually could laugh at herself was another.

GEORGE PROPOSES, CHRISTMAS, 1994

Lizzie was in the kitchen with Elaine when George asked her to go for a walk with him.

293

Lizzie didn't want to go. It had poured in the middle of the night and rain was still falling fitfully. That morning the sun never really seemed to rise and the sky was a dirty gray. It was not great walking weather. If the temperature had been about fifteen degrees colder, it might have snowed, but it hovered around thirty-five degrees. In neither of the two Christmases Lizzie spent with the Goldrosens in Tulsa had she seen one flake of snow. She doubted that it ever got cold enough to snow in Oklahoma, but whenever she offered that opinion everyone within earshot quickly brought up freezing rain. They all had stories to share. Elaine told her about trying to get to her dentist's office at Sixty-First and Yale (a notorious Tulsa hill) to have an abscessed tooth dealt with, when only her father's driving skills (he and her mother had been visiting from Montreal, where they had plenty of experience driving in snow) got her there on time, or at all. They could see cars skidding, racing their engines, trying to make it up to the top and failing. And George remembered the snowball fights of his youth and the times in Stillwater that Theta Pond froze and they'd all gone skating. Hot chocolate was mentioned several times in the retelling of these memories. Allan chimed in to remind Elaine and George of the time they were coming home from a long weekend at Silver Dollar City and an ice storm that quickly descended doomed a car that they'd already agreed was going way too fast when it passed them. They saw it later, upside down, on the side of the road, having slid through the guardrail. She wasn't sure she really believed any of them. She'd like to see it snow in Tulsa, Oklahoma, for herself.

"We're not done with the baking yet," Lizzie told him, straightening up from putting a cookie sheet in the oven. "Batches more to go before I sleep."

Out of the corner of her eye she saw George and Elaine exchange a meaningful glance. Now, this was decidedly odd. It happened that Lizzie rightfully considered herself an expert on the explication and implications of meaningful looks. Something was up. This was clearly not business as usual for the Goldrosens, whose lives, unlike the Bultmanns, mercifully lacked enough secrets to make such glances necessary.

Meaningful looks were a stock-in-trade for Mendel and Lydia. Lizzie could remember all the times when she had complained about something — the food at dinner, a classmate's behavior, the book she had been assigned to read, her head hurting (she had had many headaches as a child), and how her parents would look at one another, nod, and then Mendel would take out the notebook he always carried and carefully make a note of whatever it was that was bothering Lizzie and detail her reaction to it. Try as she might, Lizzie had never been able to find even one of the notebooks, so she couldn't be sure that's what he was doing. Still, the timing indicated it was, and what else could he be writing down so assiduously? Lizzie suspected that there were dozens of notebooks and that after each was filled, Mendel gave it to a favored graduate student to transcribe. She knew there were many dissertations based on her childhood; she'd seen the bound copies lying around the house, but she'd never found the original notes. After her parents died, the notebooks were the first things Lizzie searched for, but they were nowhere to be found. Perhaps they were in some hitherto undiscovered and now inaccessible bank vault.

"You two go on," Elaine advised. "Don't worry, Lizzie, there'll still be plenty of cookie dough left when you come home. We're nowhere near done."

By the time they got to the Arkansas River Trail and started their walk, Lizzie had descended into a bad mood. She hated the weather. She missed snow. She worried about that look that George and Elaine had exchanged. What did it mean? She complained to George that he always got stopped by every red light whenever he was driving; she carped about the fact that they had to park a few blocks away from the start of the trail; she grumped that she hadn't planned on walking that day; she grumbled about how boring the walk was, that the Arkansas might be much better known than the Huron River, but that it was nowhere near as lovely and lively, especially on this dark, dank, rain-filled day. She whined to George that the path was puddled and muddy and she was ruining her shoes. She knew that she was being both mean and unfair to George, and that he didn't deserve any of it. More importantly, she knew that she didn't deserve someone like George, so intrinsically kind and forgiving. But she couldn't help it.

Her bad mood deepened as she read aloud the engraved plaques that marked many of the benches, indicating for whom or in whose memory the bench had been given. " 'Rest Awhile: Auntie Never Met a Stranger,' " she mocked. "What sentimental crapola. 'For Our Darling Darling Nini,

Who Loved This Park.' She loved this park? Nini? Why? Oh, yeah, I know why, because she'd probably never seen a real park."

Stop, stop STOP Lizzie, she admonished herself. Just keep quiet. Be nice to George. He's so nice to you.

Throughout all of this, George remained heroically silent. He held Lizzie's hand firmly. In fact, Lizzie realized, he wasn't really listening to her at all. He was whistling the "doe, a deer" song from *The Sound of Music,* a movie Lizzie despised partly because she enjoyed being in a minority and complaining about how misguided the majority was, and partly because she hated the film's utter sappiness and predictability.

Lizzie stopped reading the plaques' messages out loud. It was actually no fun behaving this way if George wasn't responding to it, either by agreeing with Lizzie's sentiments (no way that was going to happen this time, Lizzie knew; he'd chosen to watch *The Sound of Music* dozens of times) or by arguing with her. Honestly, she'd much prefer being at home with Elaine.

Then she noticed Blake and Alicia up ahead, sitting on a bench.

"Oh, no," she groaned. "Did you know they'd be here?"

"They're pregnant," George said, continuing to ignore her comments. "Isn't that ter-rific?"

Lizzie, down for the count, didn't reply. Honestly, she was tempted to stamp her foot in utter frustration.

Alicia stood up. "Look," she said, gesturing to the plaque on the bench, "this is lovely: 'Commemorating the Sixtieth Anniversary of Helene and Franklin Brown, December 23, 1927, from Their Children, Grandchildren, and Great-Grand-children.' " She squeezed Blake's arm. "I hope someone buys a plaque for us when we've been married that long."

Against her better judgment, Lizzie said, "Really? I can't imagine being married to anyone for that long." Except Jack, Lizzie said to herself.

"Are you kidding? Why?"

"Well, Alicia, for one thing, wouldn't you run out of things to talk about after so long? It seems as though it would get awfully boring. You'd know everything about the other person already."

"I like that about marriage," Blake protested. "The more I know Alicia the more I love her."

Alicia gave Blake's arm another presumably loving squeeze. Lizzie barely succeeded in restraining herself from sticking her finger in her throat and gagging loudly.

Just when it was unclear to her whether she could control herself or whether her behavior would regress even further to that of a cranky two-year-old, George and Blake exchanged a meaningful look. Another meaningful glance in front of Lizzie in Tulsa, Oklahoma! Something was definitely going on.

"Come on, Alicia, honey," Blake said, "let's get some lunch. We'll see you guys later."

"Sure," George said. "I'll call you. Maybe a movie later this week?"

Lizzie stood watching them as they left. They were exactly at the right heights so that they could walk with Blake's arm around Alicia's waist and her head on his shoulder. They were in step — left foot, right foot, left foot, not missing a beat. It was disgusting, really.

"Sometimes I almost wish I was like Alicia, or that I was Alicia," she said to George. "Dumb, blond, and happy. Knowing everything there is to know about makeup and hair and how to dress. I mean, I hate the way she dresses, but I still wish it."

"Oh, Lizzie," George said, pulling her down next to him on the bench. "I think you're just about perfect just the way you are." He resumed his whistling; Lizzie slumped back into her bad mood.

After a few minutes George stopped whistling. "Gosh," he said. "Look at that." He pointed. "There's something under the bench."

Lizzie peered down through the slatted seat at a brown paper bag. "Ugh, just leave it, George. It might be a dead rat or something. It might have rabies."

"Don't be ridiculous. I'm pretty sure that you can't get rabies from touching a dead rat. And in any case, who'd put a dead rat in a bag and leave it here? Or put a dead rat in a bag at all? Blake or Alicia probably dropped it and didn't realize it."

"Please, George, don't touch it; it's filthy." Lizzie noticed that her voice was more than a little shrill and wondered why she was getting so upset. Oh, yeah, it had to do with a trip she had taken with her parents to Toronto when she must have been about five. It wasn't a vacation, of course. Instead, Mendel and Lydia had driven there to present papers at a conference, taking Lizzie along because most unfortunately Sheila couldn't stay with her while they were gone. It was raining then too, Lizzie recalled now. Mendel and Lydia decided they'd go to a nearby restaurant rather than eat at the hotel. While they walked there, Lizzie bent down and ran her hand through the water that had pooled at the side of the street. Mendel went ballistic, grabbing her arm and yanking it away from the puddle, yelling at her not to ever do that again. People stared at them; she still remembered how terribly frightened and mortified she felt.

Of course George didn't get angry. In fact, he didn't pay any attention to Lizzie's concerns. This was because he knew what was in the paper bag. He leaned over to reach for it under the bench. "Lizzie," he began. "I love you, you know that, right? And I get what you said to Alicia, that you can't imagine being married to someone for sixty years, but what about if we just took those years one at a time, together?"

He opened the bag and handed her its contents.

It was a gorgeous ring, a large diamond-cut sapphire (although Lizzie wouldn't describe the stone that way, not knowing the lingo; all she knew was that it seemed enormous) surrounded by smaller (but still substantial) diamonds. Despite the size of the gems, the ring wasn't gaudy. It didn't call attention to itself. It was refined, graceful, tasteful, and simply elegant. It was the sort of ring that you should probably keep in a safe-deposit box and take out only for special occasions. It was the kind of ring passed down from a grandmother to her favorite grandchild. It looked nothing like Lizzie, nothing like anything she'd ever dreamed of being, or wearing. This ring was meant for someone who was Lizzie's polar opposite.

"Oh, George," Lizzie said weakly, not knowing what else to say.

"Will you marry me, Lizzie? I can't imagine a life without you in it. Do you like the ring? It was my grandmother's, and I had the stones reset in a more modern setting that I thought you'd like."

"It's beautiful, George." Lizzie mustered all the enthusiasm she could, which was not a lot but was enough to make George happy. "But can we not think about getting married yet — can we concentrate on being engaged? Just engaged, for a while, so I can get used to the idea?"

He put the ring on her finger — it fit perfectly, of course (trust George to have found a way to make sure of that). Tears started rolling down Lizzie's face and George, being George, thought she was crying from happiness.

GEORGE & LIZZIE TELL
ALLAN & ELAINE THE NEWS

Elaine and Allan were over the moon when they learned of the engagement. Lizzie and George found them in the den. Allan was taking a nap with his head on Elaine's lap, and when George told them the news, they both tried to get up off the couch at the same time, with the result that Allan's head collided with the book that Elaine was reading and Elaine, in her eagerness to stand up, knocked over the mug of tea that she'd had been drinking, which soaked into the couch, her clothes, and the carpet.

"Oh, my darlings," Elaine said, undismayed by the potential stains. "We're just thrilled at the news. We were so hoping that George would propose on this trip so we could be with you to celebrate."

They sat around admiring Lizzie's ring. "You did a wonderful job picking out a new setting, Georgie," Elaine said. "Do you like it, Lizzie? It was my mother's."

"It's amazing," Lizzie said. That was probably objectively true. "I love it." Maybe not quite totally the truth, but still, what could Lizzie say?

"So when's the wedding going to be?" asked Allan.

"Yes," Elaine chimed in. "I've never been

a big fan of long engagements."

George looked at Lizzie, who smiled gamely back at him. "Mom, give us time to enjoy being engaged before we start planning for anything, okay?"

Later that day, though, Elaine dragged them both to Dillard's to scope out potential gifts to register for. Lizzie always enjoyed being with Elaine, but this long afternoon was a trial. She didn't really care about color schemes for towels and sheets, she was indifferent to the potential need for a good set of china as well as an everyday one, and had no opinion about silverware patterns except that she didn't like anything too ornate. "See, you *are* interested in silverware," George whispered behind Elaine's back. "That's why we have to do this." Lizzie nodded grimly. She had to do this.

George left to meet Allan for a father-and-son lunch, and Lizzie and Elaine went on to the bridal department at Miss Jackson's. After a few minutes of looking at the array of white, ivory, and ecru possibilities, Lizzie got so anxious that she grabbed Elaine's arm and dragged her away. "I have to go. I think I'm going to faint." The saleswoman wasn't noticeably fazed: she'd seen this and worse before.

Lizzie was also having trouble concentrating on the here and now, because she kept thinking how stupid Jack would find all this and how crazy she was to go along with it. She sketched out in her mind how she could break off her engagement to George in the nicest way possible when Jack came back to save her from this disastrous mistake. Please make it soon, she silently begged him. The announcers in her head loved it. "This girl's the absolute limit. Marrying someone she's not sure she loves," the second-to-the-meanest one said. "Oh, she's sure, all right. She doesn't love him at all. She's just a liar, born and bred," said the meanest one.

It soon became evident that Elaine was already caught up in a kind of wedding madness. On the way to the airport the next day, she pulled into a parking space in front of Steve's Sundries. "This'll just take a sec," she called back to them as she hurried inside. A few minutes later she came back with an armful of magazines and said triumphantly, "Look! I got a copy of every bridal magazine they had. Do you want to take some to read on the plane?"

George was inclined to accept his mother's offer of an issue or two until Lizzie looked at him sternly. "Oh, no, you keep those. We'll pick up some in Ann Arbor," he said, a bit reluctantly. It seemed he was actually

interested in weddings and their complicated etiquette. For herself, Lizzie couldn't
imagine perusing a magazine called anything like *Happy Bride* or *Modern Weddings,*
unless there was one called something like
*Weddings for the Reluctant Bride Who Is
Probably in Love with a Previous Boyfriend.*
In any case, there was really no need for her
to actually read anything on the subject of
weddings, because from then until the party
the following December, Elaine clipped
countless articles and pictures that she sent
to Lizzie, underlining the parts that she
thought were particularly relevant to the
upcoming event.

GEORGE & LIZZIE TELL
MENDEL & LYDIA THE NEWS

As soon as they got back to Ann Arbor,
George insisted that they go tell Lydia and
Mendel the big news, though he'd still not
yet even met Lydia. George hadn't been at
the last Bultmann Thanksgiving because his
grandmother had fallen and broken her hip
and George wanted to see her, even though
he and Lizzie would be back in Tulsa a few
weeks later. That was the kind of guy
George was. So it was utterly shocking to
him that he hadn't even met his future
mother-in-law. That situation needed to be

307

rectified at once. They were all going to be part of the same family.

Lizzie warned George not to expect too much from either parent. "First of all, don't count on any excitement at all," she went on. "And I wouldn't be surprised if Mendel didn't remember you. Plus they'll be annoyed we interrupted them doing whatever they were doing." George nodded but didn't believe any of these were accurate predictions.

Lizzie, however, was correct on all counts. When she and George came into the dining room, the Bultmanns were sitting at the table, smoking and drinking coffee. Mendel got up and shook George's hand, saying that he was pleased to meet him. Lizzie looked at George with satisfaction. Right again.

"You met him last year at Thanksgiving," Lizzie told her father.

"Oh, did I? There are always so many people here it's hard to keep track."

"Did I meet you then?" Lydia asked George.

Lizzie spoke before George could say anything. "No, we couldn't find you when George got here and we still couldn't find you when we left."

"I suppose you didn't check my office, did you?"

Ever since meeting George, Lizzie had made a conscious effort not to clench her teeth, but right now it was impossible not to. "No," she said. "I didn't think to check your office. It was Thanksgiving, I thought you'd be down here with everyone else."

Lydia made a noise that sounded like "pfui."

"But you should probably imprint George on your memory, because we're getting married," Lizzie added flatly.

"Married," echoed Mendel.

"Yes," George said, speaking formally, saying just what your usual parent would want to hear from the man your daughter was going to marry, that he adored their daughter more than they could ever imagine. Lizzie believed that sentence contained probably the truest words George had ever spoken. Lizzie was sure that Mendel and Lydia couldn't imagine anyone adoring their daughter.

Mendel shook George's hand again, murmuring his congratulations. Lydia got up and gave them each a traditional Bultmann hug, but that was that. Neither asked to see Lizzie's ring or inquired about when the wedding would be. They were in the house and then they were out. Ten minutes after Lizzie opened the front door, she closed it behind them.

"Whoof," George said, taking a deep breath of fresh air. It had been very smoky inside. "I might have to rethink some things that I've always believed to be true."

In the car, Lizzie leaned over and kissed George. "I love you," she said, and it might at that moment have been true. And then she poked him in the side and said, "Told you so."

MARLA & JAMES GET MARRIED, JUNE 1995

James and Marla got married immediately after they graduated; George and Lizzie six months later. Mrs. Cantor and James's mother planned it down to its final sumptuous detail. Lizzie knew that Marla thought her wedding day was almost exactly four years too late and that James was still so angry at his parents and Marla's that he could barely remain civil when he was with them.

Lizzie and Marla drove back and forth from Ann Arbor to Cleveland often that spring, because between James's and Marla's extended families and their parents' many friends there were wedding showers galore, and Marla wanted Lizzie to be at every one. After each of them, Marla would go through the gifts and give Lizzie any duplicates as well as anything that she didn't want to keep. There were many rejected items. Marla hadn't wanted to register for gifts anywhere, so the two mothers filled out the registries themselves, spending several satisfying Saturdays selecting towels and linen sets, china (both everyday and good), silver (sterling and silver plate), and kitchenware (which came in many more colors than were available when the mothers themselves had gotten married more than a quarter of a century before). This was how Lizzie and George eventually ended up with a lot of Marla and James's discarded loot, including a whistling teakettle (red), a teak salad bowl set, some dish towels, a travel clock, two books (*The Silver Palate Cookbook* and *The New Moosewood Cookbook*), and a pair of crystal candlesticks, as well as various pieces of silverware that weren't the same pattern that the mothers had registered for.

Since Marla had refused to ask James to convert, the rabbi at the Park, the Cantors' synagogue, declined to perform the ceremony. Instead the wedding took place at a big downtown hotel, with a more liberal rabbi and James's family's priest sharing the duties of marrying them. Lizzie was the maid of honor and George was one of James's groomsmen. After James had broken the glass — a Jewish tradition — and taken Marla into his arms for their first kiss as husband and wife, both of them burst into tears. Looking at the photos later, there was no sign that they'd cried. In fact, the naked happiness on their faces frightened Lizzie. It was unlikely she'd look that elated when she married George in, let's see, about a hundred and eighty days from now, although George undoubtedly would. Why, Lizzie wondered for the umpteenth time, why did he love her so much? Couldn't he see what a flawed, imperfect, pretty terrible person she was? Why couldn't Jack have loved her more? Because he obviously saw everything negative about her that George missed. Maybe she could request that there be no photos taken at their wedding. Ha! Good luck with that, Lizzie: there was simply no way that Allan and Elaine would ever let this occasion pass without several formal portraits of the newlyweds to mark it by. She'd just have to lie her way through the event. Lizzie the liar. If only George knew.

Marla and James left for a backpacking trip around Europe. They wouldn't be back in Ann Arbor until the start of grad school,

James in classics and Marla in art history. Didn't Jack say that to her? That he was leaving for the summer and would be back in August to start grad school? What if Marla never came back as well? Lizzie didn't think she would ever recover from the loss of the two people she cared about most.

But Marla returned from her honeymoon already pregnant; she decided not to go to grad school after all.

They named their daughter Beezie (short for Elizabeth, after Lizzie).

THE FREE SAFETY

Maverick told Lizzie that the free safety, Antonio Doll, had the best football instincts of anyone on the team. "To be an outstanding free safety a guy has to have a feel for the entire field. They direct the defense, just like the quarterback does for the offense," he explained. Antonio went on to play for Youngstown State, where for two years in a row he set a school record in interceptions, but forsook football after he graduated. He went on to Oxford as a Rhodes scholar and eventually became an assistant secretary of state. For no particular reason Lizzie never forgot what Maverick told her about free safeties. When she passed on that tidbit to

George, it turned out that he already knew it. "It's sort of like the point guard on a basketball team," he told her. "They run the court. Think of the free safety as the Magic Johnson of their team." And ever after Lizzie did think that, although the subject never came up again.

LIZZIE & GEORGE
TALK ABOUT NAMES

Lizzie and George were both sitting up in bed. Lizzie was turning the pages of *A Tree Grows in Brooklyn* but not really reading it. George was underlining passages in Andrew Weil's *From Chocolate to Morphine.* They couldn't be said to be conversing until Lizzie put down her book, looked at George, and took a deep breath.

"George, I really don't want to change my name to Goldrosen when we get married."

"Well, there's no need to. I certainly don't care about it. You can always stay a Bultmann."

Lizzie stared at him in disbelief. "You know that's not possible. I've been waiting my whole life not to be a Bultmann. Possibly that's why I'm marrying you. But I don't want to be a Goldrosen either."

"Why not? It's never bothered me. I like being George Goldrosen."

"Oh, George. Nothing ever bothers you."

"Not exactly true, but my name certainly doesn't."

"Look at your poor mother. I bet that Elaine wasn't happy about exchanging Lowen for Goldrosen either, but when she and your dad got married nobody kept their own names."

"Don't be silly. I've never heard my mother complain about our last name. I'm sure she loves it. But if you want to ask her yourself," he went on in a reasonable tone, "let's call. They're probably still up."

"Go ahead, George, call her. But even in the unlikely event that she says she does love the name Goldrosen, I'm not going to change the way I feel about not wanting it for my last name. I'm serious. This is serious. What would you think about shortening it to Gold? Or Rosen? I could live with either one. It's just the two parts together that I don't want."

"What do I think? I think it's not going to happen. I can't even imagine what Grandma and Pop would say about it — nothing good, I'm sure — but I know how hurt they'd be. The only two options I see that you have are staying a Bultmann or becoming a Goldrosen."

Lizzie shook her head sadly. "Now I know

what people mean by saying they're between a rock and a hard place."

"Or the devil and the deep blue sea," George agreed, somewhat coldly.

"Or between Scylla and Charybdis," Lizzie said, somewhat more coldly. "Don't be so ridiculously defensive. It's just a name that happens to be yours."

"Exactly, it's just a name. That happens to be mine. Soon to be yours. Maybe you should remember that. Elizabeth Goldrosen. I think it sounds great."

"Maybe that doesn't sound too bad," Lizzie acknowledged, "but think about all the zzzz sounds in Lizzie Goldrosen. Even you can't think that sounds good. Lizzzzzzzie Goldrozzzzzzzen. It's awful."

George shook his head and went back to reading.

Lizzie took the book out of his lap, closed it, and made one last try. "How about this? We could change our name to something neutral, like Austen, maybe. Or Bennet. Then I could be Lizzie Bennet. Elizabeth Bennet. That'd be pretty cool."

George reached for the book. "Get a grip, sweetie. It's not going to happen. Bultmann or Goldrosen, your choice."

"Wait, don't decide right away. Okay, no Bennet. But let's think of other books. You liked *A Wrinkle in Time,* didn't you? So did I. What if we became Murrys? Wasn't that Meg's last name? That sounds good, doesn't it? George and Lizzie Murry. Or Ingalls? I'd like that. But if you liked Wilder better, that'd be fine with me," she offered generously. "Or even Darling. George Darling. Lizzie Darling. That might be really fun."

"Wait a second, stop, listen to this idea," George said. "What about if we became the Littles? We could name our son Stuart. Or Seuss — then I could be Dr. Seuss. The kids in my practice would love that, I bet. Or wait, even better, let's change our last name to Of Oz. That would be cool. George and Elizabeth Of Oz. We could name a daughter Ozma. That was always my favorite book in the series."

That George could reliably make her laugh mattered a lot to Lizzie. She sometimes thought that it was what kept her from running away and spending some serious time searching for Jack.

"Dearest Lizzie, listen, we're absolutely not changing our soon-to-be joint last name to anything else. We're getting married and I'd be very happy if you chose to become a Goldrosen, but I'll certainly understand if you want to remain a Bultmann. I'm sure your parents would be thrilled."

"Jeez, George, you have never understood my parents and you never will. And I don't think you understand me either."

Well. What could George do but assure her that he did understand her parents and, even more importantly, he understood *her*. Which Lizzie never believed. All the evidence, she felt, was against it.

THE WORST THING GEORGE EVER SAID TO LIZZIE THAT WAS ACTUALLY TRUE

Finally driven to extremes during a particularly long and frustrating Difficult Conversation early in their marriage, George told Lizzie that she had the emotional age of a three-year-old.

In her heart of hearts Lizzie realized that not only had it been true when George said it, but it was probably still an accurate description years later.

WHY LIZZIE DECIDED TO MARRY GEORGE

Lizzie found that it wasn't so bad being engaged because it changed very little in her relationship with George. She began to grow very fond of her ring, although when she was in class she tended to turn it around so that the stone was hidden and all people could see (if they chose to look) was a plain platinum band. But marriage was something else entirely. If Jack should show up in Ann Arbor to see her, breaking an engagement was one thing. But what if he came after she and George got married? That would make everything much more complicated.

Marla didn't think she should marry George right away. "It's different for me and James," she said. "We planned to get married practically from the moment we met in junior high. But you, you can just go on being engaged for as long as you need to until you finally accept that Jack isn't coming back for you, ever."

"I just can't believe that I'll never see him again. That's just not possible, is it?"

"Listen, Lizzie, here are a few hard truths you have to hear. You and Jack dated for one quarter, call it three months. That's all. Yeah, I know you said the sex was terrific and you shared all that poetry, but you only knew him for about ninety days. And you're going to hang on to that long past its expiration date? You have a wonderful boyfriend who wants to spend his life with you, and you're going to mourn the rest of your natural life for some jerk who ditched you?"

"I never should have told him that was me in the article. That's why he left. The

Great Game. That was my big mistake."

"If that's really why he left, which I don't know if I believe, then he's even more of a jerk."

"It was my fault that he left," Lizzie said stubbornly. "Nobody would want to stay with someone who did such a stupid thing."

Marla sighed and reluctantly dropped the subject.

But after Marla and James's wedding, Lizzie acceded to George's desire to get married sooner rather than later. The reasons she gave herself were these:

1. She liked George well enough.
2. She loved his parents, particularly his mother.
3. She had no idea what to do next if she didn't marry George, except to continue her search for Jack. She had no interest whatsoever in grad school. Lizzie knew that she was smart, but there wasn't anything that she particularly wanted to study. She still loved reading poetry, but she hated the way poems had been analyzed to death in her undergraduate English classes. Breaking down a poem like that took away the joy of reading it.

4. Sex with George was fine. Occasionally and unexpectedly, it could be awfully nice. He was as generous and kind in bed as he was in everything else in his life.

5. George had an expansive sense of humor. He had a wonderfully contagious laugh. Lizzie loved that every time he laughed, the lines around his eyes crinkled up. (Many years later, Lizzie would hear Lucinda Williams sing "The Lines Around Your Eyes," a song that she always wanted to believe was written about George.) Lizzie egged him on in his addiction to puns and tried, unsuccessfully, to get him to stop laughing at his own jokes. Even after he got famous, George still laughed at his own jokes. His fans loved that about him. Plus, as George pointed out to Lizzie somewhat smugly, he inherited the tendency to do so from his mother, remember?

6. As far as Lizzie could see, there weren't a lot of reasons not to marry George. One, of course, was that he wasn't Jack. But Lizzie knew the big reason not to marry George

was that she probably didn't love him nearly enough.

THE MIDDLE LINEBACKER

Some fans thought that if Joe Parsons chose to devote his life to football he could rival Dick Butkus at the middle linebacker position. Joe played hard (he was a vicious tackler) and had great instincts for what was going to happen next on the field. What Lizzie remembered best about him, though, was how polite he was — the only guy on the team who opened the car door for her when he drove her home after his Friday of the Great Game was done. Following a great career with the Vikings, Joe became a noted play-by-play announcer with ESPN. His cogent analyses were a big hit with George, and the fact that Lizzie went to high school with him made listening to him even more fun. Of course Lizzie couldn't tell him that what she most associated Joe Parsons with was the Philip Larkin poem that began "They fuck you up, your mum and dad / They may not mean to, but they do," which was what she recited to herself instead of paying attention to what was going on between Joe Parsons's body and hers.

DIFFICULT CONVERSATIONS INVOLVING PLANS FOR THE WEDDING

Over the next year there were many Difficult Conversations about the wedding. They began almost immediately after Lydia and Mendel and Allan and Elaine met. The meeting did not go well. The Goldrosens flew up from Tulsa for the weekend to celebrate George and Lizzie's engagement and insisted on taking everyone out to dinner, which was almost certainly a mistake. Allan and Elaine kept trying to make conversation and Lydia and Mendel kept rigorously resisting having anything to do with their conversational gambits. When Elaine enthused about how happy they were about the engagement and how much they loved Lizzie, Mendel nodded gamely in agreement — Lizzie could tell that he was mentally writing the article that would come out of this dinner — and Lydia said that they liked George a lot too. Small talk was impossible. Politics was a nonstarter. Books were out. Nobody wanted to talk about the weather (it was cold and threatening to snow). Since the Bultmanns rarely if ever went to the movies, it was immaterial to them whether or not the Goldrosens liked any particular film. Each family was way outside its comfort zone. To the Bultmanns the Goldrosens were like exotic animals, and the only animals they were interested in were rats. To the Goldrosens the Bultmanns were equally exotic, survivors of what they'd always thought was an extinct tribe. George was dumbfounded at seeing firsthand oil and water not mixing; he kept throwing out new topics for discussion. Lizzie was mortified and promised herself that for the rest of her life she would do all she could to keep the two families apart.

Lizzie knew, from all the articles that Elaine had sent her, the exact kind of wedding that she wanted them to have, which included pretty much everything Lizzie didn't want. She didn't want a *wedding* wedding. She told George that if they were getting married, then they should just get married. She didn't want to buy a dress she'd wear only once, she certainly didn't want her father to walk her down the aisle. She didn't want an aisle. She didn't want anyone there, except his parents and Marla and James. She didn't want a party. She didn't want an open bar and an orchestra and dancing and a dinner followed by an overfull sweet table. She didn't want to cut a cake. She didn't want a chuppah to stand under during the ceremony. She didn't want the rabbi who bar mitzvah'd George to marry them. She didn't want photographs taken of the festive occasion.

Have her parents there? Forget it. They'd probably be frowning over their ever-present yellow pads of paper, making it clear that they didn't want to talk to anyone except each other, taking notes all during the supposed festivities on the behavior of wedding guests. Mendel and Lydia were so foreign, so dark and closed in, especially when compared to the sunniness of the Goldrosens and all the friends of the Goldrosens. Plus Lizzie feared that when her parents saw that a rabbi was involved in the ceremony, they would just get up and leave in disgust.

She knew she was being horribly unreasonable and was already prepared to give in as gracefully as she could manage to many of Elaine's wishes (which she knew were more than likely George's wishes as well), but she wanted to give herself lots and lots of room to negotiate.

As Lizzie suspected, George actually wanted all those things that Lizzie professed to despise.

"I do despise them, George," Lizzie retorted. "Why do you have to say 'profess to despise' as if I'm not really telling the truth?"

("We've got her back, folks," the voices in her head announced. They addressed her directly, saying, "Because everyone knows you lie all the time. Your life is a lie.")

"Okay, I apologize, you're right. I understand that it's the way you think you feel now, but, Lizzie, your parents have to be at the wedding. Just imagine how they'd feel if they weren't even invited. If we snuck off somewhere and got married without even telling them where it was or when."

"Honestly, George, sometimes I wonder just how smart you are. In the face of all evidence to the contrary, you continue to believe that Mendel and Lydia are just like your parents, only perhaps a lot more introverted. But they're not. They don't do social things like parties. They just do the bare minimum to keep the dean of the psych department happy. And we can't have a wedding in Ann Arbor. I don't want to plan it. I don't even know where I'd start figuring out how to do it. And who would pay for it? Do you want to ask them? They'd laugh in my face if I asked them."

"I don't believe that. But what if we have the wedding in Tulsa? We could let my mom plan the whole thing. She'd love doing it."

"George, please, please listen to me. I really do not want that kind of a wedding.

Dee-oh Not, with a capital *N*, whether it's in Tulsa or Ann Arbor or Timbuktu. If we have to have a ceremony, then let's just find someone to do it. Maybe James could wangle some way to become a judge for a day. Maybe we can marry ourselves."

George chuckled, but Lizzie knew he wasn't amused. "We *are* marrying ourselves," he said.

"You know what I mean. Is that even possible? Or how about if we don't get married at all? Let's just live together."

That was not going to happen. Over the course of the following year it became clear that a wedding would take place. Conversations on what this would actually entail were endless. After some tears (Elaine's), some frustration with his beloved wife-to-be as well as his mother (George), and a mad desire to just run away and hope she ran into Jack somewhere (Lizzie), they reached a compromise. They'd get married by a judge in Ann Arbor on the Sunday after Thanksgiving. The only guests would be their immediate families, which included George's grandparents and Marla and James. And Blake and Alicia, if they could get time off from work, George added firmly. Lizzie wanted to offer a mild objection to having Blake and Alicia (especially

Alicia) at the wedding but knew how much that would hurt George and didn't say anything. Maybe she'd get lucky and there would be a late-November snowstorm in Tulsa, making it impossible for anyone to fly up to Michigan.

Then, on New Year's Eve, Allan and Elaine would host a dinner (with a band and dancing and an open bar and a sweet table) in Tulsa to celebrate the wedding. It would have everything that Lizzie didn't want, aside from the chuppah and rabbi and marriage vows. Lizzie would need to buy something lovely to wear. "It'll be my special gift to you," Elaine told her.

THE BRACELET

Just hours before she was going to marry George, Lizzie was emptying the contents of her dresser drawers into a suitcase when she found the bracelet. Following the ceremony in Judge Larry Martin's chambers and the luncheon that followed it, she and George were going to move the remainder of Lizzie's stuff to his apartment (now their apartment) on Nob Hill Place. Lizzie was looking forward to none of it. In the immediate future she particularly dreaded the lunch, which would bring together Allan and Elaine, both sets of George's grand-

328

parents, and Lydia and Mendel. Plus Blake and Alicia. Even knowing that Marla and James would be there didn't make her feel much better. So here Lizzie was, emptying out her dresser drawers, waiting for George to pick her up and take her to the courthouse for the wedding.

Of course the bracelet hadn't really been lost. She'd put it there herself, underneath her socks and underwear, over three years ago, when she more or less accepted the apparent fact that Jack was no longer part of her life, and probably wouldn't ever be again. It was intended to be his graduation present, something meaningful that represented how they'd met and what they loved about each other. A book would have been the easy choice, a collection of the poems of Housman, say, which would certainly evoke their shared past. But a book didn't seem special enough. You can buy a book for anyone. Books were one of Lizzie and Jack's things, it was true, but Lizzie had been sure that there was something better out there, something amazingly wonderful that was meant just for Jack.

In July, when Lizzie was still hopeful that, despite the lack of letters, he would for sure be back the next month, she wandered through the annual Ann Arbor art fair, looking for the perfect gift. After poking through the many booths displaying sculpture, paintings, photographs, drawings, and jewelry for sale she found the present she'd hoped to find. It was a bracelet, a silver bangle bracelet, perfectly round, about a quarter of an inch wide (just barely wide enough, Lizzie would discover, to accommodate an inscription). It was both endless and somehow self-contained. It fit over your hand and was clearly meant to remain on your wrist through thick and thin, during the bad times and good, the days and the nights, the months and the years. She slipped it onto her own wrist to see how it looked. She pictured Jack wearing it, his arm, tanned from the Texas summer, a sharp contrast with the silver of the bracelet. She closed her eyes because the image made her so sad.

That night, lying in bed and unable to fall asleep, Lizzie remembered the note she'd sent Jack with the line from Millay's "Modern Declaration," and first thing the next morning she took the bracelet back to the man who'd fashioned it and asked him to engrave "Jack, shall love you always" on the inside, where it would touch his wrist.

Well. That was then, this is now, as George would often say, quoting the title of

S. E. Hinton's novel. It was his favorite book from his early adolescence and he never tired of reminding Lizzie that Hinton was also from Tulsa, and that she'd come to talk to his ninth-grade English class. And autographed his much-beat-up copy. And smiled at him and said that it looked like he'd read it more than once, which was certainly true. He'd pressed the copy into Lizzie's hands during her very first Christmas visit to Tulsa and insisted that she read it. When she dutifully finished it, she wondered if she could tell George that while she could see why he'd loved it so much, she actually felt that at this moment in her life she might just be the wrong demographic to appreciate it as much as he had when he was fourteen.

And when September came and went without a letter, without Jack, she stuck the bracelet in the back of a drawer and tried to forget it existed. But it did exist, and here it was. When she heard George coming into the apartment, she hesitated for a moment, then took the bracelet and put it on. Lizzie was ready to get married.

"I'm here," she called, somehow happier than she'd been for a long time.

After the ceremony, after the "I now pronounce you husband and wife" and after their first married kiss, after everyone had already hugged Lizzie and shook George's hand and congratulated them both and were busy putting on coats and arranging rides to the restaurant where the wedding lunch would be held, Marla pulled her aside.

"Tell me, my dear Mrs. Goldrosen, that I'm not seeing that bracelet on your wrist. Don't you think that wearing something that was supposed to be a gift for another guy as part of your wedding ensemble is a bit much, even for you?"

Lizzie grimaced but allowed as how Marla might be right. "But I didn't know what else to do with it; I was packing and there it was and then George showed up and —"

"Well, one option is that you just left it where it was. Or, I know, you could have thrown it away the moment you saw it in the drawer. It just doesn't look good for the future, you know?"

"I don't think it's that significant," Lizzie said, but Marla shook her head in disagreement.

"Look, take it off, give it to me. I'll hide it for the rest of your life. You don't want George to find it, do you? Or your kids? I can just hear them: 'Who's Jack, Mommy? Why will you always love him? What about Daddy?' How will you answer that?"

Lizzie sighed. "It's fine. It'll be okay,

really. Everybody has secrets, don't they?"

"Not secrets like this," Marla said darkly. "I love you, Lizzie, and always will. And I will always, always, keep your secrets. But this, what this means to you and George, is an important secret. It's not the equivalent of a little white lie. It'd be like me not telling James about the abortion."

"But James knew about the abortion; he was with you when you had it."

"Don't be deliberately naive; it doesn't become you. You know what I mean: some other James I was involved with."

What Lizzie wanted to say was that Marla reminded her of how, in fairy tales, there was always someone at a wedding to prophesize a tragic future, but before she could respond, Allan came up to them. "Don't hog my new daughter, Marla," he said, smiling. "You get to see her all the time. I want to tell her again how happy we are that she's part of our family."

WHY GEORGE LOVES LIZZIE

1. Her smile. When Lizzie smiles it's pretty impossible not to smile back. George has seen evidence of this with train conductors, hitherto grumpy salespeople, and little kids.

Even when he is most frustrated with her (see number two, below), her smile can almost always make everything better. Especially now that he's fixed that incisor.

2. He's never bored by Lizzie. Exasperated, yes, quite often. Very exasperated, yes, more than just occasionally. Extremely exasperated, yes, there were definitely times when Lizzie's sadness and pessimism drove George bonkers, when he knew a life without her would be easier. But all she had to do was smile (see number one, above) or laugh appreciatively at one of his puns (see number three, below) and he was back in love with her. Did this make him weak or stupid or what? George didn't know.

3. Her sense of humor. Lizzie is wonderful with sarcasm and wordplay (she shares his love of a good pun), but she's a terrible joke teller because she usually forgets the telling detail that makes the joke a joke. Here's where George comes in, since he always remembers that detail perfectly.

4. Her intelligence. George had known

smart women before he met Lizzie (Julia Draznin, for one, and his mother for another) but he soon realized that Lizzie was probably the smartest woman he'd ever met. George thought of himself as being quite intelligent (he'd always gotten high scores on standardized tests), but he'd never been quick. He liked to read books slowly and carefully (he was virtually incapable of skimming), with frequent pauses to think about what he had just read; Lizzie devoured books, one after another, like a chain-smoker with her cigarettes. She was like a lightning streak across the sky, picking up and remembering odd and interesting facts about whatever interested her, and a lot did. George would never call Lizzie a deep thinker, but, boy, she was the ideal *Trivial Pursuit* or *Jeopardy!* partner. George was frequently surprised at what Lizzie knew or didn't know. Perfectly ordinary facts like what latitude meant were beyond her, while the sort of minuscule details of someone's life — the name of Albert Einstein's first wife (it was

Mileva Einstein-Marić, George learned from Lizzie) were on the tip of her tongue.

5. Her breasts. As a late twentieth-century, well-educated male, one fully aware of the crimes the patriarchy had committed on the opposite sex, George knew that much more went into loving someone than their physical attributes, but it has to be said that he loved Lizzie's breasts. Their size and shape fit the palm of his hand perfectly.

6. Her neediness. Lizzie needed George in ways that no one else ever had or, he believed, ever would. She needed him to do the ordinary things that anyone could have done (including Lizzie if she'd been inclined to try harder: unscrew recalcitrant jars, climb a ladder to change the lightbulb on the side of the house, slice vegetables with their mandoline), and George enjoyed the feeling of being needed. More significantly, Lizzie, in George's view, needed rescuing from her own sadness, and George was convinced that he was the only person in the world who could do so.

Two Deaths

Three months after George and Lizzie got married, Lydia and Mendel were killed. Their car skidded one cold and rainy February night while they were coming home from a performance of Mozart's *Marriage of Figaro* in Detroit and I-94 suddenly became a sheet of black ice. The campus newspaper, the *Michigan Daily,* added black borders around the headline "STARS GO OUT IN PSYCH DEPARTMENT" and the first line of the story began "Family, students, and colleagues are distraught at the deaths . . ." which Lizzie found hard to take seriously. She was certainly not distraught but rather somewhat unbalanced by the event. She found it unnerving but not necessarily unpleasant to think of herself as an orphan, even when she knew, intellectually, that orphanhood was the natural state of the adult child. But "distraught" implied rending of garments and weeping until your eyes were red and your skin turned blotchy, which wasn't going to happen with her.

Actually, she couldn't imagine who if any of her parents' colleagues and students could possibly be that upset. Mendel and Lydia were respected and admired but not really liked. Friendship had never been on their minds: they were way too busy analyzing patterns of behavior. Yet there was some talk in the university community of calling off Saturday's football game against Purdue — the Bultmanns brought in a whole lot of research money — but nobody except maybe the very unpopular and soon-to-depart-for-greener-pastures-in-Seattle provost took that suggestion seriously. At the University of Michigan, football ruled. The only time a game had been canceled was the Saturday after President Kennedy was shot. The team was scheduled to play their archrival, Ohio State. Many die-hard fans were still furious about that, more than three decades after the fact. So nobody in their right mind could even expect something similar for the Bultmanns, research money be damned.

The *Detroit News* and the *New York Times* ran the same long obituary, complete with pictures of Lydia and Mendel that had been taken right after they arrived in Ann Arbor to teach, pictures Lizzie had never even seen. Her parents looked so young. Lydia had long straight hair and stared at the camera with a serious expression. Mendel had a mustache and beard and was smiling slightly. Lizzie was now older than her parents had been when the pictures were taken, another odd and unbalancing thought.

Everyone helped Lizzie make the arrangements for the funeral service and the reception at her parents' house afterward. Allan and Elaine of course flew in from Tulsa immediately and were, along with George, Marla, and James, wonderful about dealing with all that death requires the survivors to do: working out details with the funeral home, helping Lizzie select her parents' caskets, calling various governmental agencies and financial institutions to report the deaths (Allan did this, thank goodness), but it fell to Lizzie to do what she felt were the two hardest tasks.

Lydia had died instantly in the accident, despite obediently wearing a seat belt and having the driver's-side air bag work as promised. But Mendel, sitting in the passenger seat, was not as fortunate. For some reason his air bag hadn't inflated. In spite of that, he survived the collision, but with his body badly broken and his fine mind knocked silly. The doctors told Lizzie there was nothing to be done, he'd never be Mendel again, that even if his body healed and he awoke from the coma he was blessedly in, the kindest thing she could do for her father was to let him die.

Mendel and Lydia had left no instructions

for her. There was no will, nothing giving her power of attorney, and nothing at all to help her decide what was to be done with them, dead or alive. She had a slight memory of her parents coming home from an elderly long-retired Jewish colleague's funeral and Lydia scoffing at all the attendant rituals, at the procession to the cemetery, at the shoveling of dirt on the casket after it was lowered into the grave, at the professional friends and professional enemies who came together at his death to professionally mourn him. And then adding, unless Lizzie misremembered, that despite the rigmarole she'd decided that she'd like a rabbi on hand during her funeral. But nothing religious.

"That makes no sense. They're totally opposite desires," Lizzie complained to George. "But I do sort of hear her saying that in my mind. Or at least I think I do. What if I made it up? What if we do one thing and it turns out that she really wanted the other? Oh God, George, this is just like them. What do you think we should do?"

"Well, before we decide about the funeral, I think we, or you, have to decide about Mendel first, don't we? And we should do it fairly quickly, although it won't matter to Lydia if you stretched Jewish law and waited a few days before she was buried."

So this was the first hard task: telling the doctors that she wanted to end her father's life, if you could call the state he was in life. At first it seemed like a no-brainer (like Mendel, himself, at this point and now forever). But it still felt weirdly wrong when, during a meeting with her father's doctors, she told them to "pull the plug," as Allan had indelicately put it. Was it really a plug? An electrical connection? What if the God that Mendel and Lydia didn't believe in stepped into the picture with a convenient power outage so that those words wouldn't have to be said, and the decision would be taken out of her hands? In the end, the life-support system was turned off, and now neither Mendel nor Lydia could mourn the other, as she felt they would have wanted but dearly wished they had made explicit.

"Did they purchase funeral plots?" Elaine asked.

Lizzie didn't know.

"Did they want to be buried or cremated?"

Lizzie didn't know.

"What do you want to do, sweetheart?" George asked.

Lizzie didn't know. She wanted to run away. She wanted to find Jack. She wanted to be back in Terrell the Terrible's poetry class and meeting Jack for the first time. She turned to George. "Can you decide, George? Because I don't know what to do."

George considered the two options. "I'd say burial, I think."

"Okay," Elaine said, "then the next steps are to choose their caskets and find funeral plots."

"Yes," Lizzie said. "I suppose that's what we have to do."

"I'll start calling cemeteries," Allan said.

Even harder than talking to the doctors was calling the rabbi who was going to conduct the funeral service. Because the Bultmanns had never affiliated themselves with any religious institution, the first problem was locating a rabbi. "You would think," Lizzie said to Marla, "that for people who avowed no interest, zero, nada interest, in religion at all, Mendel and Lydia would have wanted nothing to do with the rituals of funerals either."

At all. But there, unable to be refuted, was Lizzie's memory of what Lydia had said. Or had not said.

Elaine called their rabbi in Tulsa for advice. After doing some quick research, he came up with the name of a young woman who had gone to rabbinical college with his own son and was now working on a PhD in

Middle Eastern studies in Ann Arbor and assisting at Temple Beth Shalom, a building into which not one of the Bultmanns had ever set foot.

Lizzie liked the sound of Rabbi Gould's voice, and she suspected that her mother would have approved of a female rabbi even if she didn't like what the rabbi might have to say. She had a brief fantasy that maybe she and the rabbi could be friends once this was all over. But first she had to convey her parents' (or at least her mother's) wishes, and could only think to say without any preamble, "My mother wanted a funeral with a rabbi, but she was a devout atheist, so she wouldn't want God mentioned at the service."

There was a long silence on the phone. Lizzie wondered if this was the first time Rabbi Gould been asked to officiate at a funeral and now, most unluckily, had to deal with such a request. Oh God, Lizzie prayed to herself, unaware of the irony, please, please don't let her refuse. I can't do this again.

Finally, Rabbi Gould spoke. "There has to be at least one prayer that mentions God. Otherwise it wouldn't be a Jewish ceremony. It's a memorial prayer called *El Maleheh Rachamim,* 'God Full of Compassion,' " she went on. "It's the first time the deceased person is labeled as deceased by name. Do you want to know how it came about?"

"Um, not really," Lizzie started to respond, but the young rabbi was on a roll.

"In Poland in the 1640s there were a series of terrible massacres — the Chmielnicki Massacres — and this prayer was a way for an entire community to be named and therefore remembered. Over time it developed into a more personal prayer that was used as a way to memorialize the dead and ask for God's protection over them throughout eternity."

"I guess that'll be okay," Lizzie replied, tired of the issue, of the last difficulty her parents had directed her way, however unintentionally. But what kind of parents would neglect to tell their daughter what she should do with them after they die? Lizzie's kind, obviously.

THE OUTSIDE LINEBACKERS

One of the outside linebackers was Brandon Melandandri (nicknamed, inevitably and, as it turned out, ironically, Dandy). The best years of Dandy's life were the years he spent in high school. Once he graduated, Dandy disappeared into drug addiction and homelessness. The last Lizzie knew he was living on the streets in Detroit. It was a pretty un-dandy ending. The other was Anoush Shashvili, who went on to become a semisuccessful writer of horror films. Be-cause Lizzie felt that real life was scary enough without the addition of the super-natural, she never saw any of his movies. In fact, she made a point of studiously avoid-ing them, and refused to let George see them either. Anoush's first film, which received a lot of praise, was *Slash/Dot/Vampire Blood.* Lizzie thought the title prob-ably said it all.

PLAYDATES

Lizzie and George loved the weekends most especially during the fall and early winter when it was pretty much all football all the time. Late in August, between James and Marla's wedding and their own, George surprised Lizzie with season tickets to both the football and basketball games. Saturday afternoons were spent either watching the Wolverines play in the Big House, as the Michigan stadium was known, or else watching the away games on television. Of course it wasn't just the Michigan games that were important. Naturally George wanted to watch Oklahoma State play, and then there were the postgame shows, and then he and Allan rehashed the OSU game and sometimes the University of Oklahoma game as well. Usually, after talking to Allan, George would call his grandfather to talk some more. The Goldrosens really loved football. Every once in a while Lizzie thought it was ironic that she couldn't tell George about the Great Game and those twenty-three guys whose names she would never forget.

The Wolverines were only a so-so team in the early years of George and Lizzie's marriage. Their best season was 1997, when the Associated Press ranked them number one, but Lizzie's fondness for the game never depended on her team winning. What she liked was learning about the different players. The quarterback who came to Ann Arbor from Selma, Alabama, and spoke with such a deep southern accent that none of the other players could understand him, and Lloyd Carr, the head coach, convinced him to become a wide receiver, where communication skills were not so vital. The linebacker who graduated from hated in-state rival Michigan State and then transferred to Michigan for his fifth year in order to study accounting and play one last season. The cornerback who won every award, including the Heisman Trophy, the first defensive player to do so. The freshman punt returner who was paralyzed the fifth play of the Wolverines' opening game. That sort of thing.

Sundays were spent watching the pro games. To please Lizzie, George adopted Detroit as his second favorite team. He saw this as an enormous sacrifice, because it practically guaranteed a frustrating Sunday, since the hapless Lions went down to defeat nearly every week. The pain of the Lions losing was always exacerbated when the Dallas Cowboys games weren't televised. "They're America's team," he'd mutter. "Why can't those idiots make them the game of the week?" And when the Cowboys lost he was pretty inconsolable for a few hours.

Lizzie especially loved the Sunday-night game no matter who was playing. She'd pop a huge bowl of popcorn, cut up some apples and carrots, and pour them each glasses of beer, and she and George would sit close to each other on the sofa and watch the game unfold, forgoing dinner. Lizzie enjoyed listening to George respond to the action on the field. She liked hearing him analyze different plays. She was happy to let him exclaim over illegal chop blocks, successful blitzes, and missed field goals. She enjoyed his rants about abysmal time management and horrible red zone calls.

George sometimes joked that he was relieved that the Cowboys didn't play the Lions in the regular season until 2002. He told Lizzie that he wasn't sure they could have handled being on opposite sides of a football game before then, when they were an old married couple — seven years! — and could deal with all their differences as adults. Lizzie couldn't tell if George intended this to be a joke or not. She rather thought not.

Lizzie was sometimes of the opinion, disloyally (whether to George or to the basketball team itself was never clear to her), that there were way too many games on the schedule. George wanted to attend as many of them as his and Lizzie's schedules allowed. She once suggested that they just move into Crisler Center during the basketball season. Lizzie found going to the games — basketball or football — exceptionally relaxing, because she knew that Jack would never in a million years attend a game of either sport, so there was no chance she'd run into him there, and that knowledge was a huge relief tinged with sadness.

One issue Lizzie had with basketball was the last few minutes of close games. To some extent the same was true for football, but the pace of a basketball game made it much more intense. Lizzie couldn't take it. She worried too much about the players who were under the enormous pressure of making a free throw when the game depended on it, or who were called for walking and were thus responsible for turning the ball over to the opposition. She couldn't stand it when a coach screamed at a player. George supposed that he understood Lizzie's feelings, but it still boggled his mind that if the score was close and the clock down to three or so minutes to play, Lizzie couldn't watch the rest of game. If they were at home she would leave the living room, go into the kitchen or bedroom, and shut the door behind her so she couldn't hear the cheers or groans. Sometimes she was unable to stay away, but mostly she just waited for George to come and tell her the outcome. It was less painful that way. When they were watching the games in person and Lizzie felt too stressed, she'd close her eyes and cover her ears, trying not to hear or see what was going on. Or if it was too excitingly nerve-racking, she'd make her way to the closest bathroom and sit on the toilet, reading the graffiti on the walls and door until the game ended and she and George could go home.

After a few too many evenings in the first year of their marriage spent like that, Lizzie would bring a book to the game.

HONEYMOON FOR FOUR

When George started college in Stillwater, Allan and Elaine called him, without fail, at nine o'clock every Sunday morning. Although the knowledge that he'd have to talk to his parents early the next day occasionally put a crimp in his Saturday-night activities, he never told them that he'd rather talk to them at, say, nine at night. The calls followed a basic pattern. He and Allan would discuss in minute detail the Cowboys' latest football or basketball game, even if they'd already been at said game together (along with his grandfather Sam) the day before and had had a similar discussion after the game was over. Their discussions were longest and most intense about football, and during these extended conversations Elaine could be heard on the extension, breathing impatiently. When it was her turn she'd lovingly grill George about the state of his emotional and physical health, then move on to the books they were reading, interesting articles they'd read, and films they'd seen or wanted to see.

She'd conclude by relating the latest

absurdity his grandmother had either said or done and the kerfuffle that resulted. This last almost never came as a surprise to George, since his grandmother had usually given her version of whatever outrage it was when he had a Sabbath dinner with them the Friday evening before, another regular occurrence. During his four years in Stillwater, at no time did it occur to George that his family was taking up an awful lot of his time. In fact, spending every Friday night with his grandparents was a good opportunity to invite his friends for a taste of real rather than dorm (and later, fraternity) food. That Gertie never liked any of the people he brought over, especially the girls, he attributed to the fact that not one of them was Jewish. She had been particularly outraged when he brought the girl he was dating sophomore year to their Passover seder and Melody came in wearing shorts, a somewhat snug T-shirt, and sandals. "Do you believe the rudeness?" George heard Gertie mutter to Sam. Did this cause him to break up with Melody shortly after the dinner? He had a suspicion it did.

The Sunday-morning conversations with his parents continued when George graduated and moved to Ann Arbor to begin dental school, but immediately after Lizzie and George got engaged they increased exponentially in duration. It turned out that Allan and Elaine now wanted to talk to Lizzie as well as their younger son every week. That took time. And now that George and Allan weren't attending football games together, their conversations about the Cowboys (both the OSU and Dallas teams) intensified and lengthened. There was much sports news to discuss.

Roughly the first six months of 1995 were taken up with discussions about the wedding: where and when and what kind it would be. Once that was settled, the conversation turned to honeymoons. Lizzie loved these weekly phone calls with Allan and Elaine, but was glad to be done with the subject of weddings.

One Wednesday evening early in July, Lizzie and George were just finishing dinner, when the phone rang. Since Lizzie refused on principle to ever answer a ringing phone except when she knew it was Marla or George, she ignored it. It was George's parents.

"Hey, Georgie," Elaine said. "Daddy and I had a great idea about your honeymoon. Can we talk to Lizzie too?"

"Our honeymoon," George mouthed as he handed Lizzie the phone and then went into the bedroom to get on the extension.

Elaine began. "I guess the first thing is, have you decided on where you're going yet?"

Lizzie waited for George to respond and George waited for Lizzie.

"No, nothing really final," George finally said. "We haven't talked about it much."

"We did think about Australia," Lizzie said quickly, "since Todd won't be at the wedding. The real wedding, I mean. I know he might come to Tulsa."

Lizzie actually liked the idea of going to Sydney. It seemed to her to be a city that Jack would choose to live in. Maybe she'd find him there.

This diverted Elaine from the subject at hand. "Yes, and even if he does come we have no idea whether he'll bring someone," Elaine said. "I swear, he goes through girlfriends like we used to go through boxes of Cheerios when you boys were little. I can't keep track of them."

"He's changed his name to Kale, did he tell you that, George? Legally changed it, I mean. I suppose that's what we'll have to call him, but I'm not sure I can do it with a straight face. Kale, a leafy green vegetable," Allan said gloomily. "It might as well be chard or parsley. I hope he's still wearing his retainer," he added in a tone that conveyed the all-too-futile hope that this might be the case.

"Oh, stop, Allan, you're getting off the point of the call. So, kids, we had this great idea, or at least we think it's a great idea."

There was a longish pause.

"Yes," George said encouragingly.

Allan said, "We'd like to pay for the honeymoon as a wedding present."

"No, Dad, that's too much," George immediately said. "You're already giving us the party. You don't need to pay for our honeymoon too."

"Well, we do have a bit of an ulterior motive."

"Uh-huh, an ulterior motive," George echoed. "I should have known. And what might that ulterior motive be?"

"So" — Elaine took over — "you know that Daddy and I have always dreamed of going on a walking trip in Cornwall, right? The South West Coast Path is supposed to be really amazing."

"You have? Since when? Why haven't you ever mentioned it before?"

Elaine brushed off his incredulity. "Oh, years and years. I can't believe we never told you and Todd —"

"Kale," Allan interrupted. "We've got to

remember to call him Kale now."

"Yes, but he was Todd when we didn't tell him, wasn't he?"

George interrupted this potentially interesting but distracting discussion about names and verb tenses. "Look, Mom, Dad, we're touched by your generosity, but please get to the point. I have to be at the office early tomorrow."

"Okay, okay, here's our idea," Allan said. "If you two really haven't any strong feelings about where to go on your honeymoon, how about if you come with us to Cornwall and we'll go on a walking trip together?"

George's chin hit the bottom of the phone, resulting in a loud thunk and perhaps internal injuries to his jaw.

"You want to come on our honeymoon?"

"Well, why not?" Allan said reasonably.

George's voice rose. "Because it's our honeymoon. Nobody's parents — nobody's sane parents, anyway — want to accompany their child and his wife on their honeymoon."

"But, George," Elaine said, "that's the point. You're not a child. We love spending time with you and Lizzie. And we wouldn't have to be together every minute. We'd just walk together. We have it all planned."

Lizzie got up from the chair she'd been

sitting in and started clearing the table. She loved the idea of spending more time with Elaine and Allan; their presence would dilute the icky stickiness of the whole honeymoon experience. Besides, did she and George really need to be alone together on a honeymoon? Lizzie thought not. They were already alone together for much of every day. "I think going to Cornwall is a great idea. It would be much more fun if we all went together. I say yes."

It appeared to be three against one and George was smart enough to recognize a fait accompli when he met one.

"I guess we could look at it as an amusing story for our children. 'Daddy, what did you do for your honeymoon?' 'Well, kiddos, we went walking in Cornwall with Grandma Elaine and Grandpa Allan. We all had a blast.' 'But, Daddy, isn't a honeymoon supposed to be just for the bride and groom?' 'Normally yes, but in this case Grandma and Grandpa asked us to make an exception. And your mommy wanted them to go with us. Oh, yeah, and Grandma and Grandpa paid for it too.'"

"Very funny," Elaine said. "Just don't think about it as a honeymoon but rather a vacation that we're all taking together. It doesn't even have to be connected with your wedding at all."

George ignored her and said, "I can see that this will give us lots to talk about at dinner parties for the foreseeable future too."

This reminded Lizzie of the time when she and Andrea had said almost exactly the same thing about the Great Game, and look how that worked out. She started rinsing the dishes so she wouldn't have to hear the rest of the conversation.

They planned to go the following May, but because of the deaths of Mendel and Lydia earlier that year, there was some discussion about whether they should cancel their trip. Lizzie had never known a family that discussed as much as the Goldrosens did. Depending on the topic and the participants' feelings about it, they chewed over, considered the pros and cons of, or thrashed out everything that came up.

Allan thought they should postpone going to Cornwall out of respect for the Bultmanns, while George and Elaine agreed that going ahead with their original plan would take Lizzie's mind off the deaths of her parents. Lizzie didn't particularly care. Her parents' deaths hadn't seemed to make any difference in her life at all. In the event, they went as planned and everyone had a wonderful time. Lizzie thought that she might never again be as happy as she was on the walk. Although the Post (Great) Game show was still going on in her head, the hours of walking in the sunshine muted the voices. Most of the time she couldn't make out much of what was said, and what she did understand — "loser," "inadequate," "fraud" — didn't have nearly the power to hurt her, or at least not so badly. Once, though, she distinctly heard someone call her name, and she stopped so suddenly that Elaine ran into her from behind.

Plus, since they met almost nobody on the path, either going their way or coming toward them, Lizzie thought the odds were excellent that Jack was not in Cornwall, also trudging along the Coast Path, so she could stop thinking about what she'd say to him if he suddenly appeared in front of her.

They walked for ten days, staying at different B&Bs each night. Starting off about nine each morning, they made their way from St. Ives to Falmouth on a path that was sometimes stony and sometimes just dirt. Sometimes they had an easy time of it, sometimes they had to climb over wet rocks where the path had been diverted because of heavy rain, or clamber up and down the cliffs overlooking the water. Lizzie soon discovered that she didn't care for edges and ledges, so occasionally she found the going extremely scary. Elaine and George tended to stride on ahead fearlessly, with Lizzie and Allan bringing up the rear.

When the walk wasn't too frightening or she wasn't harassed by the voices in her head, Lizzie found she loved being so close to the water. She marveled at how it was one shade of blue close to the base of the cliffs and then subtly changed hues the farther you looked out. It was when she was struck by the changes in the colors that Lizzie thought most acutely of Jack, how he should be there with her, rather than the troika of Goldrosens. Oh, wait, it was a quartet, wasn't it? She was now a Goldrosen too. Lizzie shook her head and kept walking. They couldn't get too far off the path, and certainly not lost, if they kept the ocean on their right, George told them solemnly. They passed coves far below them where surfers braved the waves and the icy water, paddling far out and then triumphantly coming back in for another go. The sun shone hotter as the days went on. Lizzie got a farmer's tan — her ankles and feet below her socks were stark, winter white. George insisted everyone slather sunscreen on their arms, face, and legs at least twice a day, prompting Elaine to wonder if maybe he shouldn't have gotten a job hawking Coppertone instead of going to dental school. "Or," she asked, "did you take some of the money you two got for wedding presents and buy Bayer stock?"

The day before they were to fly home, they took a train to London and stayed at a small hotel near Hyde Park Corner. They sat around at dinner and reminisced about the trip. They remembered the time in Porthcurno when a bee unaccountably dived into Lizzie's cider and the man at the table next to them advised her to "drink up, luv, that's good protein for ye." And the time Allan was so busy looking at the map that he fell farther and farther behind the other three and soon lost sight of them entirely, at which point he mistakenly took a turn inland. The ocean was no longer on his right. By the time Elaine finally noticed that Allan was missing, he had gone some distance in entirely the wrong direction. George ended up rushing back the way they'd come to try to find him. It turned out that Allan was so busy looking at the map that he hadn't seen that the path turned one way while he went the other. "Sort of like missing the trees for the forest," George said, sighing. After that they all decided it was best for Allan not to hold the map while they were walking and to stay in the middle of the group, not the back.

When dessert came they moved on to reciting the limericks they'd composed together along the way. Limerick writing began after lunch one afternoon in a pub in Mousehole (which, Allan told them, was pronounced Mauzel), when the first line of a limerick presented itself to Lizzie, and they all spent the rest of the day working on it. They found that writing the limerick took their minds off some especially fiendish climbs and descents. Finally, late in the day, they came up with one that they all agreed should be the finished version. After this success, they vowed to write limericks about all the towns they stayed in.

Their two favorites were:

A lusty young sailor from Mousehole
Hied home for his rights: they were
    spousal.
His wife acquiesced,
The sex was the best.
And he left in no state of arousal.

and

There once was a lass from Porthleven

Who died and ascended to heaven
She said, "What a treat!
There's plenty to eat.
But I'd rather have cream tea in Devon."

Lizzie cried as the plane flew back over the ocean. George tried to comfort her. "I know it's over and I know how happy you were there, but please, Lizzie, don't cry, we'll do another walk all together again. I promise." Lizzie couldn't tell him how much she dreaded going home, where the Great Game announcers were louder and went on and on and on, where she wasn't sure what to do with her life, where she might run into Maverick, or Andrea, or any of the (still, she presumed) angry cheerleaders whose football-playing boyfriends she'd fucked. These possibilities were bad enough, but what if she really never saw Jack again? When she was home in Ann Arbor, it seemed more and more likely that she wouldn't. So she wept, inconsolable.

LIZZIE MEETS KALE

Todd, now known to one and all as Kale, didn't make it to either the real or fake wedding or the Bultmanns' funeral, but came to Tulsa the next year at Christmas. The day after George and Lizzie arrived they were back at the airport, waiting for his plane to land.

"He'll be here soon," George said.

"Is that a slight lack of enthusiasm I detect in your voice?" Lizzie asked.

"No, not really. Well, maybe. He's just so damn handsome. Maybe you'll think you married the wrong brother."

"Impossible," Lizzie assured him, squeezing his hand. It wasn't that George was the wrong brother, it was just that Lizzie was still afraid that he was the wrong man. "Besides, looks only go so far."

"Plus, when he wants to, he oozes charm. That plus looks takes you even farther, right?" George said gloomily when he came into view.

"Hey, Todd, uh, Kale," George said, giving him a hug that more resembled a typical Bultmann clasp than the usual Goldrosen embrace. That done, Kale turned to Lizzie.

"And this, I presume, is my not-so-brand-new sister-in-law. Well done, Georgie Porgie. I like her already." Lizzie couldn't decide if his Aussie accent was put on just for the occasion or if it was acquired naturally during the decade he'd lived in Sydney.

At the same time that George said, "Don't

call me Georgie," in a hangdog sort of voice, Lizzie said, "You don't know me well enough to like me already," which immediately cheered George up.

They walked toward baggage claim. "I guess we should go straight home. I'm sure Mom and Dad are on pins and needles waiting to see how much I've changed."

"When did you last see them?" Lizzie asked.

"About five years ago. You remember, George, they came to Sydney for a couple of days and then flew to Auckland and took a cruise down the coast of New Zealand and ended up in Melbourne. They stayed with me, and it was a disaster for all concerned. I know you think they're the best parents in the world, George, and maybe they were for you, but I was always beyond their capabilities."

George punched his brother on the arm, not lightly. "You were an awful son, you know."

Kale winced and rubbed his arm, although Lizzie could tell he was just faking. "Well, especially compared to you, anyway, that's true. But do you ever think maybe you were too easy on them? What's your opinion, sister mine?"

"My opinion is that we should walk faster,

collect your suitcases, and go home," Lizzie said.

Kale groaned. "Okay, if it has to be done, let's get it over with. Oh, there's one of my suitcases already."

With some difficulty, George took it off the conveyer belt. "What's in here? Gold doubloons?"

"You're close." Kale grinned. "It's your Christmas and late wedding present. Emma, my former girlfriend, found it. Wait till you see it."

"What is it?"

"Lizzie, Lizzie, Lizzie," Kale said, putting his arm around her. "The Goldrosens never tell what our gifts are in advance of giving them. Haven't you learned that yet?"

Lizzie laughed, but George took his brother seriously. "I would've thought you'd have forgotten those little rules by now, since you've been gone so long."

"I've forgotten very little, actually," Todd said.

In the evenings, after everyone else went to bed, the three youngsters, as Allan insisted on calling them, headed out to one of the bars on Cherry Street and talked. Mostly Lizzie listened. Maybe it was the beer, although she never had more than a couple of glasses, but she felt as though she belonged right where she was, sitting between George and his brother in this pretty awful dive bar in Tulsa, Oklahoma. It was a rare feeling.

"I have to thank you guys for getting married," Kale said one night. "You took a lot of pressure off me."

"Your status as unmarried older brother definitely figured into our plans," George said.

"Yeah," Lizzie agreed. "We talked a lot about how it would save you from being hassled by the family so much."

"Right, that's good to hear. Now, can you continue your good works and have a kid soon? I'd like to be rid of that responsibility too."

"That's harder," George said. "It'll be a few years at least. You'll have to be patient."

"Never my strong suit," Kale admitted.

His wedding present to them was an Art Deco sterling silver coffee and tea set, which included an octagonal silver tray, a pot for coffee and one for tea, a creamer, and a sugar bowl. It was heart-stoppingly beautiful and Lizzie felt that it, like her ring, had really been meant for the next girl over, certainly not the one sitting here tonight in her in-laws' house. She couldn't imagine living up to its demands of gracious hospitality and wondered how Elaine and Allan had described her to their older son that he would think she (and George) deserved such a stunning gift.

George spoke first. "Unbelievable. Thanks, bro. Did you ransom your inheritance to pay for it?"

"Nah, I told you my ex-girlfriend found it. She haunts flea markets and antique stores and as soon as she saw it she called and told me I had to get it for you two. She drives a hard bargain."

"I wish you'd brought her, Todd," Elaine said. "We'd love to meet her."

"Did you hear me say she was an ex-girlfriend, Ma? And it's Kale." Although his smile took away some of the sting of his words, Lizzie could see how family life must have been before Todd left the red clay dirt of Oklahoma behind and moved to the other end of the world.

"You know, George," she said to him one night when they were back in Ann Arbor, "when people look at you, what they immediately see is someone trustworthy. You just have that look somehow. Solid. Todd, Kale, doesn't. I like him a lot, but I wouldn't have wanted to go out with him. He has this way of making me feel like I'm not important, like he's always looking beyond me for the next best thing."

"Do you think that's why none of his girlfriends stick?"

"Maybe. I can imagine a scenario where he takes some girl to a party, abandons her there, and leaves with someone else. Anyway, what I'm trying to say is that I'm glad you're you and not Todd." Lizzie tried not to think about another possible way to end that sentence, tried not to let the words "but it would be even better if you were Jack" even enter her mind.

GEORGE'S ROAD TO FAME

The first question reporters always asked George was what inspired him to put a thriving dental practice on hold and embark on what Lizzie called his happery-quackery crusade. His one-sentence answer was that he had a patient named Cynthia Gordon and she was sad. Then he'd add, trying (and pretty much succeeding) not to sound smug, "I realized that no matter how gratifying it might be to help people have healthy gums, it was so much more important to help someone live a happy and satisfying life."

The second question — "What influenced your theories of suffering?" — was impossible to answer in one sentence. As George grew more experienced with the media, and discovered that most reporters only have a very limited attention span, he'd worked out a short handy-dandy guide to his ideas.

When George was a senior in college, facing hours of chemistry and biology labs and studying madly for the Dental Admission Test, he decided on a whim to sign up for a class on something as different from dentistry as he could get. Perusing the catalog, he came across a course called Buddhist Insight Meditation and the Psychology of Spiritual Development. Whew! The title, which didn't appear to have anything to do with dentistry, was a mouthful and way too long to fit the space it was allocated in the catalog; it was abbreviated Budd Ins Med/ Psych of Sprtual Dev, and was popularly known on campus as Hippie 101. Dr. Robert Kallikow, aging beatnik, taught the course. He wore a beret (even in the heat of the Oklahoma summer) and the only Earth shoes ever seen in Stillwater, Oklahoma (which he wore sockless, even in the occasional chill of the Oklahoma winter). His many odd tics and traits were widely thought to have been the result of his taking part in Tim Leary's experiments with psilocybin at Harvard.

George initially regarded the class as a sort

of mini-vacation, a chance to relax in the midst of his pressured academic life. To his surprise, though, the main theme of the course — what the Buddha taught on the nature of suffering, the cause of suffering, and the way to end suffering — fascinated him, though not quite enough to abandon his career plans and go to Thailand and become a monk. At the end of the semester, he turned his full attention back to his pre-dentistry studies but remembered the course fondly and entertained a vague hope that one day, when his dental practice was well established, he could do some more reading on the topics covered in the class.

This somewhat abbreviated background (he left out the beret and Earth shoes and the psilocybin) was what he told reporters about his first meeting with Cynthia Gordon. She was his last patient on a late Monday afternoon in January of 2001. Cynthia hated her ugly teeth, she told George, and didn't believe that, given those teeth, anyone at all would ever find her attractive. George could tell at a glance that hers were the teeth of someone whose parents hadn't been able to afford braces for their daughter. Now, as a reporter for the *Ann Arbor News* who was often interviewing people for the stories she was writing, Cynthia felt increasingly self-conscious about how other people judged her teeth. "I just hate the gap between my front teeth. It's like you could drive a truck through it," she said.

(When George first told Lizzie about what Cynthia Gordon said, Lizzie wanted to be sure that George reminded her that in *The Canterbury Tales* the Wife of Bath, who's a sexy babe, also has a gap between her two front teeth. Or, Lizzie, offered, she'd be happy to call Cynthia and fill her in on the literary precedent of her dental situation. George assured Lizzie he'd relay that information to Cynthia, who turned out not to be noticeably impressed. "Chaucer, right," she said. "He wrote a long time ago and in that funny English. If she lived now she'd get them fixed too.")

George really enjoyed dentistry and sincerely liked all his patients, even the ones who blatantly, flagrantly, refused to floss, but there was almost nothing that he loved more than doing aesthetic dentistry. All the root canals, routine fillings, and crowns were swell, but it always gave George an extra-good feeling to know that through the work he did he was helping someone feel better about herself. Not to be sexist, George would add, but when it came right down to it, it was almost always a "her," only occasionally a "him."

At that first appointment, George recommended that they do veneers on Cynthia's front teeth and the two adjoining them on either side. That would fix the gap and straighten out the others. "Perfect," she said, and they'd been moving ahead on the project in weekly appointments ever since — first whitening all her teeth and then attaching the veneers. Porcelain veneers were not cheap, and George wanted to make absolutely sure that Cynthia would never feel her hard-earned money hadn't been well spent. During these appointments, he'd learned a few facts about her life. She'd grown up in Hamtramck, a small city adjoining Detroit. She'd gone to Macomb Community College for two years, and then finished up at Wayne State, where she'd majored in journalism.

About a month later, when the whitening process was over and the serious work was about to begin, George found Cynthia Gordon sitting in the dental chair, sobbing. He was not unused to tears. No dentist is. No matter how hard you might work to make things painless for the patient, it often took a fair amount of pain to ultimately ease the pain, and tears were a common response. But what he was currently doing didn't involve anything that could possibly hurt: the drills and picks and scrapers and gum-depth readers were all still on a tray, unused. Yet here Cynthia was, in tears, while George simply held up tooth-color samples to find the best shade to match her unveneered teeth.

"What's wrong, Cynthia? Are you in pain?"

If possible, although George doubted his perception, the quantity of her tears increased. "Oh, Dr. Goldrosen, I didn't get the promotion I was hoping for. I just feel so unappreciated. Like I work hard, I do. And I really wanted the chance to write a column — you know, sort of a society column, what's happening, what's hot, what's new — and now it just seems as though I'll never get to do that. And what's worse is that they hired someone just out of the J-school at Michigan State, somebody with no real newspaper experience at all. And I've been there for six years. It's just not fair."

George's first thought, luckily unspoken, was that he'd never want to read such a column, but he could see how unhappy Cynthia was. He put down the sheet of colors and sat on a stool so he was facing her.

George would have sworn that he had no recollection of what Dr. Kallikow said about suffering, but now he unexpectedly remembered bits and pieces of what he'd learned. He began talking slowly, feeling his way through his memories and trying to be as clear as possible in what he said to Cynthia.

"You know, Cynthia, I had a class in college that I probably haven't thought about since I took the final exam. But now I see how it could apply to you. Listen, most of us think that getting what we want will make us happy. You know, because not getting what we want isn't pleasant, like how you're feeling now. But if that's how you're going to define 'happiness' — getting a raise or a promotion, having a successful marriage, being the best at beer pong, whatever it is that you want — then sooner or later you're doomed to unhappiness, because we just don't get what we want all the time.

"See, what my professor said was something like what's important is learning how to respond the right way, the healthy way, when you don't get what you want. It's the difference between responding to something and reacting to it."

Cynthia's tears slowed. "I don't get the difference between 'react' and 'respond.' I'm pretty sure that I've always used them as synonyms."

The more George talked, the more his memories of the class came back to him. He could see Dr. Kallikow in full lecture mode, walking back and forth in front of the class, sockless in his Earth shoes, talking about suffering. "What he said was that a reaction is more like a reflex, sort of like a sneeze. It just seems to happen. But you can choose how to respond. Dr. Kallikow talked about how to train yourself to respond skillfully to not getting what you want."

Cynthia was doubtful. " 'Skillfully'? That's a weird word to use. Are you sure he said that?"

George nodded. He was absolutely sure because he'd had the same questions about the word that Cynthia had. "What he said when I asked was that 'skillful' in this context was more or less a technical term, which makes it sound unfamiliar. So we could say 'respond wisely' instead, or even 'respond well.' The point is, we can learn to respond so that the experience of losing, or not getting what we want, isn't a problem for us."

He paused for a moment, to see if she had any questions for him, but she just waited for him to continue. The tears had stopped.

George went on. Whole paragraphs of Kallikow's lectures had now come back to him, almost verbatim. "See, we're always writing the narrative of our lives, and when you respond badly you turn the event into a burden, something that you carry forward into the next moment, the next hour, the next day, and the rest of your life. It fills up your narrative. It weighs you down. You never forget it. But when you respond well, you have nothing to add to the narrative. You simply experience the unpleasantness, then let it naturally pass away, and then greet the next moment of your life with no trace of the last."

Cynthia seemed doubtful. "That sounds impossible. How can I do that?"

"It's not so easy," George admitted. "One problem is that trying to avoid unpleasantness only makes it worse. The smart response is to relax, to accept the experience, instead of turning away from it. It might seem counterintuitive, but that's what makes it better."

"So having an experience of failing at something doesn't mean that I'm a failure?"

He nodded. "Yes, that's it exactly. Think about it. Give it a try. But now" — picking up the sheet of colors — "here's the one that I'm thinking will work best for you."

When they'd agreed that was the right shade, Cynthia got up out of the chair and shook his hand. "Thank you, Dr. Goldrosen."

"It was amazing, what happened with this patient," George told Lizzie excitedly over dinner that evening. "It was so strange; it's never happened to me before. It must be what people who have a photographic memory can do. It's like all of a sudden I could remember in great detail everything I'd read for that class, and everything that Kallikow said. When I needed it, there it was." He began to tell Lizzie what he'd said to Cynthia Gordon but then stopped. What if Lizzie's unhappiness could be eased by the same method? How would that work? How could he convince her to try it, to start responding to her unhappiness — hell, to her life — in a more skillful way?

George didn't say anything to Lizzie about that — he needed to think about it more — but he did finish telling her what exactly he'd said to Cynthia Gordon. Lizzie replied that she had never understood a word that he'd said all throughout their married life, and now had given up any hope of doing so. George thought that perhaps that didn't bode well for his developing plan to make Lizzie give up her sadness. But he was determined to try.

The following Sunday George was showering after his morning jog when he heard Lizzie calling. He ran out of the shower, forgetting to turn off the water and neglecting to grab a towel, only to find Lizzie sitting at the kitchen table, reading the paper.

"What? What's happened?"

"Oh my God, George, look at this: that Cynthia Gordon wrote an op-ed about you in the *Ann Arbor News*!"

"What? Really? What's it say?"

Lizzie handed him the paper, open to the editorial page. "The headline's 'My Dentist Doesn't Just Know Teeth.' "

When he sat down and read the whole article, it was clear that not only had Cynthia heard what he'd said to her, she remembered most of it, nearly word for word. She either had an awfully good memory or carried a voice-activated tape recorder around with her. Since she was a reporter, either one was a reasonable possibility.

Then the *Detroit News* ran Cynthia's op-ed, and as a result *USA Today* sent a reporter and a photographer to Ann Arbor to do a story on George, which they called "The Philosophizing Dentist."

The first invitation to speak came from the Michigan Dental Association. They wanted George to talk about dealing with patients who found going to the dentist to be an "unpleasant experience." Michigan Public Radio had him on for half an hour: the response was so positive that the next time they asked him to come on the show for a full hour and take phone calls from their listeners. He started appearing on the morning show monthly. He began receiving a significant amount of fan mail from all over the country.

Scott Simon from *Weekend Edition* at NPR featured him on a segment. The dentists from Ohio came calling, and Wisconsin, and as far south as Atlanta. When the Ontario (Canada) Dental Association asked him to keynote their annual meeting, George felt himself on the verge of something big; but when he was asked to speak at the annual meeting of the Estonian Dental Association (Eesti Hambaarstide Liit), he knew his life was changed for good. And so did Lizzie.

MORE ABOUT ESTONIA

They had a wonderful time in Estonia. The dentists drove them around the country, from the Russian-speaking Narva, where the women in their babushkas looked like George imagined his great-grandmothers must have, to Kuressaare, where Lizzie dozed off in the midst of a massage. But on their last night in Tallinn, Lizzie had trouble falling asleep. Rather than wake up George, she got out of bed quietly and put on the thick towel-y bathrobe the hotel furnished for guests, rummaged through her purse for a notebook and pen, then took her pillow and got into the waterless bathtub. She listened to the voices in her head — they were quieter tonight, perhaps because they were transmitting from far away — and thought about Jack's absence from her life. She thought about how much fun she and George had when they were traveling together. Finally, she wrote a poem:

Tallinn
In this fall-away-moment, between
(ago) *that* fall-away-moment and
(then) *that* fall-away-moment, you lie,
  cocooned
under a symphony of ivory linen.
The cold has invaded my heart.

You are asleep
in room 205
Hotell St. Petersbourg
Rataskaevu 7,
Old Town,

10123 Tallinn,
Estonia,
The Baltics,
Europe, the Western Hemisphere, the
  world, the solar system.
And I am writing this — so as not to
  disturb —
in the darkness
of room 205
in this one fall-away-moment between ago
  and then.

When she finished writing she was very tempted to wake George up, give him the poem, tell him about Jack, about the Great Game, about the voices, about everything that kept her from loving him the way she felt she should. She got back into bed and scrunched as close as she could to George to absorb his warmth and finally fell asleep.

GEORGE'S SECRET

Lizzie read every newspaper and magazine story about George avidly and with great pleasure. What amazed her was that every article, every interview showed the real George, the George she was married to. She knew — from the personal experience of her own lying and devious heart, if from nothing else — that most people have a private self that's often deeply at odds with their public persona. But with George there was no persona. The real George was kind, good-natured, and evidently very concerned about the unnecessary suffering of the peoples of the world. Probably he would have eventually achieved sainthood, if the Jewish religion had saints. Certainly in the tiny world that constituted George and Lizzie's marriage, George was almost endlessly patient in putting up with Lizzie's crankiness, her emotional distance from him, and her constant pessimism.

For in George's world there were no tragedies: rained-out picnics, famine in China, lost library books, monsoons in Bali, divorce, children drinking at ten, mainlining heroin at twelve, and dead at fifteen: of course these events occurred regularly, but George refused to see them as tragedies. In his world there were no irretrievable bad choices or wrong turns. Each one was, instead, an Opportunity for Growth, which would come if you were able to respond skillfully to events as they occurred.

George understood early in their marriage that his life with Lizzie was not going to be easy, despite being desperately in love with her. He thought she was smart and beautiful and would have loved to possess the dazzlingly agile mind she had, which was able to perform backflips and front flips with ease. He was eternally grateful for Lizzie's place in his life and for his place in hers, although he was never quite sure what that place was, or how important he was to her, or how seriously she took his feelings. He knew, for example, that she didn't consider herself either beautiful or brilliant. On the other hand, so what if their life together didn't come even close to perfect? Really, what marriage is? Bring on the difficulties, George often felt, because Lizzie is his own personal Opportunity for Growth.

Lizzie was the catalyst who brought his inchoate feelings about tragedy and sorrow into focus and clarity. He believed he owed his success entirely to her, to the depth and scope of her unique unhappiness and self-hatred. Given the profundity of Lizzie's feelings, it made total sense that much of their marriage was difficult. George would give anything at all, including every bit of his fame and certainly the money he'd earned from that success, to make Lizzie happy. Where did all her sadness come from? She never told him. George was incapable of violence of any sort, but sometimes he had this fantasy of shaking Lizzie so hard and for so long that she'd be forced to tell him what was making her so damn miserable so damn much of the time.

Not surprisingly, Lizzie and George had a huge disagreement about suffering. To George, it was a valuable stimulus to emotional and spiritual growth; to Lizzie, it was merely suffering. Suffering was something she knew well. It went a long way (too long, George said, frequently) in defining Lizzie's very existence, and yet it always felt alien to her, as though she had an extra hand, or an eye in the back of her head. She knew that extra appendage should be removed because then she'd be less of a freak, but it felt like such an integral part of her that to stop suffering would be like getting rid of something necessary to her being, perhaps the purest, most honest, most important part. Despair made her a whole person. And, of course, it gave George his life's mission.

Here was a typical evening at home in Ann Arbor with Lizzie and George: they'd be sitting next to each other on the couch, shoulders touching, watching the news, Lizzie reading and drinking tea, George eating a bowl of low-fat ice cream, when Lizzie would put down her book and say, perhaps apropos of some news story, "Listen, George, I know that pain is not gain, no matter what you say. I know it's your philosophy, but you will never convince me that the lousy things that happen in this awful world wouldn't be so terrible if we thought about them differently. Maybe you've convinced a lot of idiotic people looking for answers, but you haven't convinced me."

"Oh, Lizzie," George replied sadly, putting down the bowl. "Just because you haven't come to terms with your own unhappiness, just because you wallow in it, just because you're afraid to look at it honestly and then turn away from it, is exactly why you don't believe that what I have to say is important. You romanticize suffering because you believe it gives you some crazy kind of nobility. But how else can we learn, except by using our despair skillfully?"

Lizzie always chose the words she used to counter George's statements with great care, since she didn't want George to give up on her entirely. She needed him to be pathologically optimistic. As he began his rebuttal, and the discussion segued into what any normal person would deem an argument, Lizzie, who, like many of his fans, found George's voice extraordinarily soothing, would sidle into their bedroom, with George following close behind her. He kept talking while she put on an old T-shirt of his, got into bed, piled the blankets over her, and drifted off to sleep. Meanwhile, George was still trying to get her to see the world his way.

Lizzie hoped that George, being the kind, generous, pathologically optimistic, etc., etc., person that he was, was never going to leave her despite the fact that she refused to take him seriously, refused to accept the truth of his theories, and never acknowledged or applauded his deepest-held beliefs about suffering. Yet every speech he gave, every television or radio interview he sat down for, was aimed at Lizzie, trying his best to show her how to be happy. The audiences that hung on every word he said? They were chopped liver. That was George's one great secret.

WHAT DOES LIZZIE DO ALL DAY?

This was a question that George spent much time mulling over. In the middle of drilling a patient's tooth, say, he'd all of a sudden start to wonder what Lizzie was doing at that very moment. Was she home? Was she thinking about him? Was she at one of her many and varied part-time jobs? Later on in his and Lizzie's marriage, the same thing would happen when he was standing at the lectern, waiting to give one of his speeches. It was of course a no-brainer if she'd come with him — he could then find her in the audience: she always sat as far back as she could, as close to one of the aisles as possible. He knew what she'd be doing, both before he began to speak and all during what plenty of reliable people told him was a rousing presentation: she'd be reading a book. He'd watch her long enough to see her turn a page or two and then he'd start his speech. She almost never looked up at him, except at the end, when she clapped enthusiastically. George was never sure whether she was applauding out of genuine approval or whether she was clapping because she was relieved that it was over.

But when she wasn't with him, George wondered about it a lot. He'd come home from work and they'd talk about their days, or rather George would talk about his day. When he asked Lizzie what she'd done with her time, her standard answer was "Nothing much." This was probably three or four shades darker and quite a bit bigger than a little white lie, because Lizzie was spending most of the hours from eight to five trying to find Jack using the public library's collection of city phone books, a fact that she didn't ever intend to share with George.

George wanted to bang his head against the nearest wall and pull out his hair strand by strand whenever she answered him that way.

"Come on, you must have done something. Did you talk to my mother?"

Lizzie acknowledged that, yes, she and Elaine had had a good conversation; Elaine and Allan were fine and looking forward to seeing them sometime soon.

"Yeah, and then? How did you occupy yourself for the next seven or so hours?"

"I went to the library, I walked some dogs, I dusted at Billy and Sister's, and then I did some indexing. Then I read a little, made dinner, read some more, and waited for you to come home, and now we're eating." She smiled the Lizzie smile that George loved. "So what did you do all day?"

On one of their first dates they'd talked about how they saw their futures unfolding. It was a pretty short conversation. George was going to finish dental school and set up or buy into a practice somewhere, maybe Ann Arbor, maybe Tulsa, maybe somewhere entirely new that he'd always wanted to explore, like Sitka or Salt Lake City or St. Paul.

Lizzie laughed. "That's your criterion for a place to explore, is it? Anywhere as long as it begins with an *S*?"

"I never thought of that. They all just sounded like interesting places to me. But what about you?"

"What places sound interesting to me, you mean?"

"No, what your future is going to look like. What you're going to be when you're all grown up."

"People have been asking me that since I was a little girl," Lizzie said. "I remember that once in third grade I didn't do the career assignment at first. You were supposed to interview someone who did what you wanted to do when you grew up. I mean, clearly you were supposed to interview your father or mother, which I wasn't going to do. So I just wrote 'I don't NO!!!!' with four exclamations at the top of a piece of paper and turned it in. I thought I was so clever — I mean, of course I knew the difference between 'no' and 'know,' but the teacher wasn't at all impressed with me."

"What happened?"

Lizzie shrugged. "Oh, first she wanted my parents to come in for a conference, but of course Mendel and Lydia weren't about to interrupt their busy schedules to talk to her, so they had my babysitter, Sheila, schedule an appointment with the teacher and meanwhile I pretended that being a babysitter was my goal in life, so I interviewed Sheila. The point is, I still don't know what I want to do with the rest of my life, except that I know that there's no way I would ever be a psychologist like my parents are."

"Really? That's always seemed like an interesting career."

"Trust me, George, it's absolutely not," Lizzie assured him. "It's deadly. I wouldn't major in psychology in a gazillion trillion years. So I'm majoring in English because I've always liked to read, but I'm finding those classes pretty awful too. I don't know. Maybe I'll marry someone really wealthy and not do anything. Or just live with Marla and James after they get married and take care of their children after they have them."

"That would validate your third-grade paper, right?"

Lizzie smiled appreciatively. "That's good, George. I never thought of that."

While they were dating, George refrained from bringing up Lizzie's future, but after they were married he sometimes couldn't help himself. It wasn't that George was super-eager for money or renown for himself — he really just wanted to make the world a better place — but he wanted more than anything else for Lizzie to be happy, and he had trouble understanding how she could possibly be happy when she was doing nothing with her life. It became one of their earliest and ongoing Difficult Conversations.

"That's not fair, George. I do plenty."

"Oh, right," George would correct himself. "You actually do a lot, except it doesn't get you anywhere."

Having gotten nowhere so far in her search for Jack, Lizzie was guiltily aware that George had unknowingly described her predicament. He went on, "I just don't see how you can be satisfied with all the part-time jobs you're doing. Are you? Satisfied, I mean."

"I don't know. I guess so. If this is the first day of the rest of my life, I still don't know what I want to do with the rest of it."

"I can't even keep up with what you're doing every day," George complained.

She patted his hand. "You don't need to, you know. I keep track of them."

"But . . ." he began.

"Don't let's talk about it anymore, George."

So they didn't, that night.

In fact, Lizzie considered her real job to be finding Jack, but naturally this wasn't something she was ever going to share with George. She tried to divert his concern at her lack of ambition or worry about how she was spending her days by keeping busy at several part-time jobs. Sometimes she had three or four going at the same time, so over the course of a week, say, she'd have to run from one to the other to cover them all. This led to a busy series of days, days that Lizzie considered wasted because she didn't have much time to go to the library to search through phone books for Jack. Other weeks she'd be barely busy at all and after spending time at the library she'd come home and bake cookies or, after consulting Marla and/or Elaine, concoct an elaborate dinner for George. He was happy about that too.

In no particular order, these were the jobs that had occupied Lizzie's time since she graduated from college:

Dog walker: Lizzie was an excellent dog walker, although she came to that career only after she and George married. As a child, she'd always wanted a dog for a pet, but when she was eleven and first raised the issue with her parents, they told her absolutely not, that dogs carried germs. Plus they were just too much trouble. In any case, Mendel and Lydia didn't want to find hair all over the house, not to mention fleas. Lizzie did some research and found that poodles (a) didn't shed and (b) were actually incredibly intelligent. A potential pet's high IQ was something that she felt would impress her parents; her attempt to convince them by the use of this factual information was duly noted, but their answer was still no.

Lizzie found that it was quite easy to set yourself up as a professional dog walker. One morning she posted an ad on the bulletin board at Gilmore's and by evening she'd heard from three dog owners who wanted her to start walking their beloved pets the very next day. Lizzie enjoyed the work. She found that the busyness of wrangling three or four dogs at a time was a good way to prevent her from wondering if she'd ever find Jack. She didn't mind picking up the not-inconsequential amount of poop that three dogs produced. Her regulars were Princess, Foucault, and Andrew; she took one or more of them almost every day to the park, where they could run free for an hour or so. Somewhat surprisingly to Lizzie, it turned out that she was wildly in demand by other owners. She wondered if it was the dogs themselves who recommended her to other dogs, who in turn somehow communicated with the people in their life, who then got in touch with Lizzie. In any event, there was a long waiting list of dogs eager for Lizzie's expert handling.

Indexer for the Midwest Fire Protection Association: this job involved studying magazines and newspapers in search of articles about fires, big or little. She read about house fires, forest fires, gasoline fires, electrical fires, fires set deliberately, and the occasional chemical fire. For every fire she found, Lizzie created an index card, noting where the article had appeared, its author and title, date of publication, date of the fire, pages the article was on, and a brief summary, which often included the number of deaths in said fire. The days she worked at this job she had a lot to talk to George about at dinner, although it was often gruesome stuff, and she secretly prided herself on knowing the details of any fire in the whole country that someone might bring up in the course of a conversation. Fires were only very rarely the topic of conversation, but whenever they were, Lizzie had much to contribute.

Proofreader: George was in the habit of reading the want ads while he and Lizzie ate breakfast. He'd helpfully point out any potential jobs he thought might interest her.

"Oh, look," he said one morning. "Some company called Michigan Printing and Bindery is looking for a proofreader. You'd be good at that, Lizzie, and I bet they'd love to have you as an employee. You should check it out."

It was true that as far as it went Lizzie appeared to be a natural proofreader, which basically meant that she got annoyed at the typos and grammatical errors that were constantly showing up in the books, magazines, and newspapers that she read. Radio and television announcers who used ungrammatical language were also an irritation. Though she was loath to admit it, Lizzie knew that her annoyance at misspeaking and miswriting evildoers had been passed down to her from her mother. One memory involved Lydia groaning loudly whenever someone said "between her and I." Lizzie knew she grumbled in exactly the same way.

To make George happy, Lizzie called and was invited to come in for a short interview. The specific question of her knowledge of grammar and usage was never raised. Instead the interview involved the woman in HR asking Lizzie about her background and then telling her that she seemed overqualified for the job. Evidently having an undergrad degree in English from the University of Michigan opened more doors than Lizzie had been led to believe. She'd always been told that a master's degree at minimum and even better a PhD was necessary in order to find useful work. And here was Michigan Printing and Bindery willing to hire her once she assured them that proofreading for them was exactly the kind of work she was looking for. She'd start the next morning, directly after finishing her dog-walking chores.

Lizzie didn't know exactly what she expected Michigan Printing and Bindery to actually print and bind, but when she reported for work her first day she was told she'd be proofing a manual for Bendix repairmen. The manual consisted of page after page of numbers, which she was then supposed to compare to the numbers on thousands of pieces of loose paper. The only words on each page were "Bendix Model," followed by yet another number. How could anyone proofread column after column of numbers? Lizzie admitted defeat almost immediately. Her choices seemed clear. She could either ensure — through her ineptness (and boredom) — that the repairmen who used the manual would be unable to complete their repairs correctly or she could quit. Half a day was the shortest amount of time she'd ever held a job.

Duster at Billy & Sister's: Lizzie went into

the Billy & Sister's shop for the first time when she was looking for an anniversary gift for Marla and James. She discovered that you could find almost everything there, from framed pictures of birds that actually came from the hand of Audubon himself to Sheraton sideboards, from ceramic Staffordshire dogs that always made Lizzie think of the ceramic dogs in *Anne of the Island,* her favorite of the *Anne of Green Gables* books, to a genuine Morris chair that Billy never really wanted to sell. Sister was a connoisseur of antique jewelry, so there was an exquisite (and expensive) collection of that, as well as a carefully curated section of out-of-print books. There were, for example, no Danielle Steel titles to be found at Billy & Sister's.

Before Billy hired her, Lizzie hung around the store a lot, admiring a pair of wooden sheep, life-size, with very realistic woolly coats. Sister would decorate them for every holiday with cleverly tied ribbons and nosegays and put them in the front window. Lizzie coveted those sheep with all her imperfect heart. She was sure George would love them as much as she did. But, alas, Billy refused to let them go. In her life of major regrets, not being able to buy those sheep was among the major minor sorrows

Lizzie experienced.

Perhaps to make up for not parting with the sheep, Billy asked Lizzie if she'd be interested in a part-time job dusting the merchandise and occasionally, when they were particularly rushed, gift wrapping purchases, and she agreed enthusiastically. Dusting, Lizzie felt, especially played to her strong suit of being unable to do anything that required talent. She hoped she'd never have to wrap anything, though. The resulting package would not advance the shop's reputation. Also, dusting allowed her to eavesdrop on the customers, who were almost all women, as they chatted to one another. Whenever she saw someone from high school come in, she'd tiptoe around behind them and energetically pass her dust mop over the items in whatever section they were in so that she could easily hear what they were saying. Nobody ever recognized or even acknowledged her, although this was how she learned that Andrea had gotten married to some guy she met at Stanford and Maverick was working as a sports commentator in Seattle.

George & Lizzie
Take Many Trips Together

Lizzie was happy for George in his growing success as a public speaker, even though she personally didn't buy a word of what he was telling people. She considered him not so different from those annoying door-to-door salesmen, except that he was proffering real happiness rather than vacuum cleaners or encyclopedias. He wanted his brand of happiness to go to unwashed and hungry children, to unfulfilled bespoke-suited stock traders, to housewives without hope and kindergarten teachers and butchers and mealymouthed politicians around the world. She accused him of trying to create his own religion, or at the very least his own multinational company. George half-heartedly denied it, but Lizzie was pretty sure she was right about this. It inevitably led to yet another Difficult Conversation.

Oh, George wanted to take her in his arms and tell her that everyone's Difficult Conversations, about sex, child rearing, nuclear proliferation — everything, in fact — would be much easier if people didn't insist on thinking of their differences as a zero-sum game. If you took part in these Difficult Conversations (okay, call them arguments) but didn't feel you had to come out a winner — I'm right, you're wrong — then each of these DCs was an Opportunity for Growth. Each discussion was a simply grand Opportunity to develop a deeper understanding of oneself and others, to embrace differences, to grow as a human being. To have the emotional age of an adult.

Lizzie was mightily unconvinced, although George mightily tried to convince her, just as he had convinced the thousands upon thousands of people who read his books and attended his lectures, which Lizzie somewhat snidely called the performative aspect of George's life.

After dental conventions, where no one came close to his popularity as a speaker, George got his biggest audiences at college campuses. This was fortunate, Lizzie felt, because the sole reason she accompanied George to his speaking gigs was that it meant that she could look for Jack in every city they visited, and she thought that of all the places Jack might have ended up, a college campus was the most likely. They'd normally arrive the day before the speech, and after his hosts picked him up for a round of media interviews and meet and greets the next morning, Lizzie would walk out to buy some bottles of Diet Pepsi, then find a library and settle in with the area phone book.

Whenever they got to a new hotel, Lizzie would feel energetic, ready to get started. She'd unpack their suitcases and put their clothes away neatly in the dresser, even if they were just staying there overnight. She'd fill the ice bucket and pour herself some soda. But when it became clear, once again, that she wouldn't find Jack in that particular city, she'd be in an abyss of loss, with her arms feeling so heavy that she could barely pick up the phone.

"Jack there?" she'd ask, trying to still sound nonchalant after the fourth hopeless call. "Oh, sorry, I must have the wrong number. D'you happen to know a Jack Mc-Conaghey? No? Well, thanks anyway."

She talked to a Jerusha McConaghey in Newark, Delaware; a Jon McConaghey in Pittsburgh; a Jesse McConaghey in Tunica, Mississippi; and a Jackson McConaghey in Denver, but it wasn't Jack. There were a relatively large number of McConagheys in Austin, Texas, and at first Lizzie had high hopes she'd find him there. Austin seemed like a perfect home for Jack. It was especially frustrating on those trips when she'd discover that there were no McConagheys in the city at all. How could there be not one McConaghey in Lincoln, Nebraska? It

401

seemed impossible.

But still she tried.

The Alphabetical Marriage

On nights when Lizzie slept and George sat at his desk, supposedly preparing for his next talk, he was actually compiling an alphabetical list of all the ways that he and Lizzie were different. As probably could be predicted by anyone but George, the list turned out to be profoundly depressing, but there it was.

It ran, as lists should, from *A* to *Z*. In this case, from "apples" to "zoos."

Apples: Winesaps (preferred by George); Granny Smiths (preferred by Lizzie).

Bubble gum: George was horrified when he discovered quite early in their relationship that Lizzie still chewed bubble gum. "You've got to stop," he implored her. "It's just terrible for your teeth. And your jaw." But Lizzie loved the taste of Dubble Bubble gum and adored blowing bubbles, and had not yet given it up.

Children: George couldn't wait to be a father; Lizzie couldn't wait for George to stop saying that he couldn't wait to be a father.

Dogs: Irish setters (George); cocker spaniels (Lizzie). Lizzie's preference for cockers was almost entirely due to a book called *Bonny's Boy,* which she'd checked out from the library at the impressionable age of ten. After searching for years, she finally found herself a copy at a book sale run by the Ann Arbor Public Library. The copy she bought might even have been the copy she'd read over and over as a child.

Eggs: over easy (George); over hard (Lizzie).

Forgiveness: Naturally George believed in forgiveness; it was a core tenet of his philosophy. Lizzie, as she once told George, did not have a forgiving bone in her body. This worried him, as he felt that, whatever was causing Lizzie's unhappiness, the first step to ameliorating the pain was to forgive herself. It didn't, however, look to George like this was happening anytime soon.

Grapes: green and seedless (Lizzie); red with seeds (George, because he thought the seeds made him slow down and eat fewer).

Hamburgers: George ordered his burgers medium rare, while Lizzie wouldn't eat anything that looked un- or undercooked. George couldn't fault her for this, though, knowing she had many memories of those mostly raw turkeys at the Bultmanns' Thanksgivings.

Itching: George left mosquito bites strictly

alone; Lizzie scratched them until they bled, which meant that after a Michigan summer she had scabs and scars in various stages of healing all over her arms and legs.

Jazz: George's favorite album of all time was Miles Davis's *Shades of Blue;* Lizzie only liked music with lyrics. She didn't get jazz at all and, sadly for George, found listening to jazz (or classical music) boring. "So shoot me," she said to George when he expressed amazement at this.

Kimchi: George, having been introduced to it by his Korean American roommate his freshman year at OSU, loved it. There were no Korean restaurants in Stillwater, but Jae's mother always brought some with her when she flew in from Los Angeles. Lizzie tried it once at a fancy restaurant in New York but disliked it intensely. Too spicy.

Listerine: George actively discouraged his patients from using this particular brand of mouthwash. He didn't think it was worth the trouble or was at all necessary to subject oneself to the burning sensation taking a capful would cause. Lizzie loved that sort of painful experience. It felt like an appropriate punishment for everything she'd done wrong. You might as well also add love in here too, George thought gloomily. He still held on to the hope — fat chance of it happening, though — that someday Lizzie would love him as much as he loved her.

Magazines: George's favorite magazine was *Consumer Reports*. It was his holy book, his scripture. He read it cover to cover every month and never bought anything — from towels to tires — without checking it first. One year the editors raved about the Toyota Camry and afterward George refused to buy any other make or model of car. To George's shock (and, it must be admitted, a bit of awe), Lizzie never checked any reviews at all before she made a purchase. Lizzie preferred the *New Yorker,* which she read in this order: cartoons, poetry, "Talk of the Town," stories, "Shouts and Murmurs," and finally the articles. George could never really connect with the short stories and felt that much of the time the *New Yorker*'s articles were, quite frankly, way too long. They did both read *Sports Illustrated* cover to cover.

Nightclothes: briefs (George); T-shirts belonging to George (Lizzie).

Opera: George tolerated it; Lizzie didn't have the patience to sit still through even one performance. Ditto ballet.

Patience: George had it in unlimited quantities. Lizzie had none.

Queen of spades: George played it safe while playing Hearts, only rarely trying to shoot the moon. Lizzie's favorite card in the game was the queen of spades, and whenever it looked even remotely likely she went for broke.

Regret: George didn't believe in it. There was nothing to be gained from regret. You can learn from your experiences and decide to do something different next time, but that's different from regret. Regret was a dead-end street, a dark alley on a cold night. It took you nowhere. Edith Piaf could sing (in French) with great conviction that she regretted nothing, but Lizzie regretted almost everything she'd ever done. She reveled in regret, George believed. He found it greatly frustrating.

Sex: Obviously, but George didn't want to think about that. Shampoo, then, instead. George grew up with a terrible hang-up about dandruff and thus relied on Head & Shoulders shampoo. He kind of liked the smell of it too. Lizzie hated its medicinal odor (it reminded her of Mendel) and kept begging George to switch to another brand.

Tea: No, thank you (George), give him coffee anytime; Assam (Lizzie).

Umbrellas: George appreciated the usefulness of umbrellas but only for other people. A harsh thought would never cross his mind when, during an Ann Arbor drizzle, a small person uneasily navigating with a too-large umbrella blocking much of her peripheral and even face-on vision bumped into him. Lizzie, on the other hand, took an umbrella with her if the forecast even hinted that rain was possible. Rain frizzled her hair. She bought umbrellas like other people buy packs of gum at the airport. Nearly every place she and George had traveled to, every conference, every speaking gig, she'd found it necessary to purchase a new umbrella because she'd neglected to bring one. But because Lizzie refused to spend the money necessary to buy an umbrella that might actually last longer than one or, at the most, two uses, she had accumulated a large collection of them, most now in various states of disrepair.

In downtown Ann Arbor once — because she was, indeed, one of those small people whose vision is blocked by their overly large umbrellas — Lizzie ran into a policeman who then indicated in no uncertain tones that he was not particularly happy with her. "You can't even call this rain," he snarled. "Put that damn thing away." She got the feeling that he wished he could have given her a ticket for reckless walking and endangering a police officer.

Valentines: George, blessed (according to

himself) or cursed (according to Lizzie) with extreme sentimentality, would have given Lizzie a valentine every day of the year. Lizzie considered February 14 a manufactured holiday and bought George a card only because she knew it would make him happy. "Here's your Valentine's card, George," she'd say. "You know I only got it because I knew it would make you happy." Well, in fact it did make him happy.

Wine: red (George). Red wine gave Lizzie a headache. If she was going to indulge, she'd rather have prosecco. Or Riesling. Even better was switching away from wine and drinking beer. Oh yes, and the memory of vodka, straight from the freezer.

X-Men comics: George began buying these when he was about ten. Although he lacked the earliest ones from the decade before he was born, he had what almost anyone would consider an enviable collection. In recent years he'd begun scouring eBay to fill in the ones he was missing; Lizzie didn't see the point of them and George hadn't been able to convince her to read more than one issue.

Yams: George couldn't tell the difference between a yam and a sweet potato. Unless it was clearly labeled at the store, he was unable to tell which was which. This was fine with him, since he didn't find any difference in the way they tasted either. Lizzie disagreed. They did taste different.

Zoos: George enjoyed visiting zoos. When he was in nursery school, his class went on a field trip to the Oklahoma City Zoo. Just at the point that all the kids were standing directly in front of the elephant cage, the biggest elephant trumpeted. Everyone (probably including one or two of the teachers) began screaming in panic. Was the elephant now going to wrap his trunk around the bars and twist them enough to set himself and the other elephants free, thereby trampling the mostly three-year-old crowd underfoot? But George was entranced with the noise itself and the way it echoed and reechoed throughout the stone building. He knew that old elephant wasn't going anywhere but rather just showing off for the audience. He wasn't scared at all. Lizzie, on the other hand, wouldn't set foot in a zoo. Seeing the animals caged in, no matter how spacious the cage, made her too sad.

It was all so depressing, right?

THE STRONG SAFETY
Leo deSica's dad, born and raised in Italy, taught in the Romance languages depart-

ment at the U. He really wanted a soccer-playing son instead of one who played strong safety on the football team, but when Leo pointed out to his dad that they lived in America now and his high school didn't even field a soccer team, Dr. deSica acquiesced to his son's choice. Gaby Craft, Leo's girlfriend, was one of the girls who were particularly vicious to Lizzie when the news of the Great Game trickled out. In truth, Lizzie didn't much blame her. Leo was incredibly sexy and Lizzie often wondered if his Italianness had anything to do with it. A different kind of girl might have tested this theory out by traveling to Italy and picking up men to sleep with, but Lizzie had stopped being that different kind of girl once the Great Game ended.

A LONG DRIVE WITH LIZZIE, MARLA, BEEZIE, LULU, & INDIA

Late in August 2000, James flew to Santa Fe to start preparing for his job at St. John's College. George was busy working on a book he'd sold to Crown, so Lizzie and Marla and the girls drove from Ann Arbor to New Mexico by themselves, transporting, among other possessions, a plastic swimming pool that they did their best to securely fasten to the car's roof.

It was a great trip. Beezie (four), Lulu (three), and India (two) took to the long hours in the station wagon as though they were born to travel the interstates. Marla attached India's pacifier to a piece of ribbon and pinned it onto her shirt so it would always be there for her. They stopped at every rest area (and often supplemented those stops with the bathrooms at gas stations or McDonald's) because Lulu was still nervous about her big-girl pants. Beezie read *Frog and Toad Are Friends* over and over again to her sisters, even when they weren't listening. They had Dairy Queen cones every night (it seemed that every town had a Dairy Queen near the highway) and slept in the same room, which inevitably made for unevenness of sleep quality but gave them all a lovely sense of togetherness.

They stopped in Tulsa and stayed with Elaine and Allan for a few days, then hit I-40 for the final push into Albuquerque and finally on to Santa Fe. Marla and Lizzie talked and talked and talked. It was almost like being back in college.

"Why are you still wearing that bracelet?" Marla asked. "Doesn't George wonder why you always have it on?"

"George is the most uncurious person that I've ever known. He never really notices anything. I could lose all my hair overnight and the chances are he wouldn't even comment on it," Lizzie said. "But if he ever did ask, I'd tell him I found it at a garage sale or something. He's also gullible," she added unnecessarily.

Marla took her eyes off the road for a second and looked at her. "Don't lie to George anymore, Lizzie. It's not fair to him. It's sad enough that you're really lying to him by not sharing things, but an out-and-out lie is so destructive. Is what happened with Jack still so important to you? It's been years. Why does it still matter?"

"That's sort of what George says. Oh, not about Jack, but about how much I still despise my parents, even though they're moldering in their graves. Or why I hate myself so much. He thinks that I'm much too attached to my thoughts. That I hold on to things too long. But I have no idea what he means. They're your thoughts, right? How can you not think them?"

Marla struggled to answer. "I don't know, but people do it. I think I let go of things, or at least try to. You have to, really, otherwise you're weighted down with all those cumulative bad memories. James and I used to talk about that baby missing from our lives, whether it was a boy or a girl, whether we could find out who adopted it, whether we'd ever forgive our parents, why we just didn't say 'Screw you' to them back then and get married after I got pregnant. I mean, you know, it was so present. It was always there in our lives. But if we kept that up there'd be no place for anything else. And now we just acknowledge that all that awful stuff happened, that maybe we made the wrong decision, that we were just kids. We were just kids. You have to forgive yourself eventually, right?"

Marla used the rearview mirror to check on the girls. Beezie was turning the pages of her book from back to front, Lulu was eating graham crackers, and India was napping. They were fine.

"It's going to be so hard with you not in Ann Arbor," Lizzie said. "We have to write at least once a week."

Marla agreed. "I don't really know what I'm going to do without you. We should set a regular time every week to talk too."

"We have to stay in each other's life," Lizzie said.

"Of course we will. How could we not? We're going to spend our golden years together, remember, playing with our grandchildren."

Marla returned to their earlier topic. "You

know that James and I never liked Jack all that much, right? I know you've said the sex was great. So what? It's not doing you any favors, this obsession with him. It's never done you any favors. I still can't believe you don't see that."

"I did know how you felt about him. James told me one night when I couldn't sleep, but, Marla, you didn't really know him. Jack loved me. I know he did, and I loved him."

"Okay, fine, I accept that you loved him. But, Lizzie, it's been, like, seven years since he left. You've been married to George for almost five of those years. Give it up already. Literally, give up that bracelet."

"Well, he can't get in touch with me now since I became a Goldrosen," Lizzie said. "Why did I ever let George convince me to change my name?"

Marla ignored what seemed irrelevant to her and focused on what was central to the discussion. "If he'd wanted to get in touch with you, he would have found a way. You know that."

Lizzie did know. She just didn't want to admit it either to Marla or herself.

"I still think that he was so freaked out about the Great Game he couldn't stand being with me."

"But you told me he said he was fine with it."

"I don't think I said that. Oh, he compared me to some girl in his high school who everyone would sleep with but no one would date. He apologized, sort of, but who knows if he meant it? And then he left for home so soon after that. God, I wish he'd never seen that article. I wish he'd only read the *Paris Review* and never picked up *Psychology Today*. I hate myself for what happened. And the Ouija board said so, do you remember?" Lizzie continued stubbornly. "It predicted that I'd marry a Jack M. And who else could that be but Jack? It's definitely not a George G."

"Lizzie, Lizzie, Lizzie, I cannot believe you're quoting a Ouija board. You're being ridiculous. Probably James pushed that thingy around to make you happy."

"He said he didn't. He promised."

"Let it go, Lizzie."

"If only I'd had different parents. Or if only Maverick and I hadn't broken up. Or if I hadn't known Andrea in high school. None of this would have happened the way it did."

"Oh, Lizzie," Marla said sadly. "George is right. You definitely do think too much."

DR. SLEEP (2)

Before George met Lizzie, he'd considered himself a good sleeper. That is, he'd stay up until a decent hour, say eleven p.m., watch the news, floss, brush his teeth, get into bed, close his eyes, and lie awake for five minutes or so thinking (in the fall and winter) about how the Cowboys (Dallas and OSU) were doing. In the spring and summer he was usually so tired from the pickup basketball games he played that no sooner did he close his eyes than he was asleep. The ups and downs of real life didn't cause him any trouble. That, however, was "BL" — before Lizzie showed up in his life.

George's current ongoing sleep problems were due to two issues. The first was that Lizzie seemed incapable of having a Difficult Conversation between the hours of nine and five, or even early in the evening. Whatever else happened in their bed — be it good, bad, or indifferent — for too many years Lizzie lured George into having their most Difficult Conversations just as they were moving toward sleep. This was not pleasant for either of them, yet Lizzie seemed unable to alter her behavior. The second was that Lizzie's insomnia was infectious. Sometimes George felt that Lizzie's anxiety was radiating out into the atmosphere, so that it was impossible not to inhale some of it if you breathed at all. Once George got even a whiff of Lizzie's agitation, he was a goner, and the two of them would get out of bed and sit in the kitchen together, companionably drinking hot milk.

But whenever George fell asleep before Lizzie did or if she woke up in the middle of the night and heard George quietly snoring next to her, she'd toss and turn with great abandon and, when that didn't work, she'd first kiss his back, then nudge him, not gently, and whisper, "Are you awake?" even when she knew he wasn't. In response to his reluctant admission that, well, yes, he just happened to be awake, she'd say plaintively, "I can't sleep. Will you play a game with me?"

Though he hated being woken up, George really enjoyed the word games they played, although it was a shame that the only time they played them was in the middle of the night. George was especially grateful that they didn't have to get out of bed. He just wished Lizzie would be happy playing them during the day. Having George right there in bed with her broadened Lizzie's scope of ways to trick herself into sleep. Sometimes they'd make up sentences out of five- or six-letter words. Thus "Marla" became

"Maybe a rabbi left already" or "Many accountants remembered little addition" and "Elaine" was "Even Leon and Inez nodded eagerly."

They often played $100,000 Pyramid, with the top prize being, of course, sleep.

George (host), speaking slowly and deliberately, with a longish pause between each name: George, Marla, James, Mendel, Lydia.

Lizzie (contestant): Thinking out loud, "Well, I thought I knew, but the last two make it impossible to be 'People who Lizzie loves.'" Hmm.

George added: "Allan, Elaine."

Lizzie unceremoniously gave up.

"Ha," George said triumphantly. "It's 'People who love you.' Now go to sleep."

"I strongly object. Mendel and Lydia never loved me. You know that."

"They did too. They just weren't successful at showing you that they did. Now go to sleep," he repeated.

Lizzie turned her pillow over to the cool side and tried to obey him, occasionally successfully.

THE DEFENSIVE ENDS

The two defensive ends were Richard "Dickhead" Dickman and Jeff "Stinky"

Smelsey. Richard joined the Peace Corps, was sent to Liberia, and stayed on there to teach at the high school in Tubmanburg. He sometimes contributed articles about Liberia to the *Ann Arbor News*. Stinky Smelsey became a successful podiatrist in Laurel, Maryland. If there was nothing else having to do with the Great Game that made Lizzie laugh (and there wasn't), the thought of the perfectly named Stinky Smelsey spending his days considering people's feet could almost make her smile.

A DIFFICULT CONVERSATION

It was unusual for George to get home first, but one afternoon Lizzie found him there, waiting for her. "Let's go out to dinner," he said. This was also very unlike George, who felt that because of all their traveling they ate out way too much and he'd much rather stay home and relax.

They went to Yummy Café, the incongruously named Chinese restaurant down the street from their apartment. While they waited for their food, Lizzie told George about her day. "I felt like I was running behind all day, because Foucault insisted on seeking out a fire hydrant that he'd never made use of before, so I didn't get to Billy & Sister's until way late, which was why I

419

was late getting home."

"You weren't really late. I came home at lunchtime to do some work and decided to cancel my afternoon appointments."

This was unprecedented. George never canceled on his patients. He didn't believe in it. Plus his tone of voice sounded slightly off to Lizzie.

Lizzie was just about to ask what was wrong, when the waiter came by for their order. Once he left, George asked abruptly, "Who's Jack?"

"Jack?" Lizzie asked stupidly, stalling for time and hoping that there was some innocent explanation for his question, that he wasn't really asking about *her* Jack. When George just continued to stare at her, with an expression that made it clear this wasn't a casual question, she said, "How do you know about Jack?"

"I *don't* know about Jack," George told her in the patient tone of voice you would use with someone for whom English was not her native language. "That's why I'm asking you."

Naturally Lizzie's first thought was to lie, but her second thought was that if George knew about Jack's existence, maybe he knew all about what happened and was just testing her truthfulness. Her third thought was that this didn't seem like something George would do; he wasn't the gotcha type. Her fourth thought was that maybe Marla was right, that omitting a fact or two from the résumé of your life was one thing, but telling an enormous whopper to the man you were married to was quite another. Lizzie took a deep breath, trying not to panic.

"Jack is who I dated spring quarter of my freshman year. He went home for the summer and then didn't come back to start grad school like he was going to. That's who he is, just someone I dated for a little while." Lizzie knew that the most inaccurate word in that sentence was "just." It was the word that made the statement false. She tried not to look at her bracelet. Here she was, lying even when she tried not to. It was pathetic, really.

Days, months, years went by before George spoke. The waiter brought their food, moo shu vegetables and orange chicken. Lizzie felt too sick to eat. Finally George said, "I read Marla's most recent letter to you. You know, the one you left on the counter in the bathroom. As if you wanted me to read it. That's the letter where Marla asks if there's any news on the Jack front."

"You shouldn't have read it."

"If it was so private, why did you leave it out? Do you want to tell me what's going on?"

No, not really. Lizzie definitely didn't want to tell him anything at all. "I just couldn't," she began. "I just can't seem to get over him. I think about him a lot and I'm always looking for him, wherever we go." There. Surely that was enough. She didn't have to go into a detailed description of all those phone calls in the various cities they visited for George's speaking gigs, did she?

"How come you never told me about him?"

"Oh, George, come on. Look how upset you are, and you have all that Opportunity for Growth stuff to fall back on. Of course I couldn't tell you. And anyway, what would I have said? Did you want me to say, 'No, George, I can't marry you because I'm still in love with this old boyfriend who walked out of my life and I've never heard from him again'?"

A gaping hole opened between them. George said quietly, "And are you? Still in love with him?"

This was getting more difficult by the moment. Lizzie tried to figure out what she wanted to say. "I don't know, George. It sounds crazy, even to me, to think that I could still be in love, whatever that means, with a guy I haven't seen for longer than we've been married. All I know is that I can't seem to stop thinking about him."

"Do you still want to be married to me?"

"Yes, of course! I love you, George, really. I usually think our life together is great. But it's different from the way it was with Jack."

"Of course it's different; all relationships are different, one from the other. And are you sure you remember what it was like with Jack? Sometimes you can't even remember to return your library books on time."

"Don't be mean to me, George."

"Mean to you? Are you kidding me? Don't you think your lying to me for our entire marriage justifies a little hostility on my part?"

Neither of them had eaten anything. They refused the offer of boxes to take the food home. George paid the bill and left the restaurant, not waiting for Lizzie to catch up. Back at the apartment, he pretended to watch the news on TV, and Lizzie pretended to read her book. They avoided looking at each other. When Lizzie went into the bathroom to brush her teeth, George said, "I'll sleep on the couch."

"No, don't," Lizzie said, suddenly terrified of being alone in their bed. "I don't want us to be apart tonight. Can we pretend until tomorrow that this never happened?"

They got up the next morning still without looking at one another. Lizzie carefully measured out the coffee and made sure to use the filtered water for the French press, both of which she knew were important to George and both of which she usually blew off. She sat down at the table with her toast, waiting for him to finish showering. A stranger watching wouldn't have been able to tell that it was any different (other than the filtered water and the carefully measured coffee) from virtually every other morning of their marriage, but to Lizzie it felt momentous, as though she and George were about to enter into unknown, previously unexplored territory. Everything had changed.

After pouring his coffee, George sat down across from her and began the next part of the conversation. "Look, Lizzie, I love you, but you can't have it both ways. You can have our life together or you can go off and chase your fantasy. You have to choose. You don't need to decide this minute. I'm willing to wait, but I want you to know that it can't go on this way forever. And you have to be honest with me about your feelings, even if that's hard for both of us."

Once George left for work, Lizzie called Marla, to tell her what happened.

THE END OF MANY THINGS

James was dying.

Marla phoned early one morning about a week after the Difficult Conversation to tell Lizzie that James was still coughing a lot, which of course Lizzie had noticed the last time she visited, but that now he'd started coughing up blood, which was something frighteningly new. Their family doctor immediately sent James to a specialist. The future wasn't bright.

"Ironic, isn't it, that the only thing he ever smoked was pot. He never touched tobacco," she added. Lizzie could hear that Marla was starting to cry. "Although his parents were cigarette fiends, so maybe it's all that secondhand smoke."

"Oh, jeez, Marla, I am so sorry. You don't need to deal with this by yourself. I'll see if I can get a flight for later today, or at worst I'll be there tomorrow morning."

"No," Marla said tiredly, "don't come now. My mother's been visiting us for the past few days; she leaves at the end of the week. Come then. I'd much rather have you here than her, but at least she can take care of the girls so I can go with James to his appointments. And the whole situation is . . . just so weird. It's all happened so quickly. I feel as though I'm in the middle of a particularly awful nightmare. I keep thinking that if I could wake myself up everything would be okay. Oh, Lizzie, evidently there was so much blood two days ago that James finally realized he needed to tell me, and of course I panicked and insisted he finally see a doctor, and here we all are."

"Is he home? Can I talk to him? What does the doctor say?"

"He's lying down. You're probably the only person he could bear to talk to now, but I don't want to disturb him. We have an appointment this afternoon to discuss the next steps, but nobody's hopeful. I can tell that from the way they look at us. Oh God, Lizzie, he's going to die, I know he is. I wish you were here. I always wish you were here, but I feel like I need to save you for the even worse times that are coming."

"That's ridiculous. You don't need to save me for anything. I'm coming now," Lizzie said. "And I'll be with you whatever happens."

"That would be nice, wouldn't it," Marla said, "to live in the same place again."

"I'll be there as soon as I can get a flight

to Albuquerque, and I'll rent a car," Lizzie promised, "so you don't have to come get me."

"Do you remember Mama Marla and Auntie Lizzie?" Marla asked.

"Of course I remember."

"That was a long time ago, wasn't it?"

"Yes," Lizzie said simply. "It was a pretty long time ago. Tell James I love him, and the girls too."

Nothing had exactly returned to normal in the days since George and Lizzie had their Difficult Conversation. They were being very careful with each other. Lizzie made sure to turn off the lights when she left a room (a pet peeve of George's) and to put whatever she took out of the refrigerator back in the exact same place she'd found it (another pet peeve of George's). She tried her best to roll up his clean socks the way George liked them (yet another of his pet peeves) and when she failed he didn't remind her that he'd showed her how to do it numerous times in the past and couldn't understand why she didn't grasp the process. She made dinners from George's childhood that she knew from Elaine he loved, especially the mac and cheese from *The Joy of Cooking* and the pork chops with scalloped potatoes from the *I Hate to Cook*

Book. She baked mandel bread, which took hours of her time, but since she made the decision not to go to the library to try to find Jack in the city phone books, she had a lot of time for baking. George bought a whole gallon of peanut-butter-cup ice cream because it was Lizzie's favorite. He ironed two of her blouses that she'd left on top of the dryer. He cleaned out the drains in both the kitchen and bathroom sinks. He formally thanked Lizzie for making his favorite dinners and Lizzie formally acknowledged his thanks. Besides that, and a few stray comments like "I'm going to take a bath" or "We need more Life cereal," silence reigned. When they were both home they tended to stay in different rooms, and at night in bed George didn't put his arm around her and draw her close to him, which Lizzie had always found a great comfort. Neither one slept well. A lot of warm milk was drunk, but they didn't play any word games. Lizzie thought it was like living with a ghost. George was concentrating on all the tips and techniques that he taught in order to resist looking ahead to a future that didn't include Lizzie.

As she was dialing the phone to tell George about James, a passing thought occurred to her. How had it happened, when had it happened, that nothing in her life seemed completely real until she shared it with George? Was it possible that having told George about Jack would change her memories of Jack in some way? Maybe not the specific details, but the important place that he still had in her life?

"There's terrible news," she blurted out without any preliminary niceties when he answered. She went on without giving him a chance to reply, "But, George, promise that you're not going to get all Opportunity for Growth-ish. Please don't tell me it's not terrible. I'm not one of your feel-good groupies, remember?"

"C'mon, Lizzie, don't be ridiculous. I'm not going to promise that. What's happened?"

"It's James: he has stage-four small-cell lung cancer. Marla told me that the doctors think it's probably past the point that chemo will help, but she wants to try it anyway. I don't know yet what James wants to do. I need to be there with them."

For a moment George remained silent, then said, "Of course you should go, as soon as you can."

"It's a tragedy, right? I mean, if anything can qualify as a tragedy in your philosophy of life, it has to be this. He's young, he has a devoted wife, three beautiful daughters, a job he loves and is good at, and he's going to die. And don't tell me that we're all going to die. I know we are, but it's not the same."

Once again George paused before speaking. "Do you want me to tell you what I think?"

"You might as well. I know you'll insist on telling me eventually, or it'll come up in some speech you're giving. I already know I'm going to hate what you say and totally disagree with it. You're going to say it isn't a tragedy, right? Go ahead, then, and when you're done I'll call the airlines."

Taking a deep breath, George began. "Someone backing out of the driveway and running over their child is a tragedy. The Holocaust is a tragedy. People abusing their children is a tragedy. None of those things have to happen. But it's in the nature of things for people to get sick and die, sometimes of cancer. And the outliers get it young. It's just statistics. Contrary to what you might believe, even I am nowhere near optimistic enough to believe that we can ever have a world in which there's no disease. That's the realm of science fiction."

"George, listen to me for once. James is dying. Don't you care?"

"I hear that he's dying, and of course I care. What kind of person do you think I am that I wouldn't care? I feel terrible that James is dying. I feel terrible for Marla and the girls. And you, I feel terrible for you too, because I know how much he means to you. And I feel terrible for me, because he's become a good friend. All our lives are going to change because of his death. But that's not a tragedy. Don't you see that?"

"No, I don't see. And you can't make me."

George laughed. "Are you sticking your tongue out at me? Nyah, nyah, you can't make me agree with you."

Lizzie couldn't help smiling. "I don't know why I said that. It just sort of came out that way."

"Go make your reservation," George said. "I'll be home as soon as I can. See if you can get an afternoon flight; I'll take you to the airport." He called back almost immediately. "Listen, don't go there just for a few days. I think you should plan on staying with them as long as Marla needs you. And, Lizzie, this is a good time for you to think about what you want to do with your life. Our lives."

For the next four months, the time James spent dying, Lizzie stayed in Santa Fe. Neither Marla nor James wanted their parents there. Lizzie and later the hospice nurses who came in daily to check on James were the only people they wanted to see. Lizzie slept on the trundle bed in Beezie's room, and whatever Marla wanted her to do, she did. She took Beezie to her swimming classes. She stepped in as co-leader of Lulu's Brownie troop. She took India to her speech therapy appointments. She made drugstore runs to pick up prescriptions, and supermarket trips to buy ice cream and hot fudge sauce. She made cookies with the girls. She cooked dinner and did the dishes.

Surprisingly, she and George talked every night. The evening she got there she called to fill him in on the results of James's consultation with the top oncologist in Santa Fe, who sent him to Albuquerque for more tests. The next night she felt he needed to know what the tests revealed (nothing to provide any basis at all for optimism). The next night George called to say she'd left her parka at home and did she want him to send it, and that he'd been thinking about how good it was that she was there to help out and that she should give his love to Marla and James. The next night George called to tell Lizzie that Elaine had a touch of the flu and would probably love to talk to her. The night after that Lizzie called George to tell him that his mother seemed to be feeling better but that it was good she'd called. After that it began to seem natural to share all the events, big and small, of their days — India finally learning to say *R* at the beginning of words; meeting the team of hospice nurses who would see the family through what was to come; George's invitation to speak in Reykjavik and how if the timing worked out maybe Lizzie could come with him, since he knew she'd always wanted to see the northern lights; the amazing sunsets in Santa Fe that were in such stark contrast to everything that was happening to James; Lizzie reading *Phaedo,* Plato's dialogue about the death of Socrates, aloud to James; Marla's decision to become a vegetarian; how much renting a hospital bed cost; Beezie jumping off the three-meter diving board at the pool where the girls took lessons. They never talked about George's ultimatum or Lizzie's feelings about Jack.

On a week when he had no other out-of-town travel scheduled, George flew to Santa Fe and he and Lizzie drove the three girls to Tulsa. It was I-25 to I-40, I-40 to I-44, and finally I-44 to Allan and Elaine's. They stayed for a whole week. All the way there they sang songs and tried to be the first one to see all the letters of the alphabet on license plates and billboards. Lizzie read *Alice in Wonderland* to them on the way to Tulsa and *Through the Looking Glass* on the way home. She taught them how to play "*A . . .* My Name Is Alice." George told jokes and funny stories about when he was a little boy. Elaine and Allan spoiled all of them and most importantly the trip gave Marla and James some time alone with each other.

Early one afternoon when the girls were at school and Marla was napping, Lizzie tiptoed into James's room to check on him. She expected to find him dozing — he was on massive amounts of pain medication — but he smiled when she came in. She sat down in the chair next to his bed and took his hand. "Dearest James, I know you're worrying about how Marla is going to manage, but I want you to know that of course I, George and I, will always be there for them. I promise you that with all my heart. You and Marla and the girls are my family . . ." Her voice trailed off.

James squeezed her hand. In the months since his diagnosis it had gotten more and more difficult for him to speak, but he said hoarsely, "I know you will." They sat quietly for a few moments and Lizzie could see that his eyes were starting to close, but before he fell asleep he whispered, "Lizzie, I have to tell you something. I pushed that Ouija-board thingy around, even though I promised I wouldn't. Do you think that's going to go on my permanent record?"

"Oh, James, I think I've always known you did. I love you," Lizzie said, leaning over and kissing his cheek.

The service at the graveside was not to be borne, but of course everyone had to bear it. They stood in a line, clutching each other's hands, George, India, Marla, Beezie, Lulu, and Lizzie. While James's colleagues and students spoke movingly and sincerely about how fortunate they'd been to know him, Lizzie had the confusing thought that the only way this funeral could even be marginally okay was if James were there with them, someone else was dead, someone they didn't know or at least didn't care about, and the three of them — she and Marla and James — were all completely stoned on some of his best weed, as they had been so much of the time in college. It was too bad, Lizzie thought, that the one single person in the whole world who would appreciate this thought was Marla. It was certainly no use telling George; he disapproved of drugs on principle. George. A huge wave of resentment and anger swamped Lizzie. How could George have that stupid way of looking at the world? How dare he say that James's death wasn't a tragedy? She caught his eye and said, silently but distinctly, "This is a tragedy. You are absolutely, totally, completely wrong." George shook his head, but whether he'd been able to read her lips was unclear. All those adverbs. The chances were he hadn't.

When they lowered the casket into the ground, India turned to George and said, with wonder in her voice, "That's my daddy down there."

Someone behind them heard her and let out a sob. Lizzie thought it was James's mother. George squatted down so he was close to India's height. "I know it is, honey," he said. "Should we say good-bye to him now?"

India nodded. They all said their last good-byes to James, husband, father, and dearest friend.

Later that afternoon, after everyone else had gone, Lizzie and Marla were sitting on the big screened porch, watching another beautiful sunset, while inside George played Parcheesi with all three girls. There were simultaneously shrieks of laughter and groans of despair as the four of them moved their counters around the board. From what Marla and Lizzie could tell, Lulu had just landed on the square George was on, sending his piece back to the beginning.

"George is wonderful," Marla said. "He's so good with them. They love him. Kids can tell the difference between someone really having fun playing with them, like George, and pretending to have fun, like my parents."

"I know," Lizzie said. "I know that." She sighed and spoke again. "Do you think there's a statute of limitations on being punished for all the awful things we did when we were kids?"

"I hope so," Marla said. "But when James got sick I started thinking that maybe it was some sort of retribution for giving up the baby."

"Oh, no, Marla, don't think that. It's absolutely not true. You should talk to George. He could help you see how wrong thinking that is."

"Lizzie, do you hear what you're saying? As if you listened to anything George says."

"Oh, me. Don't go by me. I'm George's only failure. The black cloud in his sky of cerulean blue. You should read his fan mail. Evidently immediately after people listen to

George, they suddenly become happy. They're cured, if that's the right word."

The Parcheesi game was over. Lulu had won, George finishing a very distant last.

A few days later Marla told Lizzie that it was time she and George went home. "I've got to see if I can do this on my own. There's a lot I have to figure out, and you guys have stuff to figure out too."

"You know that if you need me for anything, anything at all, I'll be back."

"I know that," Marla said.

Everyone piled into the car to take George and Lizzie to the Albuquerque airport. They all cried as they hugged and kissed goodbye. Lordy, we've sure done a lot of crying on this trip, Lizzie thought as they started walking into the terminal. "Wait," India yelled, bolting after them, leaving Marla, Beezie, and Lulu standing by the car. "I want to hear the story of the paste fight again." Which was probably the best thing that could have happened, because the three adults started laughing. Marla gave Lizzie a final hug and whispered, "Go home and make a life with George."

"Next time," George promised, hugging each of the girls again. "I'll tell it as often as you want."

The flight to Dallas was uneventful and

on time, but now Lizzie and George were stuck there. The terminal was shut down until a torrential rainstorm, with its accompanying lightning, passed through. It would be at least, the gate agent's voice underlined and then repeated his last two words, *at least* ninety minutes before they'd begin boarding the plane. And maybe longer. They should all just relax. Easier said than done, Lizzie thought. She'd finished reading Ian McEwan's newest novel, *Atonement,* just the night before and couldn't imagine starting another novel until Briony didn't feel quite so real to her. She thought she shouldn't have left Marla alone. Hadn't Lizzie promised James as much? That she'd always be there? What did that mean exactly, "always be there"? This was the sort of question that George most loved, and in the past he and Lizzie had many excellent Non-Difficult Conversations about issues that didn't revolve around Lizzie's unhappiness.

"I'm going for a walk," she told George. "I'll be back."

She was just getting a drink of water when she heard the static-y stutter that preceded a loudspeaker announcement in every airport that Lizzie had ever been in. She waited, thinking it might be about their flight. It was not.

"Will Dr. Jack McConaghey please check with the gate agent at gate seventeen." And once again: "Will Dr. Jack McConaghey please check with the gate agent at gate seventeen."

Whomp. Lizzie felt the same way as when she'd been slammed in the stomach trying to dodge that malevolent ball during recess in elementary school. She leaned over and put her hands on her knees and tried to breathe normally. Could it really be Jack, after all this time? Was it really possible she could walk — she double-checked the number of her own gate — twelve gates away and find him?

Yes. It was obviously possible, because she was now on her way there.

But wait. She paused and asked herself why she wanted to do this.

Because it might be Jack.

But what if it was? What would that accomplish, finally seeing Jack? Really, Lizzie, what would it accomplish to see him?

You know that I always look for him in the cities I go to. So if it isn't Jack I can just forget it and go back to my gate and wait for the plane.

Ah, but what if it *is* Jack? How would she feel if he didn't even recognize her? After all the years of his living so large in Lizzie's

440

memories, what if she couldn't pick him out from all the other men at gate seventeen? And what would she possibly say to him after more than a decade? Was she going to accuse him of abandoning her? We were in college, Lizzie told herself. In college, girls break up with the boys they're dating all the time, and vice versa. It's normal behavior that often leaves people unhappy. Look how it's made me desperately unhappy for such a long time.

But then you went and built up this elaborate fantasy that if only you were with Jack everything about your life would be different and better, she thought. And I see that that's ridiculous. First of all, James would still be dead. Second, and this is the important part, it's your own unhappiness, Lizzie. It's always been yours. Maybe, just maybe, George has been right all along, that you'll never be happy until you can believe in the possibility of happiness. Maybe you've been using Jack all these years to avoid confronting that.

Lizzie slipped the bracelet off her wrist and ran her finger over the engraved words. They had been worn down a bit, but she could still make them out. "Shall love you always." Perhaps that sentence was no longer true, although she had certainly believed it to be true, once. She started to put it back on and stopped. Quickly, so she wouldn't get cold feet, she went into the nearest bathroom and, making sure that no one was looking at her, left the bracelet on the side of a sink and walked purposefully back to gate five.

She could see George, now sitting on the floor, laughing while he did coin tricks for a little boy. George, who loved her despite everything she was or had said or done. There'd been no more loudspeaker announcements since the first two, so presumably Dr. Jack McConaghey, whether he was her Jack or not, had made his way to gate seventeen. He was there. No planes had left. She was here, moving steadily toward George, and, finally, home.

There is a kind of love
called maintenance
Which stores the WD40
and knows when to use it;
Which checks the insurance,
and doesn't forget
The milkman; which
remembers to plant bulbs;
Which answers letters;
which knows the way
The money goes;
which deals with dentists
And Road Fund Tax and
meeting trains,
And postcards to the lonely;
which upholds
The permanently rickety elaborate
Structures of living, which is Atlas.
And maintenance is the
sensible side of love,
Which knows what time and weather

are doing
To my brickwork; insulates
my faulty wiring;
Laughs at my dryrotten jokes;
remembers
My need for gloss and grouting;
which keeps
My suspect edifice upright in air,
As Atlas did the sky.
— U. A. Fanthorpe, "Atlas," from
Safe As Houses (Peterloo Poets, 1995)

ACKNOWLEDGMENTS

During the years I worked on *George & Lizzie,* I was extraordinarily fortunate to have the support of both friends and family. Thanks especially to my daughter Eily Raman, who read and critiqued the manuscript several times and was also happy to talk with me about George and Lizzie anytime I wanted to (which was frequently); to Alan Turkus, who encouraged me from the very beginning to keep writing about George and Lizzie; to Karen Henry Clark, who sent me detailed emails about the project; to Jim Lynch, who stepped in at just the right moment with helpful comments and suggestions; and to Danielle Marshall, who contributed so much to the novel's existence in the world.

I am beyond grateful to Tara Parsons for her insightful and rigorous editing, as well as the entire Touchstone team. *George & Lizzie* (and I) couldn't have asked for a better home.

Thank you to everyone at Victoria Sanders & Associates.

Thank you to Kale Sniderman for letting me use his name and a tiny bit of his life.

Thank you to Hedgebrook for two challenging and rewarding weeks in a cabin of my own.

As a favor to me, way back in 2011 Amy Schoppert asked her friend Rabbi Elizabeth Wood about Jewish funerals. The words that Rabbi Gould uses in her conversation with Lizzie in *George & Lizzie* are adapted from the answer Rabbi Wood provided. Although I doubt they remember this email exchange, I am grateful to them both.

Thank you to Terence Winch for allowing me to use his poem "The Bells Are Ringing for Me and Chagall" and to Dr. R. V. Bailey for permission to use U. A. Fanthorpe's poem "Atlas."

And thank you to all the writers whose books have given me immense pleasure over the years.

ABOUT THE AUTHOR

Nancy Pearl speaks about the pleasures of reading at library conferences and at the meetings of literacy organizations and community groups throughout the world. She comments on books regularly on KUOW-FM in Seattle, on KWGS in Tulsa, Oklahoma, and on Wisconsin Public Radio. She also hosts a monthly television show, *Book Lust with Nancy Pearl.*

Born and raised in Detroit, Nancy Pearl received her master's degree in library science in 1967 from the University of Michigan and, in 1977, a master's in history from Oklahoma State University. Among her many honors are the 2011 Librarian of the Year Award from *Library Journal* and the 2011 Lifetime Achievement Award from the Pacific Northwest Booksellers Association. She lives in Seattle with her husband.